AFTER

INSPECTOR WEST

PETER MULRANEY

Cover image: Max Sandelin on Unsplash

ISBN 13: 978-0-6481046-6-7

This edition published 2018.

❀ Created with Vellum

To Toni, for all your love and encouragement.

CHAPTER 1

'IT SAYS HERE that a bloke can expect to live until he's ninety, maybe even older if he's fit and healthy, and gets plenty of sex.'

'Paul, turn out the light and go to sleep. I'm too tired.'

'Relax. I wasn't chatting you up. I just hadn't thought about living that long. I thought I'd be dead way before ninety.'

'You'll be bloody dead before morning if you don't shut up and let me get some sleep.'

Paul switched off the light. He lay there thinking about living for another fifty years or so and wondering how he was going to pay for twenty five to thirty years of retirement living. He would just have to get serious about financial planning, once they had passed through the private school fees paying phase of middle class living. The last time he had seriously reviewed the family budget the most obvious fact was that their expenses matched their income. There was no surplus for contingencies.

His thoughts turned to Josie. It was always a challenge being next to her in the bed. He wanted sex every time he touched her naked body. Josie, however, had a different perspective. Obviously, as far as Paul could see, God had a twisted sense of humour. How else could you explain the different arousal rates between the sexes? He sees or thinks naked woman - instant

1

arousal, with lumping great erection advertising the state of his interior monologue. She requires hours of talking, coupled with gentle, slow foreplay, before she even thinks about having sex and, even after all that, she is just as likely to roll over and go to sleep, and leave him there with his dripping erection. At least, that had been his experience.

'Paul, stop tossing and turning! Every time you move you pull the covers off my shoulders.'

'Sorry. I'll try to die as soon as possible.'

She ran her smooth hand over his belly. It felt good. His penis stirred from its frustrated slumber.

'I'm sorry, honey. I'm just really exhausted and I'm finding it hard to go to sleep.'

She snuggled up to him. Within three minutes she was asleep.

It was no wonder prostitution was a thriving business, he thought. It was married men who required the services of prostitutes and supposedly celibate men, in the guise of clergy, who were most strident in their opposition to the profession. He wondered what it would be like having sex with a prostitute. She certainly wouldn't engage with the client on a personal level. After all, the client was just another transaction and, to survive as a person, the prostitute would have to shut down her emotional self while she was on the job. He decided he'd stick with Josie.

He thought of those times when they did connect and the sex was indescribable. What was the point of sex anyway? It wasn't about the physical relief, even though that was good, it was about the sacredness of intimacy and that required connection on all three levels of being: physical, emotional and spiritual. He understood why communication failure led to relationship breakdown. The blokes were too much into the physical to notice that the girls were coming from the emotional looking for the spiritual. He knew it was when he came from the emotional, and they touched the spiritual, that they had great sex in the physical.

He looked at the clock: 11:55. He got up and went down the corridor to the toilet for a piss.

He got back into bed to wait for sleep. Josie was snoring softly. He knew he didn't snore softly because Josie always woke him up and told him to stop it.

Josie wasn't the only one snoring. He could hear Matthew trumpeting away in the next room. That boy was always making noise. He spoke with a sonic boom and whenever he blew his nose you thought of a ship lost somewhere in a mid-Atlantic fog.

He drifted back to thinking about money. They were spending a fortune on the boys' education and it looked like Matthew wanted to become a musician, while Luke was dreaming about becoming the next Michael Jordan. Well, they had no-one to blame but themselves. They had encouraged the boys to go after their dreams. What was the point of insisting they go into a profession or pursue a safe career?

The alarm clock displayed the time in big red numerals: 12:36. It looked like he wasn't going to get any sleep. At least Josie had rolled over and stopped snoring. If he could only go to sleep he could stop thinking about this stuff.

Beep! Beep! Beep!

Paul's hand shot out and hit the switch to kill the electronic rooster. Josie was already out of bed. No wonder she's always tired, he thought. He looked at the clock. 6:00. Time to start the day.

He eased himself out of the bed and ambled down the corridor to the toilet for a morning piss. Then he went into the bathroom, where Josie was fixing her face in front of the mirror.

'Morning, sweetheart'.

He patted Josie's backside as he stepped into the shower to spend five minutes standing under a stream of hot water. After the shower, he rubbed himself dry with a towel and lathered up for his morning shave. By the time he had finished in the bathroom it was 6:30.

He went into the boys' rooms to play alarm clock and start the morning struggle to have them out of the house by ten to eight.

'Come on you lot, out of bed! It's already half past six. Get a move on!'

Then he went to the kitchen for breakfast: two slices of toasted multigrain bread and a cup of coffee.

'Did you sleep well, sweetheart?' he asked, as he sat down at the table.

Josie looked up and shook her head. 'I feel like I've run a marathon. Just can't get my head to switch off.'

'Why don't you call in sick and give yourself a mental health day?'

'You know what it's like at school. Taking a day off just makes more work. Besides, I've promised my year eights I'd listen to their speeches this morning.'

By seven Josie was ready to go. She searched through her handbag for her purse. Found it, opened it and revealed its emptiness.

'Can you give me twenty dollars? I'll pay you back tomorrow when I get paid.'

Paul opened his wallet. It held thirty dollars. He checked his bus ticket. It still had six trips on it. He extracted the twenty dollar note.

'Seems like we are always running out of money,' he said as he handed it over.

'Let's not go there. I've got to go.' She kissed him on the

cheek, went up to the boys' rooms, said goodbye to them and left to catch the early bus, so she could enjoy a fifteen minute walk through City Park on the way to work.

After Josie had gone, Paul made another trip to the boys' rooms to make sure they were up and getting dressed. Then he went back to the kitchen to finish cleaning up the breakfast dishes.

'Morning, Dad.' Matthew arrived in the kitchen and started making himself a bowl of cereal for breakfast.

'Where's Luke?'

'He should be here in a minute.'

Before he knew it, it was ten to eight and wouldn't you know it, Luke was in the toilet.

'I'm ready, Dad,' said Matthew as he finalised the packing of his bag.

'Come on Luke, time to go!'

Luke appeared with his tie in one hand and his overstuffed school bag in the other. They were ready.

It took ten minutes to drive the boys to school, then another ten to drive to the interchange to catch the bus. If a bus arrived just after he got there he would make it to work on time. Every morning the boys were not ready to leave at ten to eight he was late for work.

Today he had to wait ten minutes for a bus. Fortunately, it was sunny. He hated waiting at the interchange on cold, wet and windy mornings. The flat roofed, no walls, structure had obviously been designed by someone who would never have to use it.

8:30. Five buses arrived at the same time. The first bus pulled into stop A. Several people rushed towards it, only to be disappointed as the driver shut the door and pulled out. He wondered if the idiot understood he was supposed to be driving people to and from the city according to a timetable and not just driving to a timetable.

He boarded the 578, which stopped at stop B, and got a seat at the back of the bus. He looked at the thirty or so passengers on the bus.

Couples and friends were obvious. Couples touched each other. They held hands or leaned together. Some hugged and kissed as if they had to fit in as much physical contact as possible before the separation of the working day. Friends talked, smiled and laughed. The strangers sat next to each other in the intimate space of the bus seat, often sharing more body heat through the enforced contact with the person alongside them than they shared with any other person in their day. Yet the strangers ignored each other. They stared blankly from glazed eyes, read papers, magazines or novels, blissed out plugged into their iPods or feigned sleep. It was a rare sight to see two apparent strangers strike up a conversation on a bus.

Paul wondered why he didn't speak to the person he was sitting next to. He looked at her as she gazed out the window. He was old enough to be her father but he couldn't help admiring the curves of her young body. Just as well most people couldn't read auras. His would betray his lust every time he looked at a gorgeous young woman.

He wondered if young women noticed. Or did age give older men a veil of invisibility? What chance did the average forty to fifty year old male have of scoring with a gorgeous twenty something year old? He wasn't even on her radar screen. That's why he didn't talk to her. He looked away.

If he couldn't have a gorgeous young woman in his waking life, why were all the women in his dreams gorgeous young women with bodies full of sensual desire? In the dreams they came to him. They beckoned him. They opened their secret parts for him and pulled him into deep penetration. He always awoke at the moment of climax. The subconscious had a lot to answer for.

Maybe his dreams of screwing gorgeous young women were simply expressions of his suppressed sexual desires. Maybe he wasn't getting enough sex at home. No maybe about it. He wasn't.

The bus arrived at his stop in the city. He got off and ambled towards the bank. No point in rushing in for another routine day in the world of banking.

Paul started his day, like he did most mornings, sharing a cup of coffee with Henry, his team leader for the last two years. It was an opportunity to sort out the day's priorities and discuss the state of the world before they got down to the serious stuff.

'I look at the people working here, Paul, especially the ones that have been here for twenty years or more, and wonder how anyone can work in a place like this for that long and be satisfied with a basic clerical position.'

'I think I might know why. It's called economic slavery.'

'Slavery?'

'Think about it. The first workers anywhere were slaves. I mean, who built the Pyramids or the Great Wall of China?'

'I thought it was the emperor.'

'Well, he got the credit but who actually did all the work? The slaves and all they got for it was food and lodging. The emperor lived in luxury while the ordinary working man slaved away building the great whatever.'

'But you can't be serious about slavery in today's world.'

'It's more subtle these days. In the past, the rich could buy and sell slaves on the open market. They can't do that anymore and they don't have to. We turn ourselves into slaves. Think about it. The rich still own the means of production. They make all the things we need and want. They advertise all their wonderful stuff, which we can buy in their shops with money they will lend us, provided we agree to sign a mortgage, a bill of sale or credit card and work for them for minimal wages to pay it all off.'

'Paul, you're having me on, aren't you?'

'Henry, what's stopping you from resigning this morning? It's such a neat system most people don't even realise they're slaves, until it's too late.'

'I see what you mean. Well, we'd better go and do the master's bidding.'

Paul walked from Henry's office to his work station and logged onto his computer to start on the day's problems.

The telephone rang.

'Good morning, lending administration. This is Paul, how can I help you?'

Paul enjoyed problem solving but he detested the constant stream of telephone interruptions. Everybody's problem was urgent and important. To make matters worse, his department was now fielding complaints from customers about the latest fee increase.

To the customers, who had no understanding of the links between the bank's profits, its credit rating and what it paid for funds, any fee increase was highway robbery. To prove their ignorance, they rang up in their hundreds to abuse the bank's staff. Naturally, the boss man on his million dollar salary, who made the decision to raise the fee, didn't take any calls. He wrote a memo to all staff and the wage slaves, like Paul, took all the flak. At least Paul understood the rationale behind the fee increase. Most of his workmates agreed with the customers but were left with the task of handling the angry customers so they could keep their jobs.

Paul waited for the end of the caller's opening rant.

'You're ripping me off! What service am I getting for this fee anyway?'

'Sir, the fee is a way for the bank to recover the cost of operating your account.'

'That can't cost eight dollars a month! You only send me one or two statements a year and my payments are made electronically by my pay office!'

'Sir, we still have to maintain your account on our computer system every day. Your account details take up space. We have to process the electronic payments your pay office makes. Computers cost money to run. In the past we were able to cover the cost in the amount we charged for interest. We can't do that anymore, so we have to increase our fees.'

'What a load of crap! I'll be taking this to Consumer Affairs. You can't do this!'

'Sir, if you read the terms and conditions of your loan contract, you'll see that we have every right to change this fee.'

'Other banks aren't charging eight dollars a month!'

'I suggest you phone around. You'll find this is a fairly standard fee.'

'This is bloody highway robbery!'

Paul knew it was robbery. The bank had the customers over a barrel but he couldn't actually tell the customer that. The bank was getting enough bad press as it was, without him adding to it.

'You bloody banks make such high profits as it is. Why can't you look after the customers for a change instead of screwing them?'

'Well, sir, perhaps you should buy shares in the bank.'

'What will it cost me to discharge?'

Typical, thought Paul. You give the guy some good advice and he doesn't even hear you. They were all intent on threatening to go elsewhere. Time for the customer retention spiel.

'Sir, the account keeping fee on your account has increased by sixty dollars per year. The interest rate on your account is the lowest it's been for twenty years. If you want to spend a thousand dollars discharging this loan and then spend another five or six hundred dollars setting up another one, with similar fees and charges, elsewhere, I'd be happy to give you an indicative payout figure.'

'Well, now that you put it like that, I see I'm probably in a no win situation.'

'Sir, I appreciate that you're angry about the fee increase but we're stuck with it. In the current competitive environment there's no way we can avoid it.' Unless the executives all took a massive pay cut and he couldn't see that happening. More than likely they'd lay off slaves if the bottom line didn't improve.

'I suppose you're right. Thanks for listening anyway.'

'No problem, sir.'

Paul and his workmates were handling the overflow calls from the fee hotline. The last time he had spoken to the team leader of the fee response team, he had discovered the few he had spoken to had been reasonably civil. Apparently, the bank's customer base contained a large number of abusive people, under the impression that a barrage of obscene language would persuade the bank to change its decision. Fat chance. The bank wasn't even listening.

Paul's mobile phone rang.

'Paul Ford.'

'Paul, it's Rosa. Where's Josie? She isn't here and she's not answering her phone. It just goes through to voice mail. Is everything OK?'

'What are you talking about? She left home to catch the bus at seven this morning.'

'Paul, she's not here.'

'Maybe she decided to take the day off after all. She wasn't exactly full of beans this morning. I suggested she take the day off but she said something about her year eights.'

'She'd have rung me if she was doing that and she's not answering her phone.'

'Maybe she left the bloody thing at home. You know what she's like. She's always leaving it somewhere. Let me call home and get back to you.'

He ended the call, scrolled through his contacts to 'home' and pushed the 'call' button. He waited as the phone rang six times and then listened to the message Luke had recorded on the answering machine.

'Josie, it's Paul. If you get this message, please call me.'

'Where the hell is she?' he mumbled to himself, as he found the school's number and hit the 'call' button. He listened while Rosa did her formal telephone greeting before saying, 'Rosa, it's Paul. There is no answer at home. I've left a message for her to call me. She might have gone back to sleep.'

'I'm worried Paul. This is not like her. She always calls in.'

'Yeah, you're right. Think maybe I'd better go home and check. Give me a call if she arrives at school. I'll talk to you later.'

'Thanks Paul. I'll wait for your call.'

After ending the call, he logged off his computer and went to speak to Henry, who was in his office staring at his computer screen.

'Henry, got a minute?'

'Sure, what's up?'

'Josie's work has just rung to say she hasn't turned up or called in sick and she's not answering her phone or the one at home.'

'Don't like the sound of that.'

'Think I'd better duck home and check if she's okay. She wasn't feeling all that flash this morning. I was surprised she went to work but you know what teachers are like. They reckon it creates more work if they stay at home. She might have had second thoughts and gone back to bed without calling in, which probably means she's as sick as.'

'Sounds like a good idea. Give me a call if you need to take the rest of the day off. Hope she's feeling better soon.'

'Thanks. I'll give you a call.'

Paul went back to his work station, picked up his bag and told his work mates he needed to go home and check on his wife. Then he headed for the door and started retracing his steps.

Riding the bus out of the city mid-morning was an enjoyable experience. No crowd on the bus and not much traffic on the streets. He was back at the interchange before ten o'clock and driving into his driveway ten minutes later.

He got out of the car. Before going in he checked the letter box. It contained no mail. When he opened the front door there was no sign of Josie's handbag on the hall table, its usual spot when she was home. He checked the bedroom. It was empty. He checked every room, including both toilets, and then the back-yard. There was no sign of Josie or of her having returned to the house since leaving it earlier in the day.

He wasn't sure what to make of her absence. Where else would she be if she wasn't at school and she wasn't at home? He pulled out his phone and called her number. He listened to her voice mail message and left a message asking her to call him. Then he called Rosa to let her know she wasn't at home and to ask if she had turned up at school.

'I'm really getting worried now, Paul. What if something has happened to her? Maybe you should call the police.'

'Think I'll make a few more calls before I call the police. Let me know if you hear from her.'

He went into the kitchen to find Josie's address book, the one she used for the telephone numbers of her family and friends.

He started with his mother-in-law. 'Ma, it's Paul.'

'Oh hello darling, how are you?'

'Ma, I'm a bit worried. Have you spoken with Josie today?'

'No. What's wrong?'

'I don't know if anything is wrong but she hasn't turned up at work, she's not home and she's not answering her phone. I'm trying to find out where she is. I was just wondering whether you had heard from her.'

'You think something has happened to her?'

'I don't know, Ma. She wasn't feeling well this morning but she still left for school. I thought maybe she had changed her mind about going to work. If she rings can you get her to call me? I'm going to call some of her friends. I'll call you back.'

'I'm worried now, Paul. This is not like Josie. Maybe something bad has happened.'

'We don't know if anything has happened yet. I'm going to make a few more calls.'

'Call me as soon as you find out where she is.'

'Sure, Ma. Bye.' He hung up knowing she would be on the phone to the rest of the family.

Next he called his parent's number. Fortunately, his mother was home.

'Hi, Mum. How are things?'

'Fine thanks. What are you doing calling me at this hour on a working day? Is something wrong?'

'Mum, have you seen or heard from Josie today?'

'That's a strange question, Paul.'

'Mum, Josie seems to have disappeared. She's not at work. She's not at home and she's not answering her phone.'

'Well, she's not here. I haven't heard from her since Sunday. You two haven't finally had a fight have you?'

'Sorry to disappoint you, Mum. Every thing's fine apart from not knowing where she is at the moment. I'll call a few of her friends. She might just be playing truant.'

'That doesn't sound like Josie.'

'I know. That's why I'm worried. If I can't find out where she is, I'll be calling the police.'

'Are you sure you need to get the police involved?'

'Don't you watch TV, Mum? Things happen to people every day. Look, I'll call you back later. Say hello to Dad for me.'

'Are you going to be alright?'

'I'll call you back, Mum.' Paul ended the call.

He worked his way through Josie's address book. None of her close group of friends had heard from her or seen her. No doubt he had started a rumour mill among her friends. At least if any of them did hear from her he would soon find out. Some of them sounded as worried as he felt. Then he wondered whether she was sitting in that park she loved so much.

He called Henry to let him know he hadn't been able to find her and to tell him he was going to check City Park, and then call the police. Henry suggested he speak to the police first, so he called the number for police assistance on the fridge magnet stuck to the kitchen fridge and introduced himself to the female voice that answered.

'How can we help you, Mr Ford?'

'Look, I don't know whether I'm panicking or not but my wife hasn't turned up for work and she's not answering her phone. She's not home either and no-one has heard from her since she left home at seven this morning.'

'Do you have any reason to think anything may have happened to her?'

'She's a teacher. She always lets the school know if she's not coming in or if she is running late. They haven't heard from her and she's not there. This is not like her. I'm worried something might have happened to her.'

'I can understand that, Mr Ford. It's best to report it now so we can have someone look into it. Do you have a pen and paper handy?'

'Yes.'

'OK, you'll need to go to your local police station and file a Missing Persons report. Do you know where your local police station is?'

'Yes, it's about five minutes from here by car.'

'OK, you'll need to supply certain information, so write this down. We'll need a recent photograph, details of her height, weight, age, what she is wearing.' She paused to let him get the details down and then continued, 'we'll want to know if she has any distinguishing features, like scars for example, and the names and contact details of family and friends. If she has a credit card bring the card number.'

'Do you want a digital photo or a paper one?'

'Both if you have them. Does she take any medication?'

'No.'

'OK. Get those details together and go to your local police station. Once you have filed the report we'll be able look into it for you.'

'Thanks.'

He hung up and went to the study and booted up the computer. It took a few minutes to load. He opened the photo library and found three recent photographs of Josie, which he copied and saved to a CD. Then he printed the one of her that he had taken only last weekend on A4 photo paper. While it was printing he checked his email. No new messages. He shut down the computer and wrote down her vital statistics. What the hell was she wearing this morning? Then he remembered. White, sleeveless blouse and black skirt. She was carrying the black bag with shoulder strap she used for carrying students' work to and from school and, yes, those pink running shoes she used for walking, with her regular shoes in a black and white plastic bag.

He looked at the list he had written following the policewoman's instructions. Credit card. He found a statement in the file marked: accounts. Distinguishing features like scars? She had one scar, thanks to Luke's caesarean birth, but that was not visible while she had her clothes on. Having gathered together the CD, the print, the credit card statement and the piece of paper with his notes, he picked up his phone and car keys and headed for the front door.

Ten minutes later he was walking through the door of the local police station. The young officer behind the desk looked up as Paul entered and noted the photograph in his hand.

'Good morning, sir, how can I help you?'

'I need to make a Missing Persons report. My wife seems to have disappeared.' Paul put the photograph, CD, credit card statement and the piece of paper with his notes on the counter.

The officer looked at the photograph. 'When did she go missing?'

'This morning. She hasn't turned up at work. She's not answering her phone. No-one seems to know where she is. I'm worried. She always lets the school know when she's not going to be there.'

'What's your name, sir?'

'Paul, Paul Ford.'

He picked up the things Paul had placed on the counter. 'Mr Ford, come around to an interview room where you can give me all the details.' He opened the door at the end of the counter and led Paul down a short corridor into a small room with a table and four chairs.

'Bit more privacy here, Mr Ford. Just take a seat while I get the right form.'

After a couple of minutes, he came back into the room followed by an attractive woman in a police uniform that looked vaguely familiar, in Paul's assessment.

'Mr Ford, this is Sergeant Wood, she's in charge of our Missing Persons unit.'

Paul stood up and shook hands with Sergeant Wood. 'Paul Ford.'

'Marie Wood.'

They sat down on opposite sides of the table. She looked at the photograph and then looked up.

'OK Paul, what's your wife's name, and why do you think she's missing?'

'Her name's Josephine, but we all call her Josie. I don't know that she is missing. It's just that I don't know where she is and it's very unusual for her not to contact the school, she's a teacher, if she's not going to be at work.'

'Have you tried to contact her yourself?'

'Yes, I've called her mobile. She's not answering. I've been home. She's not there. I've called her mother and some of her friends. No-one has either seen her or heard from her. Look, I know it's less than four hours since I last saw her but something's just not right.'

'You're doing the right thing making this report now. Tell me about when you last saw Josie. You mentioned it was only four hours ago.'

Paul noticed that the younger officer was taking notes.

17

'She left home for work this morning around seven. That's the last time I saw her.'

'Where does she work and how does she usually get there?'

'She teaches at St Catherine's in the city. It's that girls' school on the southern side of City Park.'

'I know the one. I'm an old scholar.' She looked at Paul and smiled. 'How does Josie get there?'

'She walks to the interchange and catches a bus into the city. Usually, she gets off at the stop near the main gate to City Park on North Terrace and walks through the park to the school. She reckons that's the most peaceful part of her day.'

'If she leaves home at seven, how long does it take to get to the interchange from where you live?'

'It's about a fifteen minute walk. She would normally catch a bus around seven twenty and get off at City Park around seven thirty five and be at school by eight.'

'I take it the school rang you.'

'Yes, Rosa from the school office rang me around nine fifteen to ask me where she was. She had tried calling Josie before she rang me.'

'School starts before nine fifteen, doesn't it? Why didn't they call you earlier if she's normally there by eight?'

'Well, she doesn't have a home class this year. Maybe nobody noticed she wasn't there until she didn't turn up for the first lesson. Anyway, schools are pretty chaotic in the morning.'

'Paul, I'll need to ask you a few personal questions, is that OK?'

'Sure, fire away.'

'How long have you and Josie been married?'

'It'll be twenty years this year, in July.'

'Do you have any children?'

'Two sons, Matthew, he's sixteen, and Luke. He'll be fourteen in August. They go to St Jude's.'

'Oh, you're Matthew's father.' She looked at the photograph again. Now she knew where she had seen her before.

Paul raised an eyebrow.

'My daughter, Margaret, goes to St Jude's. She's in Matthew's home class. She talks about him all the time.'

'Seems Matthew might be keeping some things to himself.'

They smiled.

'How are things at home with you and Josie, Paul?'

'What do you mean?'

'Any tensions? How are things between you and Josie?'

'Nothing out of the ordinary. We're a happily married couple as far as I know. No domestic violence or anything like that, if that's what you mean?'

'Paul, I'm just trying to see if there are any reasons Josie might want to leave without telling you.'

'That's all right. I understand that you're just asking what needs to be asked.'

'Any money worries?'

'Just the usual middle class strain of sending two boys to a private school.'

'What's on the CD?'

'That photo and two others. I took that photo last weekend and the others earlier this year.'

'She looks pretty happy in this photo. What was the occasion?'

'We had a barbecue lunch for her mother's birthday at our place.'

'I'll get you to go through the Missing Persons report with John here, so that we will have your contact details and can start a file. You'll need to sign the report. While you're doing that I'll get these photos circulated to patrols in the city, then I'll be back with a map of the local area and you can show me the path she would take to the interchange from your place.'

The sergeant picked up the CD and left the room. With John's help, Paul spent the next ten minutes completing the Missing Persons report form. When Sergeant Wood returned she placed a map of the local area on the table and handed him a yellow highlighter pen.

'Paul, can you trace out the route that Josie takes to the interchange for me, please?'

Paul looked at the map and located his house. Then he traced the pathway both he and Josie took when they walked to the interchange: turn left at the front of the house, walk to the end of the street, turn right and walk to the interchange along the pathway through the park that ran along the river bank.

'Paul, did you actually see her go that way this morning?'

'No. I only heard her leave through the front door after she gave me a kiss and said goodbye.'

'There's probably nothing to worry about but we will keep a look out for her until she turns up. Most people who go missing, more than ninety five percent of them, turn up by themselves. I know it can't be easy not knowing where she is but she'll probably come home tonight and be all apologetic about not telling anyone where she was. Give me a call on this number when she either contacts you or turns up home. If you don't know where she is by nightfall call me.' She handed him a business card with her contact details. 'What do you intend to do now?'

'I'm going in to City Park just in case she decided to find a quiet spot and spend the day meditating.'

'I hope you find her there.'

'Thanks.'

They shook hands. Paul picked up his copy of the Missing Persons report and his notes. Sergeant Wood led him out to the front entrance of the police station.

Paul walked back to his car and drove into the city. He found a park near the gate on the southern side of City Park, close to St Catherine's. He entered the park and spent a couple of hours looking for Josie, in the parts of the park she had described to him as wonderfully quiet spots in the centre of the city. It certainly was quiet but there was no sign of Josie. He sat down on a bench in the shade of a large tree. He was hot and thirsty. It was nearly two o'clock in the afternoon. He called Rosa and then Josie's mother. Neither had heard anything or seen her since his earlier calls. He walked back to the car and just managed to evade the parking inspector waiting nearby to give him a ticket for over-staying the two hour parking limit. As he drove home, he wondered what he was going to say to the boys when they got home from school.

CHAPTER 2

MARIE TOOK the Missing Persons report back to her office. In cases like this, once she had released the photograph to the patrols, she would usually file the report and wait for the person to turn up. It wasn't a crime to disappear for a day of peace and quiet, even if a few people got upset about it. Most women came home again without any help from the police if there was no domestic violence involved.

Today she made an exception. As she processed the details against her twenty years of experience, she was left with a nagging feeling that would not subside. She couldn't put her finger right on it but something said this one was not going to be like most of the others. She had met Josie Ford, worked with her at the last school fair. She didn't seem the type to up and disappear. Something was wrong here.

She called PSS, the public security service that monitored the CCTV cameras covering the bus interchange, and asked for a copy of this morning's footage for the period between seven and eight and for them to save the footage for the previous week. Hard experience had taught her that if you didn't get in early with your request for CCTV footage it wouldn't exist when you wanted it. With so much of it these days there was no way they could keep it all.

Then she ran a database search on the Fords. No records. So, she was dealing with law abiding citizens or, at most, with people who had not been caught doing anything illegal. There were plenty of criminals who were still outside the system, so to speak, simply because no-one had caught up with them yet. Still, she had nothing to suggest that the Fords were in that class.

Fifty minutes after placing her order, a DVD containing the CCTV footage arrived by courier. With the A4 photograph of Josie on her desk, she inserted it into the DVD drive of her computer and clicked on the play symbol once it had loaded. She watched it at normal speed until the counter informed her it was up to 07:35:00. Picking up the telephone on her desk, she put in a call to the front counter and asked John to come to her office. When he arrived, she turned the monitor so they could both see it.

'John, I'm going to show you the CCTV footage from the bus interchange for this morning. Mr Ford told us his wife left home at seven and that it would take her about fifteen minutes to walk to the interchange. He said she normally caught a bus around seven twenty.'

'I'd have to check my notes, Sarge. That interview was over an hour ago.'

'You're going to have to do better than that, John, if you ever want to get out from behind that counter.'

'Yes, Sarge.'

'Anyway, we can work on your long-term memory later. Let's work on your short-term memory for the moment. Take a good look at this photo of Mrs Ford.'

John studied the photo. He couldn't help thinking she was a stunner, even if she was forty something.

'Stop drooling and pay attention.' She smiled. He was such a boy.

'You asked me to take a good look.' He grinned back at her.

He put the photograph back on the desk.

'Now, watch this and see if you can spot her.' They watched an intermittent straggle of people wander into the bus interchange, gather in a rough line at the stop for the city buses, and then disappear into the five buses that arrived in the period between seven and seven thirty five.

'I didn't see her, Sarge.'

'I can't see her either. Wherever she went this morning, it didn't include the interchange at the time her husband thought she would be there. Let's just watch the rest up to eight.'

There was no sign of Josie in the footage up to eight. Marie wondered if Paul Ford had lied to her about his wife's movements.

'John, get yourself over to PSS. I've asked them to hold footage for the last week. I want to know if Mrs Ford caught a bus yesterday morning and on all the school days in the last week. Make sure they keep the footage. If she doesn't show up tonight, we may need to see if there are any signs of her meeting someone or being followed. Get them to hold footage of the bus stop outside the North Terrace gate to City Park, where she usually gets off, as well. We might need that too.'

John started to leave.

'John, don't you think you'd better take this photo with you?' She held out the A4 photograph of Josie Ford.

'Thanks, Sarge.' He took the photograph and set off to get a patrol car and drive to the PSS control room in the city.

Marie smiled and shook her head. That should keep him out of trouble for a few hours. He was keen but a little too green for her liking. No wonder they had assigned him to her. What was it the Chief Inspector had said? Something about the lad needing an experienced mentor. She wondered whether what he really meant was that the boy needed someone to keep him out of trouble, and what she had done to be lumbered with the responsibility.

She turned her thoughts to Josie. Why would an apparently happily married mother of two teenage boys disappear first thing in the morning? Well, she was a teacher. The things they had to put up with would be enough to push anybody over the edge. Teachers didn't get much respect these days and it was becoming fashionable to blame them for everything that was wrong with today's young people. So much for parental responsibility. Now it was all some teacher's fault for not disciplining little Johnny or not teaching him properly. Parents were even going into classrooms and threatening teachers when their little darling was called to account for his latest outburst of anti-social behaviour, and it wasn't just the boys mucking up in schools. Just last week she had attended the local high school when an angry parent had turned up and threatened to shoot the principal.

She took out her notepad and made a note. Josie Ford: teacher - check out any recent parent problems/threats at St C's.

She wondered if the Ford's relationship was all Paul Ford claimed it was. He wouldn't be the first man to lie to her about the state of his marriage when reporting his wife missing. You never really knew what went on behind closed doors until you got the opportunity to look. Unfortunately, she'd had that opportunity on a few too many occasions. Still, he didn't seem a bad type and he appeared to be genuinely concerned for his wife's welfare, and she hadn't heard any comments from her daughter, who spent a lot of school time with Matthew Ford, that suggested there were any relationship issues in the Ford household. Still, if Matthew kept secrets from his father maybe he kept secrets from his friends as well, but she doubted he'd be able to keep any secrets from Maggie. She'd have to watch those two, especially since Maggie had started going home from school with Matthew and his brother.

Maybe Josie was bored and just wanted a bit of excitement in her life or maybe she felt she needed some attention. She wouldn't be the first woman seeking relief from the mother martyr syndrome. But that didn't ring true either. From what she knew of Josie, she would do anything for her boys. She didn't strike Marie as someone who would decide to do something on impulse that would cause her family a lot of stress. Time would tell.

She looked at her watch: 13:23. Time for some lunch. She looked at the map Paul had highlighted. She picked up her handbag and went out to the car park, got into her car and drove to the shops opposite the bus interchange. After buying a ham and salad sandwich and a bottle of mineral water, she walked over to the interchange, eating the sandwich as she walked, and strolled down the sidewalk that led to the pathway along the river that Paul had described earlier as Josie's intended route to the bus stop. She continued until she reached Whitbread Avenue. Nothing out of the ordinary.

She looked around. Josie had several alternatives to walking to the bus interchange. She could have turned left and walked along the path that followed the river several kilometres up into the hills. There were plenty of secluded places up there where she could spend a quiet day. Or she could have turned right when she left the house and headed in that direction instead of coming down to the park. Marie could see a street sign not far down Whitbread, so it wouldn't have taken her long to disappear from view or to walk around the corner into the next street and meet a friend with a car.

Marie turned to walk back to the interchange, but instead of using the path she walked along the river bank until she was forced to move back up on to the path. No sign of any bodies floating in the river today, at least, not along this stretch.

When she got back to the car, she took out her note book and added to her notes:

- •Early morning walkers/joggers on river pathway
- •Neighbours both sides
- •People in street joining park to interchange
- •Two streets - possible vehicle interception points

When she arrived back in her office, she called Detective Inspector Carl West to discuss her uneasy feelings, and alert him to the possibility that she would be calling him later if Mrs Ford did not turn up. When she explained to Carl that she knew Josie Ford and that her disappearance was out of character, he asked her to send him a copy of her photograph and to call him before she went home.

Carl had been a colleague of her husband, Steve, before Steve had transferred to Special Operations and got himself killed. Talking to Carl always made her think of Steve. He had been dead for five years but sometimes it felt like only yesterday that he had been killed. She knew it was probably time she moved on and met someone else. It was lonely being on her own even if she had Maggie to distract her. At least she hadn't fallen for another policeman. There was no way she was going through that again.

She took a deep breath, said a silent prayer of thanks for the blessing Steve had been in her life, and prepared a quick action plan to follow in case Josie Ford did not turn up. Then she turned her attention to her inbox to see what else had happened since she had left her office to interview Paul Ford. The world didn't stop just because one woman was reported missing.

CHAPTER 3

Matthew and Luke arrived home from school at four thirty in the afternoon to find their father sitting at the kitchen table with an empty coffee cup.

'What are you doing here, Dad?' Matthew asked.

'You OK, Dad? You look upset.' There was no hiding anything from Luke, he was almost as perceptive as his mother when it came to reading Paul's emotions. Luke sat down opposite his father, while Matthew turned into the pantry to find something to eat.

'I don't know how to say this, but your mother seems to have disappeared.'

'What?' Matthew was out of the pantry and standing in the kitchen with a packet of biscuits in his hands. 'What do you mean?'

'She didn't turn up at school this morning, she hasn't called me and I haven't been able to find out where she is.'

'Did you call her?' asked Matthew as he sat down next to his brother.

'Yeah, but all I get is her voice mail.'

'Did you check to see she didn't leave her phone home?' Luke looked at him hopefully.

'I've checked every spot I could think of. All of her hand bags, the bedroom, out by the computer, in the lounge. I've even called her number while I've been here waiting. Nothing. That phone is not in this house.'

'Did you ring Nonna? Mum tells her everything.'

'She was one of the first people I called. She hasn't heard from her either.'

'I hope nothing has happened to her, Dad. I mean, it's not like Mum not to let us know where she is. She's always insisting I call home whenever I'm out. She makes me take my phone even if I'm just going down to the shops.'

Matthew started unwrapping the biscuits.

'So what do we do now?' asked Luke. 'Do we need to call the police?'

'I've already been to the police station. I'll need to call them if your mother doesn't come home tonight. When I spoke to them today, to Sergeant Wood...'

'What, Maggie Wood's mum?' asked Matthew.

'Who's Maggie Wood?'

'She's a girl at school. Her mum's a sergeant over at the police station.'

'Come to think of it, she did mention her daughter was in your class. Anyway, what I wanted to say was she told me most people that go missing usually just turn up again. Who knows, your mother might have simply needed some time out. She looked pretty stressed this morning when she was leaving for school. I wish she'd just call.'

They sat looking at each other. Matthew took three biscuits and handed the packet to Luke.

'You may as well change out of your uniforms and get started on your homework. I need to think about what we're going to have for dinner. We can all have a laugh when she comes home, and Matthew, you can tell her off for not calling in.'

Looking out the back window, Paul noticed the forest of pot plants Josie kept on the back veranda and remembered he'd promised to water them. 'I'm going out to water the pot plants.'

'OK, Dad.'

The boys ate their biscuits and made themselves a cup of coffee before moving off to their rooms to change and start on their homework.

Paul found the watering can, filled it at the tank and started the process of giving each pot plant a drink. It took him several watering cans to cater for the twenty pot plants. He was putting the watering can back when he heard the front doorbell ring. By the time he had re-entered the house, Luke had opened the front door to his maternal grandparents.

Maria bustled in with her handbag, with Mick in her wake lugging the food basket. At least the question of what they would be having for dinner was answered.

'Hi, Nonna! Do you need a hand, Nonno?' Luke greeted them.

Maria hugged him and gave him a kiss on the cheek.

'Just hold the door open for me, Luke. Where's your Dad?' was Mick's response.

'He's out the back, watering Mum's plants.'

Paul met them as they entered the kitchen. He embraced Maria and shook Mick's hand, after Mick had deposited the food basket on the table.

'Any news?' Mick asked as he grasped Paul's hand.

'Nothing.'

Maria fussed over Matthew, who came into the kitchen to say hello and to find out what food they had brought with them. You had to hand it to Maria, she knew how to spoil her grandsons with food and affection. Paul was pleased they had come. They would help with the celebration if Josie came home or be there for support if she didn't.

Paul sent the boys back up to their rooms to get on with their homework, while Maria took over the kitchen.

'Thanks for coming, Ma. I don't know if I'll be able to handle things if she doesn't come home tonight.'

'That's why we're here, Paul. I don't know what else to do. We'll need each other if ...' she stopped talking and started to get busy with preparing dinner.

Mick found a couple of beers in the fridge and he and Paul retired to the lounge.

'What time does she normally get home?'

'About six. She likes to stay back after school to do her marking and preparation so that she can have a bit of free time at home.'

'So, what else has been happening?'

They made small talk until six o'clock came around. Paul went out to see if she was coming down the pathway along the river. No sign of her. He called her phone again. No answer apart from her voice mail greeting. He didn't bother leaving a message. A feeling of dread started bubbling to the surface of his awareness. Slowly, he retraced his steps back to the house.

'Is she here, Dad?'

'Not yet.'

Luke went back into his room. The house was quiet. Maria and Mick were silently putting the final touches to dinner and setting the table. It would be dark by six thirty. Paul decided he couldn't wait any longer. Obviously, she wasn't coming home tonight. He took out the business card Marie Wood had given him and punched in the numbers.

'Sergeant Wood.'

'It's Paul Ford. She hasn't come home.'

She waited a few moments to allow him to compose himself.

'Paul, I'll need to go public with this, are you OK with that?'

'Yes, I'm really worried now that something has happened to her.'

'OK. Sit tight. I'll need to make a few calls. Are you going to be OK?'

'Yeah. Josie's parents are here.'

'Paul, I'll call in on my way home in about an hour.'

'OK. Bye.'

They were all in the kitchen now. Maria started dishing up Matthew's favourite dish: lasagne.

The boys had lost their appetite. Luke couldn't stop crying and sat hugging Maria. Matthew picked at the food on his plate and sat in glum silence. Paul managed to eat a few mouthfuls. Mick went out to sit on the back veranda. The food trick had not worked.

They were still sitting at the table looking at their plates when the doorbell rang to announce Sergeant Wood's arrival.

Paul got up to let her in. When he opened the door, he could see several police cars in the street and officers moving off in both directions. There was a plain-clothes officer with Marie.

'What's going on?' he asked as he let Marie and the officer into the house.

'We're doing a door knock of the neighbours, Paul. We want to know if anybody saw Josie this morning. This is Detective Inspector West.'

'Carl,' the inspector said as he extended his hand.

The two men shook hands. Paul led them out of the hallway into the kitchen and introduced them to his in-laws and his sons.

Maria and the boys cleared the table. The uneaten lasagne

went back into the warm oven. Maria was aware that the boys would be looking for food later in the evening. She had heard enough stories from Josie about their legendary eating habits - especially Matthew's. Mick dragged in a couple of extra chairs from the study and they all sat around the table.

Inspector West put his notepad on the table. 'Given what you've told us about your wife, Mr Ford, it doesn't seem likely that she would walk out without telling you, so until we establish otherwise, we'll need to assume something has happened to prevent her from being here or telling you where she is.' He let that news sink in. 'While we are speaking, there is a team of officers interviewing your neighbours to see if any of them saw anything unusual around the time your wife left for work this morning.' He didn't add that they would be asking a few other questions about the Fords as well. 'In the morning, we will have a team down in the park interviewing the morning walkers and joggers. We have released your wife's photograph to the media. It will hit the late-night TV news tonight and be in tomorrow's papers.'

He paused while they took that in.

'There is one other thing. It appears your wife did not catch the bus this morning or Monday morning for that matter. Sergeant Wood has examined the CCTV footage from the interchange for the last few days. The last time your wife caught the bus as expected was Friday morning.'

After a couple of minutes of stunned silence, Inspector West turned to Matthew. 'When was the last time you saw your mother, Matthew?'

'This morning, she came up to my room and said goodbye before she left for work.'

'Does she do that every morning?'

'Yes'

'What about you, Luke?

'The same.'

'What time was that this morning?'

'Before breakfast,' Luke responded.

'Can you be a little more precise?'

'Sometime around seven o'clock, I suppose. She normally leaves just after seven.'

'Did you actually see which way she went when she left the house?'

'I don't think any of us could say yes to that,' said Paul. 'The boys were in their rooms down the end of the passageway and I was sitting in here. She went out the front door. The last I saw of her was her going through that doorway to go up to the boy's rooms.'

'What about you boys?'

'She just ducked her head in the doorway to my room and said goodbye. Then I heard the front door shut.' Luke looked at his brother.

'Same,' said Matthew.

'What about you, Mrs Kelly? When was the last time you saw Josie?'

'On Sunday. We had a barbecue here for my birthday. I haven't seen her since then. She usually calls me Wednesday night for a catch up after dinner.'

'Mr Kelly?'

'Not since last Sunday, Inspector.'

'I take it from what Sergeant Wood has told me, Mr Ford, you have contacted her friends.'

'I've rung all the likely suspects. No-one has heard from her.'

'Does your wife have an address book with her friends' contact details?'

'If you want a copy, most of them are in her email address book.'

'Thanks. We may need talk to them and her associates at work.'

Paul turned to Matthew.' Can you print out a copy of the email address book for the inspector?'

Sergeant Wood went with Matthew out to the back room that served as the study.

'Can you think of any reason why anybody would want to hurt you or your wife, Mr Ford?'

'Inspector, we are just ordinary people. We're not rich, we don't make waves, we pay our bills, we're not into drugs or anything. We don't do road rage. I've got no idea why anyone would want to hurt us.'

'Has Josie said anything about problems at school? Has she got any kids or their parents offside? I guess I don't have to tell you what parents can be like these days.'

Paul caught the brief smile in Mick's eyes at the oblique football reference. 'As far as I know, Inspector, Josie's students love her. Teaching might be tiring and school politics might be stressful but Josie loves her job. When it comes to parents she's very diplomatic. She's never said anything about having problems with parents.'

'What about other teachers? Does she have any enemies at work?'

'Josie has been back at St Catherine's since Luke started school. She's complained about a few people being hopeless teachers in that time but that's only to me. She's too diplomatic to confront people. She doesn't do confrontation in the workplace, so I doubt she has any enemies there. Still, I could be wrong. I don't actually see her in action at school. It's all second hand to me.'

'You mentioned that you aren't rich, what about your family? Any money there that might attract attention?'

'My father's a retired public servant living on his pension.

My mother never worked outside the home. I have five brothers. They all live interstate. Some of them have businesses but none of them are what you would call rich. There's no real money to speak of even if you added us all together.'

'Any reason why all your brothers live interstate?'

'If you get around to speaking to my father you'll understand, Inspector.'

'Oh. Do you keep in touch with them?'

'Yeah, we're all pretty close. It's just Dad they have issues with.'

'Maria and I could be a money target, Inspector. We own half a dozen properties.' Mick smiled at the inspector. 'We made a bit of money when we sold the business.'

The inspector made a note.

Sergeant Wood came back into the kitchen with Matthew. She placed the copy of the address book into her folder. The Inspector stood up and closed his notepad.

'Where will you be tomorrow morning, Mr Ford? I'd like to have another chat after we talk to the morning crowd in the park.'

'I'll be here, Inspector. Can't see me going into work tomorrow.'

'There could be a media contingent camped outside in the morning. I suggest you leave them to us. We will have a command vehicle at the end of the street.'

Marie Wood gave each of the boys a reassuring pat on the shoulder and then they were gone.

Paul decided it was time to warn his mother so that his father didn't see it on the TV news without knowing it was coming. The telephone rang several times before his mother picked up. His father never answered the telephone when his mother was there.

Always said it would be a waste of time. The calls were always for her.

'Mum, it's Paul.'

'Is Josie alright?'

'I don't know. She hasn't come home. The police are trying to find her.' He took a deep breath.

'Oh, Paul.'

'Mum, it will be on the late news tonight and in the papers tomorrow. You'd better warn Dad before he sees it.'

'Do you need us to come over?'

'No, Mick and Maria are here, we should be alright. I'll call you in the morning.'

'I'm sorry, Paul. This is dreadful. Are you sure you're going to be alright?'

'I don't know. I'll just have to see what happens.'

'I'll ring your brothers. You look after the boys. How are they taking this?'

Paul turned around to check on his sons. Luke was crying and clinging to his grandmother. Matthew was helping himself to a plate of lasagne.

'It's not a pretty sight here at the moment.'

'I'll be praying for you. Call me as soon as you hear something, even if it's the middle of the night.'

'OK, Mum. Bye.'

Matthew took the plate of lasagne up to his room.

'Think I'll make coffee,' said Mick. 'Do you want one?'

Nobody answered but he got up and went into the pantry to find the coffee beans to grind. One of the advantages of spending so much time in each other's houses was knowing where things were. Maria took Luke up to his room. By the time she returned, wiping tears from her eyes, the coffee was ready.

'This is not going to be easy, Paul. That boy is so close to Josie, this is breaking his heart.'

Paul motioned them into a group hug. There was no way he could speak. After a few of the longest minutes Paul could remember, Mick said, 'We'd better drink this coffee before it gets cold.'

They sat around the table drinking coffee, not game to look at each other.

'We need to stay strong for the boys, Paul,' Maria said at last. She took hold of his hands. 'And we need to stay strong for each other.'

'OK, let's all take a deep breath,' replied Paul.' We don't know that anything bad has happened to Josie yet. Let's hope it's all a misunderstanding or something. We need to stay positive. She could still come home tonight.'

'Let's hope so. Think you had better go up and talk to Luke.'

Maria busied herself cleaning up the plates. Mick went into the lounge and switched on the TV while Paul went up to comfort the boys. When he reached Luke's room he was in his bed and didn't want to talk. He gave him a hug and went to check on Matthew. He was doing his music homework and didn't want to be disturbed. He went down to the lounge and sat with Mick and lost himself in the mindless world of TV.

At nine o'clock Maria came in to join them. 'Think it's time we went home, Mick. Will you be alright, Paul?'

'Who knows, Ma? I'll try and get some sleep. You go. I'll call you if anything happens.' He stood up and gave her a hug and kissed her cheeks. He had become so Italian over the years it was scary. He even hugged Mick.

Matthew appeared to say goodnight to his grandparents, so there was another round of hugging and cheek kissing. Maria went up to check on Luke and came back to report that he was asleep.

'Well, what do we do now, Dad?' Matthew asked when they came back in from seeing off his grandparents.

'I suppose all we can do is wait and pray.'

'I need to go to school tomorrow. I've got an important test.'

'Sure you want to go?'

'Probably be easier than sitting around here waiting. At least, I'll have stuff to do at school.'

'OK. So, what did you and Sergeant Wood talk about out in the study?'

'She wanted to know if you and Mum got on or had fights.'

'What did you tell her?'

A smile spread across Matthew's face. 'I told her you seemed happy together to me.'

'What did she say to that?'

'She said I should consider myself lucky to have loving parents.'

Now it was Paul's turn to smile.

'OK, mate. Probably time you started getting organised for bed. I'll set the alarm so I can take you to school. We'll let Luke decide what he wants to do in the morning. I'm going to watch the nine thirty news.'

'Thought I might watch it with you, Dad.'

'Thanks.' They sat down next to each other on the couch to watch the nine thirty news.

After ten minutes of world and national news the focus shifted to local news. Following a story on a drug bust, the screen filled with Josie's image while the newsreader gave the details. Then they crossed to Inspector West saying that police held grave fears for her safety and asking members of the public to contact police, if they had seen Josie anytime since seven o'clock that morning.

Paul turned off the TV. The telephone rang. Within the next hour all of his brothers had rung to offer support and encouragement, and Luke was up eating microwave warmed lasagne in the kitchen.

'That sort of makes it official doesn't it, Dad? She's missing for real now.'

'Guess so, Luke, but it doesn't mean she's not coming back.'

'Hope you're right, Dad.'

'Me too, sunshine.'

By eleven he had settled Luke and was lying in bed. If he thought getting to sleep last night had been a struggle, tonight it seemed almost impossible. His head was full of a constant stream of scenarios describing all the possible things that could have happened to Josie, including the possibility that she had left him.

CHAPTER 4

WEDNESDAY MORNING ARRIVED with the usual birdsong. No-one had told the birds anything was different or that Paul had spent most of the night tossing and turning and waiting for the telephone to ring. There was no need for the alarm clock. He was awake when six o'clock rolled around. He got up, showered and dressed. At six thirty he woke the boys to see whether they still wanted to go to school. Matthew still wanted to go and complete the test he had been preparing for. Luke decided that it was probably the best course of action, as he didn't want to just sit around and wait for something to happen.

After breakfast Paul drove the boys to school. Once at school, the boys went off to catch up with their friends before classes started. Paul went to the school office to see Alice Young, the school counsellor, to alert her to the situation. Alice, who had seen the late-night news, had a copy of the morning's paper on her desk opened to the story with Josie's picture.

'Hello, Paul. Sorry to hear about this.' She waved her hand across the paper on her desk.

'I don't know what to think, Alice.'

'Sit down. I'll get you a coffee.'

'Thanks.' Paul sat in the chair that students used when they came to see Alice to discuss their problems. It had been a long time since he had sat in Alice's office. They had met, both young graduates, all those years ago when he had returned to St Jude's as a teacher. He had spent many afternoons discussing students with her in this very office. Now they were both middle-aged parents with a different set of worries. Alice returned with two cups of coffee.

'How are the boys?'

'Luke's taking it pretty hard. He's very close to his mother.' He noticed that he hadn't used Josie's name. 'Matthew's being Matthew. No open show of what's going on, staying with the pragmatic. He has a big music test today so he's focusing on that.'

'So, they're at school today?'

'Yes, they decided it was probably easier to have something else to think about and to be with their friends. The only people I'm expecting to see today are the police.'

'I know this must be hard for you, Paul. If you need someone to talk to you know you can give me a call.'

Paul took a sip of his coffee. 'I wasn't thinking about me, Alice, but I'll keep your offer in mind. I was thinking more about the boys. They might be OK today but if this goes pear shaped I think Luke's going to need some support. I'm not sure how Matthew is going to take it. He's trying so hard to be grown up about it.'

'Tell them they can talk to me anytime. It doesn't have to be at school.'

They drank their coffee in silence for a few minutes.

'Let me know if anything happens today, Paul. I'll take care of telling the boys.'

'I'd better get going. The police want to talk to me.'

'Take care.' Alice gave him a hug and he left her office and walked back to the car.

Inspector West was waiting for him when he got home.

'Hope you haven't been waiting too long, Inspector. Just took the boys to school.'

'That's OK. One of my officers saw you driving off with boys in school uniform. How are they?'

'Luke's upset. He's close to his mother.' He'd done it again, avoided her name. 'Matthew doesn't show his feelings much. He's focused on his school work.'

Paul opened the front door and led the inspector into the kitchen. They sat at the table.

'So, Inspector, what have you found out from the neighbours?'

'Seems nobody looks out on to the street in the early morning. They're either still in bed or in their kitchens or bathrooms getting ready to start the day. None of your neighbours either saw anything or heard anything, like an unfamiliar car engine, yesterday morning. None of the walkers and joggers we interviewed this morning remembered seeing your wife this week. Several said that they saw her walking towards the interchange most mornings they were in the park but not any day this week.'

'She went out that door. She must be somewhere.'

'Mr Ford, is there anything you haven't told us that might explain why your wife might have decided to leave you or why anybody would want to hurt her?'

Paul looked at the inspector. He knew he was just doing his job and these questions had to be asked, but he couldn't help feeling like he wasn't being trusted.

'Inspector, we're planning to celebrate our twentieth wedding anniversary in July. We've had a pretty good relationship over the years. A few heated arguments and misunderstandings but no big fights. We work hard on keeping our relationship alive. Sometimes that's not easy when you've got kids and the stresses of work. We talk. We spend time together as a couple and as a family. I can't believe she's left me, even if they say the husband's the last one to find out his wife has left him. Why do I say that? I know Josie. She's the sort of person that would only leave a relationship on amicable terms. If our relationship was on the rocks she would have talked it through to either mend it or end it. Besides, it's inconceivable that she'd leave the boys. No, something has happened to her.'

'What about enemies? We all have someone we have upset.'

'Like I told you last night, I'm not aware of how we would have made any enemies. We're your model citizens. We're polite, we obey the law, we talk to all our neighbours, we mix mostly with our extended family. How do you make enemies doing that?'

The inspector decided to try another tack. 'Mr Ford, if you were looking for your wife, where would you look?'

'Well, she has a close circle of girlfriends. They get together for a meal and a talkfest at least once a month, usually in a restaurant. I called all of them yesterday. Unless they were lying to me, they all said they hadn't heard from her or seen her. If she has done a runner, maybe she's staying with one of them. You've got all the names and addresses. Anna Rodrigo is her closest friend. Josie goes away with her every couple of months, for, what do they call it? Yeah, that's it, retail therapy, shopping to the rest of us, or to see a play or just to have a break. Maybe she's hiding at Anna's, but that's too obvious a place to hide if you ask me.'

'Anywhere else?'

'Well, she's not at her parents' place. That leaves her sister, Rosa, and she's the one who rang me to ask me where she was.'

The inspector looked at him, so he explained, 'Rosa works in the front office at St Catherine's.'

'What if she decided to go interstate, where would she go?'

'The only people we know interstate are my brothers and their families. They all called last night.'

'What about overseas?'

'Josie is planning to go to Italy and Ireland for her long service leave but that's not due until next year. She's been saving for the trip for a couple of years. She's got about six thousand dollars in her savings account.'

'So, she has access to enough money for a little holiday if she wanted one.'

Paul hadn't thought of that and his face betrayed that thought before he said, 'We can check her account balance if you like. I just need to log on to the computer.'

The inspector nodded his agreement, so they moved out to the study. Paul fired up the computer, located Josie's bank account log-in details and logged in to her accounts on the bank's website. They could see the details of three accounts: a special purpose savings account with a balance of $5,900.50, a transaction account with a balance of $1,980.23 and a credit card account with $1,500 available credit. The most recent transaction was a credit of $1,976.21, with yesterday's date, representing Josie's salary payment into the transaction account.

They looked at the debit transactions going back over the last three months. A series of transactions showing the same supermarket, butcher, hairdresser, gym subscription, the direct debits used to service their insurance premiums, transfers to the savings account and some cash withdrawals of $100 or less.

'I gave her twenty bucks yesterday before she left. Her purse was empty.'

'You sure?'

'She always runs out of cash just before payday. If you look at her account, you can see she runs it down to almost zero within a week of getting paid.'

The inspector reviewed the account again.

'Let's just have a quick look back over her credit card transactions.'

Their review revealed that Josie had not used her credit card for six months.

'Does she have access to your accounts?'

'No, I only have one account with a credit card attached to it. Josie kept the accounts we opened when we first started work. I had to open a new account when I joined the bank for my pay to go into. We use my money to pay the school fees and utilities and to run the car. I don't earn as much as Josie these days, one of the downsides of leaving teaching for banking.'

The two men looked at each other. It was obvious Josie hadn't accessed her accounts to fund her disappearance. That meant that either she was with someone who was paying or this was an unplanned event.

'What are your plans for the next couple of days, Mr Ford?'

'I think I'll take today off and see if I can get some sleep. I can't afford to take too much time off work, so, if I'm feeling up to it, I'll go in to work tomorrow. Don't know how much of this waiting for something to happen I can take.'

The inspector's mobile phone rang.

'Excuse me a minute, Mr Ford.' He walked out into the kitchen to take the call. A couple of minutes later he was back.

'I'm sorry, Mr Ford, there's no easy way to say this. It looks like we've found your wife's body.'

Paul just looked at him and slumped into the chair. He could feel the blood draining from his head, he was losing focus. He was sliding out of the chair. A strong pair of hands gripped his shoulders.

'Take a deep breath, that's the way. Keep breathing.'

Paul felt himself returning to something like normal awareness.

'Take your time.'

They sat together in silence while Paul regained his composure. Paul could see scenes from Silent Witness running on his inner screen. He shook his head and looked at the inspector. The pictures cleared.

'Where?'

'Over by the airport. Some walker came across the body about half an hour ago. I'll need you to come with me to identify the body. Do you feel up to it?'

'Do I get a choice?'

The inspector shook his head slowly. 'Do you want me to call someone for support?'

'No, I think this is something I best do alone. It'll be hard enough as it is.'

'Forensics are there now. They should be ready for us by the time we get there.'

They left the study, breaking one of Paul's house rules by leaving the computer on. Paul retrieved his keys and mobile phone from the kitchen and let Inspector West lead him out the front door. He stopped to lock the door and then followed the inspector to the police car waiting in the street in front of the house. Constable Priest opened the rear door for him and then returned to her position behind the wheel.

***

The trip across town to the airport through the morning traffic took an hour. Paul watched the city go by wondering how he was going to handle identifying Josie's body, and at the same time hoping it wasn't her. The inspector spent most of the trip on his mobile talking to his officers at the scene.

As they approached the airport the inspector turned to Paul. 'They've found your wife's handbag. Her credit card and driver's licence are still in her purse. So it looks like this will be a formality. My people are certain it's her. I'm sorry.'

Constable Priest turned off the street into a dirt road leading to a wooded field on the western side of the airport. The car came to a halt next to a white van and two other police cars in a parking space near where a walking trail crossed the road and led into the trees. A passenger jet roared overhead and climbed into the sky, taking people off to their holidays or business meetings, as they got out of the car. A constable appeared from the trees and escorted them along the walking trail to a small clearing, cordoned off with blue and white crime scene tape, about twenty metres in from the road.

Just like you see on TV, thought Paul, as two figures dressed in blue plastic suits wheeled a stretcher with a green body bag on it towards them. They stopped when they reached the tape. The constable lifted the tape and they wheeled the stretcher onto the walking trail.

Inspector West made the required introduction. 'Mr Ford, this is Dr Jonas, the police pathologist.'

'I'm sorry, Mr Ford, if you'll just step over here beside me.'

Paul stood next to Dr Jonas, who unzipped the top of the body bag to reveal Josie's white face staring at him, her blond hair stained with dried blood on the left side of her head above the ear. He looked at the inspector, nodded his head and managed to say, 'Yes, that's her.'

The pathologist zipped up the bag. Inspector West led Paul back to the car. Paul sat in the car while the inspector spoke with the pathologist. He looked at his watch. It was 10.15. The day was only just starting but it felt like all days had ended. The sound of another jet taking off brought him back to the present. Life goes on. Nothing stops just because someone you love leaves the planet.

The inspector got into the car and sat beside Paul.

'Constable Priest will drive you home. I need to attend to a few things here.' He eased out of the car and shut the door. The young policewoman who had driven them over slipped in behind the wheel and started the car. Before they moved off, she turned to Paul.

'Inspector West suggested we pick up your boys from St Jude's. Would you like me to call the school or do you think you can do that?'

'I think I can call to let them know we're coming.' He found his mobile phone, located Alice's number and called it as the car started to move.

'Alice Young.'

'Alice, it's Paul.' He took a deep breath.

'Are you OK?'

'No.' It came out quicker than he had intended.

'What's happened?'

'Josie's dead.' No more words would come out. Only sobs.

'Oh, Paul, I'm so sorry. Is somebody with you?'

Paul focused on his breathing. After a few deep breaths he was able to tell her, 'I'm...I'm with the police. They're bringing me to pick up the boys. We should be there in about thirty minutes.'

'OK. I'll get the boys organised and see you when you get here.' Alice ended the call.

He sat back and closed his eyes. He could see her telling the principal and then going to find Matthew and Luke, helping them pack their stuff into their bags and taking them to the privacy of her office to confirm their worst fear.

They drove in silence. What words of comfort can you really offer a stranger in these circumstances?

Paul gazed through the window at the moving blur of the busy world slipping by. His eyes saw but his brain did not register. He was lost in a black space that gave no answers to his questions. How do you process this sort of stuff? It didn't make any sense. Why was Josie lying there dead? What was he supposed to do now? How was he going to tell Mick and Maria? No point in thinking about it, just do it. There's no way to make it easy. He opened his mobile again and called their number.

'Mick Kelly.'

'Mick, it's Paul.'

'What's the news? Have they found Josie?'

'Afraid so, Mick. She's dead.'

'What?'

'They found her body over by the airport about an hour ago.' He could almost see Mick collapsing into the chair he knew was by the telephone in their family room. At least, he wouldn't have to tell Maria. Mick would have that honour now.

'Where are you?'

'The police are driving me to St Jude's to pick up the boys?'

'OK, we'll be over once I've broken the news to Maria and Rosa. Shit, Paul, how did this happen?'

'It just doesn't make any sense to me. I'll see you at home, I'm sure the boys will appreciate you being there. I know I will.'

He ended the call and then called his mother's number.

'Mum, it's Paul.'

'What's happened? Have the police found Josie?'

'Mum, you'd better sit down.' He waited to give her time to take a seat. 'They found her body about an hour ago.'

'Are you telling me Josie's dead?'

'Yes.'

'Oh, you poor darling. I don't know what to say. Oh God, this is just too much. How did this happen? Your father's going to be beside himself. What are we going to do? Where are you?'

'The police are taking me to pick up the boys. Why don't you come over? Mick and Maria are heading over. I think I'm going to need some help with this one, Mum.'

'Yes, yes, I think we might all need some help. I'll just get George organised and we'll be there. And I'll call Andrew and get him to tell the others. Oh Paul, I'm so sorry.'

'Thanks, Mum.' He ended the call and let out a long breath. It was done now.

He returned to watching the world go by and tried to stop thinking but his mind filled with a stream of questions. Why had God allowed this to happen to her? To him? To them? What did it all mean? How do you live with kissing your wife goodbye one morning only to find her dead in a paddock on the other side of town the next morning? What had happened to growing old together? What the fuck was going on? Life isn't supposed to go like this!

'Mr Ford?'

Constable Priest waited for him to look at her. 'We've arrived. Where's the best place to park?'

Paul came out of his thought maze and directed her to the parking area near the school office. She walked beside him as he approached the building in a dazed walk, and reached out to steady him as he wobbled on the steps leading up to the door. As they entered the reception area, Matthew and Luke emerged with Alice from her office. Luke's face was stained with tears. He grabbed on to his father and Paul wrapped an arm around him. Matthew stood with a blank expression holding their school bags. With his other arm, Paul drew Matthew into his embrace. They stood there holding each other up while Constable Priest took Alice aside to get her details and hand her one of Inspector West's business cards.

Alice walked over and wrapped her arms around the sad trio.

'Thanks, Alice.'

'If you need me, give me a call.'

They made their way out to the police car under the gaze of curious students peering from the windows of the surrounding classrooms. It's not every day you see fellow students getting into a police car. The real story would break soon enough.

***

Constable Priest drove them to Whitbread Avenue. Paul thanked her and took the boys inside.

It didn't feel like home. Now, it was just the house that Josie would not be returning to ever again. It felt empty as he walked in even though it was full of Josie's things. Her stuff might still be there but the connection between them and Josie was no longer detectable. The road ahead looked like a long winding path into blackness. Paul sank into the couch in the lounge and his tears escaped from the well in which he had been storing them.

Luke came in and curled up against him on the couch. Hugging each other they cried together in their grief. Matthew sat in his room in silence, lost in his own thoughts of loss but not able to cry. Maybe they would have stayed that way for the rest of the day, but about twenty minutes after they arrived home, Mick and Maria arrived. Being embraced by his nonna was the dam buster for Matthew. As soon as she hugged him the tears began to flow and he sobbed uncontrollably into her embrace, as she stroked his back and waited for the deluge to subside. When it was over a very washed out Matthew sat quietly in the kitchen, as Maria, wiping away her silent tears, started on making coffee and unpacking the hamper of food she had brought with her.

Mick joined Paul and Luke in the lounge, where all three of them sat looking sad and lost with wet, red eyes.

'Why would anyone want to shoot Josie?' Mick asked. 'I just don't get it. Why would anyone want to kill her like that?'

Paul had no answers for him.

George and Anne arrived and the crying started all over again as they exchanged condolences with Mick and Maria, then with Paul and finally with the boys. Even George burst into tears as he gave Paul a long embrace.

'I'm sorry, son.'

'Thanks, Dad.' Paul hugged him back. This was a special moment. He had never seen his father in tears before in his life.

George found his handkerchief and wiped at his eyes. 'Why would anyone do this?'

'Let's hope the police can find out, Dad.'

'I've called all the boys, Paul. They're all feeling for you,' said Anne. She gave him another hug and then went into the kitchen with Maria.

Now there were two hampers of food. Anne had brought biscuits and cakes. The boys might be upset but sooner or later they would be hungry.

'Coffee's ready,' called Maria.

They gathered in the kitchen and sat around the table sipping coffee.

'What happens now, Dad?' asked Matthew.

'We need to organise a funeral.'

'And a wake,' said Mick.

'And a gathering of the clan,' said George.

'Yeah, funerals tend to do that,' said Mick.

The doorbell rang. Maria went to answer it and came back with Rosa and Carlo and their daughters Sophie and Michelle. Another round of hugs and tears and words of consolation.

The cousins withdrew to Matthew's room to talk. Sophie and Matthew were the same age. Luke was a year older than Michelle. Having spent a lot of time together they were close friends.

The telephone rang. It was Henry from the bank.

'Paul, we've just heard about Josie on the midday news. I'm really sorry, mate. We're all thinking of you here. The team asked me to pass on their love.'

'Thanks, Henry. I'll be in touch when things settle down a bit.'

'Take your time, mate. This isn't going to be easy. I'd better let you go but if you need anything, you know where I am.'

'Thanks.'

Paul returned to the kitchen and put the telephone back in its cradle. 'That was my boss from work. He said they've been talking about Josie on the news. Guess that means we can expect more calls.'

Over the next couple of hours Paul's brothers called to give him support and to let him know that they would be coming when the funeral was arranged. The calls from his brothers were interspersed by calls from the same group of Josie's friends that he had called the previous day asking if they had heard from her.

When the telephone fell silent, Maria decided it was time they had something to eat.

While they were setting out the contents of Maria's hamper on the table for lunch, the doorbell rang. Matthew answered the door and discovered Father Mulligan standing on the porch.

'Ah, Matthew,' he said wrapping an arm around Matthew's shoulders. 'This is a sad day. Come on, let's go in.'

'Oh hello, Father,' Maria greeted him as he entered the kitchen behind Matthew.

'Hello everybody,' he replied as he gazed around the room. 'Josie was a dear friend. I know I'm going to miss her but not half as much as all of you. This is indeed a sad day for all of us.'

'You're not wrong there, Father,' said Mick as he stood to shake the priest's hand.

Slowly, in the crowded kitchen, Father Mulligan moved around the group hugging each one briefly and offering words of consolation. When he got to Paul, the two men, friends since university days, simply embraced in silence, unable to voice the emotions they were feeling. When he released Paul from his embrace, Father Mulligan suggested they take a moment to pray. The family formed a rough circle around the kitchen table, each holding the hand of two others, and bowed their heads.

'Lord, today we are hurting. We are gathered here supporting each other the best we can. We don't understand why this is happening but we trust that, in time, you will reveal its meaning to us. For now, we give thanks for Josie's life and all the gifts she brought into our lives while she was with us as a daughter, sister, wife, mother, auntie and friend. We know we are going to miss her presence in our lives because she touched us all with so much love.

We ask that you welcome her into your heavenly kingdom with all your angels and saints, and we ask for the strength we will need to get through the days ahead as we help each other to cope without her. We ask this through your son, Jesus Christ our Lord.'

'Amen.'

'Thank you, Father. We needed that,' said Maria. 'Now sit down and join us for a bite to eat.'

The adults sat around the table exchanging small talk and catching up with Father Mulligan, while the cousins retreated to the family room with plates of food.

After lunch, Rosa and Carlo and their girls went home. Maria and Mick went shopping at the local supermarket to buy the food that would be needed over the next few days. Maria's plan was to stock the pantry and come over to make sure they were eating properly. Anne and George sat with Matthew and Luke looking through photograph albums and reliving some of the moments of the family's life that had been captured on camera and lovingly scrapbooked by Josie.

Paul and Father Mulligan withdrew to the study and sat in the chairs in front of the computer desk.

'Have the police asked you to identify the body yet?'

'Yes. Inspector West was here this morning when the call came through to tell him they had found the body. He took me with him to confirm that it was Josie.'

'That couldn't have been easy.'

'I wasn't looking forward to it, but you know, once we got there it was like you see on those TV shows. Crime scene tape everywhere, people in blue plastic suits, a body bag on a stretcher, police standing around. All a bit unreal actually, even when you're doing it for real.'

'So, how are you, now that you have done it for real?'

'It's like I'm watching it happen to someone else. It was a hell of a shock when the inspector first told me. He had to stop me sliding out of this very chair. Since then, it's like I've been in some sort of a haze. Luckily, the police drove me over to St Jude's to pick up the boys. I'm not sure I could have done that myself.'

'Shock can do that to you, Paul. It lets you function during a time of crisis but it's usually followed by a black hole when reality kicks back in, so be gentle with yourself when it does. It might not be pretty.'

'You thinking Irish melancholy or worse?'

'Worse. I'm thinking grieving. It's a process and the early stages can be the hardest. It's also a process that you can't get away from. You might think you can, you might be tempted to try, but in the end, it's the only way to cope and come out sane the other end.'

'So, you're telling me I'm in for a rough time.'

Frank Mulligan looked at his friend and placed his hands on his shoulders.

'You're not going to be alone in this. You'll need to help the boys through their grieving as well. You don't want them stuffing it down and not expressing it. That only makes it worse and could lead to a couple of very angry young men. And then there's the wider family. Let them help you and don't forget your friends, we can help you but we can't do it for you.'

'Thanks, Frank. Don't know what I'd do without you.'

'And, Paul, there's plenty of evidence, scientific or otherwise, that you can't do grief effectively with the bottle.'

'So, there's no point in offering you a drink, then?'

'That's not what I'm saying. What I'm telling you is you can't drown your sorrows, no matter how hard you try. You have to sit with them, and work through them.'

'I'll keep that in mind.' They sat in silence for a few moments before Paul asked, 'Frank, how long do you think it will be before they release Josie's body to us?'

'Probably a couple of days. They'll run tests and look for evidence first.'

'I'll need to start organising a funeral. Where do I start?'

Frank pulled out his wallet and extracted a business card. 'Do you remember Ron Flint?'

'The tall guy who always stands at the back of the church?'

'That's him. He's a funeral director at Flinders Funerals. Does a very good job. Give him a call. He can arrange everything and will collect the body from the morgue.' Frank handed the business card to Paul. 'Did you and Josie ever discuss what you wanted for your funeral service?'

Paul looked at him. 'Not something we talked about really.'

'That's not unusual. Most of us don't want to deal with death. On the other hand, some of us get to deal with it quite often.

What if I pull together some ideas based on what I know about Josie and then we work it out from there?'

'Sounds good to me. I'm sure the boys will have some ideas.'

Frank stood up. 'I'd better get going. I have a couple of other visits to fit in this afternoon.'

'Thanks for coming, Frank.' Paul stood and hugged him.

'Ring Ron and tell him to call me when he has Josie's body so we can agree on a date for the funeral.'

After exchanging goodbyes with George and Anne and hugging the boys, Father Mulligan departed.

Paul rang Ron Flint and set the funeral planning in motion. By the time he had completed the call, Mick and Maria had returned with the shopping. While Anne and Maria busied themselves in the kitchen and the boys watched television, the men, ignoring Frank Mulligan's advice, started on the beer.

When everyone had gone home and the boys to their beds, Paul sat in his meditation chair staring into the darkness. For a long time, he just sat. No thoughts, only emptiness. Eventually, his mind came back online.

This certainly hadn't been part of his forward plan. Yes, death was part of the game when you played in this dimension but he hadn't counted on it playing its hand so soon. He had always believed they would grow old together gracefully, and live well into their eighties, based on their family histories. What had he been reading the other night? Yeah, that was it, living to you're ninety and having lots of sex along the way. Well, he wasn't dead, so the living to be ninety was still a possibility. He wasn't so sure about the lots of sex. He hadn't been confident of the lots of sex with Josie in any case, going on her declining interest over the last couple of years. Now even that option was gone. To be honest, he had never thought there would be a life without Josie in it. He had been convinced she would outlive him. Her grandmother had lived to be ninety. So much for that theory.

Obviously, it didn't matter how much you planned what you thought was your life. In the final analysis, you weren't actually in control of your life situation. Someone else was pulling the strings. Someone else was arranging the events that presented themselves as the circumstances of your life each day. It didn't matter whether that someone was God or your higher self or some crazed killer. The events still happened and that impersonal string of events was what made up your life situation, even if you were not impressed. It didn't matter what you did, the events still happened. All you could do was choose how to respond to the events as they showed up for you.

So, how was he going to respond to this charming little set of events that God had allowed to show up in his life? He could allow what had happened to simply be what had happened or he could rant and rave at God for allowing such a horrible thing to happen to Josie, and to him, and the boys.

Rationally, he knew that whatever choice he made would not change the event. Josie would still be dead, murdered in some senseless killing, no matter what he thought about it. The boys would still be motherless. The thing to think about was how would he be now that this event had happened?

Words he had read somewhere came to mind, words about accepting the situation as if you had chosen it and working with it and not against it, something about stopping the argument with reality. Well, his current reality was that his wife and lover was dead but he wasn't. He was very much still alive and so were the boys. His life was still happening and this event was simply part of the story. That was the bare bones of it.

The question came down to whether he wanted to spend the next six to twelve months depressed and feeling miserable, and making life for everyone around him dark and gloomy, or did he want to move on with his life in this different set of circumstances? And then there would be the reactions of everyone else. Not too many of his friends, and no-one in his family that he was aware of, was into seeing life as a learning experience for the soul. The boys, at least, had been exposed to this way of looking at life through all those dinner table discussions about the meaning of life over the last couple of years.

Others would have to cope with the situation as they chose. He couldn't afford to pander to other people's issues with death and dying and all the unfairness of it all. He could be loving and supportive but he wouldn't be playing the usual games of the sleepers. Yes, there would have to be time and space for grieving but after that he would have to embrace life and move forward, otherwise he could find himself wallowing in self-pity.

A thought floated across his mind pointing out that playing the suffering, hard done by victim of fate would probably see him rewarded with lots of extra attention from Maria. She would be just itching to step in to take care of them. After all, she would want to know how three men could take care of themselves without a woman about the house. He knew his mother wouldn't buy that one. She'd be telling him to get his shit together and get on with life because his sons needed a father, not some cry baby who couldn't cope with a speed hump on the highway of life.

He started laughing as he pictured Anne standing in front of him, left hand resting on her hip with the right pointing at him delivering that message. That confirmed it. His ego would not be getting much energy from the drama of Josie's demise. There had been enough drama already. Now it was time to centre and find that peaceful place within so that he could come to terms with the situation knowing there was nothing he could do to change it.

He spent an hour in quiet meditation and then went to bed. He went straight to sleep.

CHAPTER 5

LATE WEDNESDAY AFTERNOON, Inspector West closed the preliminary pathologist's report, shut his eyes and leant back in his chair. Reading the report had unsettled him. The pathologist had written that there was no sign of sexual assault, but had noted that there appeared to be traces of a silicon based lubricant on the walls of her vagina, indicating she had recently had sex with someone wearing a condom, and the condition of her vaginal walls suggested she had been alive at the time.

The light bruising of the knees suggested she had been forced to kneel on a hard surface. Her hands had been tied behind her back, and she had been shot through the head at close range with a 9mm pistol. The spent cartridge, found at the scene, was sitting on his desk in an evidence bag. The angle of the gunshot wound to her head suggested Josie's killer had been standing above and behind her when the trigger was pulled. The amount of blood at the scene indicated she had been shot elsewhere and the body dumped where they had found it, although the position of the body suggested someone had placed it to look like she had fallen where she had been shot. The pathologist estimated the time of death as ten pm the previous day. He would have the toxicology results sometime tomorrow.

The evidence pointed to a gangland style execution. What he couldn't understand was why anybody would want to execute this particular school teacher. If this was a gangland killing, and it was still a big if, this school teacher must have another story no-one was talking about yet. He wondered what line of business her father had been involved in and what else Paul Ford had not told him. He was bothered by the inconsistency between her being killed elsewhere and the spent cartridge being found a few metres from the body. Someone had obviously gone to some trouble constructing the scene. Another thing that bothered him was the contents of the handbag. It appeared nothing had been taken. It was as if whoever left the body there wanted to make sure they identified her straight away.

He picked up the pathologist's report, drained his coffee and went to join Detective Sergeant Nina Strong and Detective Harry Fuller, who were waiting for him in the operations room. His team occupied a space designed for ten. It wasn't only the emptiness of the space that was depressing. It was filled with furniture well beyond its use-by date. The only thing modern about the place was the technology sitting on the ancient desks. Government austerity took many forms.

'What do you think, Boss?' Nina asked as the inspector walked in.

'I think someone is playing games with us. Some of this,' he waved the pathologist's report, 'doesn't compute for me.'

The inspector walked over to the glass panel in the middle of the room with Josie's picture stuck on it. 'Josephine Ford,' he pointed to the photograph, 'reported missing Tuesday by her husband, Paul Ford. Last seen around seven am Tuesday morning. From what's in this report,' he waved the pathologists report again, 'we know someone shot her at close range around ten pm Tuesday night, and then dumped the body out by the airport. Whoever that was went to some trouble to make it look as though she had been shot where we found the body, including leaving a spent 9mm cartridge.'

He opened the report. 'Says here there are no signs of sexual or any other assault, apart from the wrist bindings and the bullet to the head. But it does appear she had sex with someone, probably wearing a condom, sometime on Tuesday before she was killed. We can start with the husband on that question.

We know that a male, claiming to be a walker, but who did not leave his name or address, called the police assistance line at eight fifteen this morning to report finding the body. The patrol that checked the location found the body where the caller said it would be. The patrol also found Mrs Ford's bag, with her credit card, driver's licence, a twenty dollar note and a pile of student papers, hanging in a tree above the body.' He looked at Harry and Nina. 'What do you make of that?'

'Strange way to bump off a school teacher.'

'What makes you say that, Nina?'

'Well, I would have tortured her to start with if she'd been one of the sadistic bitches that taught me.' She gave him one of her wry smiles. 'Seriously, this looks a hell of a lot like an execution to me, Boss. Someone clearly wanted this lady dead.'

The inspector looked at Harry.

'I wonder what she was doing between seven in the morning and ten at night. Might be interesting if the husband hasn't had sex with her for a few days.'

'Anything else?'

'Yeah, why didn't the bloke who found the body want to leave his details or meet the patrol when it arrived? That doesn't fit the behaviour we normally see. People usually want some recognition for this sort of stuff. But not this bloke, he basically just told us where it was and then disappeared. So, I thought maybe he might know more than he's letting on.'

'I hope you did something with that thought, Harry.'

'I got hold of the recording of the call and had its source identified. I think you'll like what I found out.'

'Why would that be, Harry?'

'Because it answers one of those questions you haven't asked yet.'

'What question might that be?'

'What's missing from her handbag?'

'What makes you think anything is missing from her handbag? Sounds like we got all the usual stuff, even the twenty dollars her husband said he gave her on Tuesday morning before she left for work.'

'The husband's statement in the Missing Persons report. He said she wasn't answering her mobile phone and he gave us the number. Just happens to be the same number of the phone our mystery caller used to report finding the body. And, you'll love this bit, the provider was able to tell us that the call was made through a tower located in the CBD.'

'Someone wanted to make sure we found the body today,' said Nina.

'Looks that way but the question is why?' replied the inspector. 'Nina, I want a full background check on Josephine Ford. I want to know what the hell she's been up to, who she mixed with. She's obviously pissed someone off big time. Harry, see what you can find out about the husband and the father, he said he had been in some sort of business. Maybe this is some sort of retribution. And, Harry, tell the phone company we want to know if, and when, that mobile phone comes back on air.'

'I've got them tracking it.'

'Good.'

'Boss, the last time we had one of these executions it was a drug deal gone wrong. Maybe we got ourselves a dead school teacher who was moonlighting as a dealer to the students at her school. Wouldn't be the first one. Want me to follow up with Narcotics?' asked Nina.

'Wouldn't hurt to give them a call to see if she was on their radar.'

The inspector went back to his office to study the crime scene report while Harry and Nina started on their assigned tasks. He had only just settled into his chair when the telephone rang.

It was Deputy Commissioner Thaler.

'Carl, get yourself up to my office. We've got shit flying!'

'On my way, sir.' He replaced the receiver, walked to the lift lobby and caught the lift up to the tenth floor, wondering what shit was flying besides his case.

When he got to the tenth, the deputy commissioner's receptionist waved him straight through.

'Carl, the Commissioner's just had a call from Gerard Fisher, the managing director of B&A bank. Someone called him about half an hour ago demanding five million dollars in cash by Monday and, I'm sure you'll be interested in this bit, threatening to kill the wife of another of their employees if the bank doesn't hand over the money as directed.'

'Probably explains why he wanted us to find the body today,' Carl said almost to himself.

'What was that?'

'Sorry, sir. The call alerting us to the location of the body was made on the victim's mobile phone, and there was no walker at the scene when the patrol arrived. In fact, it appears the caller was somewhere in the CBD when he made the call and not out by the airport, where the body was.'

'We need to find this bastard, Carl, and soon. There's no way we can provide protection to the five or six hundred women he's threatening. They're spread all over the city.'

'I'll need some more resources, sir. I've only got Harry and Nina at the moment.'

'I've directed Bob Reid and his team to join your case. This has to be your top priority.' He paused before continuing. He wanted to make sure Carl understood the implications of what he was about to say.

'Carl, before you do anything, you need to be aware the Commissioner specifically pointed out to me that Gerard Fisher is a close, and he stressed close, friend of the Police Minister. So we'll need to exercise a fair degree of caution in handling this. We can't have the public getting wind of it to start with. I'm sure you understand the need for speed and discretion on this one, Carl.' He waited for the inspector to nod his assent. 'I told the Commissioner I'd send you over to interview Gerard Fisher. I was told he's expecting a visit.'

'I'll get Nina and go straight over to the bank.' Carl started to leave.

'Keep me posted on this one, Carl. The Commissioner will be on my back until we get this sorted.'

The inspector took the lift back down to the third floor. This was not how he thought this case would go. As he walked in, Nina looked up and said, 'She's news to Narcotics.'

He stopped in front of her desk. 'Things have changed. We're about to be joined by DI Reid and his team. I've just been up to the DC's office. Our man's called the B&A bank demanding five million, and threatening to kill the wife of another employee if he doesn't get the money by Monday.'

'What sort of lunatic are we dealing with?'

'I'm not so sure he's a lunatic. I'm seeing some serious planning here?'

'Could be an opportunist, Boss. Just some nut acting on the media release.'

'Can't rule that out, Harry, but at the same time we need to assume he's for real. While you're waiting for DI Reid, see if you can find out if our man used the victim's mobile to call the bank.'

'If B&A's number is 85214555, the call was made about forty five minutes ago from our mobile. They're also telling me that it looks like the phone hasn't moved from the south west corner of City Park since that call was made. I've just sent a patrol over to the park.'

Nina reached for the phone book and flipped through it to locate the bank's entry. 'Think we can dispense with the lunatic and opportunist theories. That's the bank's number.'

'How do you expect them to locate a mobile phone in City Park, Harry? It's huge.'

'That bit's easy, Boss. I gave them the number.'

'Of course. By the way, just to make matters a little more interesting, apparently the managing director of the bank is a close friend of the Police Minister. He called the Commissioner direct to report the incident.'

'Oh shit. Just what we need. Political interference!'

'We'll just have to deal with it, Nina. Grab your stuff. The Commissioner's promised we'd rush over to talk with them.' He winked at her.

'Harry, you're in charge until DI Reid arrives. Bring him up to speed when he gets here.'

The inspector and his sergeant took the lift down to the lobby, walked out the front entrance and crossed the plaza to the head office of B&A bank. Bank security greeted them at the front of the building and escorted them up to the managing director's office on the 25th floor of the tallest building in town.

Gerard Fisher, who had been managing director of B&A for the last twenty years, was waiting for them with a younger man, who he introduced as Tom Makin, head of the bank's security team.

Carl introduced himself and Nina, and looked around the office. It was twice the size of the Commissioner's and had some great views. The furniture was antique boardroom but the equipment was all modern technology. Latest flat-screen monitor, sleek telephone handset. Not a paper in sight.

'Please, have a seat Inspector,' said the managing director after completing the formal introductions. Carl and Nina sat next to each other on the couch across from the managing director's desk. Tom Makin remained standing.

'Mr Fisher, I understand this must be a bit of a shock but we'll need to go over the details.'

'Go ahead, Inspector.'

'Did you by any chance manage to record the call?'

'Not all of it. Generally, we don't record telephone calls without advising people, Inspector. I'm sure you're aware of the legal implications. However, our staff can activate a recorder when they receive threatening calls. Fortunately, Mr Fisher's EA listens in on all calls to take notes, and she activated the recorder. I've got a copy here for you,' said the head of security taking a CD from the desk and handing it to Carl.

Carl passed the CD to Nina, who put it in her handbag and took out her notebook, deciding she would act as Carl's executive assistant, since no-one else seemed to notice she was in the room.

'Did the caller give any instructions regarding delivery of the money?'

'Apart from wanting cash in mixed denominations, no. He said he would call on Monday to tell us where to leave the money and, of course, to make sure we didn't set him up with you lot. The last thing he said, before hanging up, was that if we set him up he would make sure it was my wife that he picked,' replied the managing director.

'How many people in the bank know about this threat?'

'Apart from Tom and I, and Evelyn, that's my EA, no-one knows except for you, and the Commissioner of course. I can't have this getting into the media. That could ruin us, especially if this madman kills the wife of another staff member. God, it's already too horrible to think about with Josie Ford being killed. Look out the window,' he waved his hand towards the window behind his back, which framed a panoramic view of the city out to the coast. 'You can see the airport from here. You have got to stop this idiot before he hurts anybody else!'

'What are you thinking about how you want to handle this, Mr Fisher?'

'What do you mean?'

'Are you going to hand over the money or call his bluff?'

'Inspector, the money is a non-issue. We have extortion insurance, so that's neither here nor there. I'm sure you're aware of the latest nanotech tracking devices. They're so small they're impossible to see and very effective. So, we can give him the money and let him walk away with it. We won't have any problems helping you track him down. No, my concerns are keeping my people and their loved ones safe. If word got out that we put dollars before people in a situation like this we'd be ruined. And besides, my wife would kill me if I called his bluff.'

That got a smile from all the men in the room.

'Can you have five million in cash ready by Monday? I mean,

with all the electronic banking these days, do you hold that much cash?'

'I have that under control, Inspector,' answered the head of security. 'You'd appreciate we have contingency plans for these sorts of events. We'll be ready by Friday on the money side, with the trackers set up so that you can follow him and arrest him at your convenience. I can call you Friday when we have things in place.'

'Who delivers your cash? You could be being set up for a hit on your cash deliveries.'

'We've thought of that, Inspector. That's the advantage of having a contingency plan. The cash will be delivered over several shipments, starting tomorrow morning, using two different armoured delivery services. It would have to be an inside job for anything to go wrong there.'

Carl nodded and took a few moments to think. These bankers seemed to have the money side of the situation under control. It sounded like they kept a plan for these sorts of things in the top drawer and just pulled it out when required. He'd certainly like to be in a position to not be worrying about five million dollars.

'Any idea why he picked B&A? Killing the wife of one of your employees is a fairly drastic way to attract your attention. In my experience, the bad guys usually only threaten to kill someone so you'll play ball. You know, like the threat he made about your wife. This though, this is in another league. Our man has already killed someone and he's threatening to kill more. So, who has the bank really pissed off recently?'

'Going on the reports I've been getting on the reaction to the recent account keeping fee increase, around thirty thousand of our customers so far,' replied the managing director.

'I think he might be looking for something a little more dramatic than that, Mr Fisher,' said the head of security.

The managing director paused to gather his thoughts. 'Inspector, we're a bank. We turn people down for loans every day. We foreclose mortgages and evict people from their homes every week. We take people to court for non-payment of personal loans or credit card debts. Where do you start?'

'Has the bank received any other threats?'

'Not like this. The threats we generally deal with are threats to take their business elsewhere. We're a very customer friendly bank, despite all the negative press banks receive. No, this is really out of the ordinary. I have no idea who would want to do this to us.'

Carl looked at the head of security, in his immaculate three piece suit and perfectly straight tie. 'What about you, Mr Makin, any ideas?

'Sorry, Inspector. I can't identify anyone specifically at this point in time.'

'What about threats to specific individuals? I assume you have a protocol for logging them if you get them.'

'I can get those records from HR for you, if you like.'

'Thanks. That would be helpful. What about you personally, Mr Fisher? Any enemies who might be wanting to settle a score?'

'Well, I guess we all have enemies, Inspector, but I don't think I have any in this category.'

'Hope you're right, Mr Fisher. I don't think any of us want an enemy in this category.' Carl looked around the room. His eyes stopped at Nina. She gave him a small smirk of a smile. He stood up and faced Mr Fisher.

'I think we have all we need for the moment. It would be a good idea to keep the recorder on for your line in case you get any more calls. If he calls, contact me on this number.' He handed the managing director his card and turned to the head of security. 'Call me on Friday when you're set up with the tracking equipment, Mr Makin. I'll bring one of my team over to meet with you and make arrangements for using the tracking equipment.'

'Thank you, Inspector. Security will take you down to the lobby.' Mr Fisher got up and shook Carl's hand.

Tom Makin walked with them to the elevator, where one of his team was waiting to escort them down to the lobby. 'I'm sure you're aware of Mr Fisher's connections, Inspector, so an appropriate degree of discretion would be appreciated.'

'Yes, I've already been advised on that one, Mr Makin, but thanks all the same.'

The elevator doors opened. Carl and Nina stepped in with their escort and rode silently to the lobby, and then walked out into the plaza.

Carl looked across at Nina. She was displaying her 'not happy' look. 'What's eating you, sweetheart?'

'Do you think I'm attractive, Carl?'

An image of a naked Nina lying on her back propped up against the pillows of his bed popped into his mind. 'You're asking me? Don't you think I might be a little bit biased?'

'Those two stuck up pricks didn't even notice I was in the room!'

'That's not quite true. I did notice the security bloke sneaking a peek or two in your direction when I was addressing his boss.'

She hit him in the arm.

He wanted to wrap her in his arms and kiss her but they were too exposed walking across the plaza in front of Police Headquarters.

'It's still a rich, white boys' world in there.' He jerked his thumb over his shoulder as they walked. 'Did you hear them talking about five million dollars as if it was petty cash. Anyway, it's not them we have to worry about. It's the idiot out here with the gun. What do you think he's up to with this extortion threat?'

'What makes you think he's up to anything apart from extortion?' Nina replied.

'How many episodes of CSI do you think the average bloke has watched?'

'What difference would that make?'

'Think about it. Would you extort money from a bank in cash knowing what they just told us about nanotech tracking devices? And remember, what they told us is not a secret. You can look it up with Google or see it in action in any of the police shows on TV.'

'You think our man's just toying with us?'

'Or trying to distract us from the real reason he killed her.'

They reached the police building and made their way back up to their third floor office.

DI Reid and his team had just arrived. Harry's mobile was ringing as they walked into the operations room. He answered the call while the two inspectors went into Carl's office to catch up and sort out how they were going to work the case. Nina greeted the four detectives that made up DI Reid's team and helped them set up camp in the operations room.

Harry ended the call and went straight to Carl's office.

'Boss,' he waited for the inspector to look at him, 'that was the patrol I sent to City Park. They found the mobile in a plastic bag hanging from a tree.'

'Let me know once Forensics have had a good look at it, and get them to compare the voice recording we got from the bank with the one from the call to report the body. Nina's got it in her bag.'

Harry left to get the recording from Nina to take to Forensics.

'Think this guy might be wanting to tell us he knows how we think, Carl. We might be up against someone who thinks he's a criminal genius,' said Bob Reid.

'Overconfidence will be his undoing then. I've yet to come across a real criminal genius but I've met a few who thought they were. They always think they can outsmart us.'

'What did you learn over at the bank? Harry said you'd gone over to interview Fisher.'

'Hopefully the CD they gave us will confirm it's the same bloke. Apart from that, not much. They have no idea who he might be or they aren't telling us if they do. They're confident we can catch him if they give him the money spiced with nanotech tracking devices. It's almost as if they had a plan on the shelf for just this situation. Their head of security, Tom Makin, seems to know his stuff. Ever met him?'

'Yeah. He's ex-military. Not the sort you'd want to meet in a dark alley, even if he was wearing one of those smart suits, from what I've heard.'

'He made a point of making sure I was aware of the connection between his boss and ours.'

'Did he tell you about his connection to his boss?'

Carl raised an eyebrow. 'What connection might that be?'

'He's married to Fisher's daughter.'

'Should that be a problem?'

'Who knows? I've heard he's a bit of a playboy. Maybe he's the real target and not the bank.'

'I'll keep that in mind if our man actually calls in on Monday.'

'That sounds like a doubt to me, Carl. Not buying the extortion threat?'

'Would you extort a bank for cash knowing what we know about nanotech tracking devices? And, if our genius knows enough about police procedures to play mobile phone games with us, I reckon he'd know about tracking devices. So, no, I'm not buying it. We'll have to play along with the bank until he doesn't show but I think it's a distraction built into his game plan.'

'Where do you want to start?'

'Our genius has made two calls from the victim's mobile phone. Let's see if we can get any useful CCTV footage from the areas he called from and from around the entrances to City Park.'

'Might also pay to see if we can get anything from the CCTV around the airport security fence,' said DI Reid.

'That's already being followed up by uniform. And Marie Wood, you remember her?'

'How could you forget her?'

'Know what you mean. Anyway, she's already viewed the CCTV footage from the bus station and the northern entrance to City Park for the last week. We know Mrs Ford didn't catch her usual bus to work on Monday or Tuesday, but she walked into City Park through the gate on North Terrace around eight on Monday morning and turned up at work around her usual time. We have some idea why she didn't on Tuesday, but what was she up to on Monday morning?

And while we're waiting for next Monday to roll around to find out if the extortion threat is real, we need to find out as much as we can about this lady. I think our genius might be trying to convince us she was a random choice simply because her husband worked at the bank. My gut feeling is that there's another story to be unearthed here.'

'Sounds like a plan to me.'

The inspectors went out to discuss their plan of attack with the team. Carl asked Nina to organise copies of the names and addresses they had obtained from the husband and allocate them across the team for face to face interviews.

The telephone on Nina's desk rang. She answered the call and handed the receiver to Inspector West.

'Boss, you might want to take this. There's a lady on the phone saying her ten year old son has just told her that he saw Mrs Ford getting into a car on Tuesday morning, and it wasn't the first time.'

CHAPTER 6

PAUL WOKE to the sound of someone making breakfast in the kitchen. He rolled over and looked at the clock: 9:36. It was time to eat.

'Morning, Dad,' said Luke as Paul entered the kitchen.

'Morning, sunshine. How are you doing?'

Luke shrugged his shoulders. 'I don't know. It's weird knowing Mum's not going to be here anymore but it's sort of a fact, isn't it?'

Paul put his arm around Luke's shoulders and gave him a hug. 'That's what I was thinking. I really miss her but you're right. It's a fact, she's not here anymore. The question is how are we going to deal with it?'

'What do you mean, Dad?'

'Let me get something to eat and then we can talk.'

While Paul was toasting a couple of slices of raisin bread and heating some milk in the microwave, Matthew arrived in the kitchen.

'You sure you're awake, mate?'

'Dad, I've just had the strangest night. I mean, Mum's been talking to me. I couldn't see her but it was her voice. I feel like I've been wrapped in love or something. It's all so unreal.'

'What did she say?' asked Luke.

'I don't remember it all but she said not to feel so sad and to remember that she will always love us.'

'Dad, your toast is burning!'

Paul flicked the switch and watched his smoking raisin bread pop out of the toaster. The microwave beeped to let him know his milk was ready. He buttered the slightly burnt toast and stirred a spoonful of instant coffee into the hot milk and sat down at the table.

'You sure you weren't dreaming?'

'How do you tell? It's not like dead people talk to me every night. It was like she was sitting on my bed in the dark, like she does when she wants to talk about how things are going at school.'

Paul ate his toast and drank some of the coffee.

'What were you going to say before Matti came in, Dad?'

'Remember how we talked about accepting the things that are and not arguing with reality?'

'You mean that stuff about going with the flow of the river of life?' said Matthew.

'What happened to your mother is pretty horrible. She must have been really frightened. I can't imagine what it must be like waiting and knowing they are going to kill you. And who knows what else they did to her.' Paul stopped talking and let the dark thoughts move away. 'Now, we can get caught up in all the drama of thinking about that and being angry that it happened. The fact is though, it happened. We can't undo it.'

'That's sort of what I was thinking, Dad. I miss Mum heaps but no matter how much I miss her it won't bring her back,' said Luke.

'That's the point I'm trying to make. We can either spend lots of time thinking about it and feeling sorry for ourselves, and there will be days when we do, and there's nothing wrong with that, or we can accept that she's gone and start working out what that means for us. We're the ones still here. Our lives are still going.'

'That sounds like something Mum would say. I wish she'd talk to me. Why does all the good stuff happen to Matti?'

Paul put his arm around Luke. 'Maybe he's got some psychic gift you and I don't have. Maybe she's trying to talk to all of us but he's the only one who can hear her. I don't know. Let's just be thankful he got the message, even if it was a dream.'

'So, what happens now? When do we go back to school?' asked Matthew.

'Well, assuming the police release the body today or tomorrow, we should be able to arrange the funeral for some time next week. I think maybe after the funeral. How does that sound?'

The boys looked at each other. Luke shrugged his shoulders. 'Sounds okay to me,' said Matthew.

Paul turned to Luke and raised an eyebrow. 'Suits me. I've got three assignments to finish.'

'If you want to work on them, I suggest you do that over the next few days. Once the funeral date is set, this place will be overrun with family.'

'Is Nonna coming over today?' asked Matthew.

'She said she'd be over sometime this afternoon to make dinner.'

'What about Grandma?'

'She volunteered to cook for us tomorrow night.'

'Doesn't anybody know you can cook, Dad?'

'I'm sure the novelty will wear off. Anyway, they like to feel needed and I don't mind being spoilt for a few days.'

'I'm not complaining. I was just wondering when we'd have to start getting used to your cooking again,' said Matthew.

'It might be your cooking we need to get used to, mate.'

'Yeah, right.'

Luke loaded his breakfast dishes into the dishwasher. Matthew started making himself breakfast while Paul made a second coffee.

'Before you do anything else after breakfast, make your beds and make sure your rooms look presentable before we get any visitors. Hopefully, it will be a bit quieter today.'

'Some things never change even when your mother gets killed,' said Matthew. 'Someone's always telling you to clean up your room.'

Paul took his coffee out to the study.

It looked like the boys were going to cope. At least they all seemed to be on the same page. He was grateful for all the times he had discussed different life philosophies with them. That was one thing he had resolved early into parenthood; to talk things over with his sons and not just lecture them like his father had done with him and his brothers. As the boys had gotten older, he had encouraged them to read some of the books he had found interesting and had spent hours discussing ideas with them and Josie, mostly over the dinner table. Some people spent hours watching TV. The Fords had spent hours talking around the dinner table.

He looked at the computer and noticed that it was still on. He moved the mouse and the screen lit up with the wallpaper photograph of Josie and the boys. He wondered why Josie had chosen to talk to Matthew and not him. Maybe his head was so full of his own thoughts it was jamming out her transmission. Maybe it really was just a dream. Matthew had always had an active imagination. He smiled as he recalled the look on Luke's face that had revealed his disappointment that she hadn't spoken to him. What did any of us really know about the beyond? Maybe Josie had spoken to Matthew. He certainly couldn't explain it and, if truth be known, he didn't want to explain it. If Josie was choosing to communicate with them through Matthew, who was he to argue?

Then, while he was looking at the picture of Josie and the boys, the tears began. He made no attempt to stop them. It was fine to think about accepting the facts of life as they presented themselves but how was he going to cope without her? He couldn't hold back the wash of emotion surging from somewhere deep within and felt himself slipping into the void, despite all his fine intentions and efforts to stay in control.

Finally, the tide of emotion subsided and he sat there, empty, for what seemed like a long time. As he sat waiting for the fog to clear, he became aware of a series of thoughts telling him that he couldn't fall apart yet. He had to stay strong so that they could get through the funeral. How could he expect the boys to cope if he couldn't? What was the point of all those books he had read if he couldn't put any of it into practice? He started to feel a bit of a fraud sinking under his emotions and told himself to get his shit together before someone arrived. He took a couple of deep breaths and wondered how he should go about writing a eulogy.

In the distance, he heard the telephone ringing and the sound of Luke's voice answering the call. Then Luke was standing in the doorway with the mobile handset in his hand.

'It's Inspector West for you, Dad.'

Paul took the handset. 'Morning, Inspector.'

'Mr Ford, sorry to trouble you but do you, by any chance, know anyone who has a limousine with a driver?'

'The only person I know that has a limo with a driver is Anna Rodrigo's husband, Mark.'

'Do you remember what make it is?'

'I'm pretty sure it's a silver Ford, one of those stretch jobs. Why do you want to know?'

'I've been talking to someone who says he saw your wife getting into a silver limousine in the street next to the park, on Monday and Tuesday morning. Claims she walked right up to the limo, spoke to the driver, at least a man wearing a peaked cap and sunglasses, who opened the door and she got in as if she was expecting it to be there. Then the limo drove off towards the city. Says he didn't see anybody else in the limo, but then again, it had tinted windows and he was some distance away. Does this ring any bells for you?'

'Can't say it does. She didn't say anything to me about a limo. I have no idea why she was getting into a limo when she was supposed to be going to work. Maybe you'd better ask Mark or Anna to see if they sent their driver to pick her up. They've never done it before, that I know of. But I'm sure Anna would have said something when she called last night if she knew anything about it.'

'I'm sure there will be an explanation. Might just be a coincidence. My witness didn't see the number plate. Who knows how many stretch limos there are in this town. Guess I'll be finding out. By the way, how long have you and Josie known the Rodrigos?'

'Josie met Anna at some women's conference a few years ago, maybe five years at the most. I didn't meet them until a couple of years ago.'

'How well would you say you know them?'

'I've only met him three or four times. Reasonable sort of bloke, I suppose. Never lets me pay for anything when we're out. Runs some sort of import business and owns an apartment building somewhere in the city, I think. Bit of a fitness freak too. Into cycling.'

'What about Anna?'

'As I said, she's become Josie's best friend over the last couple of years, so I've seen a lot of her. She's a lot of fun, actually. A lot like Josie really. Come to think of it, I wouldn't be surprised if she had been secretly arranging something with Josie. They were always cooking up something between them, especially when they were planning their next away weekend. So, who knows if they were up to something?'

'I'd appreciate if you didn't mention this to anyone just yet. Let me make a few enquiries. I'll be in touch.'

The inspector hung up.

What the hell had Josie been up to? Why on earth would she be getting into a limo when she was meant to be going to school on the bus? She had turned up at school on time on Monday, so maybe Anna had picked her up. So what went wrong on Tuesday that led to her being shot dead? No, Anna picking her up didn't make sense. Anna certainly wouldn't have shot her. Not Anna. She didn't even like killing bugs. Besides, she had her own kids to get to school.

Did he really know her? Shit. How much other stuff didn't he know about her? They'd been married for nearly twenty years but he was starting to doubt whether he knew her at all. How often had he assumed she had left the house to catch the bus to work and she had done something else? What really happened on those weekends when she was away with Anna and he was home looking after the boys? Was she really working back after school or meeting someone with a stretch limo to do who knew what before coming home?

Stop it! You're letting your fears run amuck! What's that phrase you need here? Show me the evidence! That's it. Take a few deep breaths and get a grip before you talk yourself into believing this shit! God, the girl's only been dead a day. What on earth are you thinking? There will be a rational explanation. There has to be.

Isn't a body with a bullet in the head evidence? Well, it says you're dead but it doesn't explain why, and that's the bit I don't know. Why would someone shoot her? She wouldn't hurt a fly. Oh, Josie, what did you get mixed up in?

CHAPTER 7

ON THE FIRST day of his second year at university, Paul noticed a girl in the front row of the lecture theatre. She had the sort of body a guy couldn't ignore once she had crossed his field of vision, so he was sure he hadn't seen her before. Not only was she stunningly beautiful, she had an aura about her that said: I know you're all looking boys but get over it, I have. It was a countenance that let him know she was there to take part in a lecture, not a beauty pageant. He didn't know who she was but she was obviously comfortable being herself.

Like most men his age, Paul didn't know anything about masks and mirrors and shadow work. At twenty, he hadn't heard of the golden child projection, or how easy it was to fall in love with yourself once someone was willing to be the screen for your projections. His life would have been different, if he had been living it consciously. As it was, he was totally unaware of himself, and hadn't reached that age when he would start to wonder what had happened.

If it had been left to him, Paul would never have met Josephine Kelly.

He was starting his second year within the post-traumatic shock of finding himself no longer the centre of Amanda's life.

Apparently, he just wasn't interesting enough for Amanda, who had informed him the previous night that she wanted more excitement in her life than he was offering.

His mind might have registered the presence of a breathtakingly beautiful girl but it hadn't been able to arouse him from his feelings of self-pity, so that he could consider his prospects of being with her. He walked up to the third row and sat down with his gloom and notebook.

The one place on campus Paul thought he would be safe, while he was feeling so fragile about being dumped by Amanda, was with the chaplain. Being a daily Mass attender was one of those aspects of Paul that Amanda had found less than exciting. He could still hear her dismissive words.

'If you want to go to Mass every day, why don't you just become a priest? Going on Sundays is enough for me. I'm not wasting any more of my life with someone who thinks going to Mass every day is exciting!'

Despite Amanda's misgivings, Paul had developed a friendship with Father Mulligan, a young priest combining his post graduate studies with being university chaplain. It was that friendship that led him to Josie. When he went down to the chaplain's office for a chat over coffee later in that first week, there she was.

'Paul, this is Josie,' Father Mulligan said as he entered the room. 'Josie, this is Paul. He's starting his second year. I'm sure he'd love to show you around campus.'

It only took a couple of seconds of being in Josie's presence for the trance of that Amanda induced post-traumatic shock to become a vague and indistinct memory.

It wasn't even that she was the most beautiful girl he had ever met. Being with her just felt right. She was easy to be with, so warm and affectionate. Over the next few weeks he discovered that she was interested in everything he did and every story he told. It wasn't long before he was spending all his free time on campus with her, sharing lunch and studying with her in the library when they weren't in lectures. Josie wasn't interested in student politics or spending time in the campus bar. She was interested in her studies and him. She even attended daily Mass with him. She was the good Catholic girl match to his good Catholic boy persona. Everybody was happy, even his conservatively Catholic father.

Paul thought he finally knew what love was.

God only knows what would have happened if he had teamed up with one of those promiscuous girls his father was always going on about - the ones who reputedly led a man to hell. Well, that wasn't quite true because his younger brother, John, had fallen in love, or was it lust, with one over the summer break. Paul always wondered though where the man's responsibility lay when it came to the being led to hell part. He was fairly sure his brother had gone willingly. Anyway, it hadn't lasted. John had made the mistake of bringing her home to meet the family. One of George's sermons was enough for her to realise she didn't fit in.

It was different with Josie though. His father thought she was the perfect choice for him. Not only was she from a Catholic family, she was a regular church goer who did not believe in sex before marriage. She even engaged his father in conversation about all the doctrinal and moral issues he was so interested in.

Paul thought she was pretty special as well. He wasn't yet aware that deciding one person was special, and essential to his happiness, was the start of a journey to a lifetime of, sometimes painful, learning. If he had really been paying attention to what had been the Amanda experience, he would have been aware that it was his making her special that had ultimately led to his pain and rejection, after what had been such an exhilarating start.

Fortunately for Paul, Maria Kelly liked him. His father may have wielded the power in his family, but Josie's father was definitely in the back seat when it came to family politics.

Josie had an Irish family name but her mother was Italian. Mick Kelly liked to claim that it was the blending of the bloods that had produced his beautiful daughters; and always professed that you couldn't really see much difference between the Irish and Italians, once each side let down its guard and treated the other side as people.

One thing about Josie's parents that Paul found really attractive was their inclusive interpretation of Catholicism. They might not have spent as much time as George studying the bible, and all those other church documents he spent so much time reading, but at least they seemed to understand the gospel message about loving your neighbour.

At Josie's place, he didn't hear anything about all the special categories of sinner that populated his father's worldview. Not surprisingly, it wasn't long before he was spending more time there than at home. It helped that he and Josie were taking some common subjects in their undergraduate courses. That gave them the convenient excuse of working on assignments together.

Of course, Paul's mother wasn't fooled, and she made sure he was home on all the right occasions to keep him in his father's good books. George Ford might have been a self-righteous man at times, and he certainly kept a tight rein on their six sons, but although she loved him, she was also the one who had to pacify him when the boys crossed any of his many lines or broke any of his many rules. The Ford boys called her 'St Anne', but not when their father was around.

If there was one thing that had stamped Paul's life from the beginning it was Catholicism. He and his brothers had been baptised as infants, sent to Catholic schools and lived a home life of deeply engrained Catholic ritual. All of the Ford boys had been altar servers from age seven to fifteen. George had dragged one of them, sometimes more than one, out of bed to serve at morning Mass every morning of the year. Every night the Ford family recited five decades of the rosary. Every Friday they ate fish despite the rule changes of the Vatican Council. Every first Saturday of the month they all went to confession, whether they had sinned or not. As far as George was concerned, they were always sinning. George had preached so many sermons over the kitchen table that Paul was convinced he had missed his calling. Still, it wasn't safe to suggest that perhaps the Church should allow married priests, so that George could fulfil his obvious vocation. All such suggestions were met with hostile rebuke.

Paul and his brothers might have referred to their mother as 'St Anne' out of love and gratitude, but there were no similar sentiments in their referring to their father as 'His Holiness'.

Some of his brothers had risked the wrath of 'His Holiness' and started to relax their observances as they got older, especially after leaving school. Sometimes they didn't come home in time for the rosary. Sometimes they ate out on Fridays and they simply slept in on those first Saturdays. However, while they lived at home they all attended Sunday Mass; not because they wanted to but because they loved their mother. Paul was twenty, living at home and still conforming.

Meeting Josie probably saved Paul from turning into a clone of George. He might have had a more inclusive understanding of the gospel message than his father, but by the time Josie came along, he had become fond of the sound of his own voice, and often displayed a tendency to prefer being right over being agreeable. Fortunately for Paul, Josie was not Anne. She had her own opinions and wasn't shy about voicing them or standing up for herself. She certainly was not into appeasement. If she thought

Paul was on his soapbox she simply let him know or threw a counter argument at him. She even had the temerity to laugh at him when she thought he was going over the top. He soon changed his tune. There was no way he was going to risk losing her love and affection. He might have been a little opinionated but he certainly wasn't pig-headed. Maybe he might have successfully avoided becoming another George on his own, but being around Josie certainly accelerated his evolution into someone more agreeable.

Those three years at university together went quickly enough with part time work thrown in. Josie worked the afternoon session at the after-school care centre attached to her old school, St Catherine's. Paul worked Friday nights and weekends in the drive through bottle shop at the pub not far from his parent's place. It was so close he walked to and from work, even when he was coming home after midnight on Friday nights. They weren't great paying jobs but they provided enough money for them to enjoy the occasional concert, go to the movies, indulge each other with gifts on all those special days in their young lives, buy an engagement ring and start saving for a deposit on a house.

By the time they were ready to graduate and look for their first teaching jobs, they were engaged to be married in the semester break. No one was surprised when Josie was employed by St Catherine's and Paul returned to his own alma mater, St Jude's.

When Paul returned to his old school everything seemed familiar but also a little strange. He was no longer participating in the culture as an adolescent, subject to the rules and regulations, but as a young adult with a head full of the latest educational ideas. The one question that kept popping into his mind was:

why are we doing this? The usual answers no longer satisfied him. It might be the way they had always done it, but was it educationally sound? The old ways of teaching might have suited previous generations but the student population had changed. Now many of the boys came from homes where English was not the first language. Parents were looking at other pathways besides the traditional academic journey to university. How did he make this stuff relevant for today's young people?

Of course, in his early years as a teacher, he didn't get to bring about much overt change. All of his differences were invisible to an outside observer. He introduced change through how he was with his students – the way he talked to them, the ways in which he treated them differently than the older, entrenched teachers. No-one listened to him in staff meetings or during faculty planning days. What did he know, anyway?

'Son, they don't teach you how to teach at university, we're the ones who will show you how to become a real teacher. Just do it the way we tell you to do it, and forget all those fancy ideas that sound good but just don't cut it in the real world.'

Eventually, he discovered that no-one really knew or cared what was going on in his classroom, as long as he provided scores for the standard tests, kept them reasonably quiet and the parents didn't complain. The most empowering thing was awakening to the knowledge that he could make a difference for the ones he had in his care. He didn't have to be like the others, who had lost their enthusiasm for growing young minds, because they had been there too long and gone back to sleep, if they had ever been awake in the first place.

Once Paul realised he was basically on his own in the classroom, he started modifying the teaching program to make the curriculum more relevant to his students, without compromising their chances of performing well on the standard tests. In fact, by the end of that first year his students had become the standard setters, and some of the older teachers had started wondering what he was doing to get such results. They were too proud to ask him directly, of course, but that didn't stop them from quizzing his students. Paul was happy to share his ideas and his passion for teaching. Mostly, he only got to share them with Josie, who was enjoying a more collaborative experience in the feminine environment at St Catherine's, where the wise women were not intimidated by the enthusiasm of the young.

Fortunately, that long first year endurance test was happily interrupted by their much anticipated, and meticulously planned, mid-year wedding.

In the months leading up to their wedding, Paul and Josie attended the pre-nuptial course that the local diocese insisted on providing to candidates for the sacrament of marriage. In line with the perverse logic of the world, these courses were similar to graduate courses in education practice. None of the students had any of the relevant experience required to put the theory into context. Like the others, Paul and Josie did the required course to qualify for the next step in the process. Maybe they would refer to the notes later - if they could remember where they had filed them.

At least the session on sexuality was conducted by a married couple and not by some priestly expert. They learnt that the Church was okay with them regulating their fertility, provided they used its method, which did not involve what was described as artificial means of contraception. They ended up with a reference text on the rhythm method, to help them control their fertility without the use of contraceptive devices or drugs, like the magic contraceptive pill that Josie had told him she had no intention of taking.

Wedding preparation is mostly secret women's business. Maria, Josie and Anne did all the planning and organising. The men simply handed over the cash and turned up for the suit fittings when told. If Paul had been paying attention during this phase of his life, he might have noticed that the price for getting into bed with Josie was pretty steep. By sleeping on the job, he had already handed over control of his life, before he had arrived at the church on the big day. Like most young men approaching marriage, Paul's time horizon didn't stretch much further than the night of the big day and the honeymoon.

Paul arrived at the church early. There was no way he was going to be late. Much to everyone's surprise, Josie kept her promise and arrived on time. She even beat some of her family to the church. Of course, her newly found punctuality was short lived. Paul was destined to spend many hours waiting for her to get ready for whatever event they were attending - some habits are never really broken.

In accordance with Catholic tradition, the ceremony was a full Nuptial Mass with Father Mulligan celebrating, trapping their unwary university friends in the church for more than an hour. Paul didn't notice. This was their big day. Determined not to sound like one of those nervous weaklings he despised, he read out his wedding vows in a voice that could be heard at the back of the church, even without a microphone. Josie followed suit in a firm confident voice. Before he had noticed the passage of time, they were signing the register, being announced as Mr and Mrs Ford and walking out to be showered with rice and confetti.

It was only later, when they were flipping through their wedding album or viewing the video that they had the opportunity to enjoy the details of their wedding. Paul often wondered how people did that before the benefit of photography.

After the photography session, they moved on to the reception centre for an alcohol fuelled evening of feasting and dancing.

There might have been a few Italians in the crowd enjoying the food but there was a large Irish contingent washing it down with beer, and making a lot of noise. Even George, that bastion of Catholicity, had to be driven home that night by the ever-sober Anne, who had learnt early in her own marriage that if she wanted to get home safely after a party, it would be up to her.

Finally, the big night had arrived and Paul and Josie were alone in the honeymoon suite of the International Hilton. It didn't take them long to get undressed and into the bed.

Things didn't turn out like in the movies they had watched, in which the young lovers always knew what to do and enjoyed wild ecstasy every time they made love, even the first time. After all that time spent waiting for their first night together, Paul just couldn't control himself, and was squirting sperm all over the place almost as soon as they were naked together in the bed.

Josie laughed, and told him it was the perfect way to release all their performance anxieties, so they could focus on loving instead of just sex. Fortunately, young men reload quickly and the reloading period gave them the time to explore each other more fully, before getting closer to the movie version of love making. Well, as close as virgin lovers could on their first night together.

The next day they drove down the coast to spend their honeymoon week in a seaside hotel, where they could enjoy getting to know each other more intimately.

They had lots of sex because they wanted to and, according to the book, it was safe to do so without getting pregnant. Sometimes a guy is lucky. Paul didn't know how he would have coped if the honeymoon had coincided with one of the periods in the cycle when the book said it was a good time to get pregnant. It didn't take him long to realise that being randy and Catholic and married was going to be a challenge. He wanted to make love to Josie every time she touched him or he saw her naked. After three days, they were discussing family planning and the Church's prohibition on the use of contraceptives, and the conflict that created with their desire to make passionate love and control their fertility.

Josie was adamant she wasn't taking any pills. She didn't want to put chemicals into her body if there were other options. If he wanted to make love whenever, then he would have to take responsibility for contraception.

'If you can squirt sperm all over the place, what's the difference between squirting them into a condom and squirting them all over me?'

He didn't have an answer for that one, so by the time they were setting up house in one of her parent's apartments at the end of their honeymoon, they had taken their first steps away from the mind control of Rome and joined the ranks of sexually liberated Catholic couples; and Josie had mastered the art of rolling a condom onto his erection to make sure he used it.

It was a small chink, created by desire, but it wedged open a door they hadn't realised was closed. In the coming years that door would progressively open wider, as they re-examined all things Catholic and started wondering whatever had happened to the original gospel message. However, like lots of things in life, that journey was not linear or obvious to the casual observer.

Not long after they were married, one of the younger nuns at St Catherine's introduced them to the charismatic renewal movement. With its emphasis on the gifts of the Spirit, like speaking in tongues, hands on healing, spontaneous prayer featuring prophecy, and celebratory Masses with movement and music, this was an expressive style of worship far removed from the solemn church of their upbringing and local parish. With a little encouragement, they were soon attending weekly prayer meetings and monthly healing services, where the priest spoke of the Risen Lord, not the suffering crucified saviour. The preaching was of sunshine, not pain, the message was about embracing, not excluding. The service concluded with the priest leading a hands-on healing session that left people stretched out on the floor 'resting in the Spirit'.

Driven by a desire to spread the good news to others, Paul, like many of the newly converted to a religious way or healthy lifestyle, couldn't resist the temptation to preach about their experience with enthusiasm. It wasn't long before Paul's brothers were referring to them as the 'Jesus freaks'. It didn't take Paul long to realise that he needed to be careful about who he shared their new understanding with, because not everyone was open to the message or awake enough to recognise it when they heard it.

After the first few put downs at family gatherings, he simply stopped talking about religion or faith issues. His father didn't know the Jesus he knew and his brothers didn't want to know him. The status quo suited them just fine.

Paul and Josie moved into that space where 'Jesus is Lord' was a personal, daily awareness that impacted on everything they did and every relationship they were involved in. It wasn't long before they were moving in a different direction to their families. They were making new friends with others walking the same journey and, surprisingly, discovered that in this group of 'born again' Catholics there was very little support for Rome's views on sexuality and contraception.

The new depth of their faith redirected their teaching careers into religious education and away from their academic areas of interest. Paul found it interesting that teaching in the religious education program was the least popular choice among teachers in Catholic schools. That observation made him question why people choose to work in Catholic schools in the first place, if they were not prepared to be part of the faith development process that was the overt reason the schools existed. When he looked a little closer, he discovered that the teaching staff was as unchurched as the student body.

When he discussed it with Josie, they concluded that most teachers found it too confronting to teach things they hadn't resolved in their own lives. Most preferred to leave that to the few remaining religious brothers or sisters on staff, or the Jesus freaks, like them. Paul thought that was a pity, because their students were looking for a genuine spiritual experience in all sorts of places, including within the Church.

Without conscious awareness, Paul and Josie were surfing the charismatic movement to advance their careers and, with the decline in religious vocations, they were both faculty heads of religion studies by the time they had been married three years. With a social network of like-minded friends, they attended the national religious education conference each summer.

When you don't have children, live a simple lifestyle, earn two incomes and pay minimal rent, it doesn't take long to build a sizeable deposit for your first house, so it was no surprise when, during that third year, they bought the house in Whitbread Avenue. It was suitably placed for a couple with one car. Josie could catch the bus into the city and Paul could drive to St Jude's.

Their attendance at the religious education conference that summer was their last as a couple, as they got themselves pregnant while they were there. Life was directing their attention elsewhere, but it took them awhile to work that out.

A couple of months before she was due, Josie took a year's leave with the intention of going back to work, but before that year was up, she had decided to be a stay-at-home mother until Matthew was going to school.

On one level, these were years of wonder. On another, they were years of chaos. Moving from being a couple devoted only to each other to being parents of an infant, with his own biological clock, proved to be a bit more of a challenge than they had anticipated. It was one thing to read about the joys of parenthood; it was something else to actually experience them first hand. Matthew might have been a beautiful boy but for the first year of his life, he didn't want to sleep at night. Sleep deprivation doesn't do much for young mothers and even the most thoughtful husband can find himself being yelled at or ignored.

Paul was initially mystified at the changes in Josie's behaviour in the immediate wake of Matthew's arrival. It wasn't until his mother took him aside and explained some of the facts of life to him, as only a mother can, that he became a thoughtful husband. He also got his first experience of the postnatal celibate life that many new fathers complain about, and an understanding of the sexual frustrations that must plague the servants of Rome. Over time, things improved as Matthew gradually became accustomed to life on earth and they settled into living as a family unit.

When the sex started again, it was great but short lived. Before Matthew was two, Josie had put that book on the rhythm method to good use and was pregnant again. Whenever the question of how many children they would have came up in conversation after Luke was born, Josie simply announced that two was her limit, and that if he wanted sex he'd better be wearing a condom. It started to dawn on Paul that he might not be as in control of his destiny as he had believed.

With the responsibilities of parenthood, there was less time for attending prayer groups and healing services. They found themselves drifting back to the local parish, where Frank Mulligan was now the parish priest. Slowly their friendship group changed from charismatic prayers to young parents like themselves. All that free time they used to have for going to conferences, retreats and seminars was now taken up by being parents, and with Josie not working, they had to be a little more frugal with their spending. They had discovered that having children was an expensive choice in the modern world.

A woman Josie met at playgroup pointed them towards the next milestone on their spiritual journey. They had been discussing coping with the stresses of living with active boys over lunch, when the other mother had introduced them to the world of meditation.

Josie was the first to take the plunge into the silence. It was a question of logistics and, as she explained to Paul, she had the greater need. He, at least, got to escape from the house five days a week, sometimes six days a week if he was involved with a sporting team playing on Saturday mornings. She, on the other hand, was with the boys twenty-four-seven and, although she loved them dearly, she needed to find some way of preserving her sanity. Paul was awake enough not to argue and took charge of the boys while she attended the meditation training sessions. As it turned out, Josie was so taken by meditating that it wasn't long before she was quietly insisting, in that way that only a wife knows, that he needed it too, and so he found out about the silence.

Even though meditation had eastern religious origins in Hinduism, their experience with the charismatic renewal allowed Paul and Josie to embrace meditation as another form of prayer. A form of prayer in which you didn't use any words, except for a mantra, which was used solely to quieten the mind and allow you to pass through the door, into silence. Once you entered the silence there was no need for words. You were there to be and to listen, not to beg or praise or give thanks. The work with the Spirit allowed them to recognise the voice of God - silence. The other aspect that appealed to them was an echo of the words of Jesus about the kingdom being within.

It was years later, while exploring contemplative prayer with Frank Mulligan, that they discovered that meditation was an ancient Christian practice that had fallen into disuse, thanks to Rome Central's distrust of mystics - those troublesome monks and nuns who had had the temerity to listen to God directly without papal or priestly guidance.

The daily rhythm of a twenty minute meditation in the morning, and another twenty minute session in the evening, established an atmosphere of peace in their house that calmed the chaos and the boys within it.

Josie, with no experience of growing up with brothers or working with boys, had initially tried to protect her sons from hurting themselves, or each other, by attempting to subdue all that wild, physical play activity they so enjoyed. Anne, who had been overheard describing Josie as a 'mother hen clucking over her chicks', was relieved when, after a few months of meditating, Josie started to relax and let the boys be boys. It was thanks to meditation, and Paul's laid back attitude to play from having grown up in an all boy household, that Matthew and Luke enjoyed the freedom to explore the world of play in the backyard, instead of being penned up inside where their mother could keep them under constant surveillance.

Some kids are too timid to try new things, make new friends or pat a stranger's dog in the park, even with their mother looking on. Not the Ford boys. They believed the world was a safe place, people were friendly, and dogs just loved to meet kids. Josie met a host of people on her walks in the park with the boys, because they were always saying hello to people, joining in play with other kids or patting dogs and asking their owners questions. And they always got an answer. The people that care enough about their dog to walk it in the park are always happy to tell a small child the dog's name, and they're really impressed when the child remembers the dog's name the next time they meet. Dogs just love attention and they will let a small child do almost anything to them, although Luke did discover that some dogs didn't like having their tails pulled. He stopped doing it after a couple growled at him and reminded him they had big teeth. That put a bit more realism into the reading of Little Red Riding Hood.

Having teachers for parents meant that the boys had a lot of books read to them. So, it wasn't long before they could recite the stories just by looking at the pictures, and 'read' to each other when a parent wasn't available. From there it was a short transition to actual reading. They were both proficient readers when they started school. Luke was even more into reading than Matthew. Admittedly, he had the advantage of sitting in on Matthew's home reading lessons before he started school two years after Matthew. When he started school, his reading was so advanced that his teachers couldn't keep up with his appetite for books. Fortunately, the local librarian loved him and let him borrow a box of books every month. By the time he was ten, he had read every book in the children's section of the local library three or four times.

But bringing up kids does exact a toll on relationships.

CHAPTER 8

INSPECTOR WEST READ the email updating the toxicology report. The analysis had identified traces of alcohol and 7-amino flunitrazepam, a residue component of flunitrazepam, in Josie's blood. The pathologist had added a note informing him that flunitrazepam, a drug prescribed for severe insomnia under several brand names, also had a reputation as a date rape drug. It was known to be available on the black market in a form that dissolved quickly, leaving no visible trace, odour or taste. The ideal candidate for something to slip into a drink, especially if you wanted your victim unconscious, relaxed and with no memory of what had happened when she woke up, if she woke up.

Carl called Nina into his office and showed her the print out of the email.

'What do you think?'

'He knocks her out so he can screw her before he kills her, but he's considerate enough to wear a condom. Are we dealing with a gentleman killer here?'

'Maybe our man simply didn't want to leave any clues. Using a condom would certainly be easier than trying to wash out her vagina. Or maybe he didn't want to catch anything. You know, safe sex and all that.'

'Carl, I wonder if we have the correct sequence of events. If she got into the limo willingly, doesn't that suggest she either knew whoever it was in the limo or who sent it? What if the sex was consensual?'

'The pathologist initially thought it was, although, I suppose if she was under the influence of this drug, he could have screwed her and it would still look like consensual sex.' Carl stroked his chin. 'Guess I had better ask Mr Ford a personal question.' He looked at his notebook, found the number and rang the Ford house.

'Paul Ford.'

'Carl West, Mr Ford. I'd like to ask you a couple of personal questions. Is that okay?' These were always risky questions, so he hoped Mr Ford would not take offence, like so many men did when you asked them about their sex life.

'Suppose it depends on what you mean by personal questions.'

'Let's say I'll ask the questions and you let me know if you can answer them.'

'Okay.'

'The first question. Remember, I said it was going to be personal and I wouldn't be asking if this wasn't important. When was the last time you had sex with your wife?'

'Sunday night.'

'Did you use a condom?'

'It was always safe sex in our house, Inspector. Josie didn't want to get pregnant. Why do want to know this stuff?'

'I'll explain in a minute. But I have a couple more questions first. Was your wife using sleeping pills to get to sleep?'

'She didn't take pills for anything. She wouldn't even take an aspirin when she had a headache. She was into acupuncture and chiropractic for her aches and pains, not pills.'

'Did she drink?'

'Not much. She would have the occasional liquor or glass of wine but generally she drank mineral water'.

'Thank you for your candid responses to my questions, Mr Ford. The reason for asking is it looks like somebody had sex with your wife sometime on Tuesday before she was killed. There are traces of a sedative in her blood, so she could have been unconscious at the time, but whoever it was used a condom.'

'So you're telling me it doesn't look like rape?'

'There are a lot of forms of rape, Mr Ford. The pathologist originally thought it looked like consensual sex, until he had the toxicology report. I just wanted to find out if you had inadvertently contaminated my crime scene with a quickie on Tuesday morning before she left for work.' He paused to allow Paul to process that information, before saying, 'the pathologist has finished examining your wife's body, Mr Ford, so we can release it to your funeral director.'

'Thank you, Inspector.'

'I'll be in touch.' Carl hung up and looked across at Nina. 'Well, he wasn't the one who screwed her on Tuesday. Sunday night was their last sexual encounter.'

Inspector Reid knocked on the door and entered. 'Hope I'm not interrupting something important but I think we have stumbled across something interesting.'

'What's that Bob?'

'I was having a coffee downstairs with a couple of the boys from Organised Crime. I mentioned we were going to be interviewing the victim's best friend, a woman named Anna Rodrigo. One of them nearly choked on his coffee.'

'Why's that?'

'She's Max Spinosa's daughter.'

'Mr Mafia Max Spinosa?'

Inspector Reid nodded. 'You know him, Sergeant?'

'I've heard of him but I thought he had sort of retired.' Nina looked at Carl. 'Shit, maybe our school teacher was mixed up with drugs after all.'

'It gets worse.'

They turned back to Inspector Reid.

'She's married to the youngest son of Rocco Rodrigo.'

Their blank looks told the inspector they hadn't heard of him.

'He used to be Max Spinosa's main competition. They were always fighting over their turf, but it all stopped when two of their kids were married about twenty years ago. Our people think they're in business together, and no fighting in the streets means they can go about their business quietly, without attracting our attention. Seems they're mostly in legitimate business ventures these days. Rodrigo owns a string of commercial properties, most of which are leased to companies belonging to Spinosa. A big import export operation, several crash repairers, a local and inter-state freight business and a fleet of limousines. There are also a couple of apartment buildings leased to their employees. A couple of their operations are located down by the airport.'

'Is there anything going down with Organised Crime?' Carl asked.

'They think something's in the wind. Word on the street is someone out there thinks the families have gone soft and are ripe to be knocked off. Apparently, that someone's trying to create a bit of tension between the families but no-one knows who the someone is. Could even be an insider. There was a meeting between the families last night, so the boys think something is up. They've got their feelers out, so they don't want us stepping on too many toes.'

'Well, that's all very exciting, Bob, but let's remember we have a murder and an extortion threat on our hands. I can't see organised crime being behind the extortion threat to the bank. I suppose they could have a cash flow problem, like lots of other businesses given the global financial crisis, but I suspect they have easier ways of getting money. We need to work on finding if there are any links between the victim and Anna Rodrigo besides friendship. Think it's time we paid her a visit. Nina, give her a call and let's see if we can have a word with her today.'

Nina found Anna's number on the list they had obtained from Paul Ford and made the call. Anna was home and agreed to meet them. In fact, she suggested they come straight away so that the interview would be over before her children got home from school.

'Boss, she's home and available to see us now.'

'Bob, why don't you see what we can find out about where Mark Rodrigo fits into this little empire, and the movement of his limo over the last few days, while Nina and I go see his wife?'

They walked out into the operations room. 'Harry, how's the study of the CCTV footage going?'

'I've looked at the footage from North Terrace enough times now to see that she didn't get off a bus on Monday morning. She walks into the picture from beyond the bus zone. I thought maybe she was dropped off from a car we can't see in the footage from the gate, so I checked the footage of the traffic cameras further along North Terrace for just after eight Monday morning. We have a silver limo going west picked up by one, but it turns down a street not monitored by cameras before the next monitored intersection. We do, however, have a clear shot of the number plate.'

'And?'

'I'm not sure it's going to help us much, Boss. It's the number of a Ford transit van registered to City Florists.'

'That's interesting. Better see if you can actually sight Mr Rodrigo's limo, Bob. A photograph or two might come in handy.'

Carl and Nina took the lift down to the garage in the basement to their allocated vehicle.

'You drive,' said Carl. 'I want to make a call.'

While Nina drove them out to the leafy eastern suburbs favoured by the rich and famous, Carl called his own contact in Organised Crime to see what he had on Mark and Anna Rodrigo. Not much as it turned out.

When he put his mobile phone back into his coat pocket Nina asked what he had found out.

'Sounds like these guys are the legitimate face of the business. He manages their property holdings. She's a stay-at-home mum involved in charity fundraising for some sort of medical research. The only bit of dirt he had was Mark is a bit of a playboy. Likes younger women, apparently.'

'Sounds too good to be true to me, given what I read about Max Spinosa while I was at the academy.'

'Yeah, well let's remember that even though he's been accused of a lot of stuff, and been before a judge a few times, he's never been convicted.'

'So we're dealing with some pretty smart people then?'

'Maybe.'

Nina stopped in front of the driveway gate of what could only be described as a mansion set in a wooded park. 'Whatever these people are into, Carl, they're sure making a hell of a lot more money than you or me.'

Carl got out and walked over to the gate. He pressed the button on the intercom and spoke into the box, 'Inspector West to see Mrs Rodrigo.'

The gate opened. They drove in and realised they were entering a small gated community, not just a single dwelling. In among the trees there were two other mansions, in addition to the one visible from the street. As they moved along the driveway they noticed that while all three houses were within the one park, each house was separated off within a walled garden.

'So which house is it?'

'Number 52, the one facing the street.'

As they parked in front of number 52, the door to a room on the ground floor opened and a man dressed in a black uniform walked over to greet them.

'Can I see your identification please, Inspector?'

'Carl showed him his badge. This is Detective Sergeant Strong.'

'Thank you, Inspector. If you follow me, I'll take you to Mrs Rodrigo.' He opened the front door of the house and escorted them through to where Anna was waiting for them in her office at the back of the house. The office, with a view onto a well maintained rose garden, was almost the size of Carl's apartment.

'Inspector West is here, Mrs Rodrigo,' he announced as they entered the office.

Anna stood as they entered. 'Thank you, John. Good afternoon, Inspector. And this is?' she looked at Nina.

Another beautiful woman. This case was filling up with them. First the victim, then her sister, and now her best friend. How was a guy supposed to concentrate? Nina poked him in the side as she passed him.

'Detective Sergeant Strong, I called you earlier,' Nina introduced herself.

'Pleased to meet you, Sergeant. Please, take a seat.' Anna indicated the seats opposite her desk and sat back down behind the desk, a massive walnut barrier.

'I wasn't expecting this level of security, Mrs Rodrigo. Are you in some kind of danger?'

'Inspector, we've had security since I was a little girl. My father's always been worried about someone trying to rob us.'

'So, would I be right in assuming that your neighbours are family?'

'Yes. My parents and my in-laws have been living here ever since they went into business together, around twenty years ago.'

Carl took in the display of photographs on the wall behind her. 'So, you're a pretty close family group, then?'

'Family is important to some of us, Inspector.'

Carl let a few moments pass so he could change subjects. He wasn't all that interested in her family but he was intrigued by the security set up. He did know that both Anna and Mark had older brothers, so it was interesting that only they lived in the family compound. Still, that was something for the Organised Crime boys to worry about. He glanced at Nina to make sure she had her notebook out. Satisfied that she was ready, he decided it was time to get serious.

'Mrs Rodrigo, I understand you were a friend of Josie Ford. In fact, her husband told me you were her best friend.' He watched as Anna fought to maintain her composure. The amount of emotional turmoil contorting her face suggested she had been a very close friend.

'Yes, Inspector. We were close.' She reached for a tissue from the box on the desk. 'And yes, Paul is right, she was my best friend. Her death has come as a terrible shock.' She dabbed her eyes with the tissue. 'Forgive me. It's not easy talking about Josie.'

'Take your time, Mrs Rodrigo. I know what it's like losing a friend like this.'

She smiled weakly.

'How long have you known her?'

'It feels like forever, but it wasn't all that long really. We met about five years ago, at a conference. We got talking and realised we had a lot in common.'

'What sort of things would someone in your position have in common with a school teacher?'

She gave him a strange look. He felt a little uncomfortable but that was something that went with the territory.

'No offence intended. I'm just interested in the nature of your relationship.'

'Are you married?'

Carl shook his head. Being married was something he wanted to forget.

'Well, if you ever do get married, perhaps you'll understand that it's not always like the movies. When I met Josie, we had been married long enough for the gloss to have worn off. We'd found ourselves married to, what would you call them? Distracted husbands, men caught up in their careers. They were great fathers to their children, but not really attentive to our emotional needs.' She looked at Nina. 'You know what men are like, Sergeant. They're into sport and politics. Not into talking about personal stuff and blind to what's going on right in front of their faces.'

Nina absent-mindedly nodded her head. Carl made a mental note to stop talking about politics and start paying more attention to what Nina said to him.

'We gave each other that emotional support we weren't getting from our husbands. That's how we became best friends.'

'So you were a mutual support group. I think I can understand that, Mrs Rodrigo. Was there anything else you did together? Other common interests?'

'We had weekend escapes together. Sometimes we would go down the coast. Other times we would go interstate to go shopping or to the theatre or the movies. Moments to get away from being the always available mother.'

'No shared business interests?'

'Business, Inspector? No, we were just having fun. That was one of the great things about Josie.'

'When was the last time you saw her?'

'The weekend before last. We went to see the Phantom of the Opera.' She looked out at the garden.

'Did you have any contact with her after that?'

'Last week. I spoke with her on Thursday night. We had arranged to catch up later this week.' Anna stopped talking and looked out the window again.

Carl gave her a few moments to compose herself.

'Mrs Rodrigo, where were you on Monday morning around seven?'

Anna looked at him like he was a moron. 'I was here of course, getting the boys ready for school.'

'Can anybody confirm that?'

'Maria, my cook. John, you met him on the way in. My father. He drives the boys to school. Why do want to know about Monday? Didn't she get killed on Tuesday?'

'I take it the same people can vouch for your whereabouts on Tuesday morning?'

Anna looked confused but nodded her head. 'Why are you asking about the morning?'

'I'll get to that in a minute. I understand that you have a limousine, is that correct?'

'The business has a fleet of limousines, Inspector. Mark's always being driven around in one. He likes to play the big shot. I prefer something a little more discreet. I use a BMW.'

'Was your husband home on Monday and Tuesday mornings?'

'You'll have to ask him what he was doing at those times. He wasn't here. He's been at his apartment in the city since Sunday. He's very busy on some new project. I haven't actually seen him since Sunday. I'm expecting him home tonight, unless he changes his plans again.'

'So, what's keeping him so busy?'

'Inspector, I've learnt not to ask.'

'Fair enough. Do you have any idea who might have wanted to kill Josie?'

Anna shook her head.

'Did she discuss her work situation with you at all?'

'Sure, but she didn't seem to have any problems at school. She loved her job. Mostly she talked about the crazy things her students did that made her laugh.'

'Any problems with her husband?'

'Nothing apart from what I mentioned before. She loved Paul. She just wished he'd listen a bit more and notice what was going on in her life. The same things I think most wives wish their husbands would do. And I know, in his own way, Paul adored her.'

'So you've met Paul?'

'Yes. I've spent a lot of time at their house and we've been out a few times, the four of us, but they're not really Mark's kind of people.'

'Did she have any money problems?'

'Not that I know of. She was saving to go overseas on her long service leave. We were talking about going together. A girls' holiday. I was looking forward to it. In fact, I was intending to pay for her trip so she could spend her money on herself for a change.'

Carl stood up and took out one of his cards from the card holder he kept in his coat pocket. 'Thank you for seeing us. If you think of anything else give me a call on this number.'

Anna pressed a button under her desk and John appeared in the doorway.

'John will show you out, Inspector. Nice to meet you, Sergeant.'

Carl and Nina followed John back up the corridor from the office to the front door.

'How long have you been working here, John?' Carl asked as they emerged into the sunshine outside the front door.

'Five years, Inspector.'

'Is it just you or are you part of a team?'

'There's a team and lots of electronic surveillance. This is a twenty four seven operation.'

'So, you'd have CCTV footage of movements in and out of the driveways?'

'Inspector, we monitor the entire grounds, not just the driveways.'

'Have you had any excitement over your five years here?'

'This is the quietest job I've had. If the pay wasn't so good, I'd leave.' He smiled as he added, 'I've seen a lot of possums but not one intruder.'

'Where did you work before you came here?'

'I've always worked for Mr Rodrigo, in a way. Before I came here, I worked for the security firm that looks after the company's warehouses down by the airport.'

Carl put out his right hand. 'Nice meeting you, John.' They shook hands.

'The gate will be open for you, Sergeant.'

Carl and Nina got into the car and headed for the street.

'What did you make of Mrs Rodrigo?'

'I'd say you were lucky I came along.'

'Lucky?'

'You'd still be standing there with your bottom lip on the floor if I hadn't been here. Don't know why I put up with you.' She looked over at him. 'She seems to have you men worked out. Maybe I should come back and get some of that emotional support from an understanding friend she was talking about.'

Carl looked at her as she drove. The smirk on her face told him she was laughing at him.

'That obvious?'

'What is it with you guys? Every time you see a pretty girl you make fools of yourselves.'

'So, does that mean I make a fool of myself every time I'm with you?'

'I think you've seen so much of me you've become immune, unless I'm naked of course, and then you can't help yourself.'

'Just as well you're dressed when we're at work then - otherwise we'd get nothing done.'

'You'd get nothing done. I can work just as well without having my clothes on.' She was laughing now.

'Alright, you win. I'm sorry. Can we have a serious work conversation now?' He looked at her. 'You are dressed, so I'm in control of myself.'

She made him wait a couple of minutes before responding.

'I'd say all we got was a close friend. It didn't sound like there were any other connections, unless our pretty face is also a poker face that just spun us a story. I think we should check her out with some of the other girlfriends. They might have picked up something a loving husband would be too blind to notice.'

'I wonder whether Josie had any connection with Mr Rodrigo.'

'Why would a woman not getting what she wants from her husband link up with the husband of her friend with the same problem? That just does not compute, Carl.'

'Suppose you're right.'

'But it does sound like these two have an interesting relationship.'

'What makes you say that?'

'Well, how many husband do you know with a house in the suburbs and an apartment in the city? Puts a different spin on I'll be working back tonight, sweetheart, especially when you have a reputation as a bit of a playboy.'

'I wonder what sort of projects he would be working on, if he's so busy that he doesn't want the distractions of home.'

'That's something we'd better leave to the Organised Crime boys, Carl, you know how sensitive they get about their patch.'

'Yeah, and besides, the Commissioner's got his knickers in a knot over the extortion threat, and that's the only motive we have at the moment.'

'Thought you were cold on that.'

'I'm still not convinced it's genuine. The bit that doesn't make sense to me is why she got into the limo, and why did it simply take her to work on Monday and then lead to her disappearing on Tuesday?'

'Maybe the limo's got nothing to do with her being killed.'

'We won't know that until we find the limo. How many limo services are there?'

'DI Reid's people are checking them. I think I heard them say they had over twenty firms on their list.'

Carl's mobile started ringing. He fished it out of his inside coat pocket and answered it. Nina negotiated the city streets and headed down into the basement car park under police headquarters. By the time she had parked the car Carl was putting his mobile phone back into his pocket.

'That was DI Reid. Seems Mark Rodrigo's gone missing. He hasn't come back from an appointment and his office can't get him to answer his mobile. They can't contact his driver either. Bob said he was heading out to an empty warehouse by the airport where Rodrigo was supposed to be meeting with a prospective new tenant.'

They took the elevator back up to their office on the third floor.

'Any news, Harry?' Carl asked as they walked into the operations room.

'I got the record of calls made to Mr's Ford's mobile over the last three weeks while you were out. There's one call you might be interested in.'

'Which call would that be?'

'There's one call at eight am last Friday morning from a mobile phone number registered to Rodrigo Property Management.'

'Couldn't that be from a phone used by Mrs Rodrigo?'

'She seems to have her own number. There's a stack of calls to and from her number. I'd say these two women spent a lot of time talking to each other.'

'When's the last call from Mrs Rodrigo's number?' asked Nina.

'There are no calls after Thursday last week.'

'So, who uses the Rodrigo Property Management number?'

'I've just spoken to the office manager there. She said the number is Mr Rodrigo's personal mobile phone.'

Carl looked at Nina. 'Maybe your does not compute theory has some holes in it, Sergeant.'

'I wouldn't call one phone call proof of an affair, Boss.'

'Maybe not, but it's enough to arrange a meeting or to tell her he was sending his limo to pick her up.'

Carl took out his mobile and called Bob Reid.

'Bob, Carl. When you find Mark Rodrigo, ask him why he called Mrs Ford at eight o'clock last Friday morning.' He paused while Bob asked him a question. 'We have the record of calls to her mobile and his office has confirmed that the number for that call is his mobile.' He paused again while Bob told him something else.

'Okay, see what you can find out.' He ended the call and turned to the others. 'DI Reid just said he could see several squad cars with their lights flashing in front of the warehouse he's heading for.'

'I'll call the operations centre,' said Nina picking up the handset of the nearest telephone.

After a short conversation, she replaced the handset.

'There's been a shooting in a warehouse in the airport industrial park. Two, maybe three, victims. She wasn't sure. The call came in from a security guard from the firm that patrols the area about ten minutes ago. The guy was pretty upset. Sounds like one of the victims is a security guard.'

'Guess we'll find out who the others are soon enough,' said Harry.

CHAPTER 9

FOLLOWING the call from Inspector West, Paul called Ron Flint and set the funeral plan in motion.

Step one would be Flinders Funerals collecting the body and preparing it for burial. Step two would be Ron Flint coming around at four that afternoon so they could decide on the casket and step three, the funeral arrangements.

When he had finished the call to Ron, he called the parish office and left a message for Frank Mulligan.

Ron Flint arrived promptly at four. By five they had settled on the rosewood casket, the limousines, a Tuesday morning funeral, putting together a PowerPoint presentation of photographs to show before the service started, the design of the memorial cards, and the wording for the notices that would appear in the papers. Over coffee, prepared by Maria, they signed the paperwork and completed the transaction with Paul's credit card passing through Ron's wireless EFTPOS machine. When it was time for Ron to leave, Maria handed him the bag of clothes she had selected from Josie's wardrobe for dressing the body. Ron gave Paul the envelope containing the death certificate signed by the police pathologist.

When Ron had gone, Paul looked at the death certificate. He

didn't read it. He just looked at it and then put it back inside the envelope. He had seen the body. This was just the official piece of paper confirming what he already knew. Its only usefulness was for informing the insurance company and superannuation fund that Josephine Maria Ford was dead. Something else he would have to do. He filed it with the insurance policies so he'd be able to find it later.

Paul called his mother and went over the details, as she had volunteered to ring his brothers so they could arrange to be there for the funeral. Mick and Maria decided to take charge of arranging the wake, which would be held at Paul's as he had the largest house, and it would be his brothers doing most of the drinking. Once they had decided on who was doing what, Maria decided it was time to eat and talk about something else.

Over dinner, Maria made a point of asking the boys about school and let it slip that she had heard a rumour that Matthew had a girlfriend. Matthew glared at his father. Maria's eyes twinkled. She obviously had some inside information from somewhere.

'Don't look at me, mate. I haven't said anything,' said Paul.

'That look was a bit of a giveaway, Matti. Guess you'd better spill the beans,' said Mick.

'Nonna, I don't know who's telling you this stuff about girl-friends. I have a friend who is a girl but that's not the same as having a girlfriend.'

'And does this friend who is a girl have a name, Matti?' asked Maria.

All eyes were on Matthew. Paul looked at Maria who was smiling at Matthew's obvious discomfort. She knew she had him on this one. If she didn't get the name out of him tonight it would come soon enough.

'Maggie.'

'So, Matti, tell me how this Maggie is your friend and not your girlfriend.'

'We do music together; we're interested in the same sort of music and stuff. We just talk and help each other with our school work. She's pretty smart and'

'Sure she's not just pretty?' said Mick.

'It's not like that, Nonno. She's just my best friend at school.'

'In that case I guess we'll see her on Tuesday. I'll be keeping an eye out for her, to check her out. What do you reckon, Luke, is she pretty?'

Luke looked at Matthew and read the message in his eyes telling him to exercise extreme caution, if he didn't want to get thumped later.

'I read somewhere, Nonno, that beauty is in the eye of the beholder. You'll have to wait 'til Tuesday so you can make up your own mind.'

Paul couldn't help smiling. Where did the boy get his lines? Must be a side benefit from all the reading he did.

The boys decided to watch some TV with Mick while Paul and Maria cleaned up in the kitchen.

'So, do you know this girl, Paul?'

'I don't think I've met her but you met her mother the other night.' That stopped her in her tracks.

'The policewoman that was here the other night. She's Maggie's mother. Anyway, how come you're so interested, Ma? Who's been talking?'

'A friend of mine does relief teaching at the college. She came to see me this morning, about Josie. When we were talking, I showed her a recent photo of Josie and the boys. That was when she told me Matti was spending a lot of time with one particular girl at school. She said she saw them together every time she was at the college. I think he's too young to have a girlfriend.'

120

'I wouldn't worry about it, Ma. Half the kids at St Jude's are girls. I'm sure she's just a friend. Besides, the boy's got to start sometime.'

'You men are all the same. That's exactly what Mick said. Besides, it was something else to talk about tonight.'

Paul moved over and gave her a hug. 'It's not easy, is it?'

'I don't know what I'm going to do, Paul. It's not right. You shouldn't have to bury your daughter. Josie was more like a friend than a daughter to me. I could discuss anything with her, now she's gone. I can't talk to Rosa like I could talk to Josie.'

They stood silent for a couple of minutes, then Maria pulled out a tissue and dabbed at her eyes. 'The boys seem to be handling this better than me.'

'We had a talk this morning about the fact that she's dead and we're still here with lives to live, but I'm sure there will be some dark days. Can't say I'm looking forward to Tuesday. I think that's going to be hard for all of us.'

'What was that about Matti talking to Josie last night? Luke was very excited when he was telling me.'

'Really don't know how to take that. Anyway, at breakfast this morning, he said she had been talking to him while he was asleep last night. Guess he was dreaming but it seemed real to him. Maybe it was for real, who knows what happens after you die?'

'You think it could have been Josie?'

'Hope it was Josie, Ma. I like to think of death as a doorway and not the end of the road.'

'Isn't that sort of what Jesus told us?'

'Yeah, well as far as I know, no-one else has come back to confirm the message.'

'Maybe she'll talk to him some more,' said Maria.

'Who knows? Maybe she'll talk to all of us. After all, if she can talk to one why not all of us? And, of course, there's nothing to stop any of us talking to her.'

'She might not answer.'

'Well, that'll be different. I could get used to that.'

Maria smiled. Josie always had an answer for anything you threw at her. 'Do you think you'll ever get used to her not being here, Paul?'

'I don't think so, Ma. At one level, she'll always be here.'

'I suppose you're right but somehow we have to keep going. We can't stop living because this terrible thing happened to Josie. I don't want to end up like Signora Rosetti. She stopped looking after herself when her son was killed in that car crash last Christmas. She won't even leave the house. That poor husband of hers has to do all the shopping, everything. She's just sitting and waiting to die.'

'I'm with you on that one, so even though I'm going to be missing Josie, I still need to be here for the boys and for me. I've still got another fifty years to live yet.'

'I hope so, Paul.'

The telephone rang. Matthew answered it and then came into the kitchen.

'Dad, that was Father Mulligan. Said he'd be here in about twenty minutes.'

'Okay.'

'Well, let's get these dishes into the dishwasher and then I'll get coffee organised,' said Maria.

Together they tidied up the kitchen. Then Maria ground up a fresh lot of coffee beans, loaded up the percolator ready to put on the stove when Father Mulligan arrived, and found the biscuit tin.

Half an hour later, when they heard Father Mulligan's car pull into the driveway, Maria turned on the flame under the percolator. She knew she wouldn't have to ask him if he wanted a coffee. Like all the Irishmen she had met since marrying Mick, Frank Mulligan had been converted to Italian coffee and consumed it at every opportunity.

Over coffee and biscuits, they sat around the table talking and sorting out the details of the funeral mass late into the night. By the time Father Mulligan was ready to leave, after several rounds of coffee, they had decided on which readings to use, what prayers to include in the prayers of the faithful, and who would be asked to do what. They also had a list of the hymns the organist would play and Paul had agreed to deliver a short eulogy at the start of the Mass.

Mick and Maria left shortly after Father Mulligan.

'Do you think Mum will talk to me tonight, Dad?' asked Luke as they got ready to go to bed.

'I don't know, sunshine, but you can talk to her. I'm sure she'd love to hear from you. Just say the words in your heart, that's where she is, in our hearts, and we can talk to her any time we want. I'll be talking to her.'

'I miss her so much. I wish this hadn't happened.'

'Make sure you tell her.'

Friday morning arrived. They sat around the kitchen table eating breakfast. Josie had not spoken to any of them overnight. They were as quiet as she had been. The thought in all three minds was that she was gone. It was becoming painfully obvious that they would be travelling a long road, before they could embrace the acceptance of her death that they had discussed the previous morning.

After breakfast, the boys retreated to their rooms and their school work. At least they had something to distract themselves with. Paul put on a load of washing and went out and sat on the back veranda, while the machine he referred to as Mrs Bosch did the hard part.

By the time his mother arrived mid-afternoon, Mrs Bosch had taken care of the washing, which was now draped over clothes horses, folded and put away or in the tumble dryer. Paul had run the vacuum cleaner over the carpets, washed the floors and cleaned the bathroom and toilets.

'If you're going to get serious about cleaning, Paul, you need to remember to dust all these flat surfaces,' said Anne as she dragged a finger through the film of dust on top of the china cabinet.

'That's the bit Josie did.'

He went out to the laundry, found the dusting cloths and furniture polish, and started on the dusting. Anne went up the passageway to say hello to the boys.

Half an hour later, Paul sat down with Anne for a cup of coffee and a piece of cake.

'Are you alright?'

'Not really, Mum. I just had to do something, anything,' he waved his hand about the room. 'It's too painful to think about Josie and what her death means. I just had to have some sort of normality.'

'This is not going to get any easier for some time; you know that, don't you?'

'I'm not sure I'm going to be able to hold it all together for Tuesday.'

'No one expects you to and you won't be alone. I love all my daughters-in-law but I'm especially going to miss this one.'

The front door bell rang. Before either of them had moved, Matthew was at the door. He came into the kitchen with a girl dressed in a St Jude's uniform. She looked familiar to Paul.

'Dad, Grandma, this is Maggie.'

'Hello, Maggie,' said Anne.

'Ah, so you're Maggie,' said Paul, realising he had seen her in several band performances and at soccer on Saturday mornings.

'I'm really sorry about Mrs Ford.' She kissed him on the cheek.

'Thanks.'

'I know what it's like to lose someone close. My dad was killed during some sort of raid that went wrong.'

'Oh, I didn't know that. When did that happen?'

'When I was in year six. We came back here after it happened. That's when I started at St Jude's and Matti helped me settle in and get on with my life. I hope I can do the same for him.'

'I had no idea you guys were dealing with anything like that.'

'Not many people know about my father. Mum said it was best to keep a low profile.'

'Well, I don't think we're going to get to be low profile. Pretty hard to hide something this public,' said Paul.

'We were living in another city when my dad was killed. I don't remember it being on the news. He was in Special Operations and I think the raid was some sort of secret. They moved us here straight after the funeral. I didn't even get a chance to say goodbye to my friends.'

'That must have been tough,' said Anne, 'losing your dad and your friends all at once.'

'Well, Mrs Ford, I got Matti as my best friend.'

The beaming smile on Matthew's face told its own story.

'Then, I'd say your luck's changed, but I could be a bit biased, being his grandmother.'

'I certainly feel lucky to have him as my friend.' She looked at Matti and smiled.

'We've got some stuff to catch up on before Maggie has to go home, she's brought some notes and things from school,' said

Matthew. He led Maggie out to the hallway, where they retrieved her schoolbag, and then went up to his room. Paul heard Maggie greeting Luke and noticed that Matthew didn't shut the door to his room. He decided that discretion was the best option and stayed in the kitchen.

'She seems to be a lovely girl,' said Anne.

'Maria's going to be jealous when she finds out you got to meet her first.'

'What do you mean?'

'She was stirring Matti last night. One of her friends that does relief teaching at St Jude's told her that he was spending a lot of time with a girl at school. She gave him a hard time about having a girlfriend. Even Mick joined in wanting to know if she was pretty.'

'I can imagine. Poor Matti. Sad about her father though.'

'Yes, her mother is the sergeant at the police station where I reported Josie missing.'

'Talk about a small world. I'd better do something about dinner or we'll be eating very late tonight.'

While Anne set about preparing the evening meal, Paul went to take the last load of clothes out of the tumble dryer. As he unloaded the clothes, it occurred to him that the boys had kept the extent of Matti's friendship with Maggie a secret from him for close on 5 years, and he'd been blind to the bleeding obvious. Now that he had been introduced to her, he realised that she had been a constant at every school event involving Matthew he had attended in recent years. He wondered how much Josie had known about the relationship and concluded she probably had known everything about it.

Being the sole parent was going to be a little more difficult than being part of a team. There was so much he had left to Josie when it came to parenting, like all the emotional support stuff. No wonder the boys had told her everything and only come to him when they wanted something practical sorted out. Being emotionally available to others was one of the challenges he knew he needed to work on. Being present in the moment, listening instead of problem solving, was something he had read about but hadn't yet mastered. He wondered how on earth he was going to cope with this new life lesson without Josie's support.

Then the thought crossed his mind that he wouldn't have to do anything without Josie's support. She was still available to him. After all, it was only bodies that died. Wasn't that the whole point Jesus made? Josie was still where she always was, in the heart of God. All he had to do was remember that he was there too. That's what she had been trying to remind them of when she spoke to Matthew. She might not be with her body anymore but she was still there for them.

CHAPTER 10

THE FIRST THREE FORD BOYS, Andrew, James and Simon, were born during the years of the Second Vatican Council. Paul and John came along shortly after but Mark, fourteen years younger than Andrew, was definitely born in the post-Vatican 2 era. One of the challenges for Catholic children growing up in the post Vatican 2 world was overcoming the beliefs and practices of their pre-Vatican 2 parents. George and Anne Ford, devout Catholics, schooled in the traditions of the Church, were among the many who felt a sense of confusion and betrayal following the Council. There was a lot of change in the way things were done, including the Mass being said in English instead of Latin. They were caught in the tension created by their obligation to obey the Pope and their desire to hold onto the beliefs and practices they had grown up with. They wanted to stay with the catechism they knew and not move to the revised green book their children were introduced to at school.

In addition to his traditional religious views, George Ford was a strict disciplinarian. It might have been the swinging sixties and the start of the me generation in the world at large, but not for the Ford boys. They grew up in a household of traditional values, regular church attendance, rigid behavioural guidelines and little tolerance of transgression. They learnt to be good, to conform and to perform to the best of their abilities. Andrew and James, as the eldest, carried the heaviest burden of expectation. They had to set good examples for their younger brothers. Both excelled at school and went on to university.

Andrew became a chartered accountant and moved inter-state, to work for a big accounting firm, where he met Kathleen, a young lawyer, married her and stayed, even after he started his own firm. The professional couple, Andrew and Kathleen had no children by choice. Andrew had no desire to pass on any of his father's imprinting. George was proud of his achievements but kept his disappointment about the lack of grandchildren to himself.

James, with an honours degree in economics, joined the public service after university, where he met Sandra, a fellow economist working in the same agency. After their wedding, they moved to the federal capital to further their careers. With one of the benefits of working in the public service being maternity leave, they were the proud parents of three teenage daughters, Tamara, Tegan and Tatiana. James had a lot of sympathy for his mother, now that he was the odd man out in an all-girl household.

Simon was not academic like his older brothers. His talents lay in his hands and on the sports field. While Andrew and James had been head prefect in their final year at St Jude's, Simon had been captain of the first eleven. George had insisted that he complete year 12, but he had taken a different range of subjects than his brothers. After leaving school he took an apprenticeship with the local butcher. Five years later he was working as a butcher for one of the large supermarket chains in another city, where he found love in the form of Judy, the girl that cut his hair. They had one sixteen year old son, Sam.

John, two years younger than Paul, was more in the mould of Simon than his older brothers. He was good at sport but he was not a leader. He had been more interested in girls than his studies, and had been constantly in trouble at home from the time he was thirteen. He experimented with alcohol and cigarettes. He broke all of George's many rules and made his mother's life hell with his obscene language and angry outbursts. When he decided to join the army as an apprentice auto-electrician, George, hoping that the army would straighten him out, was only too happy to sign the papers. He stayed in the army for twenty years before he and an army mate went into business as auto-electricians, with a nice little contract servicing army vehicles. Not long after leaving the army he finally stopped playing the field and married Helen, fifteen years his junior. They had a two year old son, Nathan.

Mark, who was ten when John left home to join the army, had a very different upbringing than his older brothers. For most of his teen years he was the only one living at home. George had mellowed somewhat from the experience of raising his family, the ravages of age and the gathering of wisdom. Paul was the only brother Mark saw much of as he was the only one still living in the city; the only one who still visited on a regular basis with his young wife and family. Mark was a scholar and a sportsman. He had been both head prefect and captain of the first eleven, and had surprised them all by going to the defence force academy instead of university, and becoming an officer in the Special Air Services. With some of the traits of all his brothers, the bit he took from John was the bit about playing the field and not settling down. George was proud of his son fighting the war against terrorism, in places like Afghanistan, but each time he was on active service Anne worried herself sick and prayed until he returned.

There was a gathering of the clan at least once a year at Christmas, and they had all been home for George's and Anne's significant birthdays. The sisters-in-law had a loose association centred around Anne. They each commiserated with the others about what it was like being married to a version of George or took great delight in trading stories about the irrational behaviours of their husbands. It took Helen a couple of visits to see the funny side of her relationship with John, since she was still so much in love with her Ford. The others had had twenty plus years to find out about the foibles of their Fords by the time she joined their ranks.

Paul and Josie had often been the glue holding family functions together as they were held at Whitbread Avenue. Paul straddled the two main groupings of his brothers. He was on a similar wavelength to Andrew and James when it came to discussing politics and world events, and could pitch in with Simon and John when it came to discussing sport. Mark and John generally had no problems talking shop. The boys all avoided the topic of religion but were happy to entertain George's wild ideas about what was going on in the world. They all enjoyed a barbecue and a beer or two.

Josie, naturally gregarious, enjoyed socialising and knew how to engage with George without provoking an argument. Apart from Nathan, the new boy, the cousins had interacted on enough occasions to get along. Sam and Matthew had a common interest in music and the girls, like Luke, were all into basketball. Generally, family shows were a lot of fun.

This would be the first gathering centred on a funeral of one of them.

Paul's brothers started arriving on Sunday afternoon. Mark was the first to arrive and, knowing that none of his brothers had as much experience dealing with sudden death as he did and that someone would have to look out for Paul, commandeered the spare bed in the study at Whitbread Avenue.

After catching up with the boys and ringing his mother, Mark took Paul out onto the back veranda for a beer.

'So, how are you coping, mate?'

'I'm not so sure. I thought I had gotten to a place spiritually where I'd be able to handle this. But the more I think about it the harder it's becoming to see this as Josie just leaving her body.'

'You always were a bit too spiritual for your own good, mate. Let me tell you something I learnt the hard way in Afghanistan. You have to grieve when someone you love gets killed. If you don't, you'll end up a mess.' He took a drink from the stubby in his hand. 'I've seen too many guys try to tough it out when their best mate gets blown away. If you don't work with the process, you end up with post-traumatic shock. And Paul, we are not dealing with a normal death here. Josie didn't get sick. She didn't get killed in a car accident. Some bastard shot her. In my book, that's like a soldier getting killed in an ambush. It's a shock. Don't try and make out it's not.'

'You sound like Frank Mulligan.'

'I'd say he's had a lot of experience with death and dying and people coming to terms with it. We've got some chaplains in the Army that know how to walk soldiers through it. They've been a great help to me. I don't know how much you know about what's been going on over there. I lost two of my mates in an ambush last year. So I know what you have coming, and I can tell you, you might be able to dull the pain with these,' he held up his beer,' but you can't make it go away. You have to deal with it.'

'You sure you haven't been to see Frank on the way here? He told me exactly the same thing the other night.'

'I'm serious, Paul. Don't try to do the usual bloke thing and think you can handle it on your own or try and hide inside all that spirituality stuff. You have to embrace the pain, as one priest told me, otherwise it will hit you for six.'

'So, how did you deal with it?'

'You need someone to talk to and you need to express your feelings. I found out that grieving is a process. Sometimes it takes a long time but it doesn't have to. You're probably still in a state of shock, that's fairly normal. If you feel like crying or screaming or ranting at God, do all those things. You probably already know that you can't offend God. He knows how you feel. The worst thing you can do is try and be a saint about it. And you need to help the boys with their grief. They've lost their mother. Don't forget that when you're feeling sorry for yourself.'

'We've all been crying together and trying to work out how we will continue on without her. They're different you know. Matti tends to stuff things down, a bit like me I suppose. Luke expresses his emotions. More like his mother. You know, I'd never seen Dad cry until now. I didn't think he had it in him.'

'Yeah, well don't be like him. You're too much like him as it is. Anyway, she was like the daughter they never had. I wouldn't say that with the others around but I'd say Josie was his favourite daughter-in-law.'

'Thanks for the words of wisdom. This isn't something I'd say I was ready for.'

'It's all part of the job in a war zone. I've had more experience at this than I had planned on.'

They sat watching the birds scratching around in the back lawn, and slowly drinking their beers.

Around six o'clock they ordered in pizza. Mark spent some time with the boys telling them stories of his exploits in Afghanistan.

By eight o'clock that night the brothers, and some of their wives, had gathered at Whitbread Avenue for the first of what would be several times over the next couple of days. They might have said for coffee but there wasn't much coffee being consumed.

The brothers, sitting in the lounge, were into their second beers when the conversation turned to the progress of the police investigation.

'So what has this Inspector West said to you about what he thinks happened?' Andrew asked Paul.

'He's asked me more questions than told me anything.'

'What sort of questions?' asked Mark.

'He wanted to know if we knew anyone with a limo and a driver. Said they had a witness, who claimed to have seen Josie getting into a limo down the street on Monday and Tuesday morning.'

'Do you know anyone with a limo?'

'Why was she getting into a limo? Wasn't she going to work?' asked Simon.

'I have no idea why she was getting into a limo, but we do know someone who has a limo with a driver. The husband of one of Josie's friends.'

'Didn't know you were mixing with the rich and famous, Paul,' said James.

'Not me. Josie met Anna at some conference, one of those secret women's business things. They've been close ever since. You know, the friend she's been doing her weekend escapes with over the last couple of years. Her husband goes everywhere in a limo.'

'So did you ask him?' asked Andrew.

'No, the inspector said he would do the asking.'

'And?'

'He didn't get to ask him anything. They found his body in a warehouse down by the airport, not far from where they found Josie's.'

'Inspector West?' asked Andrew.

'No, Anna's husband.'

'Do the police think there is any connection?' asked Simon.

'Not that they've told me.'

'They tend to play their cards pretty close,' said James. A general murmur of agreement went around the gathering.

'What else did he ask you?' asked Andrew.

'He wanted to know if Josie took sleeping pills, and when was the last time I had sex with her.'

'We all know the answer to one of those questions,' said James winking at his brothers. 'The one about the sleeping pills.'

'Why did he want to know that?' asked Andrew.

'Well, he mentioned something about finding traces of sedatives in her blood, and the pathologist saying it looked like she had had sex sometime on Tuesday.'

'What, she was raped as well?' said Mark.

'He didn't actually say that. He hinted that the signs indicated otherwise but they couldn't be sure one way or the other because of the sedatives, but he did say they thought whoever it was used a condom. Pretty considerate for a rapist, if you ask me.'

'Could be the guy just didn't want to leave any DNA samples for the police,' said Kathleen, who had walked into the room.

'Hadn't thought of that,' said Paul.

'So, I take it that it wasn't you who had the sex with her on Tuesday, then?' said James.

'No. But at least I hadn't contaminated the crime scene, as the inspector put it.'

The boys laughed.

'Bloody considerate of you, mate. Do you want another beer?' asked James.

'Thanks.'

'While you're at it, James, I'll have another,' said John.

James looked around the room. 'Another round then?' they all nodded.

James went out into the laundry to get more beers out of the esky.

'Do you girls want anything?' asked Paul, finally remembering his manners.

'I'll stay with the mineral water, thanks,' said Kathleen.

'Bring me a beer, James,' said Judy.

'Perhaps I'd better give him a hand,' said Mark, who got up and went out to help James.

'So what are the plans for the funeral service?' asked Andrew. 'Who's doing what?'

'Let me get the notes I made with Father Mulligan.' Paul went out into the kitchen to retrieve the sheet of paper, which he had written on during Father Mulligan's visit on Saturday afternoon, from beneath a fridge magnet. He unfolded the sheet as he walked back into the lounge and sat down on the couch next to Kathleen.

'Andrew, I've put you down as one of the pall bearers. You okay with that?'

'Sure.'

'The order of service will be rosary, eulogy, mass, condolences as people leave the church and then the burial. After that we'll come back here for the wake.'

'What do we need to do to make the wake happen? That could be a lot of work,' said Kathleen.

'Josie's parents have taken charge of the catering for the wake. I'm sure they'd appreciate help setting up and serving food. They'll be here tomorrow morning so we can get things set up. Anybody who wants to help set up can come over in the morning, around ten.'

'We can be here by then can't we, Andrew?'

'That shouldn't be a problem, sweetheart.'

'Thanks. Mark and I and the boys will be here, of course, if I can get them out of bed.'

'If I know Mick, they won't be sleeping once he gets here,' said Andrew.

'Are you doing a slide show?' asked Judy as she took the beer Mark was offering her.

'Yes. The boys put one together yesterday. Josie's mother brought over some photos that we scanned in. We can have a look later, if you want.'

'That would be good, Paul. I'd like that.' Kathleen squeezed his hand.

'Who's doing the readings?' asked John.

'I'd like James and Mark to do the readings. I've got copies so you can have a run through if you need.'

'Yeah, that might be a good idea,' said Mark.

James nodded in agreement.

'The mothers are doing the communion procession. The cousins have been assigned a prayer of the faithful each. I've got a stack of copies out in the study for you to take with you for the kids.'

'What about music?'

'The choir from St Catherine's is taking care of that.'

'Sounds like it's all organised, then,' said Andrew.

'I still have to write the eulogy. It's not as easy as you might think.'

The room was silent. They were all lost in their own thoughts about how hard that would be.

'I intend to focus on celebrating her life.'

'That's probably a good idea, Paul,' said Kathleen. 'And, if it all gets too much just let yourself cry. Nobody's going to think you're a wuss.'

'Least of all me,' said Mark. 'I'm the bloke who cried in front of the regiment when we buried my mates.'

'Why don't we go take a look at this slide show before we all start reaching for a tissue,' said Andrew.

They moved out into the study and stood around the computer screen while Paul turned on the computer, located the file for the slide show and then set it in motion. It started with a shot of Josie as a baby, progressed through captured moments of her childhood and school days and onto her wedding. There was a selection of shots of her as a new mother showing off the boys. Then it switched to a suite of more recent photographs covering a range of family events and finished with the photographs from last weekend's birthday, including the shot Paul had given to the police, which they had all seen splashed across newspapers and television screens. As it was set on a loop it started again. They watched it three times before they had the courage to turn it off.

Andrew was wrong about the tissues.

They moved back into the lounge but the night was over. There were hugs all round, and then those sleeping elsewhere headed off into the night.

CHAPTER 11

IT DIDN'T TAKE LONG for Inspector Reid to establish that he wasn't going to get an interview with Mark Rodrigo. Shortly after approaching the warehouse, and speaking to the sergeant securing the crime scene, he knew the identity of all three victims. According to the sergeant, the one just inside the door, with his throat cut, was a security guard named Morris Abrahams. The one in front of the burnt-out limo, with a bullet hole between the eyes, was Frank Kingston, Mark Rodrigo's driver. The third victim, whose lifeless body lay face down halfway between the remains of the car and the row of offices along the side of the warehouse, was Mark Rodrigo, who had been shot in the back several times.

'What do you think happened here, Inspector?' the sergeant asked him.

'We'll let Forensics work that out, Sergeant, but my guess would be someone killed the guard and then ambushed Rodrigo when he arrived. Who found the bodies?'

'There's a security guard over there with one of my men. He's pretty shaken up. Said he came over to check on his mate when he hadn't answered his radio.'

'I would have thought a place like this would have a fire

alarm,' said Inspector Reid, looking at the tendrils of smoke rising from the burnt-out car.

'It does, but according to the guy outside, the fire alarm has been switched off. He showed us the control box. The guard's keys were still in the lock.'

'Doubt we'll get any prints. Looks like a mob hit to me.'

They waited as the sound of a 747 lifting off made it impossible to converse out in the open.

'How come you got here so quick, Inspector? I'd only just called when you pulled up.'

'I was on my way here to interview Rodrigo. His office said this was where I'd probably find him. He had an appointment here this morning. I was hoping to interview him in connection with the Ford case, about that limo over there.' He pointed towards the smouldering remains of the car in the centre of the warehouse.

'Looks like you lucked out, Inspector.'

'In more ways than one. Think I'll have a word with the security guard while we wait for Forensics.'

'Better let Operations know you're here, Inspector, otherwise they'll send someone else.'

'I suspect they'll be sending someone from Organised Crime when I tell them who the victims are, so make sure you secure this place tight.'

Inspector Reid walked over to where the police cars were parked. He found the guard leaning up against his car talking to the detective who had accompanied him on the abortive trip to interview Mark Rodrigo and photograph the limo.

'Jim, this is Inspector Reid,' said the detective when Inspector Reid walked up to them.

'Jim Adams,' said the guard extending his hand to shake the inspector's offered hand.

'Close mate?'

'Been working with Morris for fifteen years, Inspector. Didn't ever expect this.'

'What was Morris doing here?'

'Mr Rodrigo wanted the place opened up. He was showing someone through around twelve. He's been trying to rent this place for months.'

'Would turning the alarms off be standard?'

'Yeah. These places only have perimeter alarms, you know, on the doors and windows.'

'What about the fire alarm?'

'That's what got me over here. Control room called and said the fire alarm appeared to be off. I called Morris on the radio but he didn't answer, so I came over to find out why.' He picked up his radio from his belt. 'We wear these things all the time, so him not answering told me something was wrong. I thought he might have had a heart attack or something.'

'When was that?' asked Inspector Reid flipping open his note book.

'Control room called just after two fifteen. I got here around twenty to three. I was over the other side of the estate testing the new alarm system we're putting in for Spinosa Foods.'

'What did you see when you got here?'

They watched as a 737 came in to land over their heads.

'I was just telling Wayne here that there was smoke coming out the gap in the door. When I opened the door the place was full of smoke but I couldn't see a fire. Wasn't until it cleared a bit that I saw the car and the bodies.'

'That's when you called us?'

'I had a quick look around first. Once I'd checked the bodies, there didn't seem to be any point calling an ambulance. So I called you lot.'

'Did you see anybody leaving the area as you were driving over?'

'Not once I turned off the ring road and into the parking area for this warehouse. You would have seen how busy it was out there when you drove in.'

Inspector Reid nodded. 'Is there any other way out of here?'

'All these warehouses have an exit on the other side that connects to the service road that goes around the airport. You can drive all the way around to the other side, where they found that body yesterday, before you have to join the ring road again.'

'Any CCTV in use down here?'

'There is now. That's what we're putting in over at Spinosa Foods. There's nothing else. We patrol this estate day and night.'

'Anything unusual down here on Tuesday night?'

'Can't help you there, Inspector. The only person that would know is Morris; he was doing the night shift in this zone on Tuesday.'

'Have we got Jim's details, Wayne?'

'He's given me his card, Inspector.'

'Thanks for your help, Jim. Guess you'll have to stay around until Forensics are finished.'

'I've called the control room. They're sending someone over to keep me company.'

The inspector shook his hand again. 'Sorry about your mate.' He turned away and took out his mobile phone and called Operations to tell them he'd hold the fort until Organised Crime arrived to take control of the case. They told him the case was his for the time being.

Then he called Inspector West to break the news that Mark Rodrigo wouldn't be answering any of their questions, and to inform him that he and Wayne would be shifting their attention to this murder.

When he looked up a black limousine and a security patrol car were pulling into the parking lot. He watched as a man in a grey suit got out of the back of the limousine and walked towards him. A woman in a uniform got out of the security vehicle and went over to speak to the security guard.

'I've just been told my brother's been shot. What's going on?'

'Detective Inspector Reid. Who are you?'

'Michael Rodrigo. We own this place.'

'And who told you that your brother had been shot?'

'I just got a call from security. Is it true?'

'That security guard over there identified one of the bodies as being your brother. I'm sorry.'

Michael's shoulders slumped and he took several deep breaths. He looked up. 'What's that burning smell?'

'Someone torched his car.'

'Can I go in?'

'Not yet, Mr Rodrigo. We'll have to wait for Forensics to go over the crime scene. They should be here any moment. When they're finished, perhaps then, if you're up to it, you can confirm the identity of the body we believe is Mark's.'

Michael nodded that he understood.

'Perhaps you can answer a few questions for me while we wait.'

Michael nodded again.

'Let's take a walk, Mr Rodrigo. I'd like to stretch my legs.' Inspector Reid started walking towards the garden at the opposite end of the car park.

'Any idea who your brother was meeting here today?'

'This place has been empty since Vari Exports went bust a couple of years ago. Victims of the high dollar. Mark's been trying to find a tenant for months but with the state of the economy, global financial crisis and all that, he hasn't had much luck. I've lost count of the number of people he's shown through. I didn't know he was showing anyone through today.'

'Do you know if he keeps a record of who he shows through?'

'He's a meticulous record keeper, so probably. I'd have to check with his office to be sure.'

'I think that would be useful. Any idea who would want him dead?'

Michael stopped walking. 'Let me ask you a question, Inspector. What do you know about my brother?'

'Nothing really. I came out here because I wanted to know where his limo was on Monday and Tuesday morning. Guess I'm not going to find out now.'

'Guess not. Why did you want to know that?'

'Before this happened, I was trying to find out who gave someone, someone who turned up dead yesterday, a lift in a silver limo on those mornings.'

'The Ford lady?'

'Yes.'

'Shocking. My sister-in-law is very upset. Her best friend.'

'So I heard. Did you ever meet her?'

'No.'

'Why did you ask if I knew anything about your brother?'

'He's a bit of a playboy, Inspector. No, maybe that's understating it. He was always chasing skirt. He used that limo in there like a mobile bed. He generally picked up young girls in night clubs, from what I've heard from his drivers. But he also seduced other people's wives as a sport. So I'd say he had a few enemies.'

'How did his wife take to that?'

'Things aren't always what they seem, Inspector. Mark and Anna present the happy married couple for family functions to keep the olds happy, but they pretty much live separate lives. I'd be very surprised if she was behind this.'

'Property management the only thing Mark was into?'

'What do you mean?'

'Did he have any business interests outside the family business?'

'Not to my knowledge.'

'And which part of the family business are you in?'

'I'm the manager of Spinosa Foods. We import foodstuffs from Europe and export fresh produce to Asia. We have three warehouses on the other side of this estate.' He pointed to his right.

'Your security guard said you were installing CCTV over there. What's prompted that?'

'You know, Inspector, we've been operating here for close to twenty years. We've never been broken into in all that time. But in the last couple of weeks, we've been broken into three times, even though we have security patrols and alarms. And the strange thing is the first couple of times they didn't take anything. Twice they shut off the fire alarm and set a small fire in a metal drum, but on Tuesday night one of our delivery vans went missing. It was one of your people who suggested we get some cameras when we reported the van.'

'I wonder if there is a connection between that and this.'

'What makes you say that?'

'The fire alarm. Your security guard says it was turned off.'

Two vehicles pulled into the car park. A police car and a white van. Forensics had arrived.

The two men turned and walked back towards the cars.

'Have you been inside, Inspector?' Michael asked glancing at the doorway to the warehouse. The shape of a car was visible in the gloom.

'No. Enough people have been in there contaminating the scene without me joining in. I had a look in from the doorway. I'm not hopeful Forensics will find much. Everything's covered in soot. The only clear footprints will belong to your security guard, who said he checked the bodies when the smoke cleared. Forensics might be able to tell us what was used to torch the car but I doubt they'll find any finger prints or anything else to identify the killers. Looks like a well-planned operation to me.'

A third unmarked car arrived and a man in a dark suit got out and walked around to the rear of the car and opened the trunk.

'Who's that?'

'That's the pathologist.'

They watched him suit up into his white overalls and plastic bag shoes and then walk into the warehouse carrying his toolbox.

'Anything going on in your business empire, Mr Rodrigo? Anyone causing trouble apart from small fires in your warehouse? Anyone trying to muscle in and take customers?'

'There's always someone trying to take customers, Inspector. Usually they undercut our prices or offer our suppliers more money for their produce. We have to stay competitive to keep our customers, but Mr Spinosa and my father embraced what they call vertical integration these days when they started out. We grow most of the produce we sell to supermarkets both here and in Asia. We have exclusive distribution rights for a lot of the goods we bring in from Europe.'

'What about your other business interest? I understand you operate a freight company as well.'

'You seem to know a few things about us, Inspector.'

'Pure luck, believe me. I was talking to a colleague this morning. When I mentioned I was going to be talking to your brother, he gave me a summary of your family's business interests. Bit of a change really. I generally don't get to find things out until after the murder.'

'Well, we don't have the same advantages in some of our other operations. We're always competing on price. The only customer the freight company can rely on is us. All the apartments we own in the city are leased to employees. But as you can see here, we're competing with other commercial property owners when it comes to finding tenants for warehouses. We own this one and the one next door. They're both vacant.'

They stopped talking as another plane took off.

'While, we're waiting, do you mind calling Mark's office to see if they know who your brother was supposed to be meeting here today, and if they know if he kept a list of the people he has shown through the warehouse?'

'What do I say about what's happened?'

'If security told you, I guess they've told his office as well by now.'

'Yes, you're probably right.' Michael took a mobile phone out of his coat pocket and called the number of Mark's office.

Another black car arrived and parked in the car park. No-one got out.

Inspector Reid waited while Michael conversed with his brother's office manager.

'Inspector, the office manager said if Mark had the name it would be in his diary with the others, in his brief case.'

'Who's that?' asked Inspector Reid, with a nod towards the car that had just pulled into the car park.

'That's my father, Inspector. Come on, I'll introduce you. You'll have to get into the car. He's not very mobile these days.'

Rocco Rodrigo was a man of few words. Inspector Reid emerged from the back of the limousine with no more information than he had taken in, except for the impression that the old man was not as frail as he appeared. When he got out of the car the sergeant signalled that he could enter the warehouse, so he took Michael Rodrigo inside.

Michael confirmed the identities of the three bodies and went to confer with his father once Inspector Reid advised him that the bodies would be taken to the police morgue. The Rodrigo cars left the car park.

Following the departure of the Rodrigos, the pathologist and the forensics team briefed Inspector Reid. Their initial assessment was that the blood splatter on the control box indicated that the security guard's throat had been cut as soon as he had disarmed the alarms, and that the other two had been shot with a high-powered assault rifle from a vantage point up on the southern side of the warehouse. The state of the car indicated that the sun roof had been opened and the interior flooded with an accelerant before being ignited. The remains of a burnt petrol can inside the wreckage suggested the nature of the accelerant was not exotic. Any other details they could provide would be available after the autopsies and a close examination of the remains of the car back in the forensics laboratory.

After the briefing, Inspector Reid called together the officers who had responded to the call to find out what they had discovered from people in surrounding buildings. Surprisingly, no-one had seen or heard anything. No-one had seen the silver limousine or any other vehicles arrive. No-one had noticed the smoke. No-one had even turned up to find out what was going on, apart from security and the Rodrigos.

Leaving Forensics to load the wreckage onto the flat-top tow truck they had summoned, Inspector Reid returned to the city. He needed to talk to someone in Organised Crime.

He was none the wiser after a twenty minute conversation with the head of Organised Crime. They only had rumours from the street. Whatever the families were up to, it was well concealed within their legitimate business operations. The break-ins at Spinosa Foods were the only concrete signs they had of potential trouble, prior to the murders. He would have to treat it like any other homicide, as there was no evidence Mark Rodrigo was actually involved in anything criminal, let alone organised.

After speaking to Organised Crime, Inspector Reid decided to compare notes with Inspector West and his team.

'You need to find out more about that limo, Bob. Why would they burn it? What was in it that was so incriminating that the killers had to destroy it?'

'Maybe someone was in the car with Mark, someone who was part of the hit squad,' suggested Harry.

'Pretty drastic measures to make sure you didn't leave any prints,' said Nina.

'Maybe we're dealing with one very pissed off husband?' said Wayne. 'Didn't the brother tell you he was a playboy, Inspector?'

'If we are, he's formed a vigilante group and killed three people using two different weapons. I can understand the driver, he'd be seen as an accomplice, but why the security guard?'

'I think we could be dealing with professionals. They managed to get both in and out of the place without being seen. If no-one heard anything, they either timed the shots with a plane taking off or landing or they used a silencer on the rifle,' said Inspector West.

'If they drove a van or a small truck no-one would notice them down there. Be the easiest way to hide in plain sight. For all I know, they could have been parked in one of the loading yards while we were there. Maybe they used the van taken from Spinosa Foods. That would have been a perfect way to blend in.'

'So, Inspector, what was your impression of Mr Rodrigo senior?' asked Nina.

'Ever been to the zoo and stood outside the lion's enclosure, Sergeant?'

'Not since I was at school.'

Inspector Reid leant back on the desk he was using as a seat.

'Imagine a wild animal trapped inside the body of a frail old lion. He looks harmless until you look into his eyes. That's when you know that if you go into his cage it will be at your own risk. That's how I felt in the car with Mr Rodrigo. What I saw in that car was a frail old man full of burning energy. I got the impression that if I didn't find out who had killed his boy, it would not be a good idea to be around him.'

'We'd better hope Forensics come up with something, otherwise you could be in trouble, Bob,' said Inspector West with a broad grin breaking across his face.

'Anything helpful turn up on the Ford case while I was down at the airport?'

'Maybe. Forensics has a team out looking at another burnt out vehicle in the foothills. Local Council was going to tow it, before one of their crew spotted a handgun in the rubbish in the back of the vehicle. A 9 mill pistol,' said Harry.

'What would we do without Forensics?' said Inspector West.

'Even with them we don't seem to be making much progress, Boss. We have a ten year old who says he saw Mrs Ford get into a limo. We have a limo with someone else's number plate on it in the vicinity of City Park from the Monday. We think she may have gotten out of that limo on that morning but we have no proof. We have no idea where she was between the time she supposedly got into the limo on Tuesday morning and ended up dead sometime that night. No-one's heard from the extortionist since Wednesday,' said Nina shrugging her shoulders.

'We have something though, Boss. The voice on the call to the bank has the same digital signature as the voice on the call reporting the body, and we know they were both made from the same mobile phone. All we need now is a recording from someone we know the identity of and we'll have our man,' said Harry.

'Too bad that mobile phone belonged to the victim,' said Inspector West.

'Can't see how we are going to find the owner of that voice before Monday. It's not like we can listen to every mobile phone call. I think there are a few laws stopping us unless we can show cause,' said Nina.

'And think of the number of calls. I read the other day there are now more mobile phones than people. That's a real needle in a haystack proposition,' said Inspector Reid.

'We need to narrow down the field.'

'We could ask Mark Rodrigo if it was him.'

'What are you talking about, Harry?' said Inspector Reid. 'Weren't you paying attention? He's dead.'

'We have the number of his mobile. We could record his voice mail greeting. He's not going to answer his phone and I doubt they've cancelled it yet.'

'You don't really think he's our man do you, Harry? He might have given her a ride but why would he kill his wife's best friend? What's the motive?'

'Well, let's say we could eliminate him by testing the recording of his voice mail message,' said Harry.

'Have we got the equipment to do this?' asked Inspector West.

'We have a recorder. I'll have to get the lab boys to run the test.'

They watched while Harry activated the recorder connected to his telephone and then rang the number.

The room erupted in laughter when the voice of a young woman said, 'I'm sorry but Mr Rodrigo can't take your call right now. If you'd like to leave a short message with your number, he'll get back to you when I'm gone.'

'Nice try, Harry.'

'Are there any messages on Mrs Ford's phone?' asked Inspector Reid.

'There's a stack from her husband and a couple from her sister. I've already had Mr Ford's voice checked against the others. It's not him' said Harry.

'I didn't think the husband was a suspect, Harry' said Inspector West.

'Just eliminating him in advance, in case you had to change your mind, Boss.'

'Think you've been watching too many of those police shows on TV, Harry. You know, the ones where it's always the jealous husband,' said Nina.

'Wonder if we're thinking about the right jealous husband. What if Rodrigo's the jealous husband? Maybe it was the wives having the affair. Paul Ford told me they spent a lot of time together, they even went on weekend trips out of town. Maybe we need to do some snooping around the women,' said Inspector West.

'Can't see Rodrigo being a jealous husband, not after what his brother told me. Claimed he was a playboy and that he and his wife lived separate lives. I don't think the jealous husband will be a player in your case, but I wonder if he could be in mine. Someone sure wanted him dead and it sounds like he's screwed his way around town.' Bob looked around the group gathered in Inspector West's office. 'By the way, who's informing Mrs Rodrigo?'

'Uniform,' said Nina.

'I'll need to speak to her.'

'Take Nina with you when you go. She can introduce you and stop you being distracted by her beauty,' said Inspector West.

'She get the better of you, Carl? You always had a weak spot for pretty girls. I'd watch him if I were you, Sergeant.'

'Thank you for the compliment, Inspector,' said Nina, fluttering her eyes.

Inspector Reid looked at Inspector West and decided he'd better leave it at that. Wayne raised an eyebrow in Harry's direction. Harry let the ball go through to the keeper.

'There's something else you might want to consider, Inspector,' said Harry.

'What would that be?'

'Maybe Rodrigo was collateral damage. What if Kingston was the target?'

'Run a background check on him and see what comes up. The name rings a bell from somewhere.'

Harry went out to his desk and queried the police database. When the results came back he scribbled some notes on his pad and went back into the office. 'We have a Francis Robert Kingston, male, aged forty, served time for computer hacking. Been out for five years.'

'I remember him now,' said Inspector West. 'He was the guy that sucked credit card details out of B&A's system and got caught selling them in one of those forums on the dark side of the Internet.'

'Maybe he's our extortionist,' said Nina.

'Better see if we can get a recording of his voice, Harry. See if you can get a mobile number for him and try the same trick you used on Rodrigo's phone, for starters,' said Inspector West.

'Wayne, think we need to go search a couple of apartments. Let's find out where Kingston was living. It's likely he lived in the same building where Rodrigo had his playboy pad. Give Rodrigo Properties a call and tell them we're on our way,' said Inspector Reid.

CHAPTER 12

THE FUNERAL CARS arrived at ten o'clock. Paul and the boys, Mick and Maria, and George and Anne climbed into the lead limousine. Paul noted that it was a silver stretched Ford. He heard Inspector West's words floating around inside his head, and wondered what the inspector had found out.

The interstate contingent filled the other two cars. At ten minutes after the hour, they set off on the ten minute journey to the parish church. The hearse, another silver Ford, was parked in the forecourt waiting for them. Josie wasn't going to be late for her last appointment.

There was a crowd of people standing around the entrance doing what people do when they catch up at funerals - talking, hugging, laughing. The crowd fell silent and moved aside as the family exited the cars and gathered around the hearse. The six pall bearers, Paul, Mick, Matthew, Luke, Rosa and Andrew, slipped on the white gloves handed to them by the funeral director and formed up on either side of the carriage holding the rosewood casket. Father Mulligan appeared at the top of the steps with two altar servers holding candles. At least there were only a few steps to climb. The pallbearers took the weight of the casket and carried it up the steps, while the funeral attendants moved the carriage to the top of the steps. They replaced the casket on the carriage and got ready for the journey down the aisle.

'Please stand as the family enters the church.'

The family started walking behind Father Mulligan, and the altar servers with their candles, with the pallbearers pushing the casket along on its carriage. The slideshow of photographs from Josie's life was playing on the overhead screen at the front of the church. Paul noticed a block of St Catherine's uniforms in the congregation, and another of St Jude's, as he walked slowly down the aisle behind the casket. Then he was standing in the front pew looking at Josie's flower draped casket.

'Please be seated.'

Father Mulligan stood behind the lectern and led them through five decades of the rosary.

'Paul will now give a short eulogy.'

Paul walked to the lectern and took out his notes. He unfolded them, smoothed out the pages and looked out across the congregation. The church was packed. He could see people standing in the porch. He took a deep breath, and then another one, before he was ready to begin.

'Josie was born, Josephine Maria Kelly, just short of forty four years ago, not far from here. She lived her entire life in this neighbourhood. She was baptised, confirmed, and married in this church. Now, we are saying farewell to her, long before I ever imagined we would be.' He paused. He wasn't sure he was going to get through this despite all the rehearsing.

'In fact, I never thought I'd be around to deliver her eulogy going on the lifespans in her family tree.' He paused again.

'The circumstances of her death may still be a mystery, but the circumstances of her life are known to most of us gathered here. She grew up in a loving and supportive family. I'm sure many of you have heard, as I have on many occasions, Mick Kelly boasting of his beautiful daughters. Well, I can tell you Mick and

Maria, she was always boasting of her beautiful parents.' He stopped. This was getting difficult. He told himself to calm down. All he had to do was read the words. Stop thinking about them. He looked over at Josie's family.

'From all the stories I heard over the last twenty five years, I'd say Josie had a wonderful childhood. She was always close to her parents. In fact, so close I sometimes wondered how many Kellys I had married. There was certainly more than one of them in our house on many occasions. Josie enjoyed a close relationship with her mother, and I know she will be missed not only by Mick and Maria, but by Rosa and Carlo and Sophie and Michelle.'

Okay, he had gotten through that part. He found where he was up to on the page.

'When we were married, Josie became part of the Ford clan, and I'd like to acknowledge my brothers and their families who have all travelled long distances to be here today.' For some reason that let his emotions well up towards the surface. Another pause for breathing to get them under control. 'My family welcomed Josie with open arms and she formed a close bond with my mother, Anne, especially during those early years when she was discovering what being the mother of boys was all about. She also became my father's favourite conversation partner at family functions. She will be missed.'

That produced some wry smiles on the faces of his brothers and sisters-in-law. They were all happily distant and knew the baton was passing back to Paul.

'Apart from the years she spent as a full-time mother, when the boys were little, Josie taught at St Catherine's, where she herself had gone to school. I'd like to acknowledge the teachers and girls from St Catherine's here today. She loved her job and she loved her students. In fact, Josie was a teacher not only to the girls at St Catherine's but also to our sons and to me. I think I can say that without her guiding hand or her gentle, sometimes insistent, direction, there's a lot of stuff about life, the universe and all that, I would never have known. Josie, I thank you for that.

As many of you will recall, in her student days, both at school and uni, Josie performed in several stage productions. Yes, she loved to act and took great pleasure in trying out different personas on me without warning, especially in those days when she was a full-time mum. Some nights I'd come home from work to a loving wife, all affection and charm, children bathed and ready for bed. She was the picture of the perfect mother, seductive wife. Other nights, I'd come home to find a distraught woman chasing a boy or two around a house in chaos. I'd go into my saviour role and step in to restore order. She'd watch me for ten minutes or so before she'd start laughing or burst into tears, depending on which role she wanted to see my reaction to. And mind you, she had coached the boys to either cooperate with me or frustrate my efforts to restore calm. I have to admit that there were times when she had me fooled. At least life with Josie was never dull.'

There was a ripple of laughter across the church. He wasn't the only one who had fallen victim to one of her acting games.

'In recent years, she developed an interest in what I whimsically referred to as secret women's business, but in reality, it was an interest in empowerment and the development of the feminine. She was interested in finding out about the feminine, and furthering the role of women, especially through education. One reason why she was so committed to teaching girls in what she saw as a man's world, where girls don't always get a fair go.

She had many friends, as we can see.' He waved his hand across in front of him to encompass the congregation. 'But there was a special group of friends, the gang. Her favourite outing was the monthly coffee shop meeting with the gang. I got to stay home and bond with the boys, as she put it, while she and the gang did whatever it was that a group of women who had known each other forever did. I know she always came home excited from those outings, and that was secret women's business.'

That one got a laugh.

'I'd just like to say thank you to the gang. You are those special people that provided that non-judgmental and emotional support that allowed her to blossom as a woman amongst women. I know she loved you all. She might not have told me what you did or discussed together, but whatever it was, she always appreciated your time together. So, thank you.'

He paused and looked at the casket. Not much more and he could sit down.

'Friends, let's not fall into the trap of believing Josie's in that box.' He stopped and turned towards the casket, again. Then he turned back to face the congregation. 'What's in there is not Josie. It's a form, or an image if you like, that we recognised as Josie, just as those photos you see up there are images of Josie, but they are not Josie. I'm not sure where the spirit we knew as Josie is right now. I know it isn't in that box.'

A few people shifted in their seats.

'Today, we are burying a body. Today, we are celebrating the life Josie lived through that body. Today, we are remembering the person we all knew as Josie.' He paused again. Not much more, take a deep breath.

'We will all miss her in our own unique ways depending on the sort of relationship we had with her.

For me, a large black hole has opened up, a void that was the space Josie occupied in my life. I didn't realise just how much of my life she filled.' His voice faltered. He stopped to regain his composure. It took what seemed like ages to him before he could continue.

'I know Matthew and Luke will miss her as much as I do. Maybe even more.' He stopped again as tears welled in his eyes. 'It never seems right to lose your mother at a young age and certainly not in these circumstances.' He took a deep breath and looked up at the congregation.

'I thank you all for coming to show your love and support.'

He walked back to his seat, sat down and put his head between his hands. He couldn't stop the tears. He felt Matthew's arm on his shoulder and heard the sniffling and nose blowing that betrayed the tears of those around him. He thought he had cried all the tears he had. Obviously, he had underestimated the volume available.

For Paul, the Requiem Mass was a blur. He saw his brothers get up and read the readings. He heard Father Mulligan deliver his homily but he would never be able to tell anyone what was said. He watched as the young ones recited the prayers of the faithful, and stood and knelt and sat on auto-pilot. Communion and the final blessing happened, and then Matthew was reminding him to put on his gloves so they could take the casket out of the church. As they were standing alongside the casket, he heard the funeral director announce that the family would be receiving condolences at the back of the church as people filed out.

Slowly, the family made its way back down the aisle behind the casket and pall bearers. Then the casket was back in the hearse and Paul was standing next to Matthew, shaking hands and receiving condolences from what seemed like an endless line of people. He emerged from the fog when he recognised the members of the gang. They appeared as a group, all wearing a rose pink silk scarf that he knew matched the ones he would find in one of Josie's drawers at home. Her signature piece. They hugged him in turn, thanked him and kissed him on the cheek. And then there was Anna with her washed out face and tears.

She was accompanied by a young man in dark glasses that he did not recognise.

'I'm so sorry, Paul. Life just isn't fair.' She kissed him on the cheek and hugged him close. 'Take care. I'll be in touch,' she whispered in his ear. Then she was replaced by another face and the hugs and kissing continued, and he sank back into the void.

He came out of his daze again when he felt Andrew guiding him towards the waiting limousine.

'You look like shit. Here, have a swig of this.' He accepted the flask and swallowed a mouthful of Jameson's.

'Thanks.' He handed the flask back to Andrew. The bite of the whisky cleared the last of the fog. He climbed into the limousine and caught sight of Mick taking a silver flask back from Luke and slipping it into his inside coat pocket.

'Michael Kelly, don't you go getting my grandsons drunk with your whisky!' The unmistakable, sharp voice of his mother.

'A little swig won't hurt 'em! What about you, Paul. Want one?'

'It's okay Mick. Seems you're not the only one with a supply.'

His mother looked at him and then shook her head. 'You're all the same when it comes to anything painful.'

The look on George's face told him she'd caught him having a swig as well. He wondered how his father had managed to smuggle it out of the house, before realising that one of his brothers had probably slipped him a flask when she wasn't looking.

The limousine pulled out from the churchyard onto the road behind the hearse and started on the slow drive to the cemetery. The cars of fellow mourners pulled in behind and formed a convoy. It was only after they had started moving that Paul noticed Maggie sitting between Matthew and Maria. She smiled when she saw him looking in her direction.

'Mum had to go back to work. I hope you don't mind.'

'No problem. I hope these old men haven't been forcing whisky on you, too.'

'There was no forcing,' said his father, 'only polite offering, and she has more sense than these two,' he added, indicating the older women by waving his hand about.

Maggie blushed. 'I was only being polite. I didn't want to offend your father. Besides, I'd never tasted whisky before.'

'And your considered opinion of the drink of angels?' enquired Mick.

'Would that be fallen angels, Mr Kelly?'

Even Anne laughed at that one. She was starting to like this girl; she had a boldness that Anne found attractive.

'So, you'd like some more then,' said Mick.

Maggie put her hand out in his direction as if to take the flask he was offering her, before Maria intervened and redirected her hand onto Matthew's lap. 'Don't encourage them, Maggie. They'll be making fools of themselves soon enough without any help from you. Here. Look after Matti and leave him to me.'

'That was a big crowd of people,' said Luke to no-one in particular.

'Yes. I wonder how many will turn up at the cemetery,' Paul responded. 'I doubt the St Catherine's contingent will be there. They'd have to hire a couple of buses.'

'Guess we'll find out soon enough,' said George.

'There's a bus in the convoy, Dad, so there might be a crowd of St Catherine's girls after all,' said Matthew who had a view out the rear window of the limousine. 'Didn't Father Mulligan say something about a guard of honour at the graveside?'

'Oh yeah, I'd forgotten about that.'

'Just as well you typed out your speech, Dad.'

They arrived at the cemetery and sat in silence as the car made its way to the waiting grave. When the car came to a stop, they got out and stood around the hearse, while the other mourners arrived. The St Catherine's girls formed a guard of honour along the pathway, from the spot where the hearse had stopped, to the grave site some twenty metres away among the tombstones. This time there was no pushing the carriage along with the casket on top. The pallbearers took the full weight of the casket and carried it to the grave and lowered it gently onto the waiting casket lowering frame.

Father Mulligan said the final prayers and sprinkled holy water on the casket. They all joined in the Our Father. The funeral director handed a rose to each family member and invited them to say their final farewells. The St Catherine's girls formed up into a block immediately behind the mourners.

Paul walked up to the casket with Matthew and Luke. They dropped their roses, one by one, on to the casket and returned to their seats under the green canopy of the tent erected beside the grave. The rest of the family group silently followed their example. Then, the small crowd of friends, who had joined them for the burial, scattered handfuls of rose petals into the grave as the casket was lowered, and the St Catherine's girls sang the words of that song made famous by Bette Midler - The Rose.

It took Paul a while to regain his composure after that rendition of Josie's favourite song. When he looked up, the crowd had moved back to the roadway and the St Catherine's girls were trouping back to their bus. It seemed they were all dabbing their eyes with tissues as they walked along in silence. He felt Andrew's arm on his shoulders.

'Come on, mate. Time to go home. This part's over.'

Paul let himself be guided back to the limousine. He shook hands with people who were not coming back to the wake, and then they were on their way home. This time his mother had nothing to say when the whisky flasks were passed around. It was a very quiet ride home from the cemetery.

Paul wondered how people who didn't gather and celebrate coped with burying a loved one. The great thing about a wake was the opportunity to reminisce and swap memories. A wake was also a great excuse for catching up with friends and family. Reflecting on its origins, he realised a wake provided the children of the Irish diaspora with an excuse to share a feast, and drink too much.

Josie's wake was true to form. The house was full of people. The backyard was full of people. Paul's brothers took over the barbecue and manned the eskies. The words flowed freely along with the beer. The gang arrived with more food. Father Mulligan turned up with a bottle of whisky, and they had to call Grace, his housekeeper, when it was time for him to go home.

In the first few hours, every possible memory of Josie's life was aired by someone, some about real events and some imagined. Rosa told some stories no-one had heard before, but only when her mother was not within earshot. The slideshow of the pictures of Josie's life was played on the computer in the study, and the photo albums, which Josie had lovingly scrapbooked over the years, were passed around in the lounge. Slowly the conversations turned to other topics as the mood swung from melancholy towards moving on with life.

The cousins congregated in Matthew's room, listening to music and talking about school and basketball. The men talked work, politics, sport and religion in various parts of the house and standing around the barbecue, long after the cooking was done. The women talked about the men, the children and what they were doing at work.

The gathering had reduced itself down to family by the time Marie Wood turned up after work to pick up Maggie. It didn't take much of an effort from Maria to talk her into staying for a bite to eat, and then Maggie was introducing her mother, the policewoman, to Matthew's relatives. It seemed very few of them had actually met a policewoman socially, apart from Kathleen who had met quite a few professionally as well. It wasn't long before she was comfortably ensconced with the women and chatting as if she had known them for years.

The wake had kicked off shortly after one o'clock in the afternoon. By seven o'clock Paul's brothers were starting to say their goodbyes. There were planes to catch and others had long drives to face in the morning. Life had to be re-engaged.

By eight thirty, Anne had taken George home and Paul was sitting around the kitchen table with Mick and Maria, and Marie Wood. The boys were watching TV with Maggie in the lounge.

'So, what are your plans for tomorrow, Paul?' Marie asked. 'Are the boys going back to school?'

'They want to, so I guess they will.'

'I think that's probably best,' said Maria. 'You don't want them sitting around here feeling sorry for themselves. They've been home for a week as it is.'

'What about you, Paul? When are you planning on going back to work?' asked Mick.

'I'm looking at going back on Monday. I probably would have gone back sooner but Mark Rodrigo's funeral is on Friday morning. I think I should go.'

'Do you think that's wise?' asked Marie. 'It might be more of a challenge than you think. I know I found it hard going to funerals after Steve was killed.'

'You're probably right but Anna was Josie's best friend. I have to go.' He certainly wasn't feeling comfortable about going but

Anna had turned up for him. 'She came for me. I have to go for her. I wouldn't feel right if I didn't.'

'I can understand that. Just remember to be gentle with yourself.' Marie looked at her watch. 'We'd better get going. I have an early start in morning.'

'Thanks for coming,' said Paul.

'No problem. I'm glad I got to meet your family. At least now I'll know who Maggie is taking about when she's talking about them.'

Marie shook hands with Paul and Mick but didn't escape a kiss on the cheek from Maria.

'I'll keep an eye on him for you,' she said softly to Maria. 'I already have a spy in his household.'

Maria squeezed her hand. 'Thank you.'

'Come on Maggie, time to go.'

After Marie and Maggie left, Maria gave the kitchen a quick once over while Paul, Mick and the boys gathered up all the empties to put out with the recycling.

By nine thirty Paul and the boys were sitting in the kitchen on their own.

'Still planning on going to school in the morning?'

'I want to,' said Matthew. I can't afford to get any further behind.'

'What about you, Luke?'

'May as well.'

'Alright then, you'd better get yourselves off to bed.'

'Goodnight, Dad.' Matthew gave him a hug and went off to get ready for bed.

'Will you come and get me if I want to come home early?'

'If it all gets too hard, go and talk to Mrs Young. She'll call me if you want to come home and I'll come straight away.' He gave Luke a long hug. 'You'll be right.'

'I hope you're right, Dad.'

Luke went off to bed.

Paul walked out to the study and sat in front of the computer watching the scenes they had chosen from Josie's life scroll by. After watching the slideshow three times, he opened the photo library and lost himself in the thousands of digital images Josie had loaded onto the computer from her camera. He might be the artist when it came to pencils and brushes, but she had been the artist with the camera. She had left him a collection of shots from all of her weekend escapes, of every possible place you could photograph within walking distance of the house, and of all the family events they had held since he'd bought her a digital camera. He also had the vast collection of scrap-booked photographs of their early years as a couple, and of the boys growing up, which Josie had taken with her 35mm camera before that. Fortunately, she'd let him take photographs of her, so he would always have something to remind him of all the good times, and all the fun times, they had shared over the years.

He looked up from the screen and noticed that it was eleven o'clock. He turned off the computer. It had been a big day. The time he had been putting off, the moment of reckoning, had arrived. The funeral had taken place. Life with Josie was over. He was really on his own now.

No more being together forever-after. From this point on it would be after, forever.

CHAPTER 13

PAUL LOOKED at the clock sitting on the window sill as he got out of the shower. 7:30. He hoped the boys were out of bed. When he left the bathroom, to return to his bedroom to dress for the day, he heard breakfast making noises coming from the kitchen. Someone was up. Five minutes later he was in the kitchen with Matthew making breakfast when Luke walked in to join them.

Apart from cursory greetings, very few words were spoken.

Shortly after eight the boys were ready to go. The lunches Maria had made for them the previous night were packed in their bags, with their books and all the other stuff they carted to and from school. The boys decided to return to their normal routine and catch the bus home.

'If it all gets too much, just give me a call and I'll come and pick you up,' Paul said as the boys were getting out of the car.

'We'll be right, Dad,' said Luke. 'Look Matti, there's Maggie waiting for us. Bye, Dad.'

'Remember to get the meat out for tea, Dad. See you tonight,' said Matthew.

'Thanks. Have a good day.'

Paul watched as the boys carried their bags over to where Maggie was waiting for them. She gave them each a hug and a kiss on the cheek, despite the school rules forbidding such displays of affection between students. He smiled. You couldn't help but love that girl.

He drove home.

When he finally went inside, he took the steaks out of the freezer and put them on a plate on the bench to thaw.

As he was sitting down to a coffee, with the intention of planning his day, it dawned on him that this was the first time he had been alone in the house since Josie had been killed. He looked at the coffee cup. It was the last remaining cup from a set someone had given them as a wedding present. He wondered why it was still there and Josie wasn't. What was he going to do? The house was full of stuff connected to Josie. Everything he touched. Everything he saw. Even the clothes he was wearing. She had chosen them.

He picked up his coffee and walked out to the back veranda, where he sat in a garden chair and looked out across the courtyard to the garden.

The ringing of the mobile phone in his pocket startled him back to awareness. He missed the call but noticed that it was now ten thirty and his coffee was cold. He looked at the call log. He didn't recognise the number. He told himself they would call back if it was important.

He went inside and turned on the computer. When it came to life, he logged on and opened the website of Josie's bank to find out what he had to do to notify them and take control of her accounts. He filled in the required form online and then printed it, as he had to sign it before taking into their local branch. He would take it in once he had arranged the certified copy of Josie's death certificate the bank wanted.

Next, he opened the insurance company's website. They wanted to be notified by telephone and required a certified copy of her death certificate. He found the policy document in the filing cabinet and made the call. The woman that answered his call was very understanding. She'd obviously dealt with a lot of people in his position. She advised him that the funds would be released within five business days of them receiving the required paper work. She told him which form to download. She actually talked him through their website to make sure he found the correct form, and helped him find a list of persons who could certify copies of documents.

Then he rang Rosa to find out what he had to do to finalise Josie's employment at St Catherine's, and to notify their superannuation fund manager. She told him she had put all the required forms in the mail that morning. He would get them tomorrow. They told each other they were okay and promised to catch up soon.

After speaking with Rosa, he found the last update for the insurance policies and last year's statement from her superannuation fund, and did some maths. The life insurance policy would pay out $265,000. Her superannuation account had a life insurance component worth $85,000 and an accumulated balance of $210,256, as of the statement date. A quick calculation told him he'd receive around $560,000, depending on how well Josie's superannuation fund had performed since the last statement. He wouldn't have to worry about being able to pay the school fees any more.

As he would need several certified copies of the death certificate, he took it out of the filing cabinet and made five copies, using the all-in-one printer connected to the computer. He located his copy of her will and made three copies of that as well. There were some benefits to having an organised filing system. Then he set off for the Council Chambers, where a Justice of the Peace was available to certify copies of documents.

By the time he returned home for lunch, the joint bank account had been transferred into his name, Josie's savings account had been closed and the funds transferred into the joint account. He made himself a sandwich and sat down to complete the life insurance form. When he had it filled in, he walked down to the Post Office and sent it and one of the certified copies of the death certificate on their way. No point in waiting in quasi poverty any longer than required, now that there would only be his income.

When he reached home base again, he checked the frozen steaks thawing on the bench and decided it was time they went into the fridge to finish defrosting. Satisfied there would be something to eat, he went out to the study and stripped the spare bed Mark had used and put a load of washing on. Then he got the vacuum cleaner out and vacuumed the floors to remove the last traces of the wake.

Shortly after four thirty the boys arrived home from school, and discovered Paul cleaning the bathroom.

'Are you okay, Dad?' asked Luke. 'Didn't you clean in here on Saturday?'

'Just giving it a quick once over, after everyone being here yesterday.'

The boys looked at each other. Matthew shrugged his shoulders and went into his room to dump his bag, before heading down to the kitchen for a snack. Luke followed his example.

'What about basketball tomorrow night, Dad? Can I tell the coach we'll be there?' asked Luke when Paul joined them in the kitchen.

'I'm not coming,' said Matthew. 'I've got band practice until five thirty.'

'How will you get home if I take Luke to basketball?'

'Maggie said her mum would bring me home.'

'What time's the game?'

'I'll have a look.' Luke walked over and read the match schedule on the back of the kitchen door. 'We're playing at home, at five.'

'We'll have to leave as soon as you get home from school.'

'Maybe you'd better come and pick me up.'

'These early games are going to be a challenge when I go back to work.'

'I can always go with John. His mum always picks him up from school.'

'Guess we'd better speak to her tomorrow night then,' said Paul pouring his fifth coffee for the day.

'So, what did you do today, Dad, apart from clean the bathroom?' Matthew asked as he sat down.

'Well, let's see. I looked up some information on the net, got some copies of your mother's death certificate and will certified by a JP at the Council Chambers, went to the bank so we'd be able to buy food. I posted the form to the insurance company and talked to your Zia Rosa about what I had to do for St Catherine's. She said to say hello.'

'Who did the washing?' asked Luke, when he saw the sheets on the clothes line through the family room window.

'I washed the sheets and things your uncle used.'

'Sounds like you had a busy day,' said Matthew.

'Suppose so. How was school?'

'It was a bit strange this morning,' said Luke. 'Lots of kids, especially the boys, didn't know what to do or say. The girls in my class all wanted to know how I was feeling. They organised morning prayers for me.'

'How'd you go with that?'

'Okay.'

'What about you, Matti? How was your day?'

'My class did morning prayers too, and then it was just school.'

'He's got Maggie to talk to,' said Luke. 'Wish I had someone like that.'

Paul put his hand on Luke's shoulder. 'Me too.'

The telephone rang. Luke picked up the handset and disappeared into the lounge, from where Paul could hear one side of a conversation about Luke's day at school. When he heard Luke asking questions, he realised he was talking to his cousin, Michelle. Rosa's girls had gone back to school as well.

Matthew finished his snack and got up from the table.

'I've got to do some drum practice,' he said as he left the kitchen, and headed up the corridor to his room. Paul heard the door close and then the muffled sound of the striking of padded drums pervaded the house.

Luke came back into the kitchen to replace the handset. 'That was Michelle.'

'How was she?'

'She said school just isn't the same without Mum.'

The sound from the other end of the house took on an intensity that suggested Matthew was letting his emotions come out through his drumming.

'I'm going out to shoot some baskets. I can't concentrate on my homework when he plays like that.'

Luke went out into the backyard to the basketball ring standing in the courtyard. After a couple of minutes, Paul heard the sound of the basketball being bounced and hitting the backboard. The normal sounds of life.

At six o'clock he took out the steaks and frozen vegetables, and cut up a couple of potatoes. The steaks went into the frypan and the vegetables into the microwave. By twenty passed six they were eating their evening meal.

'What are you doing tomorrow, Dad?' asked Luke.

'Thought I might pack up some of your mother's stuff and take it down to St Vinnies. No point in putting it off.'

'Can I have one of her pink scarves?' asked Luke.

'Is there anything else you want to keep? I don't have to do it tomorrow if you want to think about it.'

'I just want one of her pink scarves, you know the ones she was always wearing.'

Paul nodded. 'What about you Matti? Anything you want as a keepsake?'

'I like Luke's idea. I'll have a pink scarf too. I know she had stacks of them.'

'Maybe I'll keep all the pink scarves, then. We can all have one.'

'What about Zia Rosa? She and Mum are the same size.'

'She told me she didn't want anything. Something about too many memories.'

The telephone rang. Luke answered it.

'It's Uncle Andrew for you, Dad. I'm going to do my homework.'

Andrew wanted to know how they were holding up.

Paul told him what he had done about organising the life insurance and fixing the bank accounts.

Andrew said he'd keep in touch and that Kathleen sent her love.

Paul had only just put the phone down when his mother called to see how the first day back at school had gone. She finished off her call by saying that George wasn't feeling too well. Too much to drink at the wake was her assessment. Paul said he'd come over and see them tomorrow. They agreed on lunch.

Paul decided to call Maria to see how she and Mick were coping. She was the flattest he had heard her since Josie's death. She confessed to having spent several hours sitting in the parish church, trying to understand why God had allowed Josie to be killed. It didn't make any sense to her. Paul told her it didn't make any sense to him either.

After that call Paul went out and sat in his meditation chair in the study, and was still there when Luke came out at nine thirty to say he was going to bed.

'You sure you're okay, Dad?' asked Luke.

Paul rubbed his eyes. He had no idea where he had been, and the concerned look on Luke's face suggested he wasn't back yet. 'I was just meditating. I'll be awake in a minute.' He stood up and stretched. 'What did you say you wanted?'

'I'm going to bed. I came out to say goodnight.' Luke gave him a quick hug and then retreated to his room.

The computer was still on, so Paul decided to check his email. There was a newsletter, from the art site he subscribed to, advertising a portrait drawing course. He clicked on the link, watched the video and read the course description. He hadn't touched his pencils or any of his watercolours for weeks. He purchased the course and spent the next forty minutes down-loading mp4 files so that he could complete the course at his own pace. He liked the self-paced e-learning environment offered by the Internet. As he was shutting down the computer, Matthew came in to say goodnight.

'Can we leave at eight in the morning? I need to catch up with the Math's teacher before school starts.'

'Okay, I'll set my alarm for six thirty and get you out of bed by seven. Maybe you can set the alarm on your mobile as well.'

'Alright. See you in the morning, then.' Matthew gave him a hug and left the room.

Paul decided to go to bed as well. He hated getting into the bed by himself. He had never gotten used to it when Josie was away on her weekend trips with Anna, but at least she came home after two nights. She hadn't come home for more than a week now, and it wasn't getting any easier. He wondered whether he should sleep in the spare bed, but dismissed that as being the coward's way. Life had to go on. His life had to go on. If he stopped, he might not start again.

At three in the morning he came out of a vivid dream. He had been chasing Josie through a meadow that seemed to stretch into forever. Each time he almost had his hands on her she had skipped out of his reach. She had been laughing and blowing him kisses, but she had remained just out of reach. Then she had stopped running from him and turned, reached out, touched his face and kissed him. He'd heard her say, I love you, and then felt himself falling, and landing with a thud. He was surprised to find himself lying on his back in the bed. His rapid breathing and the beating of his heart told him another story.

He got up and went to the toilet, and although he went back to bed, he couldn't go back to sleep. This was his first recollection of having dreamt about Josie since she had been killed. He had spent several long nights feeling sorry for himself and missing her. This was the first time she had shown herself to him, and what she had shown him was the happy, fun loving, Josie of their early years. She was enjoying life where she was. Was that the message? Or was he just tormenting himself?

After tossing and turning for half an hour or so, he got out of bed. He switched off the alarm and went and had a shower. By four o'clock he was back out in the study, with a coffee, working on a pencil portrait of Josie. By seven o'clock, when he heard the faint sounds of Matthew's alarm, he had the first rough portrait drawn. He decided to head to the kitchen for breakfast.

'Morning, Matti.'

'Oh, hi, Dad. You need to buy some milk.'

'Is there enough for Luke?'

'There's half a bottle.'

Paul found the note pad and pencil he had left on the shelf in the pantry and added milk to the list he had started. Then he went up to Luke's room to make sure he was getting ready so that they could leave by eight. He was surprised to find Luke, dressed in his uniform, sitting at his desk working on his school work.

'I couldn't sleep.'

'How long have you been up?

'Not as long as you. I got up around six.'

'Have you had breakfast?'

'Yes.'

'We need to leave at eight. Matti has a meeting with his Math's teacher before school.'

'I know. I'm ready, all I have to do is put these books in my bag.'

'Okay, I'll call you when we're ready to go.'

Paul returned to the kitchen and made himself breakfast. He took his toast out onto the back veranda. It looked like it was going to be a nice day. He heard the telephone ring. Shortly after, Matthew appeared with the mobile handset.

'It's Grandma. She sounds upset.'

'Hello, Mum, what's up?'

'Your father's had a heart attack.'

Bloody hell. What else could go wrong? 'Where are you?'

'I'm at University Hospital. I had to call an ambulance.'

'Is Dad still with us?'

'The doctor thinks he'll live.'

From the tone of her comment, he wondered if she was hoping for a different outcome. His father had been difficult enough to live with since his retirement, so he couldn't blame her. 'What room is he in?'

'He's still in Casualty.'

'Okay. I'll take the boys to school and come to the hospital. I'll be there as quick as I can.'

'Thank you, Paul. Take your time. I don't want you having an accident on the way here.' She ended the call.

Once a mother always a mother, he thought as he went back inside the house. So much for his plans to use the morning to start cleaning out Josie's stuff.

'What's happening, Dad?' asked Matthew when Paul reached the kitchen.

'Your grandfather's had a heart attack.' He held up his hand. 'The doctors think he'll live but I need to go to the hospital. Get yourself ready so I can take you to school.' He went up to Luke's room. 'Luke, we need to get going. Grandpa's in the hospital. He's had a heart attack. I need to go and sit with Grandma until he's in the clear.'

Luke sat down on his bed and started crying. 'What's happening to us? First Mum, and now Grandpa. It's not fair.'

Paul sat down beside him on the bed. 'You going to be okay going to school or do you want to come with me to the hospital?'

Luke reached for a tissue from the box next to his bed and blew his nose. He shook his head. 'I need to go to school. I'm already behind.'

'You can visit Grandpa as soon as he's able to have visitors. Hopefully, that will be tonight. Okay?'

Luke got up and packed the books on his desk into his bag and went into the bathroom to wash his face. Paul collected his wallet and the car keys and took the boys to school.

Luke got Maggie all to himself, while Matthew kept his appointment with his Math's teacher.

It took Paul close to an hour to negotiate the traffic and get to University Hospital. By that time his father had been moved into Intensive Care. He located his mother in the Intensive Care waiting area. She looked like she had been up half the night.

'How long have you been here?'

'Since seven o'clock. I had to call the ambulance just after six.'

'Have you had anything to eat?'

'Yes. I've been down to the cafeteria while I was waiting for you. There's nothing I can do in there.' She pointed towards the Intensive Care unit. 'We have to wait until they move him into a ward before we can see him. The nurse said he had stabilised but the doctors want to keep an eye on him for the next hour or so.'

'Why don't we go for a walk? It's nice outside and I could do with a coffee.'

Anne spoke to a nurse at the Intensive Care reception desk and they went downstairs to the cafeteria. Paul purchased a take-away coffee and they went out and strolled around the courtyard garden next to the cafeteria.

'Silly bugger had been having pains in the chest all night.'

'What, and he didn't say anything?'

'He didn't say anything until he got up to go to the toilet this morning. Came back to bed clutching his chest. He could hardly breathe. I called the ambulance straight away. It was only then that he told me his chest had been tight all night.'

'Bloody hell, Mum, anybody would think he wanted to die!'

'He might wish he had from what the doctor told me.'

'So he's not out of the woods, then?'

'He could be damaged goods because he waited so long to say anything.'

Paul spotted the nurse from upstairs walking across the court-yard towards them.

The nurse walked up to Anne. 'I'm sorry, Mrs Ford, your

husband had a massive heart attack just after you left. We've lost him.' She wrapped her arm around Anne and waited.

'I suppose it's for the better.'

The nurse looked across at Paul.

'What happens now?' Paul asked.

'If you want to see him before we move him to the morgue, you'd better come up now. I'm sorry, but we need the bed.'

'You okay to go up, Mum?'

'I'll be alright.'

Anne let the nurse lead her back into the building. Paul followed behind as they made their way across to the elevators and up to the third floor. At least his father was nearly seventy six and had died from what they called natural causes. He wondered how the boys, especially Luke, who had a close relationship with his grandfather, would take it.

The nurse took them into a room just inside the entrance to the Intensive Care unit, where George's body lay on a gurney ready for its trip to the morgue. As they were standing looking at the body, the young doctor that had spoken to Anne earlier came in and offered his condolences. As he was leaving, he gave Paul the envelope containing George's death certificate.

While Anne sat with the body, Paul went out to reception to see about the paperwork and to find out what to tell the undertakers, who would need to collect the body. George had told him several years ago that he had taken care of all the funeral arrangements, even down to the readings he wanted used during the funeral service. All Paul would have to do, once Anne had provided him with the details from George's pre-arranged, pre-paid funeral plan, was make a telephone call.

With the paperwork finalised, he went back into the room to wait for Anne. She was ready to go as soon as he arrived.

'No point in sitting here all day.'

'Okay. You right to drive home or do you want me to take you?'

'You'll have to drive me home. I came up in the ambulance.'

They took the lift back down to the lobby and walked over to the car park, where Paul had left his car. After paying the toll, they started towards home.

'Whoever thought we'd be having two funerals within a week of each other,' said Anne.

'Life is full of surprises.'

'I couldn't call Josie's death a surprise. More of a shock than a surprise, if you ask me. At least your father was getting on in years.'

'I wasn't expecting it. It's not like he's been sick.'

'I think Josie's death hit him pretty hard. He might not have said much about it but he spent a lot of time brooding over it.'

'I have to admit, that day we found out Josie had been killed, that was the first time I had ever seen Dad cry.'

'Your father loved Josie. He always said that out of all the daughters-in-laws, she was the only one that made him feel welcome.'

The feeling of tears forming persuaded Paul that it might be best if he didn't try to respond to that one. He took a couple of deep breaths and wondered why his mother seemed so together. Maybe she was still in shock; like he had been the morning they had found Josie.

'I still wasn't expecting it.'

'This must be hard for you coming right after Josie's death.'

'This is different. Like you said, Dad was getting on in years. You sort of know in the back of your head your parents are going to die. In a way, you're kind of ready for it. I still haven't got my head around Josie getting killed. Maybe I never will.'

They rode in silence for a while.

'How do you think the boys will take this?' Anne asked.

'I'm worried about Luke. He was pretty close to Dad. He was upset when I told them Dad was in hospital.'

'When are you going to tell them?'

'Think I'll wait until they get home from school.'

'We'd better ring your brothers when we get home. I hope Mark is still in the country. Did he say anything to you?'

'No, but he might have said something to John.'

Once they arrived at his parent's house, Paul rang each of his brothers to break the news. Anne located the details of the pre-paid funeral plan in George's alphabetically organised filing cabinet. Turned out he had contracted Flinders Funerals. Paul called Ron Flint to set things in motion while his mother made lunch, and rang Father Mulligan before sitting down to eat.

***

After lunch he rang Mick and Maria, and then he didn't know what to do, so he sat and read through the funeral service his father had planned, while his mother called her circle of friends. Around one thirty Father Mulligan arrived. Paul let him in through the front door.

'Pretty tough couple of weeks, Paul. How are you feeling?'

'I don't think this one has hit me yet.'

Father Mulligan placed a hand on his shoulder. 'Have you told the boys yet?'

'No, decided to leave that until they get home from school.'

'I'll drop around later.'

'Thanks, Frank.'

'Where's your mother?'

'She'll be out in a minute. Apparently, a tracksuit is okay for an emergency visit to the hospital, but it's not presentable for visitors. Come in to the kitchen.'

They made their way to the kitchen and sat down.'

'Just like your father to suffer through the night, not wanting to disturb anyone.'

'Yeah, well that turned out to be his undoing.'

Footsteps sounded in the corridor as Anne made her way in to join them.

'Hello, Father. Thought it might be you.'

'Hello, Anne.' Father Mulligan stood and embraced her. 'My condolences. This must be a bit of a shock.'

'I wasn't expecting it but he didn't help himself either. I can't believe he didn't wake me up earlier. But it's done now. He's dead.'

'Well, let's take a moment to give thanks for his life and ask God to support us as we come to terms with his passing.'

They joined hands and stood in silent prayer.

'Father, we give you thanks for the life of George Ford, our husband and father, and ask that you receive his soul into the communion of saints and send your love upon us who mourn his passing. We ask this through Jesus, your son. Amen.'

'Thank you, Father. Can I make you a cup of tea?'

'Thanks, Anne.'

'What about you, Paul?'

'I'll have one, thanks.'

Anne made the tea and cut up some of the fruit cake she had made the day before. Father Mulligan and Paul sat on the chairs around the kitchen table.

'Dad's got the whole funeral service planned out. The readings, the hymns, the prayers. I'll get you a copy.' Paul got up and went into the lounge where he had left the folder containing his father's funeral details. When he returned, he handed the folder to Father Mulligan.

Father Mulligan flicked through the pages. 'Looks like he's thought of everything. He's even got a list of pallbearers.'

'George said that was the easiest bit to work out. He simply wrote down the boy's names,' said Anne as she poured Father Mulligan's tea.

'No eulogy?'

'George didn't believe in eulogies. He wants a rosary the night before and then a Requiem Mass. No picture show. You should have heard him carrying on about the picture show you did for Josie. I told him to pull his head in.'

'It might be his funeral but he isn't here to argue, so we could change this if you want to,' said Paul.

'See what I have to put up with, Father? And this one's supposed to be the good son.'

'Perhaps we should agree on the details before the others arrive.'

'Good idea, Father. I promised George we'd stick to this. So this it is.'

Paul held up his hands in mock surrender. 'I'm not going to argue. I'd be the last person to change Dad's plans. He'd probably come back to haunt me, in any case.'

'Stop that.' His mother poked him in the side.

'How many copies do you have of this?'

'He made several copies and I'm sure it will be on his computer somewhere,' said Anne.

'I'll take a copy but if you can find the electronic version, I'd appreciate that. Makes it a lot easier to get it printed.'

'I'll see if I can find it for you before I go home and email it to you.'

When they finished the tea and cake, Father Mulligan left to make another visit. Seemed he was always visiting someone. Using the details his father had written onto a card stuck to his desk, Paul logged onto his father's computer and searched through the files. Fortunately, his father had applied the same naming system that he used in his filing cabinet, so it didn't take long to find the file he was looking for. He searched through the desk drawer and located the USB stick he had given his father on his last birthday. It was still in the packaging. He copied the file onto the USB stick and slipped the stick into his pocket.

As he was packing up Mick and Maria arrived to sit with Anne. After a quick round of hugs and kisses, Paul decided he'd better head home so he'd be there when the boys arrived.

'I'll bring the boys over after tea. They'll want to see you.'

'Why don't you bring them over for tea? That will give me something else to think about.'

'Okay.' He gave her a kiss on the cheek and headed for the car to go home and break the news to the boys.

On the way home, he dropped into the shops to buy milk, thanks to the yellow sticky note Matthew had left on the dashboard. When he arrived home, he went out to the study and logged onto the computer. After reading the emails in his inbox, he connected the USB stick he had taken from his father's desk and emailed the file containing his father's funeral service to Father Mulligan. He knew his father had died but he felt somewhat removed from the reality of it.

As he sat contemplating his different reactions to Josie's death and to that of his father, he heard the boys entering the house through the front door, along with the unmistakable sound of Maggie giggling. Before he could get himself out of the chair Luke was standing in the doorway to the study.

'How's Grandpa?'

'I'm sorry, mate. Grandpa had a massive heart attack after I got to the hospital. He didn't survive.'

Luke's shoulders slumped. He came into the study and sat on the bed. 'Did you get to see him before he died?'

'No, he was still in Intensive Care.'

'That must have been hard.'

'Yes, but there wasn't anything I could do about it.'

'How's Grandma?'

'I think she's okay. She didn't react anything like I thought she would. She seemed more upset when your mother died.'

'It's a bit different, Dad. Grandpa was an old man. You know old people are going to die. Mum wasn't old.'

'So Grandpa's dead too?'

Paul looked up to see Matthew standing in the doorway, with Maggie peering around him.

'Afraid so.'

'What happened?'

'He had pains in his chest last night but didn't say anything to Grandma until this morning. When he told her about it, she called the ambulance. He'd had a heart attack during the night. He had another one, a big one, just after I got to the hospital, that killed him.'

'Oh.'

Maggie pushed her way passed Matthew. She gave Paul a kiss on the cheek. 'I'm really sorry, Mr Ford. Your dad seemed like a nice man.' She sat down next to Luke on the bed and patted the quilt to indicate to Matthew to come and sit next to her. Matthew complied.

'What do we do now?' asked Matthew.

'If you feel up to it, you could give Grandma a call. We're going over there for tea, so if you want to do any homework, you'd better get organised.'

'Does Nonna know?'

'She was at Grandma's when I left.'

'Will you have to organise another funeral?' asked Luke.

'Grandpa's already done that. Guess which funeral home he chose?' Paul waited a couple of seconds, and then added, 'Flinders Funerals.'

'What, the same one we used for Mum?'

'Yes, and he made his arrangement years ago. Bought one of those pre-paid funeral plans. He even had the funeral service all drawn up. I've just emailed a copy to Father Mulligan.'

'Where did you get a copy from?'

'Come on Luke, anybody could break into Grandpa's computer. He's got the password stuck on his desk,' said Matthew.

'So when's the funeral?'

'I don't know yet. Mr Flint is working that out with Father Mulligan. We should know sometime tomorrow.'

Matthew stood up and looked at Luke. 'Come on, let's go call Grandma. Then we can get something to eat before we start on our homework.' He shifted his attention to Maggie. 'We need to get that music assignment finished before your mum comes to pick you up.'

Luke and Maggie stood up and followed him out of the room.

'Do you want a coffee, Mr Ford?'

'Yes, thanks.'

Paul heard Matthew and Luke talking to their grandmother. Then he heard Maggie giving her condolences over the phone. Next he heard the sound of the coffee grinder. Then it was silent. He assumed they were eating. A few minutes later he heard the sound of coffee bubbling up in the stove top percolator. Then Maggie appeared with a coffee cup in one hand and a plate of biscuits in the other.

'There you go, Mr Ford.' She placed the cup and plate on the desk. 'We'll be up in Matti's room working on our arrangement, if you need anything.'

'Okay. Thanks.'

She left him to enjoy his afternoon tea.

Paul watched her walk away through the doorway until she disappeared into the kitchen. It was hard to believe she was only sixteen. She was the most poised sixteen year old he had come across. He thought Matthew was pretty lucky to have a friend like her, then he remembered what she had told him about how Matthew had helped her after her father's death. They were lucky to have found each other.

He sipped his coffee and ate one of the biscuits, and wondered if all of his brothers would come for this funeral.

CHAPTER 14

THE CAR PARK at St Lawrence's was full of expensive cars by the time Paul arrived. He signed the book and found a spot, next to a group of young men, just inside the entrance to the church. He looked around and took in the sombre atmosphere, of respectful silence, emanating from a congregation dressed in black. The men in their mourning suits. The women in black dresses of every available fashion. When the hearse arrived and the family came in with the casket, the congregation stood as one in silence. Anna and her two boys walked in behind the casket and followed it up the aisle to the front of the church. Behind them walked two elderly couples and what was, Paul assumed, the rest of the families.

There was no slide show or eulogy. The service was a traditional Requiem Mass straight from the Roman missal, with singing by a professional funeral singer. The volume of the responses indicated that either these people were very respectful or they were not regular church goers. At the end of the service, the funeral director announced that the family would take condolences in the front pews, and reminded the mourners that the burial would be a private family service.

It was almost an hour before Paul was offering condolences to people he didn't know. Then he was standing in front of Anna. She smiled briefly when she saw him and they embraced like two lovers lost in a forest.

'Not much fun, is it?' she said to him.

'No, but they tell me you can get through it.'

'Thanks for coming, Paul. It means a lot to me.'

He kissed her on the cheek and released her from his embrace. He couldn't say anything else. They held hands briefly and then it was time for her to go.

He watched as the family followed the casket back down the aisle and disappeared into the waiting daylight. He wasn't ready to leave just then, so he sat in a pew facing the altar and reminded himself to breathe. He had been okay right up until he had embraced Anna. She reminded him so much of Josie that he was having trouble keeping himself together. Someone sat down beside him.

'Are you okay, Mr Ford?'

He looked up. At first he didn't recognise her in her black dress, then he realised she was one of the officers working on Josie's case.'

'Nina Strong,' she said to help him place her face.

'What are you doing here?' he asked.

'Right now, I'm making sure you're all right. Before that, I was mingling to see who was here.'

'I see you dressed for the part.'

'No point in standing out in a crowd like this. So how are you feeling? You looked like you were losing it just then.'

'I'm feeling better now that you've distracted me.'

'I was surprised to see you here, so soon after your wife's funeral.'

'I came to support Anna; after all, she's a friend.'

'Will you be okay to drive home or would you like a lift?'

'I think I'll be right. Any news?'

'Not yet.'

They stood and made their way out of the church. The expensive cars had gone. A few older men were standing around smoking and talking. No-one took any notice of them as they walked to their separate cars and departed.

It was lunch time by the time he had driven from the affluent suburbs around St Lawrence's to the humbler dwellings in Whitbread Avenue. He changed out of his suit, ate a sandwich, and then went up to the bathroom and started on the clean out he had planned to start the day before. He managed to clear Josie's stuff out of two drawers in the vanity unit, before his mother rang to find out how he was and to let him know that his father's funeral would be on Tuesday morning.

'I hope that's the end of it,' he said after she had told him.

'What do you mean?'

'That will be three for me. Aren't things supposed to happen in threes?'

'And I thought you weren't superstitious.'

'Something I picked up from you. Anyway, I don't think I can take any more, so don't you going dying on me.'

'I'm not going anywhere. There's still plenty of life in this old girl.'

'Hope you're right.'

After the interruption of the call, he sorted the items he had taken out of the drawers into two piles - used and new. He dumped the used items into the bin and placed the new ones into a box to take to St Vinnies. By the time he had cleared all of Josie's items out of the bathroom vanity, he understood why it had always seemed like there was never any room in the vanity for his stuff. Next, he went into their bedroom and emptied out the drawer in which Josie had kept her perfumes, and the tubes of night creams she had used just before getting into bed. One of the perfume bottles was still in the packaging, so he put it into the box. The rest joined the rubbish in the bin.

The next job was more of a challenge. He emptied the drawers that held her underwear into a garbage bag and then sat on the edge of the bed trembling. He couldn't look at her knickers and bras. The feel of them, as he had picked them up and dropped them into the bag, had been enough to undo his resolve.

How could she do this to him? What had he done to be punished like this? He threw the garbage bag across the room and went out to the study and sat in his meditation chair. Not that he meditated. He was too angry to meditate but he knew he had to do something or he would explode with rage. He decided to focus on his breathing and was surprised at how fast it was. Gradually, as he paid attention to each inhalation and exhalation, his breathing slowed.

'I know I'm supposed to accept what is, but that doesn't make it any fairer,' he said to whoever was listening.

There was no answer.

'Why? Why did you allow this to happen?'

He sat there looking out the window waiting for God, for someone, to answer his questions.

His mobile rang. He pulled it from his pocket.

It was Luke. 'Dad, are you coming to get me for basketball?'

Paul looked at his watch. 'Sorry, mate. I lost track of time. I'm on my way.'

They got to the basketball stadium ten minutes before the start of the game. The coach was pleased to see Luke, his star player. When Luke walked onto the court, his team mates cheered. The team went into a huddle that broke up with a round of high fives. Luke was back. The parents of the other players, who had not seen Paul since Josie's death, expressed their condolences and then left him to his thoughts. That allowed him to get engrossed in the game. It was always exciting watching Luke play. He had a range of ball skills Paul could only dream about, and was one of those players gifted with the ability to read the play, so that he was always where the ball was about to be before the pass was made. It was no wonder he wore out his sneakers so quickly. He was all over the court. At the end of the game, when you expected him to be exhausted, he was pumped whether they had won or lost. The trip home was always a post-game analysis, Luke telling Paul how he had seen the game and where they could improve.

Listening to Luke's post-game analysis as he drove home, Paul realised that their life was returning to some sort of normality.

When they got home Mick and Maria were there. Maria was preparing a meal in the kitchen. Mick was watching the start of the Friday night football with Matthew.

'How was the Rodrigo funeral?' Mick asked when they walked in.

'Very sombre. A real black suit job. Just as well I decided to wear my dark suit, otherwise I would have been out of place. Didn't realise they had so many rich friends. Never seen so many mercs and beamers in the one place at the same time. For Italians, they sure seem to like German cars.'

'That family owns a fair slice of the commercial property in this city, so I guess they're not short of cash.'

'How was Anna?' asked Maria from the kitchen.

'She looked like death warmed up,' he said, as it dawned on him that she had been surprisingly soft and warm when she embraced him. A little voice told him to store that and think about it later. He sensed a hidden message that some part of him had understood, even if his conscious mind had missed the signal.

Maria joined them in the lounge. 'Did you go to the cemetery?'

'Fortunately, they had a private family burial, so I didn't have to face that part today. That will be hard enough next week when we bury Dad.'

'See anybody else there you knew, Dad?' asked Matthew.

'I thought some of the gang might be there, but I didn't spot any of them. The person I did see was someone I hadn't expected to see.'

'Who was that?' asked Maria.

'Nina Strong. I don't think you've met her. She's one of the officers investigating Josie's murder.'

'Sergeant Strong? That cute little number that came out to talk to me and Maria. Who could forget her?'

The look on Maria's face told him that the sergeant had made an impression on Mick that she didn't approve of.

'What was she doing there?'

'Said she was mingling. I guess they're also trying to work out who shot Mark.'

'Rumour has it there's more to that family business than meets the eye. Pat reckons he's heard stories of mob connections with that name.'

'Michael Kelly, stop spreading your brother's idle pub gossip!'

'We'll see how idle it is when the police find out who shot him. Certainly looks like a gangland shooting if you ask me.'

'Our daughter wasn't a gangster but her murder looks just as much like a gangland killing. So why does he have to be a gangster?'

Maria went back into the kitchen, from where the sound of saucepans being moved around betrayed her emotional state.

Matthew got up and went to join her, while they waited for Luke to finish his shower.

Mick and Maria went home shortly after they had finished eating. Paul and the boys watched television until it was time to go to bed.

Paul's brothers and their families arrived over the course of the weekend. They gathered for lunch at the local hotel on Monday to finalise arrangements for George's wake. As George had set aside a small fortune for them to spend on celebrating his life, there was no arguing over whether there would be a wake, only a discussion as to where they would hold it. In the end, they decided to hold the wake in the hotel and made arrangements with the manager. Anne handed around copies of the order of service for the funeral, so that they would all know their parts, and asked them to join her for the rosary service at seven thirty that night. They all promised they would, even the ones who had not said a decade of the rosary since leaving home.

It seemed attending rosaries had gone out of fashion. Family members made up the bulk of the small group that gathered to recite one last decade with George. One thing about the rosary is the simplicity of the prayer makes it easy to remember, even if you haven't said it for years. By the time they completed the decade, the gathering had taken on the feeling of one of their long ago family evenings. George lay in state in his plain wooden casket. If a plain wooden box had been good enough for his favourite Pope, George had decreed it would be good enough for him. They followed up the rosary with supper at home. After all, the Ford house was just down the street from the parish church, and Anne insisted they join her for a cuppa before they went their separate ways for the night.

Despite Anne's brave front, Paul suspected she did not want to be alone in the house. Just as well John and Helen had decided to stay with her again. That meant she had Nathan as a distraction from thinking about George.

Tuesday was the first day it had rained for weeks, and it rained a steady drizzle all day. Despite the proliferation of black umbrellas, they got wet carrying the casket into the church. Apart from the family, the congregation was made up of the remaining elderly members of the cohort of parishioners George had spent so much time with over the years, and Anne's circle of friends. George had attended the funerals of most of his workmates. The couple still alive were ensconced in aged care facilities and too frail to venture out. It was another sombre event. It had none of the energy of Josie's funeral. It felt like the end of a long, drawn out life.

It wasn't until he was listening to the readings his father had chosen that the floodgates holding back Paul's emotions gave way. He knew the tears were not for his father. The tears were for himself, the self left behind, alone. There is an apparent finality about death that cuts you off from the one who has crossed that threshold. Jesus might have pulled off the resurrection thing but it didn't look like anyone was going to do it again any time soon. By the time the Requiem Mass was over, he had retreated deep inside and re-closed the floodgates. He was sufficiently functional to follow the funeral director's instructions and help his brothers return the casket to the hearse for its final trip to the cemetery.

At the graveside, they were protected from the rain by the undertaker's tent, while Father Mulligan recited the final prayers from under the biggest black umbrella Paul had ever seen. He was too numb to feel anything when they lowered the casket. He was glad Andrew was there to catch their mother, when at the sight of the coffin going down into the grave, her calm demeanour broke and she collapsed into Andrew's arms. Paul stood with his arms tightly folded and waited for his emotions to subside.

They took it in turns dropping sodden flowers onto the casket, and then returned to the cars for the trip to the hotel. This time they were passing the whisky flask to warm up cold bodies and not drooping spirits.

At the hotel, Mick and Maria joined the Ford family in a private room off the main dining area to share a meal over drinks, and to reminisce over life with George. The volume of conversation among the boys increased as they relaxed with each round of drinks. By the time the main course had been eaten, the brothers were sharing stories about 'His Holiness' and laughing about the things they had done behind his back. One of the rules they had imposed on themselves, by way of circumventing George's many, was - 'What Dad doesn't know about he can't worry about, so keep it to yourself.' So, they had a few secrets to share. It transpired that John wasn't the only one who had been led astray by a wicked and willing woman. He was the only one unwise enough to bring one home to meet the family.

'I only did it to wind him up, and I still reckon it was worth every minute of it,' protested John.

'Yeah, like we believe you, mate!'

'What are you lot confessing to now?' asked Anne.

'Some things are best kept secret to protect the innocent,' said Andrew.

'I don't remember any of you lot being innocent,' said Anne.

The boys laughed.

Kathleen took the opportunity to turn the conversation to what Anne was planning to do now that George was buried.

'I need a holiday. Once I get myself sorted out, I want to go away somewhere, anywhere. George wouldn't take me anywhere.'

'Why don't you come and stay with us?' said Kathleen.

'Andrew's the executor of the estate, so he'll sort out your affairs for you. I can take some time off and show you around. We can go shopping and you can spoil yourself with some of that money George left behind.'

'Sounds good to me,' said Anne.

'When do you want to come?' said Andrew.

'Let me think about it. I might need some time to get used to the idea that I'm on my own.'

The coffee and cakes arrived.

'I'd like to suggest we do something about meeting in more joyful circumstances,' said Simon.

'What do you have in mind?' asked Andrew.

'Why don't we plan something for Christmas this year?' said Mark. 'It's been ages since we were all together for Christmas.'

'I have to work over the holiday season,' said Simon.

'Why don't we do Christmas at our place then?' said Judy.

'Sounds like a plan,' said Mark. 'You okay with that, Paul?'

Paul looked at Matthew and Luke. They looked at each other and then at Maria, who nodded.

'It's okay with us, Dad,' said Luke.

'We're in,' said Paul.

There was a general buzz of excitement as the news spread among the cousins.

'Doesn't a mother get a say?' said Anne.

'You can have a say, if you want,' said Simon, 'but it sounds like we've decided for this year.'

'Besides, Mum, this way you won't have to do any work, not like all those times we had to have Christmas at your house,' said Sandra.

'I might come, then,' said Anne.

'Please come, Grandma,' said Tamara. 'It won't be Christmas without you.'

'Come on, Grandma, say you'll come,' said Luke.

'How could I refuse such loving grandchildren?'

'That's settled then. Christmas at our place,' said Simon.

By four o'clock the party was over. People had planes to catch or long drives home. Mick and Maria drove Anne home, while the younger ones walked to Anne's place, where they had left their luggage and cars. Those going to the airport organised taxis. Those driving took their leave. By five o'clock Paul and his boys were the only ones left. They stayed to share a light meal with Anne.

'How did you cope on those first nights?' Anne asked while they were doing the dishes.

'I remember, when I was falling apart one night, seeing a picture of you in my mind's eye telling me to get my act together.'

'Did it help?'

'Made me laugh. I had this picture of you standing there with one hand on your hip and pointing the other at me.' He did an impersonation for her benefit.

She laughed. 'But are you coping?'

'It's still lonely every time I get into bed. Some nights I cry myself to sleep. Some nights I'm so tired, I just fall asleep. Some nights I wake up every couple of hours. It's not easy.'

'What I find hardest is the quiet. No snoring. I didn't think I'd miss that.'

'It's funny what you miss. I didn't think I'd miss the sight of bras hanging on door knobs either, but every time I don't see one it reminds me that she's gone.'

She hugged him. 'I'm so sorry, Paul. It must be a lot harder for you, she was still young. At least George had a good innings.'

'You'll miss him.'

'Yes, I suppose I will. But you know, in a lot of ways his dying has set me free. He was such a control freak at times. Do you realise this will be the first time in my entire life that I won't have to ask someone for money or for permission to buy something for myself.'

'Oh. I hadn't realised it was that bad.'

'I never said anything while he was alive. He couldn't tolerate criticism. I learnt a long time ago how to live with him.'

'Honestly, Mum, why didn't you leave him?'

'That might be the way of the young ones these days but it wasn't our way. I married him for better or for worse. I had some of the better and I had some of the worse. He had his short comings but he was also very loving. He was so dashing when I first met him. Swept me right off my feet, he did.'

'I think they call that lust at first sight these days.'

'Even if it was, there wasn't anything you could do about it back then, until you were married.'

'Well, I admire your sense of commitment.'

'Thank you. Now I think it's time you took the boys home. They must be tired. It's been a long day.'

'It's been a long couple of weeks.'

He roused the boys from in front of the television. 'Time to go. You guys have school tomorrow and I need to get my act together for going back to work.'

They said goodnight to Anne, climbed into the car and headed for home.

'Bit different to Mum's funeral,' said Matthew.

'Your mother was more sociable than Grandpa. She liked being with people and making friends.'

'Most of Grandpa's friends are dead. He told me that at Mum's funeral. He reckoned he was the last one left. He told me all his school mates were dead, his brother was dead, and his last surviving friends from work may as well be dead. He said the last time he had visited them they didn't remember who he was,' said

Luke. 'He was sad that Mum had died but I think he was sad that he was still alive.'

'Think I've had enough of funerals. Three in a week is too many.'

'Yeah, I'd like to get back to something like normal. All these people dying is messing up my school work. I'll be behind again after today,' said Matthew.

'Perhaps you can ask God to put his death program on hold for you, Matti.'

'Bit late for that, isn't it? Mum's already dead,' said Luke.

The rest of the ride home was silent.

It was seven thirty when they got home. The boys went to their rooms to do what homework they could before it was time to go to bed. Paul made himself a cup of coffee and sat in his chair in the study. He drank the coffee and took out his journal for the first time since Josie had been killed.

I can't explain why I don't feel anything about Dad. Maybe it will hit me later but there's no room for grieving his death in my heart. I'm full up with grief for Josie. It's been two weeks - the longest two weeks of my life. Will it ever get any easier? I'm struggling through every day. The boys seem to be doing better than me. Guess I should be grateful for that. Her death is still a mystery. The police have come up with nothing. How do you get closure if you don't know what happened? Maybe I'll have to give myself closure. What would Josie do? A ritual. Yes, she'd do a ritual. I wonder if there's something in that book of rituals she bought.

He drew a flag in the margin to mark that thought.

Tomorrow I'm going back to work. Hope I can handle it. Don't want to make a fool of myself. It might be good to have something else to do to distract me from myself. Wonder what I'll find in my inbox. Worry about that tomorrow.

I need to start thinking about what to do with the insurance money. Maybe I should think about what I could do once it arrives. I think I need to consider the field of possibilities that could open for me with 500k in the bank. Maybe I can give myself a holiday from work but I don't want to make any rash decisions. Let's see how things pan out for a few weeks. What do they say? Every black cloud has a silver lining. Maybe I can get something positive out of this but I want to make sure it's something I want to do.

He sat back in his chair and closed his eyes. He knew Josie's death wasn't the end of the world, even if at times it seemed that way. He knew he wouldn't feel like crying for ever, even if he felt like that now. He knew he had choices, if he wanted to make them. He knew he wasn't a victim. Life may have dealt him a tough hand but life had no say over how he would respond. He might be down for the count at the moment but he didn't have to stay down. He could choose to get up and move on. He could choose to stay down for as long as he wanted. The choice was his and he would make it when he was ready. For now, the cloak of grieving was warm about his shoulders.

CHAPTER 15

PAUL RANG the doorbell and was surprised when Father Mulligan, and not Grace, opened the door to the parish house. They embraced in the doorway.

'Hello, Paul. How are you?'

'Hi, Frank. I've been better.'

'Let's go down to my study.' Father Mulligan led the way down the corridor to his private study at the back of the house, away from the parish office.

Once they were safely inside, Father Mulligan closed the door. They made themselves comfortable in the armchairs, purposely placed in the room for these sorts of conversations.

Paul looked at Father Mulligan's collection of books. 'This grieving stuff is hard work. Got any helpful books on it?'

'Probably, but why don't you tell me how it's going for you?'

'I thought it would have gotten easier by now, but I can't stop feeling angry. I really want to punch God out, but it's coming out in me being short with the boys. I just don't understand why God allowed something like this to happen.'

'Feeling angry is part of the process, so don't feel bad about it. If you're aware of it, hopefully, you can spare the boys. And it's okay to be angry with God, he doesn't mind. It's natural to blame him for things we don't understand or don't want to accept, but as I'm sure you already know, there's not much point in blaming God. It doesn't help, does it?'

'Then what do I do?' Paul might have understood on a rational level but he still wanted to blame someone. 'It's hardly my fault, and I can't believe she set out to get herself killed.'

Father Mulligan sat back in his chair. 'You'd be surprised by the number of people who blame the person who died, for dying on them. What I've learnt over the years is that blaming someone for dying may be a natural instinct but it isn't very helpful. Sooner or later you realise it doesn't change anything even if you find someone to blame. You still have to live with the fact, they're dead.'

'I don't know what to do. I know I don't want to go on being horrible to the boys. It's not fair on them. They're coping with her death and Dad's as well. At least I can accept Dad dying. He had his three score years and ten, plus a few more as well, but Josie didn't get hers.'

'And how are they doing?'

'They seem to be doing better than me. Even Luke. I thought he'd be hit really hard by Dad's death but he seems to have taken it in his stride. They're both missing their mother but they don't seem to be losing it like I am.'

'The young are always surprising us. Sometimes they're teaching us more than we're teaching them.' Father Mulligan joined his hands together as if he was about to pray. 'Paul, it comes down to how you choose to look at life. The way I see it, life is a series of unfolding events. When things happen we can choose to believe they either happen to us or for us. Peace comes from seeing the event, no matter how uplifting or traumatic, as containing a blessing for you. Sometimes it takes a long time to recognise the blessing, but I assure you, it's always there.'

'I've read something like that somewhere.'

'Well, now it's time to transform that knowledge from something you've read into something you understand. Time to realise that how you respond determines how you experience the event. If you don't make space for the blessing to make itself known, you won't be able to see it.'

Paul became aware that he had folded his arms across his chest. He relaxed and sank into the chair. It was more comfortable than his meditation chair. 'Maybe I've read too many books. Maybe I just like the reading part. It's a lot harder to do the things they recommend.'

'That's probably true for all of us. Do you remember the first time you met Josie in my office at uni?'

'That's a day I'll never forget.'

'Meeting her was an event. You met lots of girls in my office. They were all events. What made the meeting Josie event so memorable?'

'Josie.'

'No, it was how you chose to respond to meeting her. That response is what led to all the subsequent experiences you know as your married life. None of it would have happened, if you had responded to meeting Josie the same way you responded to meeting Jane Ellis. Do you remember her or any of the other girls in that group?'

Paul felt a shiver run up his spine. 'I'd rather forget Jane Ellis. Just hearing her name gives me the creeps.'

'I think that just goes to prove my point. They were both beautiful girls but you chose to respond differently to what you perceived in them.'

'Hmm, I hadn't thought of it like that.'

'Most of us don't think about it. We think life happens to us and we have no say in it. We're victims of a whimsical God.'

They sat looking at each other for a few minutes.

'So, are you suggesting that I can change the way I'm feeling by changing the way I'm looking at this?'

'Paul, you can go one asking God why he did it to you or you can wonder why Josie's death happened for you to respond to, and then consider all the ways you can choose to respond. There is no right answer. It's your life. Choose the experience you want to have.'

'You make it sound so simple.'

'Most secrets are simple. Mind you, simple does not mean easy.' The smile lines on Father Mulligan's face moved. 'Are you still meditating?'

'Yes, but sometimes it's almost impossible. I can't stop the voice in my head. It keeps asking the same question over and over - why?'

'Remember the ritual. Focus on your breathing. Count your breaths.'

'I always start out with that intention but I end up with that question going around and around in my mind.'

'Have you tried simply waiting for the answer to that question to come?'

'What do you mean?'

'Ask the question as the intention for your meditation and then focus on your breathing until you move into silence, and wait for the answer to present itself.'

Paul nodded that he understood.

'Let's do a meditation now, remembering that Jesus said that where two or more are gathered in his name he would be there with them.'

Paul closed his eyes and set his intention. He let his body relax, took several deep inhalations and exhalations of air, and focused his attention on his breathing. Each time he became aware of a thought, he started counting his breaths on the intake until he lost awareness of the counting. After what seemed like twenty minutes he opened his eyes. The chair opposite was empty. He looked at his watch. An hour had passed. Father Mulligan came back into the room carrying a tray with two cups and a pot of coffee.

'You look a bit spaced out.'

'I have no idea where I've been.'

'Sounds like you may have dropped into your soul for some recalibration.'

'I feel rested, and that voice in my head has stopped talking.'

'Well, now you know how to stop it whenever you need to. Join me in a coffee?' Father Mulligan poured the coffee from the pot into the cups.

'Soul recalibration? That's a new term.'

'You like it?'

'Yes. It's sort of modern and technical sounding.'

They laughed.

'Something I picked up from one of those Internet sites the bishop doesn't like me talking about. It's a way of describing what's going on in deep meditation. The guy I was listening too was talking about awareness at the level of soul, as opposed to awareness at the level of personality. Made perfect sense to me. After all, didn't Jesus say that the kingdom was within? So, I figure that's where the soul is and that's where your awareness goes in deep meditation.'

They sat in silence drinking coffee.

'How's your mother? I haven't seen her around.'

'Seems to be doing better than me. She's gone over to stay with Andrew for a couple of weeks. I think it's the first holiday she's had in years.'

'Probably do her good.'

'She was pretty chirpy when she called the other night to see how we were.'

'What about yourself? Why don't you take a break away?'

'I'm thinking about going down the coast or over to the peninsula with the boys for a few days in the school holidays.'

'Make some concrete plans. Book a place. Get your leave sorted out at work.'

'Work, that's something else I'll need to sort out. Not sure I want to stay on at the bank. These last few weeks have been really depressing. I'm not getting any enjoyment from my work anymore.'

'You might want to give yourself a bit more time before you start making those sorts of decisions.'

'I know, but at least I want to put it on the list. I don't want to find myself there ten years from now. I'm not enjoying it, I'm feeling undervalued. I don't have to stay there for the money any more. Like you said before, I've got choices now, some I didn't think I had before.'

'Got anything in mind?'

'I might even go back teaching but I'll probably need to do some study first. Might look into that Masters in Education I talked myself out of when I was quitting teaching.'

'I think you should come over and meditate with me more often.'

'What makes you say that?'

'Listen to yourself. That's the most positive I've heard you in weeks.'

Paul placed his empty cup back on the tray. 'I've had time to think. Sometimes I've forced myself to look at options just so I won't spend all night missing Josie.'

'Matthew told me the other day that you've been spending a lot of time drawing portraits.'

'Yes. I might be overdoing it. I think I've done about twenty portraits of Josie since I started drawing again. Almost a compulsive obsession.'

'Hmm, you might want to move on to drawing someone else.

Sounds like you could be holding onto Josie.'

'No sounds like, Frank. It's not easy to let her go. I know I'll have to.'

'You will. When you stop drawing her you'll know that you're moving on and returning to the world of the living.'

'I'm glad I came to see you. Talking to you I can see that I haven't been spending all my time down in the dumps, even if it feels like that at times.'

Paul got up out of the chair. 'I'd better get going or the boys will think I've abandoned them.'

'Give them a hug from me.'

As they left the study Grace came out of the kitchen with a carrot cake wrapped in plastic.

'Take this home for the boys, Paul. I know it's Matti's favourite. He's always eating it when he's here.'

'Thanks, Grace. Matti might get some competition for this.'

Grace went back into the kitchen to work on the evening meal, while Father Mulligan walked Paul up to the front door and let him out onto the veranda.

'Thanks again, Frank.'

'You're welcome, Paul. See you Sunday.'

They embraced in a warm hug and then Paul walked over to his car to start the journey home. He wondered whether Grace had simply noticed that Matthew was always eating whenever he was around food. Now that he had sole responsibility for the food shopping, he was amazed at how much Matthew actually ate without seeming to gain any weight. Luke on the other hand, who appeared to be more active with all the basketball he played, only ate half as much as his brother. He certainly didn't expect Grace's cake to last very long once he got home. He'd have to cut himself a piece, as soon as he walked in, if he wanted to have any. Now he understood why his mother had always cut herself a small piece before serving him and his brothers.

When he arrived home, Maggie was sitting at the kitchen table with Matthew. The table was covered with books.

'What are you two doing?'

'Hi, Mr Ford, we're working on our history assignment.'

'Team work, is it?'

'Yeah, Dad. What have you got there?'

'Grace gave me a cake.'

'Is it her carrot cake?' Matthew didn't wait for an answer. He cleared a space on the table and got up to get a plate and a knife.

Paul unwrapped the cake and cut it in half. He placed one half on the plate Matthew had placed on the bench and cut it into slices. He wrapped the plastic around the other half so there would be some left for later.

'Don't be shy, Maggie, or you'll miss out.' Paul walked over to the door that opened onto the corridor leading to the bedrooms. 'Luke, do you want some carrot cake?'

Luke appeared within seconds.

'What do you guys want for tea?'

'Mum's bringing pizza.'

'Is she?' Paul looked at Matthew.

'I invited her,' said Matthew. 'I said we'd probably be having pasta, so she said she'd bring pizza and we could have the pasta for the second course.'

'What time is she coming?'

'Around six thirty.'

'Don't eat too much of that cake then. I'd better get some water on and you'd better move your books somewhere else. It's already after six.'

Luke went back up to his room to work on his homework. Matthew and Maggie transferred their pile of books to the floor of the lounge and continued their assignment research. Paul placed a large saucepan, three quarters full of water, onto the cooktop, added some salt and lit the flame so that the water would be boiling when Marie got there. He was surprised to find himself looking forward to her arrival.

Paul was opening a jar of pasta sauce when Marie arrived with a family size pizza, a large bottle of Coke and a bottle of red wine. After an exchange of greetings, Paul dropped the spaghetti into the boiling water and they got the table ready for pizza eating. The smell of pizza attracted the young ones into the kitchen. He didn't expect the pizza eating to take up much time once the boys got started.

'You'd better grab some if you want some,' Paul advised Marie.

She placed a piece on her plate before opening the wine and pouring two glasses, while Maggie was pouring Coke.

'How was your day, Mum?'

The boys didn't seem to notice but that question gave their gathering a familiar tone Paul hadn't felt since Josie's death. He sat there with a piece of pizza in one hand and a glass of red wine in the other wondering what Marie would say.

'Tiring. Think I could do with a holiday. What do you say to going away for the school holidays?'

'Sounds good to me,' said Maggie.

'Me too,' said Paul. 'I was only discussing going down the coast or over to the peninsula with Father Mulligan this afternoon.'

The boys exchanged glances. It was the first they'd heard of it.

'That would probably be a good idea, a change of scenery and some fresh sea air will do you all the world of good,' said Marie.

Paul got up and stirred the spaghetti. Then he poured the sauce into a saucepan to heat it up while the spaghetti finished cooking. When he sat down again there was one piece of pizza left for him to finish. By the time he'd eaten the pizza the spaghetti was ready. While he was organising the spaghetti, Matthew took the pizza box out to the bin and Maggie got up to carry the bowls of spaghetti over to the table.

The conversation over spaghetti centred on school and all the assignments that had to be finished in the last three weeks of the semester.

When the meal was over, Marie helped Paul with the dishes and the young ones disappeared to work on those very assignments they had discussed over the meal. Once the dishes had been washed, Paul and Marie sat in the kitchen drinking wine.

'How are things going for you? My spy tells me you've been a bit of a grump.'

'I'm finding it really challenging. How did you cope with Steve's death?'

Marie twirled her wine glass before answering. 'In the early days I didn't want to cope with his death at all. I just wanted to die. Fortunately, I had Maggie to look after and she was younger than Luke at the time.'

'Obviously you made it, so what happened?'

'A couple of things. First, the Commissioner decided we weren't safe where we were, so he transferred me back here, and that happened really quickly. I had to pull myself together to cope with that, and getting Maggie set up in a new school.'

'You know, I only found out after Josie's death that was when Matti met Maggie. She told me he had been a great support for her at school. He hadn't said anything at home that I was aware of.'

'Josie knew. We'd spoken several times over the years. I used to see her at school functions, especially those music fundraising nights.'

More secret women's business that no-one had thought to inform him about. 'What was the other thing?'

'I didn't have the family support you have. I'm an only child. My parents divorced when I was a teenager. I haven't seen my father since, and my mother moved back to England a couple of years after I joined the force. Anyway, that meant I needed to find someone to talk to. Work provides counselling services, so I started with one of them. She introduced me to a support group of other officers who had lost a partner on the job.'

'What you're telling me sounds like having a support group of people who have gone through the same thing worked for you.'

'It certainly helped put things into perspective. It's so easy to think that you're the only one this has happened to. Hearing their stories helped me see that there was a journey to go through but it had an end.'

'Can't say I've come across too many people in my situation.'

'There's at least one. And she'd be happy to help you. You only have to ask.'

He looked at her. 'Would you?'

'I've walked the journey. I know there is a way to the end. I can help you get there.'

'That would be good.'

'What's the thing you feel the most at the moment?'

'Anger. I'm really angry with God for allowing it to happen.'

'I wanted to blame someone too but I wasn't game enough to blame God straight away. At first, I blamed Steve instead. Why did he have to join Special Operations? I used to tell myself if only he hadn't joined, he'd still be alive. It was only when I accepted that it didn't matter who I blamed, he would still be dead, that I started to heal.'

'Sounds like you've been reading the same script as Frank.'

'No script, Paul. Just an awakening to the truth of the matter. I can't tell you what a relief it was to wake up from that black space, where everything was darkness and there was no hope. I don't ever want to go there again.'

'Is that why you haven't remarried?'

'Probably. If there was one thing I decided after I came out of the pain, it was I would never get myself into a relationship with another policeman.'

'I think I can understand that.'

'What else did Frank have to say?'

'He was talking about the event being neutral and my experience being determined by how I was responding to the event and not by the event itself.'

'He has some unusual ideas for a priest.'

'I've known Frank for a long time. He's very widely read and, despite the bishop's concerns, he's open to exploring spirituality through unorthodox means. I've learnt a lot from him over the years.'

'What's he said about grieving?'

'The first thing he told me about grieving was that I wouldn't find the answer in a bottle.'

'He's right there. I've tried that approach. All you get is a hangover.' She topped up their wine glasses. 'But sometimes it's fun to blot the world out for a few hours.'

'We did a meditation while I was at Frank's. It was the first time I'd blotted out the world, and my mind, since Josie died. It felt really peaceful. Do you know what Frank called it when I said I had no idea where I'd been?'

'What?'

'Soul recalibration.'

'Think I could use some of that myself.'

'Do you meditate?'

'On and off. I know you're supposed to make it a daily ritual but sometimes I just don't seem to be able to find the time.'

'I think it's the only thing keeping me sane.'

'Perhaps you can teach me how you do it.'

'Well, it doesn't mix well with red wine.' They clinked their glasses and laughed.

The sound of giggling came from the lounge.

'Do you think we should be concerned about those two spending so much time together?'

'It's young love, Paul. Leave them alone.'

'She's a pretty special girl. I've never met anyone like her before. My mother and Maria both think the world of her, and Mick hasn't stopped teasing Matti since the funeral.'

'She might look like me but she's a lot like her father. He really knew how to connect to people. That's the thing I miss about him the most. I always felt special with Steve.'

'Yes, I know what you mean. Luke is so much like Josie in a lot of ways. Matti's more like me.'

'And what are you like, Paul?'

'I'm one of those quiet ones that my mother said girls always had to be wary of.'

'I'd better stay on guard, then.' She took a sip of her wine. 'What's this I hear about you being a portrait artist?'

'I don't know about being an artist but I like to draw. I find it relaxing. It's more relaxing than watching TV.'

'Can I have a look?'

'Okay. Come out to the study.'

They went out to the study and Paul showed her his collection of portraits. Most were of Josie but he had also done some of the boys and even a couple of himself.

'Would you do one of me?'

'If you want. I haven't done any life drawings since my student days.'

'I can send you some photos if you'd like.'

'Perhaps we can do both. I'd like to try a life drawing. I can always use the photos to help with the finer details but it could be fun working with a model.'

'These ones of Matti are pretty good. What does he think of

them?'

'He took the best one.'

'I have to confess to having seen that one before tonight. It's on the wall in Maggie's room.'

'Wondered what he'd done with it.'

They walked back out to the kitchen.

'Are you serious about taking a break during the school holidays?'

'Yes. I think the boys need one.'

'Why don't you come with us? I have a beach house over on the peninsula. Nothing flash. I bought it to escape to after Steve died. You and the boys will need to bring some air beds or something to sleep on but there's plenty of room.'

'Should we ask the kids?'

'Okay, let's do that and then we'd better be on our way. It's been a good night, don't you think?'

'Yes. Thanks for coming.'

They gathered the children and discussed the plan for a joint holiday. Not surprisingly, Matti and Maggie were in agreement. Luke asked if he could ask Michelle to come with them. Paul, aware that Luke had become close with his cousin since Josie's death, said that he'd speak to her mother to see if she could come. Marie didn't have a problem with her joining the expedition. So it was agreed. They'd spend the school holidays on the peninsula.

When Marie had gone home and the boys had finally gotten over their excitement, Paul took stock. He could hardly believe what had just happened. One minute they had been talking about portraits. Then the next thing he knew, they had agreed to spend two weeks together in a beach house. How did that happen? He had no idea. The more he thought about it, the more he liked the idea.

He rang Rosa and arranged for Michelle to join them. That sealed it.

CHAPTER 16

A WEEK after agreeing to the holiday on the peninsula, Paul was cleaning out Josie's drawer in the filing cabinet when he came across her journals. He knew they existed but had forgotten where she kept them. She'd obviously thrown some of them out, as there were only six of the exercise books she had used as her journals at the back of the drawer. The one at the front of the group had writing on the first few pages but the others were full of her thoughts. At first he hesitated, not sure whether he should read them or just throw them out. When they had started journaling, they had agreed not to read each other's journals, unless invited to read a passage the writer wanted to share. Over the years, their journals had become next to sacred, and rarely shared. They might have shared some insights recorded within them, but the journals had remained hidden texts. In the end, the temptation to look into some of her secret women's business triumphed. He lifted the journals out of the drawer, sat down in his meditation chair and opened the one with the most ancient date. It contained her thoughts from five years ago.

He flicked through the pages, not knowing where to start. Some of her handwriting was indecipherable. Some of it looked like it had been written in code. Some was in Italian. Paul had never learnt the language. Other pages were neatly printed and some were illustrated with doodles and pictures. She had obviously gone through a phase where she used different coloured biros on different days but none of the pages were dated, as far as he could tell. He spotted his name on a page.

I don't seem to be able to reach Paul these days. He's withdrawn into himself and won't talk about how he feels. I think he's really angry at or about something but he doesn't want to talk about it. He might think he's keeping it hidden, and maybe he is from himself, but his energy is really black. I can feel it as soon as he walks into the house. And he's so abrupt with the boys. I wish he'd just talk to me about it instead of hiding out there in the study.

What had been going on in his life five years ago? He'd been at the bank for three years by then, but was still being plagued by the anguish that had driven him out of school. And, by then, he'd discovered that working at the bank was boring, and there wasn't much of a career path to look forward to. He had been marking time. He hadn't been able pull himself out of the black hole that had opened up in his life after he had walked from teaching, following the confrontation with the principal at St David's. Five years ago, he had been feeling like a failure and describing his life to himself as dull, colourless and boring. He had been too ashamed to talk to Josie about it. At the time, he believed that he had let her down. Too late to apologise now. Then he remembered that she had given him a book for his birthday that year. A book about accepting how things were in your life. That book had helped him climb slowly out of that black hole. Somehow, she had worked out what he needed and encouraged him to do it. Now that she was gone, he was actually thinking about leaving the bank and going back to what he was passionate about. He wished he'd done it back then.

He flicked through some more pages and stopped on one with a bright blue line across the top.

Matti told me about a girl at school called Maggie. Apparently she arrived towards the end of last year. Came to St Jude's after her father (policeman) was killed in some sort of accident. Says she is his best friend. They do music together. The other boys are giving him a hard time but he doesn't care. He said he didn't want me to tell anyone, 'especially not Dad'. He thinks his father will stir him. I said he would understand but he said, 'Dad's not good with secrets.' Maybe that's why they come to me for their emotional support and only go to Paul for practical help like Math's home-work and fixing things. Sad really. I'd like them to have a good relationship with their father. He's an important figure in their lives and they need to get to know him as more than just a problem solver.

They wouldn't have much choice now, would they? And neither would he. Who else was going to be there for them when they hit the inevitable bumps in the road? He hoped he would know what to say when the time came. He chuckled to himself. Hadn't he heard the unsaid message in Luke's request to have Michelle come on the holiday? God, what was happening to him? It seemed he was becoming perceptive in his old age. He spotted a page with an Italian flag drawn in the top right hand corner.

I want to go overseas. Just watched a travel show on European holidays. I have to go to Italy and Spain and Ireland - and I want to go on my own! A girl's got to have some freedom in her life. I'm sick of putting myself last. I want to spoil myself and I want to get away from here for a break. I could sure use a break from Mr Misery. And I could use a break from being the always available parent. I'm starting a separate savings account next payday and putting money aside each payday - think I can do that online, won't even have to go to the bank. Thank God for computers and the Internet. I'm setting a goal like they say in all those books - I'm going for my long service leave and if things haven't improved by then, maybe I won't come back. I found out last week that because Mum was born in Italy, I can get Italian citizenship and an EU passport. Think I'll make an appointment with the consulate after school this week and see what I need to do.

He thought about the night she had told him about her plans for her long service leave, and informed him that it would be a great opportunity for him to bond with the boys. He smiled at the memory. They had just had the best sex in months and were lying entwined in each other's arms when she told him. He hadn't expected it, and his initial reaction was one of disbelief. But she had been adamant that she was going and about going on her own. Something about never having had an opportunity to do anything on her own. What was he scared of anyway? She wasn't leaving him, just going for a holiday, where she wouldn't have to worry about any of them, not him, not the boys, not her parents, not anyone for six weeks. She deserved a break after all she had done for them. In the end, he had simply agreed. What would have been the point in arguing with her? She had known how to get him to agree to anything - the gentle art of sex based persuasion. Maybe that should be listed as a weapon, he chuckled to himself, as he acknowledged her expert use of it.

He wondered if she had gone ahead with the EU passport. She hadn't said a word to him about that. He opened the file that held her personal papers and flipped through the papers and envelopes she had stored in it. Inside an envelope, with passport written on it, he found her EU passport bound to her Australian passport with a rubber band. She had been good at keeping secrets. He wondered what other secrets he would uncover and whether he could live with the knowledge. He wondered if she had lied to him about not leaving him. He almost put the journals back, but the power of curiosity was greater than his fears. He stopped at a page with a small photograph of a pink rose, glued in place, like a colourful initial letter at the beginning of the text.

Gang meeting today. We signed up for the Goddess Within workshop next weekend - it's all about connecting with who you are as a woman and bringing power and wholeness to your life and relationships. Sounds exciting and only $300. Who knows what will come out of it. I wonder if they have something similar for men. Paul could certainly use some help getting in contact with himself.

It turned out there had been a workshop for men. He had found out about it when she had persuaded him to attend a 'Wild Man' retreat weekend organised by Father Mulligan. Another notch in the belt of her weapon of persuasion.

The thing he remembered most about the Goddess Within workshop was it was where Josie had met Anna. She hadn't told him much about the workshop but he had heard all about this amazing woman called Anna.

Another thing he realised was that after that workshop, she had stopped trying to get him to talk about his feelings or to understand how she was feeling. She had just started doing what she had always accused him of doing, and their relationship moved to one based more on companionship, cooperative parenting and less frequent, less satisfying, physical sex. Outwardly, they looked and acted as a loving couple. Inwardly, he had been lost and clueless in knowing what to do about it. He certainly hadn't felt comfortable enough to talk to anyone about it. As usual, he had just gone along with what she wanted. Looking back now he could see that he had given most of his power away, and hadn't even realised it. The term 'dickhead' came to mind as it dawned on him which head he had been operating from. He turned to another page.

The sadness of all that promise lost, the loss of all that love. What's happening to us? What happened to the young lovers we started as? Once we saw each other as the most important aspects of life. We went out of the way to keep each other happy. Now we're sitting in our own corners most of the time - except for brief loveless sex. I just can't give myself to him anymore. I wonder if he even notices that I'm not there when he's fucking me. Men. They're so fixated on sex and he thinks it fixes everything. I know deep down he loves me but I wish he would get in touch with that part of himself again. He used to be so much fun. Now he's a wet blanket, a grey mist, a dead weight.

I love him so much it hurts that I'm not able to show him anymore. I have to look after myself. I can't afford to go under trying to drag him out of himself. I'm relying on you, God, to do your bit to wake him up to himself. He's locked himself in a dark cave. All I can do is send him love and hope he eventually comes out. I wish he'd talk to someone, it doesn't have to be me, but I've given up trying to draw him out of himself. Whatever it is that he's so frightened of, he's buried it deep. Classic case of denial. He hasn't been happy, despite what he says, since he left teaching. I can't understand why he's staying at the bank when he hates it so much. He's such a talented teacher. He could easily get another teaching job but he bites my head off every time I mention it.

I'm amazed at how committed he is to being a father, despite all his issues. Must be something he decided to be so that, no matter what, they wouldn't have the same experience he had as a boy. Must have been horrible having someone as rigid as George as a father. It's like he's putting all his energy into being a good father. He's always supporting them with their sport - he's been all over the place with basketball for Luke, even joined the committee to help raise money for the state carnival last year, and last month he took time off work to help out at Matti's music camp. Anne told me his father was never there for him or his brothers, always too busy with either work or church. No wonder most of them went away as soon as they could.

I wish I could make him happy but I can't, and you know what? I don't feel guilty about that anymore. That's one thing I've learnt from the GW - I'm not responsible for his happiness - that's his responsibility. For now, I'm focussing on my happiness. If he's not available to share my feelings and thoughts with, there are others only too willing to share.

He closed the book. He didn't want to confront what those words were bringing up but it was already too late. An ugly thought formed and arose from the cellar in the depths of his mind. She'd left him emotionally five years ago. She'd cut him adrift and found her emotional support elsewhere, and he'd been too asleep or too engrossed in his own dramas to notice. All that time he had believed that if she was having sex with him, she was there for him. It dawned on him that he had been having sex with himself. She had simply provided a body for him to fuck. A small pebble dropped into the pool of his consciousness. He didn't like the ripples it created on his awareness. He had noticed that the sex had taken on a more physical tone, except for those times when she had used it persuasively to get him to agree with some plan she had, but he had pushed the meaning of what that might have meant down into the cellar of his mind, deep down where he kept all of his black boxed secrets.

What was the point of loving her if he couldn't express that love? His love for her wasn't a secret. It was his self-loathing that was the secret. He didn't want to admit that leaving teaching had been a mistake based in pride. He couldn't bring himself to admit that he had been wrong all along. Shit! He was pig-headed, just like his father. God, he'd put so much effort into not being like his father, and look what had happened. He heard a voice from somewhere within his head whisper, 'You manifest what you put your attention on.' Yeah, well he'd done that, hadn't he?

Somewhere, he'd read something along the lines that your world is an illusion, constructed from the thoughts you think and influenced by the thoughts you try to suppress. He leant back into the chair. The illusion that had been his picture of his relationship with Josie was fading. He'd had a picture of being happily married, of being in a committed relationship, of being in love. The words in her journal were not nourishing that picture. They were destroying it. He hadn't even finished the first journal. What else was he going to find out? Did he want to find out anything else? He couldn't help himself. He opened the second one from the pile to a page with a gold star stuck on it.

First $1000 in my travel account, hurrah! I can see it happening. Mum said she'd give me some spending money when I'm ready to go. She was so excited when I told her when she and Dad got back from their trip. They seem to have more money now that Dad and Uncle Pat have sold the business. Dad's been talking about buying some more apartments. He's always liked property investments. Wish I could talk Paul into that but let's not go there. He's such a worrywart when it comes to money. He's always going on about juggling the bills. Another reason he should get out of the bank. The place might be full of money but they don't send much of it home with him. I should be happy that at least his black mood has lifted. He's not such a pain in the arse to be around these days. He even seems to enjoy Anna's company when she's here. She's such a flirt at times but at least she gets him laughing. Mark's more than a flirt. Those two always seem to be flirting with other people but not much with each other. Their relationship's even more strained than ours, but they're play acting for the outside world just like we do. I wonder what the real story is there.

I'm not sure I could trust myself being alone with Mark. He's got so much animal magnetism. You can feel his sexual energy when he walks into the room and he's always touching my bum when he gives me a kiss to say hello. I wonder what it would be like being fucked by someone like that. Can't image him being anything like Paul. Might be fun finding out but I don't think I'd want to be in a relationship with him.

He'd always wondered whether Josie had sexual fantasies. Now that he knew, he wasn't all that surprised she fantasised about fucking Mark. After all, he'd fantasised about fucking Anna, and lots of other women he'd seen in the street. He was a bit mystified by her comment on Anna and Mark's relationship. They'd seemed like a happy couple to him. He read the words again. This time the reference to play acting stood out. He knew Josie was good at acting. He'd seen her in action on many occasions, and been the victim of some of her feigned dramas, but he hadn't seen himself as play acting in their relationship.

He thought he'd been himself, even if they had experienced some of the little problems everybody seemed to have in long term relationships. No relationship was going to be up all the time. There had to be some down. Why was she referring to it as strained? Obviously, she had seen it differently. Had the whole thing been a sham all this time? Why hadn't she left him then? The boys. She would have stayed for the boys. Maybe that's why she had play acted the happy wife and mother, at least on the surface. Now that he thought about it, in light of what he'd read, some of her behaviour, especially towards him, over the last few years took on a different sheen. He could hardly believe he had turned a blind eye to it. There was some stuff about him, about them, about her, he hadn't wanted to face. Maybe she was right after all, he had been play acting and it was himself he had been fooling.

He wondered who else she had shared her thoughts with. Who else had she told that their relationship was all play acting? He didn't think she had told her mother. There had been no change in the way Maria had related to him. She wouldn't have told Anne. No way could he image that happening. He wondered how much of their secret women's business had been about their relationships. Did women talk about those things? He knew blokes didn't, until it was too late. He'd only ever heard about a mate's marital problems after his wife had left or kicked him out.

The statistics, from a survey he'd read about recently, claimed the woman instigated separation in more than seventy percent of cases. He was starting to understand why. If most blokes were like him, they had no idea what was going on. Paul, like most blokes, thought he'd done everything right according to his rules. Now he understood he hadn't done anything right, according to her rules.

How many times had Josie told him it wasn't about him solving her problems or fixing things? That it was about listening or sharing what he was feeling. How many times had she expected him to just know what she wanted, as if he had been a mind reader? He didn't know what he was feeling most of the time, and he sure as hell didn't know how to talk about it.

He had tried to listen but she was always angry when she wanted to talk and, it seemed to him, as though it was always him she was angry about. It was like he had to be the scape goat for all the oppression of women at the hands of men. He couldn't handle that. He'd never been violent towards her or anybody else. Why did he have to take the blame? She would shout. He would walk away. He didn't like confrontations. Look what had happened when he had confronted that prick of a principal at St David's. Who had been the one forced to leave?

He noticed he was breathing rapidly. He wanted to hit someone or something. He stood up. He sat down. It seemed like his whole life had become a lie. She had lied to him by not being honest with him. And now, she was the one who had walked out and wasn't coming back to talk it over, ever. He threw the book across the room. It crashed into the bookshelf and fell to the floor.

He wasn't sure he could read anymore, but he couldn't bring

himself to throw them out or burn them. He wished he had honoured their original agreement. Now it was too late.

He flipped open the one she had written in last year. It was written in Italian. It may as well have been encrypted. There was no way he would be getting it translated. Who knew what other secrets it held? He certainly didn't want anybody else knowing about them. His fear of exposure pushed him to action. He gathered up the books. They had to be destroyed. He took them out into the backyard and released their secrets to the atmosphere from within the Weber barbecue.

He wished he had done that straight away. Now, thanks to his curiosity, he'd found out about things he didn't want to know. Finally, he understood Humpty Dumpty. His version of reality lay shattered before him and there was no way he could restore it. The truth might set you free but sometimes, it seemed, liberation was painful.

He sat in his meditation chair and wept as he realised that he was responsible for her leaving, that he was just as much to blame for the state of their relationship as she was. He hadn't done anything to keep it alive. He'd taken it for granted. He'd taken her for granted. He hadn't been brave enough to ask for what he wanted or for what she wanted from him.

Slowly, he cried himself out and his tears gave way to sniffles. Finally, he was able to slow his breathing and quieten his agitated heart. He found his own journal and made an entry.

Josie, I'm so sorry I was too stupid to realise what was going on, that I was too proud to confess to you what I felt and too scared to talk to you about it. I'm such a coward. Will you ever forgive me? Oh God, will I ever forgive myself? I've been such a fool. I wonder what would have happened if she hadn't been killed. Would she really have left me? Would she ever have confided in me? Would she have trusted me enough? Would I ever have been brave enough to really open up? Shit, seems like all the so called spiritual work I've been doing has been a waste of time. I don't seem to have made any progress at all. If I'm really honest with myself, I have to admit that I like reading about it but I'm not so keen on actually doing the work required to identify and work through my issues. If I had, maybe I wouldn't be sitting here feeling sorry for myself because I've discovered how broken our relationship was. Maybe if I'd done the work I would have been brave enough to talk to her about things.

Bloody hell, what's the lesson here? If all events come in to your life to teach you something, did Josie have to get killed so that I could read her journal to find out that our relationship was on the rocks or maybe even over in everything but name? All those stories you read about people not getting it until after some shock. Is this my shock?

I can't believe that's the way things work. That's not fair! What sort of God arranges such a universe? What sort of bloke doesn't talk to his wife, the woman he claims to love?

Maybe I know nothing about love. I thought I was in love with Josie, and I thought she was in love with me. Would lovers really do what we did to each other? Would lovers, real lovers, keep secrets and be too scared to talk about their fears and hurts? What was it then that we were doing? Were we just parenting? Cohabiting? Was it lust all along? I can't believe that. I don't want to believe that even if it's true. We were so much in love when it all started. What happened to me? I used to trust her with everything. We had no secrets once. What happened to us? What happened to me? How did I come to let her down so badly? How did I come to let myself down so badly?

God, how many other lies have I told myself?

I wonder how many other people know. The Gang? Anna? Would she have told them? God, how do I face them?

It was bad enough losing the love of my life, now I've lost my cover story as well. Who am I? What sort of man am I?

What do I do now? I can't dishonour my memories of her. I can't shatter the boy's version of reality. I can't talk about this with Maria or Mum.

I'm not even sure I'll ever be able to forgive myself for reading her journal. If I hadn't been so nosey I would have been none the wiser, and could have held on to my deluded beliefs. Looks like I have a shitload of issues to clear here. God, if grieving wasn't enough, now I have to face being honest with myself. God, give me the courage to be honest with myself, and the courage to live with myself.

He looked at his watch. It was nearly five o'clock. Mick and Maria would be back with the boys for tea soon. He put his journal away and went to wash his face. The play acting would have to continue until he had sorted himself out.

CHAPTER 17

THE BEACH HOUSE was located in a small coastal town on the western side of the peninsula. A couple of streets back from the foreshore, the house was protected from the ravages of the salt spray blown in off the ocean. The front yard was an expanse of buffalo grass, kept in check by a local contractor. Out the back, a veranda, which also served as a carport, stretched over a paved area edged with garden beds holding an assortment of bushy shrubs. On one side of the paved area, someone had built an impressive gas-fired, brick barbecue.

The house itself was nothing to look at. It looked like it had seen better days, but at least it was constructed from materials that required minimal, if any, maintenance. Inside, it consisted of a large central room furnished with a dining table and chairs, a cane lounge suite and a modern kitchen. Three bedrooms, a laundry and a bathroom opened off one side of the central room. The main bedroom had an en-suite. On the opposite side, a door opened into the guest wing - a louvered sleep-out with its own bathroom down the far end.

'How much did you pay for this?' Paul asked Marie as they unpacked the cars.

'I got it before they started on the resort further down the coast. That really pushed up prices in these little places. What do you think I paid?'

'When you told me where it was, I had a look at the real estate prices over here. This place would be worth two to three hundred thousand going on its position. So if you got it before the spike in prices, what a hundred?'

'Eighty.'

'You're kidding?'

'It was a deceased estate. It didn't have that kitchen and we've done up the bathrooms.'

'What's it like in the summer? Does it get hot?'

'Not anymore. Didn't you notice the vents? Evaporative cooling. And that's the gas heater over there. Which reminds me, I need to check the gas bottle. Come into the sleep-out and I'll show you how to turn on the hot water booster. It's solar, but it will need boosting this time of the year, or some of us will be having cold showers.'

They explored the fuse box with the switches for all things electrical and satisfied themselves they had enough gas. Then they gathered the children to organise who would be sleeping where.

'Why don't you bunk in with me, Michelle?' said Maggie.

'The boys and I can use the sleep-out. There's plenty of room and that should simplify the bathroom arrangements,' said Paul.

The boys picked up their air mattresses and sleeping bags and staked out their territory next to the bathroom. 'Dad, you can sleep down that end,' said Matthew.

Once they had settled in, Paul went out the back and became acquainted with the barbecue, while Marie supervised salad making in the kitchen. As he stood over the hotplate turning sizzling sausages and hamburger patties, he wondered what he had done to deserve this. They'd been there for less than an hour and he was already feeling relaxed, and as if this was home.

There was so much laughter coming from the kitchen, he wondered what was going on inside the house. He smiled and told himself two weeks of this could only be good for him and the boys. He was glad Michelle had come. She was good for Luke and her being there would allow Matthew and Maggie some space as well.

Over lunch, they sorted out some house rules and set up a cleaning roster. The boys cheered when Marie said there was a dishwasher. After lunch, the young ones went for a walk along the beach, while Paul and Marie went food shopping at the local supermarket, the smallest supermarket Paul had ever experienced. If they wanted to buy anything not stocked in the local supermarket they would have to drive to the next town down the coast, which supported a larger population and the nearby resort.

'At least you don't have to deliberate over which brand to choose,' Paul joked as they filled up their trolley.

'The simple life. That's what I like about coming over here.'

He couldn't argue with that. 'Already I'm in love with the place.'

'Told you you'd like it.'

For the first few days they lazed about, read books and went for long group walks along the beach. Then Marie persuaded Paul to get out his drawing equipment and they spent an afternoon drawing portraits under Paul's tutorage. Paul and Michelle were the only serious artists in the group, but by the end of the session, they were able to mount an exhibition of drawings on the inside glass of the large front window. There was a lot of laughing as they surveyed the output of their afternoon. Luke had drawn a series of group portraits in his primitive, stick figure style. Matthew had spent the afternoon drawing cartoon portraits of Maggie, and she had returned the favour. Michelle had drawn the boys. Marie had attempted to capture Paul's likeness, while Paul had drawn Michelle and Luke.

The following morning, Marie posed and Paul started working on the portrait he had agreed to paint. The young ones escaped to the beach with the cricket equipment. Even the girls were eager to play.

For the first half hour, Marie sat relatively still while Paul drew several quick sketches to capture her likeness and focus on the position of her eyes and mouth.

'How are things going, Paul? You haven't said much over the last few days. Are you okay?'

'This place is like magic. I feel really relaxed, as long as I don't think about Josie.'

'Know what you mean. I found it really difficult to think about Steve in the months after he was killed. I didn't know if I was going to cope but it does get easier.'

'When did you find this place?' Paul stopped sketching.

'I came over here for a weekend with one of the members of the support group I told you about. That was about six months after Steve was killed. I spotted a for sale sign on this place on one of my walks. I had the insurance money sitting in the bank and, as they say, the rest is history.'

'Did coming here help?'

'Once I'd bought the place, we came over every weekend for a couple of years. I come here every time I have holidays. It's a really good place for reflection, and no-one asks any questions. The locals are friendly enough but they don't go out of their way to get to know us blow ins.'

Paul decided to take that as a yes answer. 'Did you have a good relationship with Steve?'

'I think so. He was a pretty special guy. I don't know too many other men as open about how they feel, like he was. He was willing to share what was going on in his life and he was a great listener. Ironic isn't it, that's what got him killed.' She looked up into Paul's mystified expression. 'He was the negotiator on the Special Operations team. He got shot trying to talk some crazy kid out of killing his girlfriend.'

'How did that put you in danger?'

'The girlfriend was the daughter of some criminal. He blamed Steve for her death, and even though he was inside at the time, I got death threats. It was pretty scary.'

'You feel safe now?'

'You know, life can be really funny. When he got out of prison last year, he sent me an apology through the Commissioner. I actually met him a few months ago. The girl was his only child. I think he found her death more of a punishment for his life of crime than prison. So, yes, I feel safe now.'

'Unexpected deaths have a way of making you question the whole purpose of your life,' said Paul.

'They certainly give you an opportunity to reassess how you've been doing, don't you think?'

'Yeah, and I can't say that I'm all that proud of some of the stuff that's come up.'

'Don't feel like you have to tell me, but if you want to talk about it, I'll listen. When you're ready.'

'Do you want a coffee?' Paul walked into the kitchen and turned on the kettle. He wasn't sure if he wanted to voice his secrets but he had to tell someone.

'Yes, thanks.' Marie looked at his sketches. She hoped his final drawing would be a little more realistic. 'This makes my face look skinny.'

'I'm just getting a feel for where your bits go, you know, seeing where your eyes are in relation to your ears and so on.'

'Oh.'

He came back with the coffees. 'I'll do the layout for the final drawing once I'm satisfied I've got the relative positions noted.' He sat down beside her on the lounge. 'What I've discovered from all my navel gazing is that I have been deluding myself, hiding the truth from myself, for years.'

Marie waited for him to continue, giving him the space to decide whether he wanted to talk or chicken out.

'I thought we were happily married. That's the story I told myself. That's how I always acted. I actually believed it. But now I'm not so sure.'

'The boys seem to think that you and Josie were very much in love.'

'We were committed to being loving parents, and we supported each other in lots of ways but,' he stopped speaking.

'What's happened, Paul? You didn't sound like this when you came to report her as missing.'

For a few moments, Paul didn't say anything while he struggled with his guilt feelings.

'I found some of her journals. I should have destroyed them but I couldn't resist the temptation to have a look.'

'I can understand that. I would have looked in Steve's if he'd kept one. I take it you didn't like what you found.'

'One part of me wishes I'd never opened them. Another part says I had to be confronted with the truth. Otherwise I wouldn't learn anything from the whole experience.'

The sound of footsteps in the driveway, followed by the thud of the cricket bag being dropped on the back veranda, announced the return of the children.

'It's raining,' said Luke, the first to appear inside the house.

'I'm starving,' said Matthew.

Marie touched Paul on the knee and said, 'We can talk later.'

Then she got up and moved into the kitchen area to supervise the preparation of lunch.

Michelle came over and sat down next to Paul. 'How's the drawing going, Uncle Paul?'

He showed her the sketches and discussed his plans for the portrait with her until Marie called them over to eat.

By the time they had eaten lunch the rain had stopped. The children decided to watch a DVD, while Paul and Marie rugged up and went for a walk along the beach. For a while they walked in silence. Paul found the repetitive sound of the waves crashing on the shore especially soothing. Their walk took them around a bend on the beach into a small sheltered cove, where they sat on a rock out of the wind.

'I've spent hours sitting on this rock,' said Marie. 'This is where I came to shout at God.'

'You too?'

'Steve was the best thing that ever happened to me. He was my rock, my safe harbour and he was taken away. Who else was I going to blame?'

'Frank reckons it's okay to be angry with God, but he did say not to stay there.'

'Frank might know a thing or two about death and dying, I suppose. He deals with it a lot more than we do, but I think there's a difference between serving the grieving and being one of the grieving. What do you think?'

'With Dad dying so soon after Josie, I think there might be different types of grieving. I don't feel anywhere near as cut up over Dad as I do about Josie.'

'I think I'm still grieving for my father, and as far as I know he's still alive. He may as well be dead, I suppose. I haven't seen him for thirty years. At least my mother keeps in contact.'

'That must be hard.'

'Not as hard as losing Steve, so I guess I'm agreeing with you

about there being different types of grieving. My grieving for my
father is on a slow burn. My grieving for Steve was like a furnace
that almost consumed me, but I think I've reached a point where
I can let him go. You have to live in the present at some stage.'

'That's pretty philosophical.'

Marie shrugged her shoulders. 'Maybe. Tell me how you see
it going for you. Are you planning on grieving forever?'

Paul watched the seagulls twisting and turning in the sky and
waited for his thoughts to settle.

'Josie's only been gone for a couple of months. The first few
weeks were really hard. That's when I was swearing at God. But life
was still happening. The boys needed me to be their father. School
didn't stop for them. I went back to work.' He paused and looked out
to sea. 'The pain's changed. It's more of a dull throb instead of a
sharp stabbing pain now. You know, having someone like you to talk
to makes it more bearable. I don't know what would have happened
to me if I'd tried to do it in my usual style, on my own.'

'You should be thanking Josie's mother. She asked me to talk
to you. She thought I would understand what you'd be going
through, after I told her about Steve. Matti told me that Josie told
her mother everything. So I think she might know what you're
like.'

'How many spies do you have in my house?'

'Two. And one's only there on a temporary basis. Luke
doesn't tell me anything. He's very loyal to his Dad.'

Paul thought of his boys. One confiding in his girl-friend and
her mother, the other in his cousin. At least they were talking to
someone, and not bottling it up based on his modelling. That was
something to be grateful for.

'After what I read in her journal, I think Josie had some
secrets she didn't share with her mother. She certainly didn't
share them with me.'

'You don't sound all that happy about that.'

'Do you remember me telling you that she was planning to go to Europe for her long service leave?'

'Yes.'

'I found an EU passport hidden in a folder in the filing cabinet.'

Marie raised an eyebrow. 'What makes you think it was hidden?'

'She never said anything to me about it. She's had it for around five years. I only found it after reading about it in her journal, on a page where she wrote she was thinking about leaving me at the time she organised it.'

'And you had no idea?'

'Seems I wouldn't know if my arse was on fire.'

'Don't be too hard on yourself. From what I hear, most husbands are a bit like that.'

Paul hung his head and looked at the sand between his sneakers. 'Think I might have lost her twice. Once, when I got so lost in myself after quitting my teaching job, and again when she got shot.'

'Sounds like you've had some practice grieving then.'

'Suppose you're right. Can't say I understood it as grieving then, and I was in a dark hole for a long time.'

'Want to tell me about it? Might make it easier if you get that old stuff out of your system.'

It started to drizzle. They stood up and walked back the way they had come.

'When I went into teaching, I wanted to make a difference in kids' lives. Education is a vehicle you can use to do that. I had a lot of fun in the first few years, but things changed when they made me the faculty head for religious studies.'

'So what happened?'

'Politics. I wanted to change things, the way we did things, the way we interacted with the kids.'

'And you found out that people don't like change.'

'You know, I thought it would be different in schools. I thought people would be open to lifelong learning. It was all words. People are interested in power and the status quo, just like in the rest of society.'

'So you got disillusioned and quit?'

'Not straight away. I thought maybe I should try somewhere else. I'd been a student at St Jude's and some of the people resisting my ideas had been my teachers when I was a boy. I got a transfer to St David's.'

'How long did you last there?'

'Three years.'

'What was it like? Was it different from St Jude's?'

'Don't get me wrong. They're both great schools but I was pushing the envelope in religious studies. The principal was threatened by the reaction of some of the more fundamentalist parents and pressure from the bishop. In my third year there, he cut my funding so I couldn't run the senior school retreat program off campus. We had a big fight. He was more concerned about his precious reputation and keeping his job than with what I was trying to do. I resigned at the end of that year.'

'How did you feel about that?'

'That's the sort of question Josie would ask.'

'That's how we girls process the stuff that happens. We look at the feelings that come up when things happen. So how did you feel about leaving?'

'Honest answer. I was so angry I wanted to kill the bastard. Everything I had worked for in that school came to a stop, because he didn't have the balls to back me. Do you have any idea what it feels like to be betrayed by the people you're counting on for support?'

'Whoa! There's still plenty of anger there, and this happened how many years ago? Sounds like you're still holding on to that anger.'

'Everything's been coming out of the cellar since Josie died. I thought I'd dealt with it and moved on but after reading her journal, and reflecting on how I behaved at the time, and in the years since, I have to confess that all I did was stuff it into a black box and store it in the cellar.'

When they reached the shelter with a park bench, located above the beach not far from the house, they sat huddled together against the wind and looked at the sea through the drizzle.

'Want to explain this code of black boxes and cellars to me?'

'It's just my way of saying I've locked unprocessed stuff away. You know, putting it in boxes down in the cellar, where you don't have to look at it as you go about your daily life in the rooms above.'

'Why do you call them black boxes?'

'You know, like in computers. The black box is the part with all the mysterious bits in it. The one with the warning on the outside that says it's not to be opened by anyone except a qualified technician. Someone who understands how all the bits inside work.'

Marie laughed. 'You guys are so technical, even when analysing your own shit. I like it. Black boxes in the cellar. Makes perfect sense in a way.'

'Works for me.'

'I suppose you talked this all through with Josie.'

'Yeah, she was really supportive when I was making up my mind whether I'd stay or leave. I don't think I would have had the courage to do it, without her support and agreement. In the end, we decided it would be best if I had a break from schools.'

'You didn't consider going to another school?'

'I'd had enough of school politics at that point. I needed a break from all those closed minds.'

'Fair enough. How'd you end up at the bank?'

'Old scholars' network. I didn't know what I wanted to do. I mentioned to someone at an old scholar's function that I was looking for a change from teaching. Next thing you know, I'd been offered an opportunity to try out banking, you know, give it a go and see if I wanted to stay.'

'How long have you been at the bank now?'

'Eight, nearly nine, years.'

'Is it a better place to work?'

'It was different. I got to work in different sections until I found my niche in lending administration, doing the real back office stuff sorting out problems, mostly stuff ups by the bank. But you know, it didn't take long to work out that it wasn't all that much different to school. The games being played were the same. Power games by management and not rocking the boat by the crew.'

'How did you feel about that?'

'That's the bit where Josie started calling me Mr Misery in her journal. I was disappointed, to say the least, but instead of working through it, I pretended that it was okay. I didn't know how to admit that I'd made a mistake. I didn't know what else to do. I was too proud to go back to teaching.'

'So, you weren't open with Josie about how you were feeling. Is this where you stuffed this issue into one of your black boxes?'

'Think I might have had a whole stack of black boxes by then. One with the anger from feeling that I was forced to leave teaching, another with the disappointment of finding things were the same at the bank, another with my anger with myself for being such a coward.'

'You done any forgiveness work?'

'That sounds like a Frank Mulligan question.'

'Maybe, but have you?'

'What sort of forgiveness work are you talking about? I've given up that confession shit, if that's what you mean. Had enough of that forced down my throat as a boy.'

'Sounds like another black box.'

Paul looked out to sea. He couldn't believe what he was doing. He hadn't talked like this to anyone for a long time. He'd never confessed to anyone, except Josie, how he felt about his father.

'The forgiveness work I'm talking about is the work of forgiving yourself. It's funny how you think you need to forgive other people for the hurts they have caused you, until you find out that the only person you have to forgive is yourself, because no-one else can hurt you.'

'Where did you learn this stuff? Sounds like something I've read in a book or heard at some conference.'

'It's what saved me from going insane after Steve was killed. I'd love to help you come to the same understanding. It will give you peace.' She reached out and squeezed his hand. 'Let me help you.'

Paul turned and looked into two blue eyes, and felt himself falling into a depth he couldn't fathom.

'Why are you doing this for me?' His voice was barely above a whisper.

'Let's just say that I want to pass forward a kindness that was given to me, because I can see that you're hurting.'

'Thank you.'

Marie stood up. 'Come on, let's go and see what the kids are up to. They're another reason I want to help you. They are such lovely boys and they need you whole.'

They walked up the road to the house. The children were spread out over the lounge furniture watching the last minutes of their movie.

Over the next ten days, they shared their stories with each other and talked through issues as they came up. Mostly Paul talked through his issues with prompting from Marie. She knew how to ask the probing questions he didn't know how to ask himself. She also knew how to listen and reflect back without judging. For the first time, in a long time, he felt safe enough to expose his fears and secrets. They spent a long time talking about intimacy and what it meant in relationships. Paul finally understood why Josie would have turned to her friends for emotional support. He didn't feel good about himself and his failure to recognise what she really needed from him, but with Marie's help, he was able to start work on forgiving himself instead of stuffing the guilt into another black box.

They discussed his desire to return to teaching and what that might involve, seeing that he had been out of the classroom for eight years. In the end, Paul resolved to make some enquiries when he got home, so that he could start on any required refresher training as soon as possible. His intention was to enrol, resign from the bank and start applying for teaching positions.

Marie also reminded him that grieving was a journey he would have to walk. Sometimes the walking would be easy, sometimes hard, but the walking had to be done, if he wanted to come out the other end. She also reminded him that she had done it, and would be there for him for the hard parts.

There were days when he couldn't believe his luck to have found someone like Marie. There were days when she reminded him what a friend Matthew had been to Maggie, when her father had been killed. Sometimes he wondered who was directing his life, because he had no idea what was going on.

By the time they were ready to head back to the city, Paul and Marie had painted each other's portraits. Paul's portrait of

Marie was realistic and she was pleased with his effort, however, thanks to guidance from Matthew, her portrait of him was closer to a cartoon. Paul announced he would be having it framed as a reminder of the holiday.

On the final night of their stay in the beach house, Paul and Marie went for a walk along the beach while the children played cards in the kitchen.

'Do you know if they're making any progress on the case?' Paul asked as they approached the beach.

'My involvement with the investigation finished when it moved from Missing Persons to Homicide,' said Marie.

'Have you heard anything? That Inspector mate of yours hasn't exactly been forthcoming with news.'

'Carl's a good detective, one of the best. I've known him for years. He was Steve's closest mate on the force, when I met him. You have to be patient. These things take time. Sometimes it takes months or years before we get to the bottom of a murder. It's not like on those TV shows where everything gets solved in sixty minutes or less.'

'I guess you're right. I've never been involved with a real murder investigation before. I'm curious to find out what happened, of course, but I'm also worried about what the outcome of the investigation is going to mean for me and the boys, apart from more press coverage of a painful event in our lives?'

'I know what you mean. I knew who shot Steve, but that didn't make any difference really. It was still painful every time someone mentioned it.'

'The thing I'd like to know is not so much who shot her, but why? And how'd she get herself into a situation where someone wanted to kill her? That's the bit I don't understand. Who'd want to shoot her? Be terrible to find out it was a random act.'

'Don't go there. I have a friend who had to deal with that.

Not good.' Marie stopped and looked at the moon sitting on the horizon line. 'Do you think she might have been having an affair?'

'Who knows? I thought I knew her but now I'm not so sure. You know, you assume people are doing certain things, like going to work or going away shopping with a girlfriend for the weekend but really, what do you know about what's going on when the other person is out of your sight?'

'I guess that's what trust is all about.'

'Think my trust has been blown.'

'Do you really think so? I feel like you've trusted me.'

'Talking to you is different, you're a friend. What I mean is I don't think I'll be rushing into another relationship in a hurry.'

'I can understand that. Look at me, it's five years since Steve was killed, and I haven't been game enough to start another relationship. Plenty of blokes have tried but I'm sworn off policemen.' She laughed. 'You're the first bloke I've ever brought over here.'

'I'm touched. These couple of weeks have been really good for me. I think the kids have had a great time too. I'm sorry to be going home.'

'Me too. That's why I come here as often as I can. I love the sea. I can sit and listen to the sound of the waves rolling in and out for hours.'

'It's a great way to meditate.'

They found a large rock on the foreshore and sat listening to the waves, until it was time to go back to the house.

In the morning, they packed up, cleaned the house, and then set out in a two car convoy for the city.

In the weeks following the beach holiday, Paul resigned from the bank and enrolled in the master's course he had put off when he quit teaching. With the insurance payout and Josie's superannuation money in the bank, he decided he could afford to study full time and complete the masters in one year and then get himself back into the game.

As time marched on, the pain of Josie's death slowly receded into the background. It was always there but it had lost its edge. It was no longer a stake through his heart. It was more like a painful memory blended with all the joyous memories of the times they had shared as lovers.

Without any firm planning, he found himself seeing more and more of Marie Wood. She lived within walking distance of Whitbread Avenue. Maggie spent time at his house most nights after school, and they shared meals together. On weekends, when Marie wasn't working, they escaped to the beach house and spent hours walking along the beach, talking through their feelings and thoughts on everything under the sun.

Blissfully unaware of their destination, Paul and Marie journeyed on towards becoming lovers.

CHAPTER 18

ANNA WAS SITTING at a table by the window when Paul arrived at the coffee shop. She had chosen the Brasilia, on North Terrace, across from the entrance into City Park. He knew it had been her favourite spot for meeting Josie for coffee, before they set out on their walks in City Park. She waved as he entered. He walked over and kissed her on the cheek, without paying any attention to the young man, in dark glasses, sipping a coffee at the table opposite the entrance.

'What are you having?'

'A skinny latte.'

He walked over to the counter and ordered, before joining her at the table.

'It's been a while, Paul. How are you doing?'

'I thought I was doing okay, until I walked in here.' He worked on suppressing the tears threatening to escape, and failed. They started sliding silently down his cheeks and dropping on to the crisp white table cloth. Anna reached over and touched him on the hands. Here was the vulnerable Paul that Josie had so much wanted to see. She waited for him to compose himself.

The waitress arrived with the coffees. She was sensitive

enough to take her cue from Anna's eyes. Paul found his handkerchief and wiped his eyes as he regained control of his emotions.

'How are things with you? Been a bit strange not seeing you every weekend or hearing about what you two were planning to do next.'

'It hasn't been easy since Mark's death. Then, you already know what that's like.'

'You seem to be handling it better than me.'

'It's been six months. Besides, there are a few things about me and Mark that make it a bit different for me. For starters, our marriage was nothing like what you and Josie had going. Ours was more of a family arrangement.'

Paul looked at her. He had never heard anyone describe their marriage as an arrangement. He'd read about arranged marriages but thought they belonged to another place, another time.

'I thought those things went out with the Dark Ages, unless you were Hindu or something.'

'In a lot of ways, my family is still in the Dark Ages. At least, they behave as if they were. Did Josie ever tell you she had met my father?'

He shook his head. He was getting the firm impression that Josie had been a lot better at keeping secrets than he had thought. Maybe it was only his secrets she hadn't kept.

'Does the name, Max Spinosa, ring any bells for you? I know it didn't for Josie.'

He'd heard that name somewhere. He waited for his subconscious search engine to filter through his memory banks. A memory of a headline from a late-night news bulletin hit his screen. Oh, shit!

'Your father is the bloke who's supposedly the local mafia kingpin?' Paul's head was spinning. What had Josie got them into mixing with the daughter of a reputed mafia mobster?

'Don't look so worried, it's not true anyway. My father's just an old-fashioned businessman that played hard in his younger days.' Anna flashed a smile at him.

'The Spinosas and Rodrigos spent years trying to cut each other out of the fruit and veg market. I gather some of their methods, when I was little, were not what you'd call strictly legal. I think that's where the mafia rumours started. Anyway, after one incident, when someone got seriously hurt, they called a truce, and decided to join forces and corner the market, instead of trying to destroy each other. They arranged my marriage to Mark to seal the deal. Youngest Rodrigo son joined to youngest Spinosa daughter, me.'

'How did you feel about that?' Shit, what was he doing? He'd asked the sort of question Josie or Marie might have asked.

'I didn't have any say in it. I was eighteen. I did what my father said I had to do in those days. Besides, Mark was, well you know, handsome and I didn't know any better. I hadn't been allowed to have a boyfriend while I was at school. It all seemed so romantic and exciting to be getting married to someone my parents had chosen.

It was only later that I realised Mark and I were hostages. Anyway, it meant the families were in business together making money instead of losing money fighting each other. It made a lot of sense at the time, and the partnership has prospered for close on twenty years'

'So how did you find the marriage? I can't image what it must be like marrying someone you hardly know.'

'As it turned out, the marriage wasn't such a bad deal. Once we got over the awkward part, we decided to do like the royals. We put on a good show for all to see. We were the happy couple. We produced the required heirs, one for each side of the family, and came to our own arrangements. I didn't ask any questions about what he did or who he was having an affair with. He didn't ask if I was having any affairs. We had sex whenever he wanted to. I got to indulge my interests, go to uni and play the loving wife as required. We had access to money, servants and a nanny for the kids. All in all, we had the life lots of people dream about.'

'Sounds like one of those TV shows. So what went wrong? What was Mark into that got him killed? Hard to imagine that property management is that dangerous.'

'I don't know yet why he got killed, but that's not what I want to talk to you about. I've told you a bit about me and Mark so you could understand what I really want to tell you.'

That didn't sound encouraging. He decided to wait for her to continue.

'When I met Josie, she was such a refreshing change from the people I usually mixed with.' She stopped talking and looked at him. She didn't want to break his heart but she knew that, shortly, she would be doing just that.

There was something about the tone of her voice that caught his attention.

'You're trying to tell me something here that you don't think I'm going to like, aren't you?'

'Paul, you're a dear friend and a great father to your boys. I don't want to hurt you but you need to understand a few things. Josie thought the world of you, but she felt she didn't really know you anymore and that you didn't really care how she felt.'

'What do you mean? How can someone not know you after spending twenty years married to you?' He knew he was being defensive. Then he realised he was about to get hit with a brick.

'Can you tell me how Josie felt about getting old, or who her favourite writer was, or why she cried herself to sleep those nights you were up watching some current affairs program on TV?'

She watched his eyes. Josie had told her she would see the shutters come down whenever she was trying to get him to open up. His eyes started to well up again as he slowly shook his head. Something had clearly changed since Josie's death.

'I wish I'd found out about this intimacy stuff before this happened, and that I hadn't been such a coward when it came to facing my fears. I've missed out on so much and now there is no way I can ever get any of it back.' He fished out his handkerchief and blew his nose.

They sat quietly while they finished drinking their coffee.

'Come on, let's go for a walk.' Anna took his hand and led him outside into the sunshine. They crossed the street and headed into City Park. Paul didn't notice the young man leaving the coffee shop and following them, at a discrete distance, as they entered the park.

Anna hooked her arm through his and they walked among the trees, looking like lovers taking a stroll in the park. It was great just being out in the sunshine with another human being. Both of them were thinking of the last time they had strolled through the park, arm in arm, with Josie.

Paul was the first one to break the trance. One thing he had learnt, from being married to Josie, was that if a woman wanted you to know something, you were going to be told. It didn't matter whether you wanted to know or not. He decided he may as well get it over with.

'So what is it you want to tell me?'

'Let's go and sit down there.'

They walked along a path leading down to the lake. Anna steered him towards a bench under a tree just off the path. They sat down next to each other.

'Paul, I'll understand if you hate me after this.' She put her fingers to his lips. 'Josie and I were more than friends.' She stopped and looked down at her feet. Her voice was very soft when she continued. 'We started out friends sharing walks in this park and then weekends away. We ended up sharing more than hotel rooms.' She lifted her head and looked him in the eyes. 'We were sharing beds.'

'You were lovers?' He said it so softly she hardly heard it.

'Yes. I don't think I understood what love was until I met Josie. I certainly hadn't felt anything like it with Mark.'

'How? How does something like that happen?'

'It just happened. When we met, we were at a stage in life where we needed someone to confide in, someone to share our thoughts, our feelings and concerns with. You boys were off in your own worlds and didn't seem to care what was going on in ours.'

They sat looking at the lake for a long time. Finally, Paul turned to her and said, 'I'm sorry it wasn't me who was there for her when she needed someone. At least you were there. Why didn't she say anything?'

'What do you say? Honey, I've just had the most wonderful weekend having sex with Anna. I hope you don't mind.' She smiled at him coyly.

'No, not that. I mean, why didn't she tell me what she needed from me?' He sat thinking. Some of those pages in her journal started to take on a new significance. 'Maybe she did and I just didn't get it.' He looked at Anna. She looked fragile.

'There's something else I need to tell you. Mark found out and we had a big fight.'

'What do you mean? I thought you said you had an arrangement.'

'I discovered that there was a big difference between having a discreet affair and having that affair exposed, especially when Mark had his big macho ego to defend.'

Paul noticed that her face smiled but there was no twinkle in her eyes.

'Josie and I didn't become lovers straight away. It happened gradually, you know how it is. As we got to know each other we started feeling comfortable about being together. When we started the affair, we were really careful, but then we got more relaxed about being together, especially when we were away from home. Mark had as much idea about what we were doing as you did.'

Paul knew what he had known about the affair.

'So what happened?'

'Someone with access to a very good camera made sure he found out. Do you remember the Phantom of the Opera weekend, the last time Josie and I went away?'

He nodded.

'We stayed in a room on the sixteenth floor. Josie wanted to see the city lights, so we didn't bother closing the curtains. We should have. When I got home, Mark was waiting with a video and a spread of photos of us making love in that room.'

'Shit!'

'Is that all you can say? Mark had a lot more to say than that.'

'I might have too if I had been the one with the photos. So what happened after that?'

'Mark went ballistic. Claimed he didn't give a shit about the affair. Said that was fair enough. He'd been having affairs for years. But he was pissed off that someone had photographed me fucking my girlfriend. Said he could have lived with photos from an affair with a bloke, but having someone flashing around photos of his wife having sex with another woman. That was too much. It made him look like a complete idiot. He was worried about what it was going to cost him to stop them being published online.'

'So, he was more worried about his image than anything else? Did Josie know about the photos?'

'Of course! I told Josie straight away. She had to be warned in case she bumped into Mark. I didn't know what he'd do. I'd never seen him so angry. His big macho ego was all offended. I was worried sick. He was so impulsive when he was upset. Would have been better if I had been screwing you.' She looked at him and fluttered her eyelashes. 'Just kidding.'

'So why are you telling me this now?'

'A couple of reasons.' She paused, before saying, 'Mostly because I feel guilty. I'd like to ask you to forgive us.'

Paul reached over and placed his arm around her shoulders.

'What's there to forgive? I'm just as much at fault here as you or Josie. Come on, let's go down to the lake. It was one of Josie's favourite spots in the park.'

They stood and started walking towards the lake.

'I have to admit, Paul, I'm a little surprised at how you've taken this. I thought you'd be devastated or, at least, angry at me or Josie. Don't you feel betrayed? I feel like I've betrayed your friendship.'

'If Josie was still alive, I'd be angry. I'd probably be as pissed off as Mark was with my ego screaming abuse. I'd be worried about those photos becoming public knowledge. That would have been the end of Josie's teaching career.' He slowly shook his head from side to side. 'But not now. You get a different perspective on life when someone shoots your wife. Nothing's as devastating as having the person you love shot dead. This? This affair, you've just told me about, it's nothing more than an interesting footnote in the story of Josie's life. And if Josie loved you, then you're someone special.' He placed his arm around her shoulders and squeezed her close. They continued on down to the lake.

'What do you miss about her the most, Paul?

He gazed out over the still water of the lake. 'What I miss the most is her presence. Life is so empty without her. Every time I come home, the energy of her presence is no longer there. There's no trace of her. No bras hanging on door knobs. No knickers in the washing. No shoes under the bed. No handbag on the hall table. No laughter of her being on the phone with you. No-one to cuddle up to in bed. Nothing. She's gone. And what's worse, she's not coming back.'

'Are you getting any help or are you doing the usual bloke thing? You know, stuffing it all down. If you need someone to talk to, I could be that someone.'

Paul turned and looked at her. She looked as miserable as he felt. 'And what about you?'

'You didn't answer my question. Are you getting help or bottling it all up?'

'It's a strange world, Anna. The policewoman I filed the Missing Persons report with turned out to be the mother of Matti's girlfriend. She's been a great help. Her husband was killed a few years ago. Shot on the job, actually. She's taken an interest in my welfare having been there, so to speak. So, no, I'm not bottling it all up. She's a great listener, bit like you really. Think I've learnt a lot about intimacy from talking with her. I just didn't realise it was about self-disclosure and listening without wanting to fix things, and being prepared to feel things like sadness or failure. Still doesn't make it easy. What about you?'

'I'm talking to a therapist. Decided I needed some professional help. It's not like I could open up to any of my friends about something like this. It's taken me all this time to build up the courage to tell you. I was frightened I'd lose you too.'

'I need all the friends I can get, so I won't be casting you out, even if you are the evil, other woman.'

She turned to face him. 'When Mark was killed I got scared. I told my father the whole story. He didn't care that it was another woman. In fact, my old-fashioned father liked Josie and was happy that I had found a friend. He wasn't happy about the photos though, especially about the fact that someone had sent them to Mark. He thinks Mark's death is the opening shot of a war to put them out of business. He's afraid someone thinks he really is the local mafia, and they're planning on taking his patch.'

'Are you safe? Is it safe for you to be meeting me? Is it safe for me to be seen with you?'

'It was my father who asked me to meet with you. He thinks that maybe the same people killed Josie. He doesn't want anything to happen to you or your boys.' She looked at him. There was a cheeky twinkle in her eyes. 'It's safe to meet with me, as long as you don't do anything stupid.'

'What do you mean?'

'We are not alone. Dad's assigned a squad of body guards to watch over me since Mark was killed. He's worried that I might be the next target. I have one with me all the time. Didn't you see the hunk sitting in the coffee shop with the dark glasses? He's my new 'boyfriend'. And I have another one to drive my car.'

Paul looked around, and noticed a well-built young man standing in the shade of the trees about ten metres behind them.

'So, it's possible Josie got caught up in this war, simply because she knew you.'

'I don't know, Paul. I really don't know anything about how the real mafia works. My father and my father-in-law might be tough businessmen who drive a hard bargain, but they're not criminals, despite the TV news.'

'If I remember correctly, the case against your father was thrown out of court for lack of evidence.'

'That's right.' Anna looked at her watch. 'I have to run. I have to meet with some lawyers before I go home.' She hugged him and signalled to her body guard, who joined her as she walked back towards the North Terrace gate.

Paul watched them go. Then he returned to the bench they had been sitting on and put his head in his hands. He had a few things to process.

He couldn't believe Josie had betrayed him right under his nose. Who was this woman he had been living with and making love to? She didn't sound anything like the person he thought he knew as Josie. He'd heard of people leading double lives but this was ridiculous. Bloody hell, she was good at acting but this was sounding like an Oscar winning performance. She'd certainly fooled him. How many other people had she fooled?

How many other affairs had she had? Perhaps she was fucking Mark, as well as Anna, going by the comments he had read in her journal. Perhaps he shouldn't have been so quick to destroy them. Too late now, those secrets were lost.

God, what did it say about him? She obviously thought she could do whatever she liked? Why did she bother staying with him? Was it him or the boys that had kept her with him? Maybe she had just been using him as a front so she didn't have to come out. It wouldn't have been easy in their family circle. Now she'd left him to handle the embarrassment all on his own. He wondered how much of the story would get out.

Who could he trust? Had Anna told him the whole story? What if the mafia stuff was actually true? She didn't seem like a mafia wife, at least not when compared to the ones he'd seen in the movies. Where did you get to see real ones anyway? Maybe Anna didn't know the whole story either. What did any of this have to do with Josie being shot? Maybe nothing. Maybe Anna had just wanted to get their secret off her chest to appease her guilt, as she had told him.

He wondered if Anna had shared the secret with him so she could share the information with the police trying to solve the riddle of Mark's murder. He wondered why he hadn't asked her about that. Shock he supposed. He'd have to talk to the police about the affair and the photos.

He took his mobile phone out of his pocket and called Anna's number. She answered on the second ring.

'What's up, Paul? Missing me already?'

'Anna, is it okay to tell the police about the affair and the photos?'

'Sorry, did I forget to tell you that? I've told the police all about it. That's one of the reasons why I wanted to tell you, so it wouldn't be such a shock when they told you.'

'When did you tell them?'

'Just before I met with you. I'm really sorry I forgot to tell you.'

'I'm not surprised. Making the confession would have been hard enough.'

'Paul, let me know how it goes with the police. The lady sergeant was understanding, but the men looked at me as if I was a witch.'

'I'll call you. Take care.' He hung up.

Maybe she was a witch but she'd be a white witch. He didn't think there was a mean bone in her body. He checked the time display on his phone, before slipping it back into a pocket, and decided he'd better head for home. The boys would be back from school in a couple of hours. As he headed towards the gate his phone rang. He looked at the caller ID. It was Inspector West.

'Hello Inspector. I was just thinking about calling you.'

'You were?'

'Yes, I've just had an interesting conversation with Anna Rodrigo.'

'Where exactly are you, Mr Ford?'

'I'm in City Park, heading toward the North Terrace gate to catch the bus.'

'There's a coffee shop on the corner, Brasilia's, do you know it?'

'I had coffee there with Anna.'

'Wait there. I'm sending a patrol car to pick you up. We need to talk.'

'Yes, I suppose we do.'

Obviously, Anna had made an arrangement with the police to give her time to break the news to him. It occurred to him that this meeting was going to be embarrassing, but there was no way out of it now. He wondered if Marie had said anything to Inspector West, about what he had told her about his relationship with Josie or her journal. He hoped not. She had told him that she was not on the case. He needed someone to trust after what he had just learnt. Surely she wouldn't betray his confidences? He would have to talk to her after this meeting.

He called Marie while he was waiting and gave her a brief update. She volunteered to meet him after work. They decided they'd have tea together, as Maggie would already be with the boys. As he ended the call, a patrol car pulled into the curb. He walked over and slipped into the back seat.

'Hello, Mr Ford. Remember me?'

He looked into the smiling face of the young policewoman who had driven him home from the crime scene, the morning they had found Josie's body. 'Constable Priest, isn't it?'

'That's right. How are those boys of yours?'

'They're fine. They've got school to distract them.'

'And how about yourself? How are you coping?'

'Depends on the day.'

'I dare say it does. Now, if you'd like to buckle up, I'll take you to your meeting with Inspector West.' She turned her attention to the traffic and eased the car onto North Terrace.

Five minutes later she dropped him off at police headquarters, where Sergeant Strong met him in the car park and escorted him up to Inspector West's office.

CHAPTER 19

CARL WEST PREFERRED SOLVING crime riddles. He was not comfortable being baffled. As far as he was concerned, there was no such thing as a perfect crime. The perpetrator always left a clue that would undo him. All he had to do was find that clue. The trail in the Ford case hadn't gone far enough to reveal that clue just yet, but it would.

The extortion threat had come to nothing. B&A bank had not received any further calls with instructions about where to leave the money. The extortionist had vanished, if he had ever existed beyond someone's idea of a joke. The more he thought about it, the more he was convinced his initial intuitive response had been correct. The murderer had simply been playing games with him. No-one took cash in a bag these days. Even the amateurs knew about tracking devices. It was only the desperate that robbed cash, and they preferred convenience stores or bottle shops. There was too much security in banks.

It was certainly a challenge. The only evidence linking the victim to anyone was the eye witness account of a ten year old boy, possibly corroborated by some CCTV footage showing the victim walking up to the North Terrace gate of City Park, coupled with footage from a traffic camera located on North

Terrace showing a silver limousine in the vicinity of the gate at the same time. Circumstantial? Yes. But also interesting, when you considered the number plate on the limousine displayed the registration number of a delivery van.

Harry had spoken to the owner of that van. The number plate had not been stolen.

That same number plate was attached to a burnt-out van, found in the foothills a couple of days after the Ford murder, along with a 9 millimetre pistol that appeared to be the murder weapon. At least it marked shell casings identically to the casing found with the body. The burnt-out van was identified as being the van reported stolen from Spinosa Foods on the night of the murder.

The number plate connected the vehicles and the murder but didn't tell him much else, unless he could positively identify the limousine in the North Terrace footage. Despite examining photographs of the rear ends of fifty six silver Ford limousines of the same model, they hadn't been able to find the car. It might have been easier if their owners hadn't been so obsessed with keeping them spotless.

The only known link between a silver Ford limousine and the victim was the fact that Mark Rodrigo, the husband of her best friend, was chauffeured around in one. No-one they had spoken to had any idea why Josie Ford would have been picked up by a limousine at seven in the morning, when she was supposedly heading to work. Every other morning, it appeared, she caught the bus. He had CCTV footage showing her doing that every morning in the week before her murder.

Rodrigo and his driver had been killed before anyone could question them, and the number plates on their burnt-out limousine matched those of its registration details. There was no sign of the other number plate in the burnt-out vehicle, not even a plastic residue that might have suggested its presence.

They weren't making much progress on that case either, although Forensics had turned up one interesting detail on Rodrigo's limousine. It had been fitted out with high-end digital video cameras covering the passenger compartment. The cameras provided their feed to a computer in the trunk. Unfortunately, the fire had destroyed the hard drive, so there was no record of what had been recorded on the day of the shooting.

They had discovered another set of cameras linked to a computer in Rodrigo's apartment. The hard drive of that computer held some interesting video recordings. What was more intriguing was that an edited version of those recordings, along with some additional video taken in the back of the limousine, was found on the hard drive of a computer in Frank Kingston's apartment. The videos had been edited to remove all images of Mark Rodrigo. What you saw was a series of women doing a striptease routine, and then laying back on the bed in Mark's apartment or on a bench seat in the back of a limousine. After watching the recordings, Carl suspected the action had been choreographed. The women always got undressed in the same corner of the room or while perched on the same seat in the limousine. Some of them looked as if they were aware of being on camera.

Over several months, Bob Reid and his team had tracked down and interviewed a number of the women. Several were reluctant to talk. Some of them said it had been a one night fling with a rich playboy, who had plied them with drinks in a nightclub and taken them back to his apartment for sex. Others said they had had a brief affair with Mark, claimed he had an animal magnetism that was hard to resist, and complained about his short attention span. The girls that looked like they knew they were performing for the camera turned out to be high-end prostitutes, who had been paid for their performance both for the camera and in the bed.

A couple of them admitted to having had sex with Mark in the back of his limousine on the morning after, before he dropped them off home. Apparently, Mark knew some secluded spots around town, where he would enjoy, what the girls said he called his morning after hit, while his driver went for a walk.

It looked like Rodrigo and Kingston had been compiling soft porn videos based on Rodrigo's encounters. The question was why? Carl could understand a playboy compiling a record of his conquests, but this was more than that. Maybe they were supplying images for the porn market. He wondered what else they might have been up to. It wasn't like Rodrigo needed the money, and he had been paying Kingston good money as his driver. Neither of them appeared to be into drugs or gambling. Perhaps they were doing it just because they could. Maybe Rodrigo was a bored rich bloke playing games.

After the discovery of the images, Bob Reid had interviewed Anna Rodrigo again. She had admitted knowing about his playboy habits. In fact, she hadn't denied that story when Bob had interviewed her shortly after Mark's murder. However, she claimed to have no knowledge of the videos or of Frank Kingston's computing skills. She only knew him as one of Mark's drivers. She wasn't even aware of the cameras in the limousine.

That morning, Anna Rodrigo had come to see him and told him about her affair with Josie Ford, and about the video and pictures Mark had claimed someone had sent him. She didn't have a copy of the video but she had handed him copies of some compromising still shots, obviously taken with a high definition digital camera. She thought they had been taken from outside the room, but Carl wondered if the camera had been set up within the room. Someone had obviously gone to a lot of trouble to get the pictures, given that the room they had been taken in was on the sixteenth floor of a hotel.

Anna had agreed, when he'd said Mark's reaction was somewhat hypocritical, given his own affairs, but added that Mark was more concerned with his image than about what she and Josie had been doing. When he had asked if she thought Mark might have killed Josie, she had replied that he was capable of anything when he was angry, but she didn't think he'd hurt Josie. Then she'd laughed, and said he had been trying to get her to have sex with him ever since they'd met.

When he had asked her why she had come forward with this information now, she had replied that she had discussed what Inspector Reid had told her with her father. He had suggested that maybe Mark had videoed someone's daughter, girlfriend or wife, and sold the images to some porn site, and that someone had found out and was not impressed. According to her father, those videos attached a different message to the pictures of her and Josie. Someone was telling Mark they were on to him. Maybe that was why he was so pissed off about it. Maybe that someone had also killed Mark to make sure he wouldn't do it again.

Anna had also told him her father was so concerned about her safety that he had insisted she have a body guard. When Carl had asked where this body guard was, she had said she trusted him, so she'd left her body guard downstairs, in the lobby.

He had agreed to give her a couple of hours to break the news about the affair to Paul Ford, before he called him in to discuss the implications of what she had told him.

Once she had gone, and he had relayed her information on to Bob Reid, he realised that it didn't appear to help with the investigation into Josie's death, until he wondered whether Mark had used the pictures to blackmail Josie into having sex with him. It still didn't explain why he would have killed her, unless he really was a jealous husband, as well as a playboy. He'd met stranger men.

Nina escorted Paul Ford into Carl's office.

'Thanks for coming in, Mr Ford.'

The two men shook hands.

'Afternoon, Inspector. Thought we'd be talking after what Anna just told me.'

'Take a seat, Mr Ford.' Carl indicated the chair on the other side of his desk. 'Am I correct in assuming that what Anna Rodrigo told you came as a bit of a shock?'

'That's one way of putting it. I knew they were close but not that close.' Paul shook his head and sat down in the chair opposite the Inspector.

'Yeah, well they say the husband is usually the last one to find out,' said Nina.

'Bit late to do anything about it now, don't you think?' said Paul.

'Might be for you, Mr Ford, but it puts another spin on our investigation.'

'Meaning?'

'Did Anna Rodrigo tell you anything about her husband's, shall we say, hobby?'

'Hobby? She told me they had an open arrangement and that he'd had his share of affairs. Is that what you mean?'

'It went a bit further than that, I'm afraid. It appears Mark Rodrigo and Frank Kingston, the guy that drove his limo, were video recording all of Mark's sexual encounters with women, both in his apartment and in the limo. There was an edited version of the recordings on the hard drive of a computer in Kingston's apartment, which only has images of naked women.'

'What, like pornography or something?'

'Looks that way.'

Paul looked at Inspector West. He wasn't sure he understood where this was going. 'So, why would he be upset about someone taking photos of Anna and Josie?'

'That's a good question. Sort of makes the open arrangement a bit one sided, don't you think?'

'According to Anna, he was worried about how it would make him look if those photos got out.'

'How do you feel about those photos getting out?' said Nina.

Paul turned to face her. 'If I'd found out about them when Josie was still alive, I guess I'd have been livid. As it is, it's not doing anything for my ego knowing Josie was having an affair with her girlfriend. To be honest, it's pretty humiliating. If I'd found out about the photos before this, it would have been the end of our marriage, for sure.'

'What about now?' said Nina.

'It's still humiliating but it's all academic now, isn't it?' When she didn't reply, he continued, 'Besides, over the last few months, I've discovered a few things about myself, things I'm not proud of, that might explain why Josie turned to someone else for love. But as I said to Anna, now, now it's just an interesting bit of the story.'

'Do you want to see the photos?' asked Carl. 'Anna Rodrigo had copies of the stills.'

Paul shook his head. It was embarrassing enough knowing about them and having to talk about them, without having to let anybody see his reaction to seeing them.

'I'd prefer this didn't become public knowledge, if at all possible.' He looked up at the inspector.

'I'm sorry. I can't promise that. It all depends if they lead us anywhere.' Carl couldn't look him in the eyes. 'I'm wondering if these photos were a not too subtle message that someone sent to Mark Rodrigo, to let him know two could play his game. It's also possible the images have already been posted on some porn site.' Carl looked up from his desk.

'I see.' Paul could feel himself shrinking under an imagined spotlight as people became aware of her betrayal. He couldn't bear to think that photos of her having sex, with someone else, were out there somewhere in cyberspace for all those perverts to masturbate over.

'Could be a bit tricky for you if your sons, or any of their friends, are a little curious in that area,' said Nina.

The concern in her voice surprised him. He hadn't expected any sympathy from them. It was enough to bring him back into the present moment. 'I'll have to handle that one when it happens, Sergeant. Does anybody else know about the photos?'

'We've handed all the images from Frank Kingston's computer, and the photos Anna Rodrigo gave us, to the federal pornography task force. They will attempt to cross reference them with any of the sites they have under surveillance. We'll let you know if they get a match.'

'So where does that leave us?'

Carl shifted in his chair. He didn't want to go where his next line of thought was leading but felt he had no other choice. This would be the best time to ask, as he figured Mr Ford couldn't possibly feel any more humiliated than what he was feeling now. 'Given that Mark Rodrigo had the photos, I wonder if he might have used them to blackmail your wife into meeting him for sex. Anna Rodrigo told me that he had been trying to get your wife to have sex with him, before he found out about their affair.'

Paul's mind whispered the words from Josie's journal to him. He decided some secrets should stay hidden, as he didn't want to confess that he had destroyed the journals. 'Who knows?'

'She didn't say anything to you?'

'She hadn't told me about the affair with Anna. Why would she tell me about having sex with Mark to keep it quiet?' Paul sank back into his seat. 'What makes you think he might have blackmailed her?'

'The call log on your wife's mobile lists a call from Mark Rodrigo on the Friday morning before she was killed. It might explain why she was seen getting into a silver limo on the Monday and Tuesday mornings before her death.'

Carl waited while Paul absorbed the implications of his suggestion.

'Maybe, but it doesn't explain why she ended up dead. I mean, if Mark was blackmailing her for sex, why would he need to kill her? It's not like threatening to tell me, or anybody else for that matter, that she'd been screwing him in exchange for his silence would be much of a threat. Someone like Mark wouldn't have been afraid of anything I could have done.'

'It joins a few dots but yes, you're correct. It doesn't solve the puzzle.'

'Do you think Josie's murder might be linked to Mark's?'

'To be honest, Mr Ford, I don't know, but it's starting to look like a possibility.'

'Inspector, there's something else bothering me. When Anna was explaining her marriage to me, she told me she was Max Spinosa's daughter. Is there any truth to the stories about him being a mafia big shot?'

'Nothing we have been able to prove, and believe me, we've been looking into Spinosa and Rodrigo pretty closely since Mark's murder.'

'That's what Anna said, but I didn't know whether to believe her. It's not like it's something people would tell you, is it?'

'Doesn't mean they aren't. Just means that if they are, it's so well hidden we can't find it,' said Nina.

Carl put down his pen and came around to where Paul was sitting. 'Thanks for coming in, Mr Ford. I appreciate that this can't be easy to deal with.' He offered his hand to Paul.

Paul stood up and they shook hands. 'Life takes some interesting turns, don't you think, Inspector?'

'Yes, I suppose it does. I'll be in contact if anything turns up.'

Nina escorted Paul down to the lobby.

'I'm sorry you had to find out this way, Mr Ford.'

'Me too, Sergeant, me too.'

She watched him walk across the square to the bus stop and then went back up to the third floor, where Carl was waiting for her.

'Don't think I'd like to be him right now,' said Carl as she came back into his office.

'Me neither, Boss, especially if he has to explain the pictures to his kids.'

'What do you think the connection might be? If you'll excuse the pun, all I'm seeing here are dead ends.'

Nina sat in the chair Paul Ford had vacated.

'Harry's suggested to DI Reid that there might be a connection between the limo being torched and the images shot in the car. They're trying to identify every girl videoed in the back of that car. DI Reid reckons it's a long shot but Harry thinks it might be the missing link.'

'Who'd have believed there'd be so many girls willing to take their clothes off for a bloke like Rodrigo?'

'Do I detect a little envy?'

Carl looked up to make sure Harry was out of earshot. 'There's only one girl I want to take her clothes off for me.'

Nina laughed softly. 'I'll see if I can persuade her to come around and see you later.'

'You do that. Now get out there and help Harry before I forget where I am.'

'Yes, Boss.'

Carl watched her wiggle her bum as she walked over to join Harry at his computer. His fantasies were interrupted by the telephone on his desk. He answered the call and learnt that the images he had sent to the federal pornography task force, and the video of Anna Rodrigo and Josie Ford, were indeed available from a website hidden in the depths of the dark side of the World Wide Web. The site was so far removed from the cyberspace most people thought of as the web that he thought Paul Ford's sons were unlikely to ever see it.

He went out to where Nina and Harry were cross referencing photographs from the social pages to their collection of naked women.

'You might be on to something, Harry.'

'What makes you think that, Boss?'

'Appears we've helped the feds identify the source of some images on a porn site in the deep, dark recesses of the Internet, and they've returned the favour by letting us know that the video Mrs Rodrigo told us about is also available in cyberspace.'

Nina and Harry stopped what they were doing.

'We have a connection between some of our dots,' said Harry.

'Yes,' said Carl.

'I still have a problem here.' Nina looked at Carl, who raised an eyebrow inviting her to continue. 'If they published the video of his wife, wouldn't that have balanced the score with Rodrigo? So why did they kill him and Frank Kingston? Why kill Josie Ford?'

'Sounds like you're assuming the same party is behind both murders. What if they're not?'

'Harry, why do you have to make it more complicated?'

'Let's just say Harry wants to keep all possibilities on the table,' said Carl. 'Of course, it would be convenient if your assumption was correct. For now, I'll go with our resident sceptic. We have two killers to find.'

'So, what now?'

'Keep looking. One of those girls is connected to the someone who took the video of Anna and Josie.'

Carl left them to continue with their search and went to find Bob Reid to give him the news.

'Looks like we have more than the suggestion of a motive. How's Harry going with identifying those girls in the back of the limo?' said Bob after Carl's update.

'I think we might have to change tack and go public with the faces.'

'Yes, I was thinking the same,' said Bob.

'Okay, I'll get Harry to compile a set of images for you to release to the media.'

'Thanks.'

Carl returned to the operations room.

'Harry, time to move this up a notch. How many unidentified girls have we got?'

'Eight.'

'Prepare a set of images for DI Reid. Digital and hard copy. He's going public. And, Harry, faces only, we want people to come forward not hide in shame.'

'That shouldn't be a problem, Boss,' said Harry. 'Thanks to Frank Kingston's editing skills, I should have what you want in about twenty minutes.'

Carl called Paul Ford and Anna Rodrigo, and gave them the news that the pictures were on the Internet. Although he stressed that they were on a porn site that his sons and their mates would probably never come across, the tone of Paul's response conveyed that he was not happy with the turn of events. Anna Rodrigo thanked him for his call in a tone that suggested she was beyond caring if the pictures were posted all over the Internet.

Three days later, Inspector Reid received a call from the office manager of Rodrigo Properties, who told him they had discovered what appeared to be a secret office, located in an apartment that the books showed as being leased to a non-existent employee of Spinosa Foods. When he added that the apartment contained several computers, and material that indicated it had been used by Mark Rodrigo and Frank Kingston, Inspector Reid didn't have to be asked twice to come and take a look.

The highly skilled technicians from Organised Crime needed two days to crack the encryption locks on the computers. It took them a further day, to open enough files to determine that the computers had been used to run a sophisticated identity theft operation. Once they were in though, it didn't take them long to realise that, although no-one had logged onto any of the computers since the morning of the day Mark Rodrigo and Frank Kingston had been shot, they had been compromised by an intrusion over the Internet that had successfully penetrated their heavily fortified firewall a few days after the murders.

By the time the computers had yielded their secrets, Inspector Reid knew who the remaining eight naked beauties were.

Nina and Harry scored the job of interviewing them and working out the web of their relationships. The interview process was very uncomfortable for the women, once they had been shown their video recording and been informed that it was available from a pay for view service on the Internet. They had interviewed six women before they got a breakthrough.

Georgina Okawani, a twenty two year old bank teller with physical assets other women paid plastic surgeons good money for, told them she had had a six week affair with Mark. He had taken her to some fancy nightclubs, places she couldn't afford on a bank teller's salary, and bought her some really nice clothes to take off in front of him in his apartment in the city. On the nights she slept over, he would drive her home in the morning. It was on one of those mornings they'd had sex in the back of his limousine. Shortly after that, he'd ended the affair.

At the time, she hadn't known he was married. She had been under the impression that he was a rich playboy who liked being seen with younger women. She had seen him with other young women before she had met him. She said the affair had been a lot of fun. She'd certainly had a good time while it lasted.

Then her sister's boyfriend, who worked in some surveillance job, wanted to know who she'd been screwing in the back of a limousine. When she had asked him how he knew about that, he told her that he had seen a video on the Internet of her taking her clothes off and having sex with some guy in a limo.

When he had shown her the video he had downloaded from the Internet, she realised it had to be Mark Rodrigo. A couple of days later he had shown her a video of her taking her clothes off in Mark's apartment. Mark wasn't in that video but she recognised the clothes and the furniture, and besides, she hadn't done that sort of thing for anybody else. It was sort of a fetish he had. He had insisted she do a strip tease routine for him before they had sex. Well, you do anything for a guy who buys you expensive stuff, and who's good in bed, don't you?

She hadn't known what to do. After all, it had been consensual sex. It was the videoing of it that she wasn't happy about. First they thought she should get a lawyer, but Mark was really rich, so her sister's boyfriend suggested that it might be easier to get some serious money out of him in return for not pursuing the matter.

When Nina asked how Mark had responded to their request, she told them that, initially, he hadn't taken them seriously. After a little further prompting from Nina, Georgina explained that things got interesting when her sister's boyfriend discovered that Mark's wife was staying in a hotel, that his company did the security for, with another woman. He'd set up some surveillance cameras in their room when he realised they were more than friends, and couldn't believe his luck when they had sex with the lights on. He'd captured some very compromising images.

Armed with their images, they had started the negotiations with Mark again. He had paid them an initial instalment of ten thousand dollars but claimed he couldn't do anything about the images on the Internet. So John, her sister's boyfriend, had posted the images on the same site. Then someone shot the other woman and Mark was killed before they could conclude the negotiations. Scared shitless by the shootings, they had decided their best option was silence.

Inspector Reid paid Georgina's sister's boyfriend a visit. He wasn't happy that Georgina had revealed his activities but agreed to talk, once Inspector Reid gave him the choice of cooperating or facing a string of charges. Although the inspector didn't think John or Georgina had any part in the murders, he was interested in finding out how John had gone about getting access to the images in the first place, and how he had managed to sell his images to a porn site.

John explained how he got bored watching surveillance screens night after night and had started surfing the net to entertain himself. He'd strayed into a couple of porn sites and was surprised to see his girlfriend's younger sister taking her clothes off, and having sex, in the back of a limousine. At first, he'd thought it was probably a look alike, but when he had shown her the video, she had turned white and collapsed onto the floor of his apartment in tears.

After she told him about her affair with Mark, they decided to see if they could get some money out of him. John had called Mark and threatened to take him to court for breach of privacy unless he paid up, but Mark had laughed at him. It was only after he had sent Mark a copy of the images he had, of his wife and her girlfriend, that Mark had agreed to do a deal. And getting those pictures had been a gift from the gods.

Sent interstate to fill in while someone took his holidays, he couldn't believe his luck when Mark's wife had shown up with her girlfriend. They had been all over each other in the hotel lobby, like a couple of schoolgirls.

He'd simply slipped into their room, while they were out on the town, and set up some cameras linked wirelessly to the hotel's security system. Ten minute job. Then, he had erased his image from the security video covering the corridor leading to their room. Piece of cake when you were the one in charge of the equipment.

When Inspector Reid asked how he knew the woman in the hotel was Mark's wife, John explained that after Mark's initial response to their threat he'd decided to do a bit of research, to see if Mark had any weak spots he could exploit. That's when he found out he was married. He'd stalked his wife and taken photos but he hadn't been able to get anything to use against Mark, until she turned up at that hotel with her girlfriend.

Anyway, Mark had handed over ten thousand dollars in exchange for an undertaking not to pass the photos to the media. Negotiations had broken down when Mark wouldn't agree to have Georgina's pictures taken down from the Internet. Mark had claimed that he didn't control the site; he was just a supplier of images. John had decided that two could play that game, so he had sold his video to the same porn site. Unfortunately, Mark had been killed before he could rub his face in it. And when he discovered that the other woman in the video had also been killed, he got scared and talked Georgina into keeping quiet about the whole affair.

When Inspector Reid asked him how he had gone about

selling his video, John told him that it was like uploading a video to any other photo or video sharing site. You became a member, set up an account, uploaded your images, they did a quality assessment, provided you with a rating and, when you accepted the rating, they made a monthly royalty payment to your nominated account, using some innocuous sounding business name like Marty Smith Publishing.

At the end of the interview, Inspector Reid asked John where he had been at the time of Mark Rodrigo's murder. Fortunately for John, he told the inspector what he had already confirmed with John's employer - he had been at work. Before leaving, Inspector Reid advised John not to share the pictures with anybody else, otherwise he'd be back with an arrest warrant.

Back in the operations room, the inspectors concluded that although the video material was titillating, it didn't seem to be directly linked to the murders. John and Georgina were the only ones to admit knowing the images from Rodrigo's recordings were on the Internet, and to have done something about it. They still had the ten thousand dollars, and they both had alibis for the time of the murders of Mark Rodrigo and Frank Kingston. There appeared to be no connection between them and Josie Ford.

They would have to wait and see what Organised Crime came up with.

Carl was frustrated. He hated dead ends.

CHAPTER 20

PAUL HAD JUST GOTTEN off the bus, when Inspector West called to let him know that the video of Anna and Josie was available, from a pay for view porn site, on what the inspector called the dark side of the Internet. Although the inspector claimed that it was unlikely that the boys or their mates would ever stumble across the images, Paul was not reassured.

As Paul was approaching the house, his mobile rang again.

'Paul, it's Marie. Carl West just rang me. Are you alright?'

'Not really.'

'Where are you?'

'I'm walking up the driveway, at home.'

'Put the kettle on. I'm on my way.'

'Thanks.'

A picture of a guardian angel popped into Paul's mind. The picture was from his childhood. He hadn't thought of guardian angels for a long time. He wasn't even sure he believed in them anymore, but it looked like there might be some around. Who would have guessed that Inspector West was a guardian angel? He could entertain the thought of Marie being a guardian angel. But Inspector West? That was a stretch too far.

Marie arrived as the water was boiling. He made her a cup of tea while his coffee brewed in the percolator. Paul looked at the clock as they sat down at a corner of the kitchen table. They had about half an hour, before the children would arrive home from their after-school activities.

'How much did he tell you?'

'He told me about the affair, the pictures, and the fact that they're available on the Internet. Is there anything else?'

'No, that's pretty much it.'

'Bit of a shock, isn't it?'

Paul leant back in his chair and considered the flower pattern on the rim of his coffee cup, one of a set Josie had bought him on one of her trips away with Anna.

'I can understand the friendship she had with Anna. As I've told you before, I wasn't exactly the most supportive of husbands when it came to the emotional stuff. In a way, I suppose I blame myself.'

'I can understand why you'd want to do that but remember, there are always two sides to a story. Josie made some choices too.'

'That might be true but to be honest, I'm not feeling very good about myself right now. I feel like I've let myself down. If I'd been more attentive, maybe none of this would have happened. Now it's all over the Internet.' Paul drained his coffee. 'See this cup? She bought this for me on one of those weekends she spent away with Anna.'

Marie watched as he slowly put the cup down onto its saucer. She'd half expected him to drop it onto the floor. 'What are you upset about? That she had the affair or that the pictures are on the Internet?'

'You know, I told Anna that the affair was just an interesting footnote in Josie's story, and I suppose at a rational, intellectual level, it is. But deep inside, I can feel that black hole opening up again. I don't know whether I'll be able to get out again, if I fall back in there. And then there's all the shame and embarrassment

I'll have to face if the boys, or heaven forbid, anybody else finds out.'

Marie reached over and held his hands. 'You don't have to fall back into that black hole. I'll support you no matter what comes up, but I want you to promise that you'll keep talking to me.'

'I don't know what I'd do without you. You know, when you called earlier, a picture of a guardian angel popped into my mind. Is that what you are?'

'If that's what you need.'

'Tell you what though, I'm finding it a bit hard to see Inspector West as a guardian angel. Why do you think he called you?'

'I've known Carl for a long time. Underneath that gruff exterior there's a big softy in there. He knows we've become friends, so he knew who to call to make sure you got looked after.' She squeezed his hands.

'I hadn't expected it of him. I suppose we forget they're people too. We just see them as the police, until we get to know them.'

'I hope you don't see me as just the police,' said Marie looking him in the eyes.

'No. Not even in your uniform.' He smiled one of those smiles his mother had warned her about.

She leant across the corner of the table and kissed him gently on the lips. 'Be careful where you flash that smile, it could get you into trouble.'

'Thanks for the advice, but I think I'm already in trouble.'

'Well, before you get into too much more, just remember that the kids will be here soon.'

'Speaking of the kids, how am I going to stop them finding out about this? By the way, what's this dark side of the Internet the inspector keeps going on about?'

'It's a part of the Internet used by organised crime, and

anybody else who wants to conduct their affairs anonymously. Basically, from what Carl explained to me, it's a maze of secretive networks you have to be invited to join, but there are ways of breaking into the maze. The feds have a task force tracking the users of child pornography sites, and our organised crime unit is always poking around in there as well. That's how we located the photos.'

'So, it's not likely the boys are going to see the pictures?'

'I hope so, but Carl doesn't know how the pictures got there yet. They could be released some other way, so you'd better be prepared just in case.'

Paul put his head in his hands and stared at the table. 'So, is it better to just tell them everything or wait until they find out? How will they feel if they find out and I haven't told them?'

'Whatever you decide, I don't think rushing into it is a good idea. I think you should let yourself come to terms with it first, don't you? Besides, it looks like the pictures have been on the Internet for months, and nobody we know has noticed. They might never see them.'

They were interrupted by the sound of a key operating the lock in the front door, followed by Maggie and the boys coming in from school. Matthew and Maggie entered the kitchen. Luke disappeared up the corridor. They heard the bang of his door shutting behind him.

'Hi Mum, what are you doing here? Hi, Mr Ford.' Maggie breezed in and gave them both a hug.

'Hello, Mrs Wood. Probably just as well you're here.' Matthew looked briefly at his father, and then looked towards the door opening to the corridor behind him. 'Dad, we've got a problem.'

Paul looked in the direction of Luke's room and then at Matthew, who was looking at the floor. 'What sort of problem?'

Matthew looked at Maggie. 'Some boys at school have been saying some terrible things to Luke about Mum.' Matthew stopped talking, sat down next to Marie and started crying. It took him several minutes to get himself sufficiently under control before he said, 'Maggie, you better tell them.'

Paul and Marie looked at Maggie. She was looking at the floor. Finally, she looked up.

'They're saying they've seen some pictures on the Internet, not very nice pictures, and they've been saying stupid things.'

Paul held up his hand to signal that she didn't need to say anymore. He looked at Marie. 'Looks like I'm not going to get that time to let this sink in.'

'Apparently not. How do you want to handle this?'

'You know about the pictures?' said Matthew, looking from Paul to Marie.

'That's why I'm here, Matti. We found out about them today. That's what we were talking about before you got home from school.'

'Guess we may as well tell them everything, then. I'll go and get Luke.' Paul went up to Luke's room to get him. It was a full five minutes before he reappeared with a red eyed Luke.

They sat around the table, with Luke between Paul and Marie, and Maggie practically in Matti's lap.

The inside of Paul's mouth felt like the bottom of a dam at the end of a ten year drought. 'This is not going to be easy and I might need some help.'

'Why don't you let me start? I have some experience explaining sticky issues.'

Paul nodded. Guardian angel, indeed.

Marie looked at each of the boys in turn. 'Your Dad's had a

bit of a rude shock today. First, he found out that your Mum had been having an affair.'

'Is that true, Dad?' asked Luke.

'Afraid so.'

'Who with?' asked Matthew.

'Mrs Rodrigo,' said Luke, almost to himself but loud enough for the others to hear.

'How'd you know that?' said Paul. He looked at Marie in disbelief and back again to Luke. 'How did you know that?'

Luke looked at his hands. 'It wasn't hard to work out. They spent lots of time together, and the boys said the pictures were of Mum and another woman. Who else would it be?'

'Yes, well that brings us to shock number two,' said Marie. 'We also found out that someone had taken, what we call compromising photographs, of your Mum and Mrs Rodrigo, and posted them on the Internet.'

'So much for the inspector's dark side of the Internet,' muttered Paul.

'What did you say, Dad?' asked Matthew.

'We thought the pictures had been posted to a pay for view pornography website, so I'm surprised your friends at school know about them,' said Marie.

'They're not my friends,' said Luke. 'If they'd been my friends they wouldn't have said what they said about Mum. Anyway, it was Robertson's big brother who found the pictures. He's an idiot. He was always in trouble when he was at school. He was the one that got busted selling drugs to the year twelves, a couple of years ago.'

'I remember him,' said Marie. 'Nasty piece of work.'

'So, how did this all happen?' asked Matthew. 'I thought you and Mum were really in love.'

'So did I,' said Paul.

'How did you find out?' asked Luke.

'I had coffee with Mrs Rodrigo today. She told me about the affair and the photographs. None of us knew the photos were on the Internet, until Inspector West found out this afternoon.'

'Who took the photos?' asked Maggie.

'We don't know that yet, but we'll find out,' said Marie.

'Has this got anything to do with Mum getting shot?' asked Luke.

'We don't know that either. Apparently, Inspector West found out about the photos as part of the investigation into Mr Rodrigo's murder,' said Marie.

'This is getting messy, Mum. I wonder if the two murders are connected.'

'Leave the detective work to Carl, honey.'

'So, how do you feel about this, Dad?' asked Matthew.

'I'm not sure I really know yet. It's all pretty embarrassing having to tell you guys. I certainly had no idea she was having an affair.'

'How do you feel about it, now that you know?' Marie looked at Matthew and then Luke.

'Knowing about those photos on the Internet makes me sick. I'm so ashamed. Why did she have to do that?' Luke glared at his father. 'What did you do to her?'

'It's not what I did to her, it's more what I didn't do for her.'

'Like what?'

'Like not listening or not talking to her about how I was feeling about things.'

Luke looked at him with a blank stare. 'I don't get it.'

'It means I wasn't there for her when she needed me. Anna was. I guess one thing led to another. What can I say? I'm really sorry it happened.'

'She had me fooled. I thought she really was in love with you, Dad,' said Matthew.

'Maybe she was. Maybe being in love with me wasn't

enough.' Paul stopped talking. The river of tears that had been building up behind his eyes escaped from confinement. He dropped his head into his arms on the table and sobbed. Inside his head, the picture of their happy marriage was fading into nothingness.

Marie signalled to the children to withdraw. She wrapped her arms around him as Maggie and the boys went up to Matthew's room. Gently, she coaxed him onto his feet and led him out to the study, where she guided him into his meditation chair. She knelt on the floor next to him and held his hands.

Paul slowly came to himself. 'I feel such a failure. I feel like I've let them down just like I let her down.' He stifled the tears that wanted to follow those words.

Marie handed him the box of tissues from the desk. He blew his nose.

'It doesn't mean you're a bad person. We all make mistakes. That doesn't make us failures, but I understand why you'd feel that way. It's okay to feel that way. Don't try and stuff that feeling. You don't want any more of those black boxes you keep telling me about, do you?'

'No, I have enough of them.'

'Okay, sit here and feel what you need to feel, and process what comes up. Write it in your journal. We can talk about it when you're ready, if you like. I'll go and talk to the boys, and get tea organised.' She kissed him on the cheek.

He didn't know what he had done to call her into his life. 'You sure you're not an angel?'

She had a smile that was as deadly as his own.

'No.' She tousled his hair, and left him to feel the feelings he needed to feel.

When Marie closed the door on her way out of the study, Paul took several slow, deep breaths, and tuned in to that part of his mind that wanted him to fall into despair. He could hear a voice inside his head, a voice that sounded like his voice, telling him how stupid he had been to have placed his trust in someone like Josie. Look at how she had treated him? She'd betrayed him, and, to make it worse, she had been so careless there were now pornographic photographs of her spread all over the Internet. She'd humiliated him, shamed him publicly, made him look a fool. She must have thought he was worthless to do something like that. What did it tell the world about him? What were people going to think of him now? What did his own sons think of him? What had she done to her sons?

He could feel himself sinking into a dark vortex. Then, something arose from deep within his being, something powerful, something resisting the vortex. He stood up and looked at his reflection in the monitor on the desk. A fragment of dialogue from a movie about the workings of the ego, which Frank Mulligan had related to him, burst into his awareness. He looked his reflection in the eyes and said the line out loud.

'I'm on to you!'

He found his journal and started writing.

I might have listened to you before but you'll destroy me if I listen to you now. I have a choice. The power of choice is mine and I choose not to listen to you. What you're saying is not true. My value is not determined by what other people think. I might have made a few mistakes - that doesn't mean I'm worthless. It simply means I've given myself some learning opportunities. If Josie chose to be in love with Anna as well as me, who am I to judge her? It's only betrayal if I think I owned her or that she was answerable solely to me. What sort of relationship is that where you think you own the other person or that the other person only exists to serve your needs?

It's hardly her fault if some dickhead took photos and posted them online. It's not like she asked for the photos to be taken. Who'd expect to be photographed in a room on the sixteenth floor? So give me a break. Stop talking crap!!!!

People can think what they like. Pretty obvious that Marie doesn't think any less of me because this happened. The relationship I had with Josie was a loving relationship. It might not have been prefect but it was loving. Just because she was having a relationship with Anna as well doesn't mean she had stopped loving me. It just means she was sharing a part of herself with Anna that she was not sharing with me. Why do you want to make such a big deal out of it? Feeling sorry for myself isn't going to change anything. All that will do is make me feel miserable. I have had enough of your misery, thanks!

Sometimes shit happens and you just have to deal with it. This is one of those times. I can choose how I want to feel about it. If other people have a problem with it, well that's their problem. I don't have any control over what other people choose to think. I can't change any of what's happened either, but I can choose how I will respond to it. Sure it's upsetting and embarrassing but let's be honest, it's not the end of life as we know it!

What sort of example will I be giving the boys if I fall apart? I want them to know that they are not defined by the things that happen, but rather by the way they choose to respond to the things that happen. They've done pretty well with the way they have responded to Josie's death. I'm sure they will survive this as well with my support; they need me to be strong. No, I choose to see it as a neutral event. It happened. It doesn't have any power over me unless I choose to invest power in judging it, or interpreting it as some form of attack on my person.

He closed the journal and let it drop to the floor. He sank back into the chair and closed his eyes, and became aware of the rapid beating of his heart and the shallowness of his breathing.

Adrenalin was rushing through his system. It felt like he had just run a hundred metres in nine seconds. He laughed to himself. He had pushed through a barrier. It felt good.

He allowed his breathing to slow and focused on taking deeper breaths. His heartbeat slowed to normal and then gradually dropped to the level he experienced during meditation. He spent the next half hour in deep, silent meditation. His ego was too afraid to disturb him.

As he opened his eyes, the sounds of meal making coming from the kitchen entered his awareness. The river of life may have swept Josie away downstream, but it had also delivered a guardian angel into his life. Before getting up, he offered a silent prayer of gratitude. Then he went out to love his boys and the new women in his life.

CHAPTER 21

Paul walked into a kitchen enveloped in the aromas of freshly cooked food. Marie had roasted the chicken he had taken from the freezer that morning, and left in the fridge to thaw. She'd found enough potatoes and onions in the pantry, and frozen vegetables in the freezer, to make a meal for five. She'd even made gravy. That was something he'd have to learn.

She looked up from the bench as he came into the kitchen. 'How are you feeling?'

He walked over to where she was standing and hugged her. 'I think I've had a break through.'

'Oh.' She stopped cutting up the chicken and turned to face him.

'Yes, I felt myself being dragged into that black hole I was telling you about, being drawn in by a voice telling me how worthless I was, and how hurt I should be feeling, blah blah blah. Then, a line from a story Frank told me, about a guy fighting with his ego in some movie he had seen, popped into my mind from somewhere, and I realised I had a choice. I didn't have to listen to that voice. My value isn't determined by what happens to me. I can choose to see what's happened anyway I want. I'm choosing love over fear.'

He stood there beaming with his arms around her.

'What movie was that? I think I might want to watch it, if one line from it can do this to you.' She pushed him out to arm's length, so she could get a better look at him. 'I was fully expecting to be putting you into bed with a hot water bottle, before I went home tonight.'

'I can't remember the name of the movie, but the punch line was the guy telling his ego that he was on to it, and that's what I did.'

She stroked his face. 'That's wonderful. Have you thought about what you're going to say to the boys?'

'It will come out once I start talking.' He knew thinking about it would make it harder. Best just to start and let the words flow.

'I've had a talk with them. They're lovely boys. You and Josie have done a marvellous job with how you brought them up.'

'Thank you.'

'No need to thank me.' She turned back to the chicken. 'Anyway, we talked about remembering the mother they knew. The whole affair thing has come as a bit of a shock to them. They've seen a side of their mother they hadn't known about.' She paused to gather her thoughts. 'Luke's pretty upset about the way the other boys talked about the pictures. He wouldn't repeat the names they used, but I think we can imagine the sort of language adolescent boys would resort to. But he told me, she's still his mother no matter what she did.'

'What about Matthew? He's the one I worry about. He doesn't let much out.'

'Maybe not to you, but you forget I have a secret weapon.'

'What, you're doing the guardian angel trick on him as well?'

'No, I have my apprentice on the job. Between the two of us,' she winked at him, 'I think we might know every thought and feeling Matti has. He's a very open book in the right hands.'

'Sounds like something Josie would have said.'

'No doubt.'

'So what's the prognosis?'

'He's worried about you. He's already told me that he knows he doesn't have to buy into any of the other stuff. He knows that his mother loved him and still does. Has he told you about his dreams?'

'Not recently.'

'He says she comes to him in his dreams nearly every night, so he knows she's okay. What he's worried about is whether you're going to be okay.'

'Sounds like I've had my breakthrough in the nick of time.'

There he was worrying about how they were going to cope and what were they doing? Worrying about him as if they were the adults and he was the child.

'Why don't you go and call them down for tea, and we can celebrate your insight together.' She turned him around, pointed him towards the door and gave him a gentle push. 'Don't be long otherwise this will get cold.'

When he opened the door to Matthew's room, Paul discovered the boys showing Maggie through one of their photo albums. He was surprised to see that it was the album holding the photographs of Josie's life that had formed the basis of the presentation used at her funeral.

'What's going on here?'

'We're remembering Mum the way we want to remember her,' said Luke.

'Can I join in?'

Paul sat on Matthew's bed and looked at the pictures as Matthew and Luke told Maggie the stories behind the photos. After about five minutes Marie appeared in the doorway.

'I thought you'd come up here to call them down for tea?'

'Sorry, we were sharing a precious moment.' Paul stood up. 'Come on guys, let's go eat.'

They took the album to the kitchen with them.

Marie served the food and Paul started the meal with a prayer, simply letting the words flow as they came to him.

'Father, today's been a pretty tough day. We found out some things we'd rather not know. Some of us have heard others say hateful things about our mother. We know their words have no power unless we give them power. We choose to remember Josie the way we want to remember her, as a loving mother and a loving wife. She may have had a life outside this house, that we didn't know about, but that doesn't change the life she had here with us.

We thank you for reminding us that we have the power to choose how we see things, to choose how we interpret events and how we will respond. We thank you for sending Marie and Maggie into our lives, and we thank you for this meal we are about to share. Amen'

'Amen.'

'That was a good prayer, Dad,' said Matthew. 'Sounds like you're going to be alright.'

Paul looked at his older son. 'Yes, Matti, I've decided to be grateful for the life we had and for the love we shared. We all make mistakes, but we can choose to forgive any imagined hurts.'

For the next few minutes they concentrated on eating.

'This chicken is good.' Paul put down his utensils.

'Cooked with TLC, what else would you expect?' Marie's smile spread across her face.

Paul turned his attention to his sons. 'So, how are you guys feeling now you've had some time to think about today's news?'

'I'm sorry I blamed you before,' said Luke.

'That's alright. I wanted to blame me too, but I realised that would only make me feel worse.'

Matthew put down his fork. 'It's a bit weird really. Who'd have thought Mum was a lesbian?'

'That's just another label, Matti,' said Marie. 'You don't have to use it.'

'I guess you're right. I'd rather think of her as Mum. I don't want to think of her as someone who had an affair.'

'Maybe it was an adventure or a game more than an affair. You know how she liked to play games and act out different roles,' said Paul.

'Yeah, right, Dad,' said Matthew.

Paul shrugged his shoulders. 'I can think about it anyway I choose, and so can you.'

'Okay. Point taken,' said Matthew.

'What about the photos, Dad? What are we supposed to say about the photos?' asked Luke.

'We could say she auditioned for a movie, and someone stole the film and released it on the Internet to embarrass her,' said Matthew.

Paul looked at Marie, who was shaking her head. Matthew had been quick on the uptake of his suggestion.

'Not sure that would go down with your grandparents,' said Maggie.

'What are you going to say if they find out?' asked Luke.

'That's a good question, Luke. I'd rather they didn't find out but if they do, I guess I'll tell them the truth. In the end that will be easier than making up a story.'

The conversation stopped as they finished eating the chicken and vegetables.

'Anyone for sweets? There's ice cream and sliced peaches,' said Marie.

Everyone at the table raised a hand. 'I'll take that as a yes all round, then. Matti, can you get the ice cream out of the freezer, please? And, Luke, can you open the peaches, please?' She turned to Paul, who was sitting next to her, 'can you find the dessert plates for me?'

'Don't I get a please?'

Marie squeezed his knee and mouthed, 'Please.' Then she stood up and said, 'Maggie, can you help me pack the dishes into the dishwasher, please?'

They moved to their assigned tasks and then regrouped for ice cream and peaches.

'Dad, there's something else I want to ask you,' said Luke.

'And what might that be?

'What's going on with you and Mrs Wood?'

Paul looked at Marie. 'We're becoming friends. What would you say, Marie?'

'Your father thinks I'm his guardian angel, and maybe I am.'

'I think he's lucky to have you for his guardian angel.' Luke gave her one of those smiles that revealed his heart, just the way his father smiled. 'Can you be my guardian angel, too?

'Yes, of course, darling.' She tousled his hair, blond like his mother's, with her hand. 'For as long as you need me.'

Matthew shrugged his shoulders. He knew where his guardian angel was - sitting next to him eating his ice cream.

When they finished eating, the young ones went to do their homework. Life might give them the occasional big issue to deal with but the demands of school were a constant in their lives. They all had assignments due by the end of the week.

Paul and Marie sat at the kitchen table drinking coffee.

'So, what is going on between us?' Marie asked him.

'Something's happening. I think I might be falling in love

with you. I know I like being with you. What do you think is going on?'

'Much the same but I think we need to go slowly. It's only six months since Josie died. It's taken me five years to get to the point where I feel comfortable being with another man. I don't want anybody to get hurt by rushing. Besides, we've got the children to consider.'

Paul twirled his coffee cup on its saucer. 'I think the boys might have fallen in love with you too.'

'Hmm. That's what I mean. We're adults, so we should be able to handle it if things don't work out, but the boys are vulnerable right now. Luke especially, I wouldn't want to break his heart.'

'Might already be too late to avoid that.'

She leant over and kissed him. 'Looks like I'll just have to stay with you then, and hope for the best.'

'I thought guardian angels were assigned for life.'

'That can't be true. This isn't my first assignment. Who knows if it will be my last?'

'Are you enjoying the assignment?'

Marie looked at him. What she saw was a larger version of Luke with dark hair and the same open hearted smile. 'It's growing on me.'

CHAPTER 22

THE EVIDENCE, extracted from the computers left behind by Mark Rodrigo and Frank Kingston, revealed that they had belonged to that select group which exploited its skills to plunder other people's accounts through cyberspace, and to trade in stolen credit cards and identities.

The trace of the hack into their system led to a server, connected to the Russian mafia, buried deep within the dark side of the Internet. When the Organised Crime team investigator located a file containing thousands of credit card details, that appeared to have come from that same server, on the computer used by Frank Kingston, he called Inspector Reid.

'Inspector, I think we might know why Rodrigo and Kingston got themselves killed. It looks like they got a little too greedy.'

'Want to be a tad more specific, Sergeant?'

'It looks like they hacked into a computer belonging to the Russian mafia and stole a shit load of credit card details.'

'And, I suppose the Russian mafia managed to find out who took their stuff.'

'Looks that way.'

'Anything else of interest on those computers?'

'There's enough stuff here to keep us busy for months. Not

much else of any use to you, but we did come across something that will be of interest to Inspector West.'

'What would that be?'

'There was a USB stick in a drawer of the desk Rodrigo used. One of the boys accessed it today. I'll send it over. It's got a very interesting video on it.'

MARK CALLED JOSIE, while she was walking to school through City Park, on the Friday morning after the Phantom of the Opera weekend. He was straight to the point, a simple choice for her to consider - sex or exposure. While she listened, he explained that she could meet him for sex or he could send the photos to Paul, and to the principal of her nice, little, Catholic girls' school. He laughed, and suggested that Paul might forgive her, he was such a sap anyway, but he wasn't laughing when he said he couldn't see her keeping her job at that nice, little, convent school, once she had been outed as an adulterous lesbian. His final barb was that he was sure her father would love to see the photos.

Josie stopped walking. Her mind was racing, along with her heartbeat. There was no way she could keep the boys in school if she lost her job, and she certainly didn't want her father seeing the photos. She had been shocked enough when Anna had shown them to her. He might be right about Paul, but she didn't want to risk that either.

'When do you want to meet for this sex, Mark?'

'Monday. I'll meet you on your way to school. Don't worry, you won't be late for work. I'll be waiting for you at the end of your street, where you cross into the park.'

Where your car will be invisible from the front of our house, she thought. 'Okay, but I have one condition.'

'I'm not sure you're in a position to set conditions.'

'You want the sex?'

'What's your condition?'

'I'll agree to sex, if you agree to wear a condom.'

'And, if I say no?'

'Make sure you have enough copies of the photos to go round.' She wasn't getting pregnant for him, or anyone else.

'No problem, Josie. I got enough kids as it is. See you Monday.'

The phone went dead. She looked at her watch. Eight o'clock. She had time to calm herself down before getting to school, so she headed off the main path and found a bench under a tree. She wished she'd thought about things going wrong before she'd started the affair with Anna. She hadn't considered being discovered, let alone finding herself starring in a secretly recorded pornographic video, or being featured in a spread of high quality photographs, suitable for one of those plastic-wrapped men's magazines.

She took a few slow, deep breaths and turned the situation over in her mind. She'd often wondered what it would be like having sex with Mark. He had what could only be called animal magnetism. Might be exciting having sex with him after all these years of doing the same thing with Paul.

She smiled, as she recalled what Anna had told her about his love making. Apparently, he wasn't much into foreplay, just a quick feel up and then a quick fuck. As long as he got what he wanted, he was satisfied. He didn't care much about whether she did or not. And he liked her to make noise. Sounded a bit like Paul really, so maybe it wouldn't be all that different after all. Could she fake it? Take on the role of a prostitute? All she had to do was call on her acting skills from all those drama classes she'd taken at uni.

Hadn't she been pretending for Paul over the last few years anyway? In fact, she was quite proficient at making her body available to Paul when he wanted sex. He didn't seem to notice she wasn't there. Would serve him right if she actually enjoyed screwing Mark.

What had happened to that good, Catholic, convent girl? Life hadn't turned out the way she had hoped. She was bored and wanted some excitement. She'd risked one affair, and look where it was taking her? Right into another one, with blackmail thrown in to boot. It was the perfect opportunity to let her naughty girl out for some more fun. She laughed and headed off to work.

That night, on the way home from work, she slipped into the shops and spent the money she had put aside for lunch, on a box of lubricated condoms. The same ones she bought for Paul. They made it easier to slip him in if she was a little tight. No point in leaving it all to chance when a little insurance could enhance her upcoming performance.

Monday morning, she left the house as usual, just after seven, dressed the way she usually dressed for school - skirt and blouse, and wearing her pink walking shoes with anklet socks. No point in arousing anybody's interest by dressing out of the ordinary for her first date with Mark.

When she reached the intersection at the end of the street, there was Mark's silver limousine parked in the side street. His driver, one she hadn't seen before, was standing by the rear door on the driver's side. When she approached, he opened the door and she slid in next to Mark on the rear seat. None of them saw the small face peering out of a window in the house that faced the street.

'Nice of you to join me, Josie. I've been looking forward to this all weekend.'

He smiled. In reality, he'd wanted to fuck Josie ever since he'd met her, and couldn't believe his luck.

'Me too,' she said, as she looked around the limousine.

It was just as she remembered it from the last time they had been out as a foursome. Three leather bench seats in a space that was more than ample for what they were about to do. She knew there was a bar fridge, and several other cupboards, hidden away somewhere within the upholstery. A solid glass wall separated them from the driver. She could vaguely make out his form through the glass.

'So, how do you want to do this?'

The car started moving.

'Sit back and relax. We'll go somewhere a little more private, and then you can show me a good time.'

The car came to a stop in a parking lot surrounded by trees. The driver got out and walked away towards the trees. Josie didn't pay him any attention, so she didn't notice that he was facing towards the car, or see the iPad he was holding. This was routine for Frank, but he was wondering what Mark was up to with an older woman, even if she was pretty. He knew better than to ask questions.

Mark pushed a button. The door locks clicked into place and the back of the car filled with light as the sunroof opened. He directed Josie over to one of the seats running along the length of the space and moved onto the other, so that they sat facing each other.

'Okay, Josie, let's see your tits.'

She bent over and removed her shoes and socks. He ran his fingers through her hair. She hadn't been surprised by his opening remark but she was a little surprised by the gentleness of his touch. Sitting up she undid her blouse, took it off and placed it on the seat next to her. She'd never been shy about taking her clothes off in front of others. Living in a small house with one bathroom and three males, she didn't give a second thought to getting undressed in front of any of them. Motherhood could do that to you.

'Ready for the tits?'

'Can't wait any longer.' A boyish look of anticipation spread across his face.

They're all the same, she thought. Every man she had ever met couldn't keep his eyes from straying to her breasts. Removing her bra, she casually dropped it on top of her blouse, put her hands behind her head and arched her back. That should give him an eyeful.

He slid forward on the seat and fondled her breast and caressed her erect nipples. Again, she was pleasantly surprised by the tenderness of his touch. After a few minutes of fondling her breasts, he said, 'Let's see the rest of you.'

She leant back in the seat and removed her skirt and knickers in one move, before dropping them onto the pile of clothes next to her on the seat. She reached over to where her handbag was on the floor and took out the condoms, a packet of tissues and a small container of wet ones. She placed them on top of her clothes.

'I see you've got all your supplies.'

'I don't like to leave a mess.'

She let him feast his eyes on her and stroke her breasts and thighs. He pulled her towards him, pushed his hand between her legs, cupped it about the outside of her opening and stroked her gently.

'So, what have you got under those clothes?'

'Why don't you come over here and find out?'

She crossed the gap between them, rested her knees on the

edge of the seat and started undressing him. As she opened his shirt he continued gently stroking the inside of her thighs with his hand. She let herself enjoy it as she undid his belt and unzipped his trousers. She slid her hand into his underpants and gently grasped his erect penis. It felt hard and warm in her hand. Looking him in the eyes she caressed its tip with her fingers. He sure liked that. The tip was already wet from his dribbles. She reminded herself to stay aware of where that wet tip was, until she got the condom over it. He lifted his body from the seat, and she helped him pull his trousers and underpants down. He left them around his ankles. She was confronted by the sight of a trim male body with one very erect penis. He was certainly in better shape than Paul.

'That's a big one.' She bent over and put her mouth over it and ran her tongue over that wet tip. One way of getting that first rush of dribbles out of the way, and she knew it drove Paul mad with desire, so it would probably work a trick here as well.

She moved into a kneeling position and wrapped her legs around him so that her pubic bone rubbed up against his erection. She could feel his wetness smearing on her belly, so she knew where that wet tip was. She moved up and rolled her breasts across his face. Time to get the condom onto him, before he got any other ideas.

She leant back. He brushed the back of his hand across her breasts as she picked up the condom packet and tore open the wrapper with her teeth. She moved off his lap to sit beside him on the seat, and rolled the condom onto to him, making sure she left a free zone at the end. She didn't want any of his semen journeying up her canal. Marvellous how some skills, learnt earlier in life, came in handy when you needed them. Who ever thought she'd be using her condom fitting skills, acquired in the honeymoon days of her marriage, to roll a condom onto another man's erection in the back of a limousine. She looked up and smiled.

'Ready to come in?'

She'd never had a no to that question.

Without waiting for an answer, she straddled him again and raised herself above the level of his erection, by kneeling and lifting her bottom off his lap. Keeping balance with her left hand on his shoulder, she used her right hand to guide him into place. When she felt him enter her, she slid herself slowly down along the lubricated condom. It worked, just as she knew it would. All that practice playing prostitute to Paul was paying a dividend. She let a soft moan escape from her throat, as she slowly moved herself up and down along that shaft. She saw his eyes close as he let her move. Then he grabbed her by the hips and increased the rate of her movement until he ejaculated. He stopped moving almost immediately after coming. His performance was just as Anna had described. She kept moving up and down slowly and moaned as she faked an orgasm. It was obvious he had no interest in whether she had come or not. She gently eased his drooping member out from her vagina, making sure not to let any of the sticky mess dribble out of the condom.

She decided to complete her service by cleaning him up. Turning, she reached for the tissues and wet ones. He watched through half closed eyes, not sure what she was going to do. She felt him relax when she eased off the condom, wrapped it in tissues and wiped his penis, making sure to gently squeeze out the last dribbles, before wiping it down with a wet one. She dropped the mess into one of the rubbish containers at the end of the seat. Then she used a wet one on herself, to remove the sticky liquid he had dribbled onto her belly before she had gotten the condom on to him. She didn't want the smell of dried semen about her when she arrived at school.

'There you go, sir. Was that to your liking?'

She finished wiping herself down and threw the wet one into the rubbish container with the others.

'Can't understand why you're fucking Anna.'

'If I wasn't fucking her, I wouldn't be here fucking you, would I?'

That got a smile from him before he started pulling his pants up. Obviously, that was it for today. She moved back to the opposite seat and put her clothes on, wondering how much of a mess he had made of her face and hair.

It was definitely a 'quickie' in her book, but he looked satisfied. She liked the fact that he was a silent fucker. It made it all seem so familiar, and much easier to pretend that she was a prostitute on the job.

She finished tying her shoes and returned her items to her handbag.

'So, what now?'

'I'll see you tomorrow morning for a repeat performance. I like the way you fuck, Josie, but tomorrow, I'll show you how I like to fuck.'

She wondered what that meant. 'That sounds interesting. I hope it means a girl gets a good time.'

'I haven't had any complaints.'

'I'll make my own assessment tomorrow, as to whether you're up to standard. Want to take me into town so I can go to work?'

Mark pressed a button and the driver's side window slid down. When the driver acknowledged the signal, he sent the window back up.

By eight o'clock they were on North Terrace. 'Where do you want to be dropped off?'

'The gate to City Park will do fine, thanks.'

The driver pulled up behind the line of buses at the stop in front of the gate, and came around to let her out onto the footpath. He touched his hand to his cap as she alighted, and closed the door as she headed for the relative safety of the park. She didn't look back as the car re-joined the stream of morning traffic making its way into the CBD.

Once inside the park, Josie headed for the restrooms just inside the gate, where she spent several minutes making sure that her clothing and face were in order, and wondering how many women had been fucked in the back of that limousine. She knew he was a bit of a playboy. According to Anna, he preferred younger women, so she wondered what he was really up to with this sex with her. Anyway, it had gone pretty well from her perspective. He was just like any other man when it came to being seduced by her body. She checked herself over again. Satisfied, she headed off to school.

Tuesday morning arrived too soon. With Paul tossing and turning all night, and her anxiety about this sex thing with Mark, she was amazed she had been able to get any sleep. She'd regarded the affair with Anna as an adventure, but this being blackmailed for sex was something altogether different. She wasn't sure she really knew what he was up to. He could have asked her for sex anytime. Why did he think he had to blackmail her to ask? Maybe he didn't think she'd agree otherwise. Men, they were so insecure. She probably would have fucked him just to see what he was like. She was sure as hell bored with fucking Paul.

She spent extra time in the bathroom in front of the mirror, making sure she was presentable, but Paul still noticed she was a bit off colour. The usual story about staying home creating more work had shut him up. She remembered to get some cash from him before leaving. At least, she'd be able to buy lunch today.

By the time she had walked down to the limousine, she had slipped into the role of being a prostitute ready for her customer. Mark was dressed very casually this morning. In fact, he looked as if he had just walked out of the bathroom. He was still wearing his bathrobe. His clothes were hanging against the side window. It didn't take her long to realise he wasn't wearing anything else, once they had reached the parking lot and the driver went for his walk.

'Get your kit off, Josie. Do it nice and slow like you did yesterday. Today though, I want you to stay on this side.'

She wondered what difference it made what side she sat on. After all, no matter where she sat she would be within touching range. As she undressed, he moved to the seat opposite her. She saw his erection poking out of the bathrobe as she removed her bra and put her hands behind her head and arched her back so that her nipples pointed right at him. He didn't reach over to fondle her but simply indicated for her to take the rest of her clothes off. As she slipped off her skirt and knickers, he took a condom from her pile and slipped it on before removing the bathrobe and spreading it out on the seat alongside her.

He lay her down on her back on the bathrobe, and sat looking at her displayed before him. She wondered what he was waiting for. He used his hands to signal that she should open her legs, so she slowly parted her legs and looked at him expectantly. Before she could make another move, he was on top of her, rubbing and then sucking her breasts. He was certainly being rougher than he had been the day before, but she felt herself becoming aroused by his sexual energy. She felt his fingers slip into her vagina and his thumb working on the spot above her clitoris. Then he was driving his erection up into her. Right up her. She had never felt one up that far. He grabbed the cheeks of her bum and rammed himself up and down hard and fast. She didn't have to fake the moaning this morning. It hurt, but he was hitting that spot that

Paul never seemed able to find. She felt herself climaxing as he moaned and slumped on top of her. Engrossed in the wave of her orgasm, she kept moving to get the most out of it. It felt good when she came the second time. He smiled at her as he extracted himself from her, being careful not to spill anything on her.

'That's what I call a fuck!'

'I could take more of that,' she heard herself say.

'Well, you should have considered me sooner. I've wanted to fuck you for ages.'

That certainly explained a lot of the sexual energy she had always felt around him.

She handed him the tissues and watched as he cleaned himself up, wondering how many more times he would want to fuck her this week, if at all. Anna had told her that he quickly lost interest in his girlfriends, once he had fucked them a few times.

He took some wet ones and used one to wipe her breasts, another to wipe over her pubic hairs, and a third to wipe around the opening to her vagina. Returning the service, she thought.

'Okay, sweetheart, get dressed!' It was more a command than a reminder.

Mark left the bathrobe on the seat and put on the clothes hanging under his suit coat.

Once he was dressed, he turned on the computer screen in the back of the seat behind her.

'Come here and take a look at this.' He pulled her over to sit next to him on the back seat.

On the screen, she saw herself taking off her clothes, bathed in soft sunlight in the back of a limousine, arching her back and pointing her breasts towards the camera, before laying back to reveal a full length shot of her naked body, including a close up shot of her parting her legs, before Mark's back came into view as he moved in to fuck her. Fuck! Now she was a star in two, maybe three, pornographic videos.

'Want to tell me what's going on? Didn't you have enough damaging evidence of my fucking around?'

'Josie, you're a great fuck, but this isn't about you. I don't care if you're fucking around, that's Paul's problem. And I don't give a shit about your precious Catholic school. '

'So, all that blackmail shit was just talk to suck me in?'

'Getting to fuck you was too good an opportunity to pass up.'

'Why the video? How'd you take it anyway?'

He pointed out the cameras to her. Now, she understood why he had insisted on her using that seat, and why he had waited before launching himself into her. 'How did you do the zooming? I didn't see you playing with any controls.'

'Frank does all that. He's got some wild apps on that iPad of his. By the way, he reckons you have great tits.'

He laughed. She hit him in the arm.

'If it's not about me, what is this about?'

'The video is for my collection, so I can look back and remember what a great fuck you were.'

'And?'

'I'm doing this for Anna.'

'For Anna?'

'I'm giving Anna a little reconciliation gift, to remind her that she belongs to me.'

'What, a video of me fucking you? You must be nuts. She'd chuck it in the bin as soon as I told her how you tricked me into it.'

'Not the video, Josie. Weren't you listening? The video is for me. I've got something else in mind for Anna.'

'Well, I hope she likes it.' She looked at her watch. 'Can we get going? I don't want to be late for work.'

'Okay, let's just have a drink to celebrate a successful shoot, and then I'll take you into town.' He opened one of the hidden cupboards and took out two small glasses and a bottle of Fra

Angelico. He turned to the side away from her line of sight and filled the glasses, keeping the one he had marked for her on his right.

It was a bit early for a drink but she thought that if she refused, he might make her late, so she took the glass he offered her.

'Cheers!'

She sipped the liquor. Fra Angelico, her favourite. She drained the glass and handed it back to him. He topped it up, and she enjoyed another glass as he drained his second. It was early for a drink, she knew, but things started swimming inside her head almost as soon as she relaxed back into her seat. She couldn't keep her eyes open. She'd never been this tired after sex before.

Mark congratulated himself on how easy it had been to get her to drink it. Knowing her weakness for Fra Angelico had helped.

As she drifted off, she thought she heard him say he would be gift wrapping her for Anna, in a shroud. Her mind tried to raise a question but she couldn't get her thoughts into a coherent pattern. She felt the car start to move and then lost consciousness.

When she woke, she was lying on the floor in a dark room, with her hands tied behind her back. She couldn't work out why her hands were tied and had no idea where she was, or why she was there. Her brain was a complete fog. Someone came into the room and switched on a light. It was blinding to her eyes. Strong hands grabbed her and forced her onto her knees. Then it all went dark again.

'Stay still, you stupid bitch, while I wrap you up for Anna.'

Josie heard a noise that sounded like something metallic

sliding into place. In her confused state, she had no idea what it was.

Josie's body fell forward onto the plastic sheeting as the round hit her in the side of the head.

Mark bent over and removed the bag he had slipped over her head. It had stopped the blood from splattering all over the place. He placed some old towels under her head where her blood was pooling. He searched for and retrieved the cartridge. He needed that to link the killing to the pistol he had acquired especially for this job.

He waited until she stopped bleeding. Then, he wrapped the body in a sheet and carried it out to the van parked in the warehouse. Once he had the body in the van, he returned to the room and rolled up the plastic sheeting with the blood-soaked towels inside. He secured the sheeting inside a large plastic garbage bag. He collected her handbag and her mobile phone, which he had charged while he was waiting. He removed the condoms from the handbag, and put them into the garbage bag. He left everything else in the handbag. He wanted the body to be identified when it was found in the morning.

Satisfied that there was no trace of her in the warehouse, Mark drove the van around to the woods on the other side of the airport, without turning on the lights. The airport service road was deserted at that time of night.

He parked the van next to the intersection where a walking track went into the woods. He took her handbag and hung it in the tree he had picked the day before. Then he carried the body into the woods, unwrapped it from the sheet and positioned it face down, as if she had been shot there. Lastly, he dropped the spent cartridge a few metres away from the body, as if it had flown there from the pistol. He didn't know how smart the police were, but he was leaving them a trail of mixed signals to maximise the entertainment value of their inevitably futile search for her killer.

After setting up the crime scene, he drove the van into the foothills on the other side of the city, where he parked it behind some trees at the end of a dead-end gully. He took his bicycle out of the back of the van, before torching the van and its contents, including the pistol, the rubber gloves and the outer garments he had been wearing since he entered the room to shoot her. Satisfied that the van was well ablaze, he mounted his bicycle and started pedalling.

Mark looked like any other training-mad cyclist in lycra, as he headed home to his apartment in the city, chuckling to himself about the next steps in his plan. His only disappointment was that for the plan to work, he couldn't be with Anna when she found out that Josie was dead.

He took consolation in the knowledge that she would be devastated, whether he was there or not.

A NOTE FROM PETER

If you enjoyed *After,* you can help other readers share your enjoyment by telling them about the book and writing a review.

Drop by at **www.petermulraney.com** and join my **Crime Readers Group** to download a free copy of *Deadly Sands* and be one of the first to know when my next book will be released.

ACKNOWLEDGMENTS

Writing a book is one thing. Getting it ready for publication is another challenge altogether.

I'd like to express my gratitude to my son, Francesco, for his assistance in editing the manuscript and providing feedback on the final design for the cover.

Thanks also to my wife, Toni, for her feedback on the original draft of the manuscript and her assistance with proof-reading.

Murder. Kidnap. Redemption.

Inspector Carl West investigates the murder of seventy-five year old Kieran Moore and the disappearance of his ten year old great-grandson, Toby, after the pair secretly steal away for a holiday weekend.

If you like mystery mixed with intrigue, you'll love the twists and surprises in The Holiday, the second book in the Inspector West series.

CHAPTER ONE

Helen woke with a start. She looked at the alarm clock. It was nearly ten o'clock. She had slept in. Terry would be arriving any minute to pick up Toby to take him to the game.

She slid out of bed and went to see if Toby was ready. He rarely slept in on Saturdays. It was the only day she let him watch TV in the morning. He was always excited whenever Terry took him to the football. They were football mad and their team was having a great season, so she fully expected to find him ready and waiting to go.

She wondered why Toby hadn't come in to wake her.

There was no sign of him in the TV room. There were no dirty breakfast dishes on the table or in the sink. There was nobody in his bed. She was the only one in the house.

She looked into the backyard through the laundry window. There was no sign of him. She checked the back door. It was locked from the inside. She checked the front door. It wasn't locked, but the security door was locked from the outside. Maybe Terry had come while she was asleep. She went into the kitchen, to see if they had left her a note on the white board attached to the side of the fridge - nothing.

Typical bloody Terry, she thought. She went back into her bedroom to fish her mobile phone out of her handbag.

Before she could call him, she heard Terry's truck pull up in the driveway. When she opened the front door, he was standing there, alone.

'Hi, Helen. Is Toby ready?'

'I thought he was with you.'

Terry looked at her. He hadn't expected that response.

'How could he be with me? I only just got here.'

The colour drained from Helen's face, as it dawned on her that she didn't know where Toby was.

'If he's not with you, where is he?'

Terry managed to catch her, before she hit the tiles on the front veranda, and carried her inside. When she came out of the faint, he checked the house. He opened all the wardrobes that Toby could be hiding in and looked under the beds. He went out into the backyard and checked the small shed where the garden implements were stored. Toby was nowhere to be found.

When he returned to the living room, Helen told him that Toby's backpack and red parka, which he had left next to the front door before he went to bed last night, were gone. It looked like he'd taken off on his own. They looked at each other in disbelief.

'God, what if he's run away?'

Helen felt warm tears running down her face.

Terry did something he hadn't done in a long time. He hugged her. It felt so good she was reluctant to move out of his embrace.

'We'll find him,' he said softly, as he stroked her back, like he used to do when she was upset over something. 'There has to be a logical explanation.'

They called their parents to see if Toby had turned up at either of their houses. Toby spent a lot of time with his grandparents in the after school hours. While Terry asked the neighbours if they'd seen him leaving, Helen called the mothers of Toby's group of school friends. No-one had seen him.

Terry called the police to report him missing and then they waited, not knowing what to expect. This was so unlike Toby. He was such a good kid. He had never given them any trouble.

'What have we done to him?' Helen asked.

'What do you mean?'

'Think about it, Terry. What do you think our separation, and all the fighting that went before it, has done to Toby?'

'Hadn't thought about that.'

'You not thinking about things is half the problem.'

Terry reached over and held her hands. 'Let's not get into a fight?'

Helen glared at him. 'What if they can't find him?'

'Don't go there. He can't have gone too far. He's a ten-year old on foot. The police should be able to track him. They said they'd bring a dog.'

The twenty minutes it took the police to arrive seemed a lot longer to Helen and Terry. They were relieved when a patrol car pulled up in front of their house. Five minutes later a second patrol car with a police dog and its handler arrived. The dog was introduced to Toby's scent and immediately appeared to pick up his trail at the front doorway of the house. The dog crossed the front lawn and stopped at the kerb in front of the house next door. The trail ended there.

The policeman handling the dog spoke to the sergeant interviewing Helen and Terry, and then returned the dog to the back of his patrol car.

'Looks like your son probably got into a car in front of the house next door,' said the sergeant.

'What does that mean?' asked Helen.

'Means we have a bit of a problem, Mrs Moore. It looks like either your son has been taken or he had help.'

'If he got into a car, he could be anywhere by now.'

'Do you have a recent photo of Toby, Mrs Moore?'

'The school photos came last week. I haven't even paid for them yet.'

'Where are they?' asked Terry.

'On the TV,' said Helen.

Terry got up and went into the TV room off the kitchen. He wanted to have a look at the photos before they handed them over to the police. One of the downsides of living at his parents' place, while he and Helen were sorting themselves out, was missing out on things like seeing Toby's school photos when they arrived. He pulled out the large portrait of Toby and handed it to the sergeant.

'Nice looking lad,' said the sergeant.

'What happens now?' asked Terry.

'Two things. First, we'll distribute a copy of this photo to every patrol car in the State.'

'How do you do that?' asked Terry, thinking that could take forever.

'We'll scan this photo into the system in the car. It will appear on the screen of every other patrol car within seconds.'

The sergeant handed the photograph to her constable, who went out to the patrol car.

'Okay, and the second thing?'

'When I get back to the station, I'll release details to the media so we can get Toby's picture and description out to the public. They're our eyes and ears. Hopefully, they'll help us locate him as soon as possible,' said the sergeant.

'And, what do we do?' asked Helen.

'Stay here in case he comes home. Give me a call if he does. If you come up with any ideas as to who he might have gone off with, call this number.' The sergeant handed Terry a card and stood up to leave. 'If you hear from anyone who claims to have taken him, call me. I'm sorry I can't make it any easier for you. This is going to be tough until we find him or he comes home.'

As the police were leaving Helen's parents arrived.

———

Kevin and Mary Sloan waited for the police car to leave before alighting from their silver Mercedes. The police car had been parked in Kevin's favourite parking spot in front of the house. He liked to look out through the front window and see his Mercedes in the street.

Mary waited for him to check that the electronic locks had engaged, and then she followed him across the small patch of lawn to the front door. Terry opened the door before they could knock or ring the doorbell.

'Any news?' said Kevin.

'No. They've only just left to start looking for him.'

'Where's Helen?' asked Mary.

'In the living room,' said Terry, stepping back to allow them to enter.

Mary pushed past Terry. Kevin stood on the veranda. 'What did the police have to say?'

'They think he got into a car in front of next door.'

'How'd they work that out?'

'They used a dog. It followed Toby's trail across the lawn and stopped at the kerb just over there, about a car's length in front of where your car's parked.'

'Any sign of forced entry?'

'No. It appears he let himself out the front door. Took his backpack with him. Helen thought he'd packed a few things for the football. Looks like he had other plans.'

'So, he's run away from home.' Kevin took one last look at the car and entered the house.

Terry closed the door and followed Kevin into the living room. If Helen hadn't been distressed before her mother arrived, she was now.

'Hello, darling,' said Kevin.

'Hello, Dad,' said Helen. 'Thanks for coming.'

'Terry, have you called Sean and Louise?' said Mary.

'I've talked to Dad. They'll be here once Mum gets home from the hairdresser.'

Louise Moore visited her hairdresser and manicurist every Saturday morning. It was a treat she gave herself as a reward for surviving another week picking up after Sean. She'd given up trying to change his habits after thirty years of marriage, and now simply used his credit card to compensate herself. She reasoned that if Sean could throw good money away on the horses, he could afford to look after her in the style of her choice.

He'd only protested her credit card bill once. A month of no sex had been enough to persuade Sean it was better to pay the monthly account, regardless of the balance, without asking questions.

Mary glared at Terry. She blamed him for everything. He was so much like his father - irresponsible and self-centred. Mary regretted ever having supported Kevin, when he insisted Helen marry Terry, once they had discovered she was pregnant with Toby. Helen would have been better off as a single mother, in Mary's opinion.

'You realise this wouldn't have happened if you two hadn't separated,' said Mary.

'For God's sake woman! Our grandson, their son, has run away from home and you want to blame them. Where's your compassion woman?' Kevin didn't particularly like Terry either, but he didn't see any point in inflaming an already strained relationship.

'It's okay, Kevin,' said Terry. 'She's probably right. We love Toby. I'd do anything to have him walk back through that door.'

'Would you grow up and accept some bloody responsibility as the boy's father?'

Everyone in the room stopped as Mary's outraged shout washed through them.

Terry looked at the floor. He knew Mary didn't think much of him. She wasn't all that good at hiding her feelings, especially when she was attacking him for what she regarded as his immature behaviour. She'd taken him to task several times over the years for his gambling and drinking. He looked at Helen. She was waiting for him to answer.

'Yes, Mary, I'd be willing to do that.'

The fight had gone from Terry. The three weeks he had been apart from Helen had been the longest three weeks of his life. At first, it had been a relief to have a break from their constant quarrelling. Then it had turned into agony. He missed being with her so much it hurt.

He'd planned to ask Helen if they could get back together this weekend. He'd already admitted, to himself, that it was his fault they had been fighting, especially after his mother had opened up and shared what is was like living with his father.

Louise had even advised him to find another job. Spending all day with his father, she'd told him, would not help, if he wanted to change his habits. Terry didn't know if he could do that, he enjoyed working with his father. They were a good team, and they were making good money. But he did know that for things to work out with Helen, he'd have to give up going to the pub and betting on the horses, for starters.

Helen smiled. She'd seen Terry beaten before, but there was something about his energy this time that suggested his perspective might have shifted. There was no fire in his response. She hoped he'd stay with her until Toby came back. She didn't want to have to cope with this on her own.

'What say we call a truce and have a coffee?' said Kevin.

Before anyone could answer, the doorbell rang. Terry opened the door to his parents, Sean and Louise Moore.

The stink of cigarettes wafted in with them as they entered. Sean had obviously had a quick smoke between the car and the door. Louise did not allow smoking in her car. Sean could smoke in his work truck if he wanted to, but she drew the line at the front door of the house and inside the family car, the one she regarded as her own.

At the time of Toby's birth, Louise and Helen had invested a lot of energy into persuading Terry to stop smoking. That was one victory that still gave Louise joy, and it had helped cement her relationship with Helen.

'We think we might know who he's with,' said Louise, breezing into the room, looking radiant with shining hair, highly polished nails, and firm breasts bouncing under a tight pink sweater, thanks to her Berlei lift and shape bra.

That got everyone's attention. Except for Kevin, who was momentarily distracted by the movement of Louise's pink sweater.

'Who?' said Mary.

'Kieran.'

'What makes you think he's gone off with Grandpa?' said Terry, who was having a few problems believing Toby would go off with the grumpy old man he knew as his grandfather.

'The two of them have spent a lot of time talking on Skype over the last couple of weeks. Kieran even dropped in to see Toby after school on Tuesday. First time I'd seen him since Martha died,' said Louise. 'They took the dog for a walk down to the park.'

'Any way you can contact Kieran?' said Kevin, now that he had tuned into the conversation.

'I've been trying to get him on his mobile ever since Louise joined the dots,' said Sean. 'He's either got it turned off or he's out of range. I've left him a message to call me.'

'Can't you go around to his place?' asked Helen.

'We called by his place on the way here. He wasn't home,' said Sean.

'His next door neighbour said he'd heard Kieran leaving around five thirty this morning,' said Louise, who wasn't shy about asking people for help.

'Wouldn't he have said something if he was taking Toby somewhere?' asked Mary. 'Surely, he wouldn't kidnap his own great-grandson, would he?'

Kieran was a mystery to Kevin and Mary. They'd only met him briefly at a couple of family events, and he hadn't been all that friendly. Mary had been repulsed by his tattoos. He was simply too taciturn for Kevin, who liked to engage people in conversation to see if they offered anything he could take advantage of, even if it was only a connection to someone else who might be interested in what he was selling.

'I'm pretty sure Kieran wouldn't see it as kidnapping,' said Louise. 'He probably thinks he's helping these two get their act together, giving them something to think about apart from themselves. He's a man of action. He does stuff and thinks about the consequences later.'

'We'd better call the police, Terry. The sergeant said to call if we thought of anything,' said Helen. 'Where'd you put that card she gave you?'

Terry took out his wallet, extracted the card the police sergeant had given him, and went into the kitchen to use the telephone attached to the wall above the sink. After a couple of minutes, he came back into the lounge and asked his father to come and talk to the sergeant. They all listened as Sean told the police Kieran's mobile phone number, described his van and told them where he lived.

'He's semi-retired. He's got a little courier business, does runs between here and the Riverland, two or three times a week. Okay, I'll ring as soon as I hear from him.'

Sean put the handset back into its cradle.

'She said they'd look up the registration number and send out an alert,' said Sean, as he rejoined the others in the living room.

'I hope you're right about him being with Grandpa,' said Terry.

'Let's hold on to that thought until we hear otherwise,' said Louise.

'What do we do now?' asked Helen.

'Well, we can sit around and starve or we can do something about lunch,' said Mary. 'Louise, why don't you and I go down to the shops and get some fresh rolls and cold meat?'

'Sounds good to me,' said Louise. 'Do you have any cheese, Helen?'

'You'd better get some of that, too,' said Helen.

'I'll put the kettle on,' said Kevin, who was dying for a coffee.

After an hour of polite conversation over lunch, Sean and Louise went home. Sean wanted to place some bets and Louise needed to have a lie down.

Shortly after, Kevin and Mary decided to go home as well, so that Kevin could prepare for the open inspections he had booked for Sunday.

'Are you two going to be alright here together, or do you want me to stay?' said Mary, as they were preparing to leave.

'We've been together for eleven years without killing each other, Mum. I think you can go,' said Helen, with a forced smile.

After her parents had gone, Helen turned to Terry. 'What are you planning on doing?'

'When today started, I was planning on asking if I could move back in with you and Toby. Now, I'm planning on staying.'

'I'd hoped you'd say that. I don't think I can do this on my own.'

They sat looking at each other across the kitchen table.

'I'm sorry, Helen. I'd like to start over.'

'Do you think we can?'

'I had a really long talk with Mum last night, when Dad was at the trots,' said Terry.

'You mean you didn't go with him?'

'No. Mum asked me to stay home and talk things over with her. She pointed out a few home truths. Some stuff, in fact a lot of stuff, I didn't want to hear.'

'What sort of stuff?'

Helen was starting to understand where the change in Terry's energy had come from. He'd been enlightened by his mother.

'For starters, she told me I was an idiot for the way I've been treating you. Then she told me that Toby needed a father, not a big brother.'

'How come it seems to mean something when she tells you? Isn't that what I've been telling you?'

'I don't know. I couldn't or didn't want to hear it before. She made me look, really look, at the way my Dad treats her.'

'And how is that?'

'He treats her like a slave. He doesn't even put his dirty undies in the washing. He just leaves them on the bathroom floor for her to pick up. He expects her to meet his needs, but he's not interested in knowing what her needs are. She said I was the only reason she stayed with him when I was growing up.'

'Why does she stay now?'

'Now she stays for the money and what it lets her do. It's become a game for her and Dad doesn't know the half of it.'

Helen wondered whether Louise had found herself a lover. That might explain why she spent so much money on clothes and beauty products, and the way she flaunted her body. Must be nice not to have to work, even if your husband is a jerk.

'So what does that mean for us?'

'I don't want to treat you the way he treats her.'

'Do you have any idea what that might mean?'

Terry looked her in the eyes. 'It means doing what your mother said - accepting my responsibilities as a husband and a father. It means being here for you, and not being in the pub. It means putting you and Toby first.'

'Do you want to do that? Do you think you can do that?'

'The other side of that coin is life without you. After the last few weeks, I don't want to do that.'

'Do you know how hard it is to break habits? We're talking some seriously addictive habits here. Do you think you can give up the horses and the pub, and your mates?'

'Ask Mum. I haven't had a drink or placed a bet for a week.'

'A week! I read somewhere the other day that it takes forty-two days to change a habit. You've got some way to go yet.'

Terry noticed she was smiling. 'At least I've started.'

Helen reached across the table and held his hands. 'I love you, Terry. Let's start again. I don't want to end up living like your parents, or mine.'

They were wrapped in the afterglow of their reconciliation when the telephone rang.

Cooking 4 One

Sanity Savers

Living Alone (Collection)

Novella

The New Girlfriend

Everyday Business Skills

Everyday Project Management

Everyday Productivity

Everyday Money Management

Writings of the Mystic

Sharing the Journey: Reflections of a Reluctant Mystic

A Question of Perspective

My Life is My Responsibility: Insights for Conscious Living

I Am Affirmations: The Power of Words

Beyond the Words: Reflections on I Am Affirmations

Mystical Journey: A Handbook for Modern Mystics

Sharing the Journey Coloring Books

Mandalas

Mandalas by 3

Sharing the Journey Coloring Journals

Sharing the Journey Coloring Journal

Discovery

Reflection

www.ingramcontent.com/pod-product-compliance
Lightning Source LLC
Chambersburg PA
CBHW020701110726
47901CB00001B/267